Murder at the Tremont Theatre

To Helen Cox, a Boston History Buff,
with appreciation and wishes
for a New Year of Peace, Joy &
Good Health.

[signature]
2011

This book is a work of fiction. References to real people, events, establishments, organizations, or locales are intended only to provide a sense of authenticity, and are used fictitiously. All other characters, and all incidents and dialogue, are drawn from the authors' imaginations and are not to be construed as real.

Designed by
Frank Cullen & Donald McNeilly

Inkhorn Press
New Mexico 2010

Printed in the United States of America

ISBN # 1-453-75052-5

EAN # 978-1-453-75052-0

Also by Frank Cullen & Donald McNeilly

Vaudeville, Old & New:
An Encyclopedia of Variety Performers in
America (Routledge Press, 2007)

Acknowledgements

Florence Hackman, our partner in many ventures, for her expertise, advice and friendship.

Peter DiForte, Jr. of *Celebrate Boston* for sorting out the rapid and complex development of Boston's public transportation system that was underway in 1908.

John Flemming of Boston City Hall who provided detailed maps of Boston of the period.

Donna M. Wells, Records Manager & Archivist of the Boston Police Department for researching and writing the history of the *Boston Police Department* [Arcadia Publishing series of Images in America, 2003, isbn 13-978-0-7385-1302-7] and for answering our many questions.

Teddi & Tony Andres, Anne Brinton, Sharon Morrison & John Harrington, Nina Simonelli and Ernest W. Sturdevant for reading the manuscript in its various stages and for their friendship.

Margaret Moreland Stathos for years of encouragement and good advice.

Murder at the Tremont Theatre

by
Frank Cullen & Donald McNeilly

The First Porridge Sisters Mystery

Florrie & Lavinia

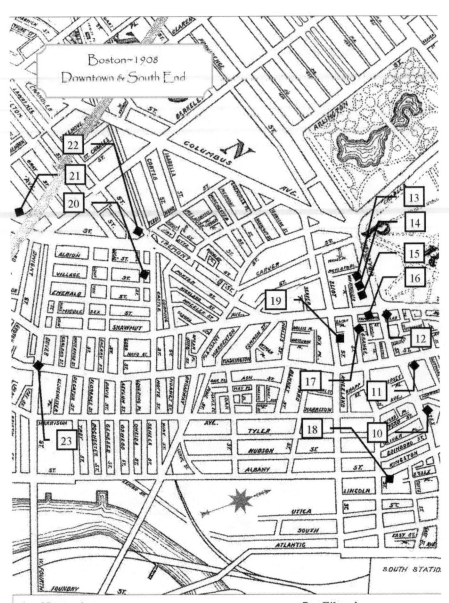

1. Haymarket
2. Old Howard Theatre
3. Friend/Union Subway Station
4. Pemberton Square—Police Station & Courthouse
5. Parker House
6. Gilchrist's
7. Filene's
8. Boston Common
9. Keith's New Theatre
10. Chauncy Street
11. Globe Theatre
12. Tremont Theatre

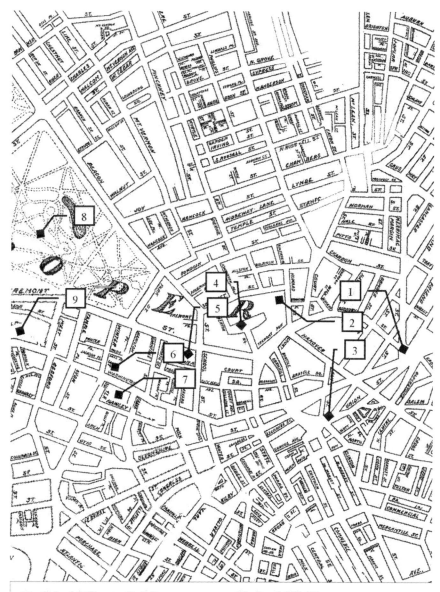

13. Colonial Theatre Building
14. Shraffts
15. Liggett's
16. Touraine Hotel Apartments
17. LaGrange Tavern
18. Chinatown
19. Jacob Wirth's
20. Portridge Arms
21. National Theatre
22. Castle Square Theatre
23. Dover Elevated Station

GLOSSARY:

at liberty: unemployed and awaiting engagements

bill: (like bill of fare) the line-up of acts appearing that week at a vaudeville theatre

center stage fancy: ornate opening, representing a grand interior entrance, cut within a painted canvass drop placed far upstage

charts: (also called sides) musical arrangements for each orchestra instrument

close-up magician: one who specialized in hand manipulations (cards, coins, etc.) rather than large scale illusions, and thus able to work *in one* rather than a full stage

colored: the preferred term of the era—along with 'Negro,' among African American and African Caribbean American people

drops: scenic backgrounds painted on canvas to represent interiors or exteriors

Gerry Society: Society for the Prevention of Cruelty to Children under the leadership of Eldridge Gerry, who evinced more concern for children who worked on stage than those who had to work on the streets or in sweatshops

house: theatre

in full: the full four quarters of the stage area from apron/footlights to rear wall and side to side

in one: the stage area between the apron/footlights and the front curtain

in two: the front half of the stage, from footlights to midway back

in three: (seldom employed) the front three-quarters of the stage

jump: distance and time spent in travel from one engagement to the next

proscenium: the decorated large square or arched opening (directly behind which was hung the front dress curtain) that acted as a frame for the stage and separated it from the orchestra pit and audience

mufti: civilian clothes in place of the usual uniform

sides: see 'charts' for music. In drama: the pages of a script

split week: two- three- day engagements, usually the end of a week or a weekend

Theatrical Syndicate (or Trust): a largely successful attempt by a group of theatre businessmen led by Abe Erlanger to dictate terms and blunt competition on the dramatic stage by creating a vertical monopoly of legit theatres, performance rights, and central booking to dictate what played where and when and by whom for how much

trades: publications intended for a specific trade: automotive, construction, textiles—even show business

trouser roles: male roles assumed by females: most prevalent in music hall, pantomime, extravaganza and old-style burlesque

U.B.O.: United Booking Office, founded in 1906 as the successor to the Vaudeville Managers' Association, and dominated by the large Eastern circuits that controlled bookings of performers for vaudeville theatres and eventually covered much of the USA and Canada

CHARACTERS

Portridge Arms Personnel:

The Porridge Sisters (Flora & Lavinia), co-proprietors of **Portridge Arms,** 'a boardinghouse for theatricals' in Boston's South End.

Flora (Florrie) Portridge, 53, manages provisions and kitchen (in which she is chief cook); is older sister of Lavinia

Lavinia Portridge, 49, manages finances, room reservations and building maintenance. Younger sister of Flora

Florrie Lavinia

Tommy Agnes

S. A. Boniface

Sidney Austin Boniface, late sixties, retired actor who resides at Portridge Arms and assists in its maintenance

Agnes Rigney, 17, full-time dogsbody who cleans and assists in preparing meals

Tommy Shields, 9, newsboy, lives at Portridge Arms in exchange for performing chores

Cora Williams (seventies) and **Ida Banks** (early thirties), part-time housecleaners who reside off premises

Vaudevillians lodging at Portridge Arms this week:

Victor Greeley & Company (**Doris Greeley**), early fifties

Hennigan Brothers (Ned & Mike) 22-23, dancers

Franklin Sisters (Marla & Paula), 21-22, dancers

Mrs. Renee Cormier, 60, manager of (her daughter Alice's (10) song-&-dance kid act with two young boys (7)

Vetter Trio (Andras, Karel and Dietmar), mid-twenties, acrobats.

Other Principal Characters:

Rosetta Rice, mid-forties, vaudeville singer and victim

Nathan Furst, mid-fifties, booker for the United Booking Office in Boston.

W. Dudley Pierce II, 56, Rosetta Rice's attorney.

Inspector Malachi Brody, 40, assigned to the murder at the Tremont

Patrolman Frankie Moore, 22, the local beat cop.

Ira Wood, 73, founder of Ira Wood Enterprises a small circuit of vaudeville houses including the Tremont.

Joshua Wood, 45, son of Ira Wood and vice-president and manager of Ira Wood Enterprises.

Owen Yates, early seventies, office manager/bookkeeper for Ira Wood Enterprises

Jane Markey, mid-sixties, Mr. Yates' assistant and Ira Woods Enterprises receptionist

Laurence Simpson, 50, Tremont Theatre manager

Mo Weiss, 60-ish, box office manager and bookkeeper of the Tremont Theatre

Emily Stropell, 70, assistant to Mr. Weiss

Ed Gilly, 40, Tremont Theatre stage manager

Petey Martin, 67, stage door tender at the Tremont

Earl Findley, 44, pit band leader at the Tremont Theatre

Pop and Buddy Declan Plunkett (senior & junior), railwaymen/arsonists

Nicky Nikitin, mid thirties, fence of stolen goods

Pemberton Square Police HQ: Chief Inspector Watts and **Ass't Chief Dugan,** both in their fifties

Station Four police: desk sergeant **Danny Riordan, Captain Walsh, Lt. Culhoun, Sgt. Crowder, Patrolman Dan Madden** and **Patrolman Paul Kelsey**

CHAPTER 1

Friday afternoon, 1908: Haymarket, Boston

"Onions, ten pounds for a quahta! Onions, ten pounds for a quahta, get 'em while dey last."

"Lettuce! Fresh lettuce, t'ree fuhra dime!"

"Get yer fresh tomaytas here; fifteen cents a dozen."

"Peppers, right offa da vine!"

"Potatas, five pounds for a quahta."

"Peahs, t'ree for a dime."

"Hey, foah for a dime over he-ya!"

Although the competition sounded fierce, some families owned several pushcarts, and cutting each other's prices was one way to steer customers towards produce that buyers thought was a bargain but the sellers wanted to move before it spoiled. Next time around, the family would throw the sale to another cart.

Prices were crayoned on small brown paper bags pegged by clothes pins to a bushel basket or stuck on garden stakes in the middle of an appetizing pyramid of fruit or vegetables. All the prices were better than fair; the trick for the peddler was to array the good stuff at the front of the cart while putting the produce that was bruised or going to rot behind the good. As the peddler, like a stage magician, reached with his fingers for the smooth peach in front, he palmed one of the less lovely ones from behind the pile and dropped both into the bag, He repeated his move with such rapidity that the buyer was caught without uttering an objection until it was too late—the bag tossed on and whipped off the scale and thrust at him with the demand for "fifteen cents." It took more than a few trips to Haymarket for a customer to learn the game.

"Imagine. Five cents for one rutabaga!"

"The man's just trying to make a living."

"They weren't even proper white turnips." It always nettled Lavinia that she couldn't negotiate a bargain as deftly as Florrie. "And this late in the day. What does he think he's going to do with a bushel of rutabagas after the market closes?"

Lavinia, weary and laden with groceries, allowed herself to be carried along in the stream of shoppers on their way to the streetcars and subway trains that would carry them home.

"Lavinia—"

To hesitate in the onrush was to be buffeted about by bags filled with produce and wielded like shields by people plowing past each other along the narrow corridor of pushcarts. Lavinia feigned not to hear her sister.

"Lavinia, hold on!" Florrie knew her sister would not leave her far behind. "Salvi, I want a dozen pears. No, thank you, I'll pick the ones I want. No, thank you; either I choose what I want or I won't want any."

Salvi found it easier to let Florrie have her way. It was a weekly skirmish—one that he never won—with a good, steady customer, so he turned his attention to another woman who, odds were, would prove a more compliant buyer. It took Florrie only a few seconds to select her dozen boscs—she was as practiced in assaying the ripeness and weight of produce as any merchant—and she presented three dimes to Salvi.

With three large hemp sacks filled to overflowing, Florrie rearranged items and nestled the pears amid several heads of lettuce, a secure yet soft place, before she launched her considerable bulk into the traffic fray and was on her way. Florrie found Lavinia waiting at the next corner.

"What did you buy now?"

"Pears. Bosc pears. They're just ripe but firm. I'll poach them for desert. A dribble of Bird's custard with a soupçon of brandy and they'll be delicatish." Florrie was as inventive with words as recipes.

"If you don't eat them on the way home."

"And maybe a walnut and current tea bread for tomorrow's brunch. This week's lodgers have been a good lot, and we ought to send them off with a tasty morning meal."

"Better to worry about getting home and putting a decent dinner on the table before the actors have to get to the theatre."

"Lavinia, when have we missed getting a meal to table on time?"

"There's always a first time," Lavinia was poised to mutter, but Florrie had dropped her bags at Lavinia's feet and lurched off in the direction of a newsboy hawking the *Boston Evening Record.*

Florrie returned in an instant with the tabloid caught under her arm "Got his last copy."

"Why won't you buy a respectable newspaper? ..."

2

"Our lodgers want to check the baseball scores—the men anyway, and the women like to read the crime stories."

"So do you." Catching Florrie looking at her under a raised eyebrow, Lavinia admitted, "And so do I, sometimes. But we should be supporting a decent newspaper like the *Christian Science Monitor.*"

"Yes, we should. And if you can find a newsboy selling it, I'll be glad to buy it and read it with you, but most show folk are looking for news about the theatre and sports—and the funnies."

"The *Monitor's* only been publishing a year."

"Somehow I doubt that the Katzenjammer Kids or the Boston Braves will ever find their way onto Mary Baker Eddy's pages."

"Hey, ladies." The newsboy was at their elbows, and Lavinia moved a step away as quickly as she would from a purse-snatcher.

"Oh, hello. I paid you for the newspaper, didn't I?" Florrie again rested her shopping bags on the sidewalk; Lavinia held onto hers.

"Yes, Ma'am, but you bought my last rag, so I figured maybe I could help you home with your bags? You got a lotta stuff there."

Lavinia picked up the three bags she had been toting. "We're headed to the subway station, boy. We won't need your help."

"I'm going that way."

"Which way?," snapped Lavinia.

"To the subway."

"And then?"

He paused a moment and judged the odds, "Down Washington Street."

"How far?"

"Never mind, Lavinia." Turning to the boy, Florrie asked "Will a dime and your carfare do?"

"Sure will." He grabbed all three of Florrie's sacks and started off.

"Stop!" Lavinia took two of Florrie's three from the boy and gave him one of her own bags. "Two will be enough for you to manage. And don't get too far ahead of me, boy."

Lavinia and Florrie fell into step behind the small, sinewy lad as they wove their way through the late Friday afternoon crowd on Blackstone Street. "I wasn't going to let him carry the bag with the pears in it."

"Oh, Vinny, he's all right, I'm sure."

"You think everyone's all right. Experience should have taught you better. And *don't* call me Vinny."

Twenty minutes later, the subway train rose out of the bowels beneath downtown Boston and up a newly elevated rail track over Washington Street before it screeched into Dover Station. Lavinia and Florence pulled their bundles together in readiness to exit the train. When Lavinia reached for the bags the boy was holding, he told her that Dover was his stop as well, and he followed them off the train. From the Dover Street platform above Shawmut Street, there were two long, steep flights of metal stairs to descend before they reached the street. Once there, Lavinia again reached for the bags the boy held, but he insisted that he was headed their way.

"And which way is that?"

He gestured vaguely, trying to encompass a probable route. A pause let him know that more was needed to satisfy Lavinia. "Where do you live? I'll carry the bags the rest of the way. I need to make some more money to take home to me Ma."

"Where do you and your mother live?"

"Up, off Northampton."

Lavinia relented. They had bought six bags of groceries instead of the usual four and the walk from the pushcarts on North Street through Dock Square and Adams Square to the subway at Friend Street had been the shorter part of the weekly shopping trek to Haymarket. "How much do you want to go to Castle Street? We're at the far end, near Albion. You know where that is?"

"Yes, Ma'am." It was twice the distance as from the pushcarts on North Street to the Friend Street subway, but he decided not to push his luck. "Another dime, and how about an apple?"

"What's your name. I can't keeping calling you boy.

"Tommy Shields."

"Well, Tommy, pick up those two bags. We're late. Come on Florrie. It's well after four. Agnes must be in a fine sulk by now."

They made an odd trio: a small boy followed in line by two women who, although sisters, shared few physical characteristics. Lavinia was a lean, five feet and seven inches tall. She held herself straight as a ramrod and strode ahead like a drill sergeant. Florrie was only an inch or so shorter than her sister but bulkier. She slouched, and her clothes, including at least one colorful scarf, flapped about her. Easily distracted by the flight of a bird, passersby, shop windows, even the odd copper penny in a gutter, her pace was uneven, halting, then scurrying to catch up to Lavinia and Tommy.

The late October sun had warmed them during the afternoon—a blessing of the fast-fading Indian Summer—but the sun was setting earlier each day, and by the time they left the train station, the sun had slid behind the five storey buildings that lined the streets and alleys of their South End neighborhood. Their bodies were chilled, their shoulders, back and arms ached, and their fingers were nearly numb. Fortunately, Lavinia and Florrie had worn gloves. Florrie noticed that the boy hadn't.

"Poor boy, I didn't realize how small he was until the train. I doubt he's more than four feet tall, and I'd be surprised if he weighs 50 pounds dripping wet."

"Stop fretting, Florrie. You and I have enough to do to carry what we've got. You always buy too much." They walked in silence for several minutes. "He's enterprising, I'll give him that."

"Those bags must weigh at least 20 pounds together..."

"What do you think bundles of newspapers weigh? He may be small but he looks wiry."

"How old do you think he is? Eight? Nine at the most. Poor dear..."

The sisters' two brick row houses fronted on 146 and 144 Castle Street at the corner of Albion Street. Unlike most row houses in Boston, those along Castle Street did not back up to the rear of another set of row fronts on the next street parallel to and behind theirs. All the houses and back yards along Castle Street were a block deep. The main front entrance was at 146 Castle, up a flight of brick steps to the exterior double door where a brass plaque over the doorbell proclaimed "Portridge Arms, Lodgings for Theatricals."

After household shopping expeditions, however, the sisters used the descending half-flight of steps from the sidewalk that curved under the main exterior staircase and led down through a basement entrance into the kitchen, scullery, pantry, furnace, storage rooms and a stairway to the upper floors.

The boiler room, scullery, linen storage and pantry were to the right, and, dead ahead at the end of the basement hall, the kitchen took up the entire rear width of number 146.

The land alongside Portridge Arms sloped downward several feet to a long back yard leading to Paul Street, allowing rear access directly into the kitchen at 146. This was the entrance used by hired help and for deliveries and service calls. Number 144 Castle was a mirror image, but the space formerly used for kitchen and scullery had been converted to storage.

When one entered the basement and kitchen level from Castle Street, as did Lavinia and Florrie, the coal room was to the right, and a coal chute led up and outside to a square metal cover set amid the bricks in the sidewalk. An identical cover concealed the chute for number 144. Truckers for the Metropolitan Coal Company used both to fill the bins that fed the furnaces in both houses.

Dusk was settling and, despite Tommy's help, Lavinia and Florrie were sore and cold when they reached Portridge Arms. "Here's your 20 cents," said Lavinia after she had pressed the doorbell firmly three times before turning back to look Tommy square in his eyes. "Mind you give it to your mother."

"And here's your apple," winked Florrie, palming an extra one as she had seen the pushcart vendors do and sticking both into the pocket of his jacket."

Tommy doffed his cap and ran off, turning back once to wave before he skidded round the corner back onto Albion Street.

"I saw that." She rang the doorbell again.

"Did you, Vinny? Too bad you don't catch the peddlers when they try it."

"They're slicker than you. Agnes is ignoring us."

"Use your key, then, I'm chilled. Did you notice? He didn't have gloves."

"Gloves are for December." Lavinia pushed open the outer door. "Agnes! Give us a hand. Didn't you hear me ringing?"

Agnes bustled toward them, dithering and wiping her hands on her apron, "I've been trying to make dinner, and I have to set the table, and those actors will be expecting their meal and…"

"And *we've* been on a holiday, I suppose?"

Agnes sniffed pettishly and carried Lavinia's two bags from the doorway and set them on the long pine counter opposite the stove. "The bread should be done in about twenty minutes, so I put the chowdah on top of the stove to warm. It's nearly five."

"It's twenty minutes before—unless your wee people have been fiddling with the clock."

"It's all right, Agnes," put in Florrie. "I'll pull together the desert while you do the salad. And here's Mr Boniface to set table. Hello Mr Boniface. How are you?"

"Well, thank you, Miss Flora, and it will be my pleasure." Tall, thin and modestly groomed, his long white hair brushed close to his head, the old man relieved Florrie of her bags and brought them to a far counter. He moved with a minimum of fuss, gliding among cupboards, sideboards and counters. "And how are you this crisp October afternoon, Miss Lavinia? And you, Miss Agnes?" Lavinia acknowledged his greeting with a nod and Agnes squeezed out "Fine," as the four of them executed a kitchen pavane as they had many times past.

"Are those pears, Miss Flora?"

"Poached pears for desert, Mr Boniface, with a brandy and pecan custard sauce."

"Lovely."

CHAPTER 2

Friday afternoon: Passage to Providence, RI.

Nate Furst marveled that he could leave his Boston office at noon and reach Providence, Rhode Island, on the Old Colony railroad out of South Union Station in Boston in less than two hours. If he left early in the morning, he could reach Providence, conclude his business and be home for dinner that evening. Normally, he regarded time spent away from deal-making as wasted, but trains relaxed him. Had he been able to command the locomotive and make it go faster, he would have, but, as he couldn't, he read the trade papers, gazed out the window at the passing countryside and enjoyed the rare time away from his desk. Sometimes, he simply idled and thought with satisfaction about how far he had come on a longer journey.

His surname confused some people. It sounded German, but because he was a booker in the entertainment industry, many assumed he was Jewish, an impression reinforced by his given name, Nathan. That, too, suited him. If they wanted Jewish, he was Jewish. If they preferred German, then he was German. It made no difference to him other than how it factored into each deal. As to the truth, who knew? His parents had come to America before the Civil War. They crossed on board a ship filled with German and Scandinavian farmers. At least that is what Nathan had been told. He was also aware that some people in the profession played with his name to the effect that it was "Nate Furst, all others second." Long ago Nathan Furst ceased to care about any reputation he acquired except that it reinforced his aptitude for business.

Instead of journeying on with the rest of the passengers to the farmlands of the Midwest, where a deed for an entire farm sold for less than the cost to rent a single year's land tenancy in the German provinces, his parents probably remained in New York City because that is where Nate spent his childhood. His earliest clear memories were of the Bethlehem Lutheran Children's Home in Manhattan. What became of his mother and father no longer concerned him; he cherished no mental picture of them.

The orphanage wasn't bad. He got three meals a day and a foundation in the three Rs. He fared well enough in the reading, writing and the speaking of English that permitted him later to communicate effectively with those both above and below his social register. He aced the arithmetic that provided the passport to his later success.

In the 1850s, do-gooders organized the first Orphan Trains that transplanted orphaned and abandoned children to the supposed wholesome rural environment of Kansas. After the Civil War, when an uneasy peace settled over the USA, rumors resounded within the orphan asylum that the Orphan Trains once again would run and transport some of the older lads from Bethlehem Lutheran to the hard work and moral rectitude of farm life—a future with little appeal for boys yearning for adventure.

In the dark of one early morning, young Nathan slipped away before his number was called. By then between ten and twelve years old, as well as he or anyone knew, he soon found life on the streets too rough and, following some other lads, jumped a freight train that was rousted by railways coppers when it came to a halt in Fall River, Massachusetts.

After several months of hawking newspapers in that mill town, Nate added as many years to his age as seemed believable and parlayed his talent for rapid and accurate calculations into a series of short-term jobs, each an advance on its predecessor, topping out by the age of twenty as the assistant bookkeeper at the *Marine Journal* in nearby New Bedford.

His newspaper work with the shipping industry and newspapers had brought him in contact with several theatres located not far from the New Bedford wharves. The gossip and flamboyant behavior of theatrical folks intrigued young Nate far more than seafarers and the staid atmosphere of shipping industry offices, so he began freelancing on the side, handling advertisements and accounts for several theatres.

Working for stock companies was useful experience but would never pay the kind of money young Nate dreamt of earning. When he realized that vaudeville was on a rapid rise throughout New England, he found work as a bookkeeper in an actors' agency and in less than a few months worked his way to a position as an agent on behalf of vaudeville acts. As his skill as a negotiator grew, he drew the attention of the opposition who decided that Nathan Furst was just the kind of booking agent that managers needed to defend their interest in bargaining with performers' agents. It had all worked out nicely—to his employers' satisfaction and his own.

After checking into the new, downtown Hotel Providence, Furst placed a phone call to the Narragansett Hotel and made an appointment to meet in two hours, which allowed him time to freshen up and enjoy a good lunch.

Nathan was hardly a stranger to Providence. He went there every month or two for his current employers, the freshly minted United Booking Office, to scout acts playing the city's small-time vaudeville houses: young, new acts or old performers with new acts. If an act were sufficiently polished and entertaining to merit a route, he booked it for several weeks in some of the lesser houses in outlying areas of Boston. He never let the acts—or their agents—know they were being tested for engagements on the big-time Keith circuit.

When he liked a new act enough to give it a short, trial route on a Keith-affiliated circuit, he called in the act's agent and proceeded to dicker about another of the agent's acts. The acts agents were always summoned to Nate's personal office, a small room on the third floor of an old building situated on Chauncy Street near the corner of Essex. Two blocks away from his official office in the U.B.O. suite on Mason Street behind Keith's New Theatre on Washington Street. Most small-time agents remained unaware of Furst's employment by the United Booking Office. They remained equally unaware of his objectives.

Nathan invariably passed on the acts he initially inquired about, and the agent, anxious to salvage something from the encounter, quickly offered various other acts under his management. Few agents ever caught on that they had shaved an act's price in order to sell it to Nathan Furst who already wanted it. Invariably, Nathan bought the act he sought at a price below what would have been asked.

Nate felt good about those negotiations when they went his way. He figured that he got what he wanted below a price any other booker in the nascent United Booking Office could have wangled. The agent got to brag to his client that he had managed to boost the act out of the smaller, small-time vaudeville houses and get them a trial booking on the Keith circuit, and the act was thrilled to have the opportunity, believing that the first four weeks of small money would be followed by a longer U.B.O. route at a more rewarding salary.

Content and confident after a lunch at a nearby, small, German restaurant, Nathan Furst decided to walk to the

10

Narragansett rather than engage a hackney. A brisk walk on an autumn afternoon would give him time to restore his edge dulled by lunch and to review the odd particulars of the negotiation he was soon to begin. Never before had he been allowed such latitude, yet he was still determined to secure the best price under the circumstances.

The formally attired desk clerk at the Narragansett took Nathan's name and rang Miss Rosetta Rice's apartments. Upon confirmation that Mr Furst was expected, the desk clerk summoned a bellhop and directed him to escort Mr Furst to a drawing room on the mezzanine where he could await Miss Rice.

Tiring of endless travel, Rosetta Rice hadn't worked vaudeville since 1902 when she quit to take a soubrette role in one of the Rogers Brothers' annual shows. She appeared with them for three seasons, but their stands in Manhattan lasted only about two months, so she had to spend the balance of each season touring with the shows. A few years ago, still on the bright side of forty, she decided she could make as much money staying home and cutting the coupons of bonds in which several wise men had encouraged her to invest. Other, less wise men, had found that giving her securities encouraged her to forget all else that had transpired.

Nathan had seen the singing comedienne several times and admired her talent, costuming and the ease with which she connected with her audiences, but he had never met her until she walked into the drawing room. She was simply but expensively garbed, and her gloved hand extended in greeting. As he rose, he noted that she was less tall than she appeared on stage but just as shapely.

"Miss Rice, thank you for seeing me on short notice."

"Quite all right, Mr Furst. I have a few minutes before my party arrives. What is our business?"

"First, let me tell you how much I've enjoyed your performances many times. You got a great act." He was improvising, trying to get her measure but distracted by her unexpected forthrightness.

"Thank you" was all he received in response.

"Have you thought about returning to vaudeville?"

"No. I was happy to leave it."

"But you haven't worked in a few years."

"Mr Furst, unless you come to the point of your visit, I shall consider such remarks impertinent and undeserving of an answer."

'Undeserving' he knew, and he guessed accurately at 'impertinent.' "Forgive my bad manners. I'm Nathan Furst—that you know. I represent the United Booking Office, and I've come here personally to offer you an engagement in Boston at the Tremont Theatre."

"I choose not to work, Mr Furst, and my circumstances allow that."

"You no longer have representation, Miss Rice?"

"No, and I doubt, Mr Furst, if you'll forgive my being blunt, that I shall find the need for an agent any time soon."

"I'll get right to the point. I'm prepared to offer you a fine salary for one week, next week in fact, at the Tremont Theatre."

"Mr Furst, you have a poor hand to play. I don't need the stage. I'm well-and safely invested and live as comfortable a life as I could wish."

"Then, Miss Rice, if money isn't important ..."

"I didn't say money wasn't important. But because I don't need more, I can afford to demand a lot."

Nathan detected in her seeming rejection a willingness to consider the engagement. "Because I admire your talent so much, I will do whatever is necessary to make you happy in Boston."

Rosetta Rice looked at the tiny watch set in a bracelet of gleaming jewels. "What's my spot and how much?"

"You're on fourth, a great spot, Miss Rice. They love you in Boston."

"How much, Mr Furst?"

"For you I can go as high as $400.

Nathan's offer elicited no reply.

"Okay, $450." That offer also failed to prompt a response.

"Miss Rice, you're killing me. $500. For that Albee will be killing me. You're a big Broadway success. Why quibble? You said you don't need the money."

"Right, Mr Furst. That's why I can turn down $500. And $600, too.

"Tell me, what do I have to do?"

"I don't need vaudeville. Why don't you just get someone else?"

"Darling, where am I going to get on a Friday night a big star like you for next week? Besides, they asked special for you. Only you. That's why I'm pleading with you. $650, darling. That's it. The top. I got no further I can go."

"It's getting late, and my guests should be arriving any moment. Here the deal, Mr Furst: $750, my transportation and hotel, only two shows a day, my photograph in the lobby and billing as a special attraction."

"Now you've killed me—but you got it. Don't worry about the Monday matinee, just get there before five for the evening show. You remember, maybe, Earl Findley? He still leads the pit band. He'll pick up fast on your tempos. A half-hour band check before dinner, and it'll be like old times."

"Old times are what I left behind. Let's keep it straight, Mr Furst. I'm doing you a favor. An expensive one, but a favor nonetheless."

CHAPTER 3

The Portridge Family

Friday evening's dinner was served on time, although several hungry actors had been cruising like cats between the adjoining dining and sitting rooms upstairs well before the food was put on the table at 5:30.

Vaudeville theatres customarily began their matinees anywhere between 2:00 and 3:00 p.m. Generally the show lasted two hours or a bit more. Acts from the first half of the show usually had time to shop, sightsee or stop for a few drinks on their way back to their boardinghouses before the evening meal. They were expected back at the theatre no later than an hour before curtain for the evening shows that began at 8 or 8:30 p.m.

Acts that performed on the second half of the bill were expected to arrive on the half hour before show time, but some headliners didn't show up until the intermission. As they customarily stayed at the better hotels, dinner was a more leisurely affair in the hotel restaurant.

Originally, Portridge Arms had been built as two adjoining town houses but, around 1890, the South End no longer fashionable, Abner Portridge bought both buildings and converted them into rooming houses. He willed one each to his surviving daughters, Flora and Lavinia. Prior to his death, the sisters had lived with their father in the family home in Atlantic, a community south of Boston and adjacent to Quincy proper.

Neither sister had given much thought to marriage, and they were not especially concerned that they were regarded as spinsters by neighbors. Lavinia surprised everyone, and perhaps herself, when, nearly forty, she married Jim Salter, a merchant seaman whom she had met at the local Congregational Church that she attended with her father.

During his courtship of Lavinia, Jim agreed to give up seafaring and set about finding land work, which he got as a pipe-fitter in Quincy at Watson's Fore River Ship & Engine Company, shortly after it opened in 1885. Lavinia didn't want children, should they have any, to grow up in a household whose father, like hers, had been absent for long periods at sea.

After a small wedding in the back-yard orchard of her family home during the spring of 1886, Lavinia and Jim moved to Quincy

Point and set up housekeeping. Less than two years married, Lavinia and Jim were childless when, in 1888, he was killed at the shipyard when a crane fell on him while working on the construction of the *Rhode Island,* a battleship commissioned by the U. S. Navy.

As the weeks following the funeral wore on, Lavinia realized she couldn't heal and get on with life if she continued to live in her married home. Equally true was that there was no way she could afford to continue to live there without Jim's weekly salary, so she joined Florrie who, still unwed, had remained in Atlantic and kept the Newbury Street house for their father who had retired a few years before Lavinia's marriage. Abner Portridge seemed still in the best of health in 1902, when, just before his seventy-first birthday, he died in his sleep.

Abner had long outlived his bride, Jennie, who succumbed following a rapid onset of cancer—of a type never made clear to her daughters, still in their teens. Their father never remarried and continued to hire out to shipping companies as a captain, content that his daughters had proved sufficiently mature to live responsibly on their own and take care of their home during his long absences.

There were three Portridge daughters, each different in appearance and temperament. Unlike most girls her age, Florrie, the eldest, evinced little interest in boys as she matured. She had favored her mother Jennie in genial temperament and artistic interests, if not in willowy, feminine form and appeal. Florrie's enthusiasms consumed her, and in that she was much like her mother and youngest sister, Mayme. Together the trio traipsed to museums, the theatre and an occasional lecture on Sundays.

If the lecture's topic was sufficiently practical, Lavinia, the middle sister, consented to join them. More often she preferred staying home with her father; both were content to read while they enjoyed each other's nearly silent company.

For Abner, reading was a habit acquired during decades of long voyages, and he had developed a particular thirst for histories and scientific speculations, subjects that intrigued Lavinia as well. Like her father, who had learned as a captain to maintain a formal distance with his crew, Lavinia had little patience for frivolous chatter. When she and Abner spoke, it was for a purpose, whether to discuss politics, plumbing, the books they were reading, or simply inquiring how one felt or what one wished for lunch.

Mayme seemed to draw from both her older sisters as well as her parents. Like her mother and Florrie, she loved the stage, especially anything musical. Her taste in clothes was theatrical—a bit more so than Jennie's, whose taste was disciplined—but not nearly as eye-poppingly bizarre as Florrie's. Mayme, like her mother, was a beauty, yet beneath her fair looks there dwelt a very practical and focused mind and a firm resolve, and in these, if no other traits, Mayme was like her father and sister Lavinia.

Inclined to more sensible clothes, Lavinia always chose fabric and stitchery above color and cut. Even after a period of mourning considered respectable by most people, Lavinia seldom strayed beyond greys and blacks in her attire except on festive occasions when she donned her indigo taffeta best, added a brooch at her breast and a Spanish comb to her chignon.

Abner always returned home from the sea with gifts for his wife and daughters. The fabrics they sewed into draperies and clothing were the envy of other women in the neighborhood. Florrie could always be counted upon to choose exotic scarves and shawls, and select the most problematic of patterns, giving little thought to whether material would run up well or hang properly.

While Abner was at sea, after the death of his wife, all of the organizing and much of the work fell to Lavinia who had watched with interest and a keen eye as her father took care of minor plumbing and other repair problems. She also handled the family finances and dealt with tradesmen.

Mayme, when she wasn't gallivanting with her young friends, too many of whom were boys for Lavinia's comfort, could be persuaded to don a cute apron to dust or fold laundry—even starch and iron, the type of chores that prettified their home with artfully swagged drapes, crisp curtains, neat arrangements of bric-a-brac and cut flowers, frequently changed linens and meticulously maintained clothing. She was uncommonly handy with needle and thread but more inclined to making flattering alterations in her own clothing than routine repairs.

Wisely the family employed a laundry service for neither Mayme nor Lavinia were likely to do that chore. Florrie had been all too eager to give it a try, but she neglected to distinguish between fabrics, and she was relieved of the chore after she bleached too liberally and scrubbed delicate fabrics too vigorously.

Like her father, Florrie was solidly built, and she was receptive to any chore that demanded wholehearted physical effort and did not require chasing dust balls. Her prescribed method of cleaning was to drown a floor, scrub it on her hands and knees and then mop up the mess. When she took the rugs out to the backyard and hung each one over a low, horizontal branch, she whaled at them like a *taiko* drummer.

Florrie particularly enjoyed working in the garden, digging, planting, hoeing and weeding, but as much as she loved their flower, herb and vegetable gardens and the large apple and pear trees that extended front to back along one side of the long deep yard on Newbury Avenue, Florrie had always longed to live in Boston with its museums, libraries, concerts and variety of churches and temples.

Mayme did not merely long to leave Atlantic. She left. At sixteen, two years shy of completing school and while her father was on a voyage to Venezuela during the early autumn of 1878, Mayme confided to her sisters that she had decided to go on the stage. As she didn't explain how soon, Lavinia and Florrie discussed the matter as though they had a voice in it, while Mayme and one of her girlfriends abruptly left town with a show. Confident of her stage appeal and talents, Mayme had her mind set on comic opera, but she didn't blink at the interim expedient of joining a burlesque troupe as a chorus dancer.

She had never studied dance, but she held herself proudly, moved prettily and quickly learned and remembered dance patterns. Those qualities and a passably proportioned figure were all that harried dance directors of the day expected. The Columbia Amusement Company producers expected their sketch and dance directors to churn out a complete road show each week, and the talent and looks of the chorus girls were no better than could be attracted by the salary of twelve dollars a week and unpaid rehearsals. Thus the routines the dance directors devised were little more than drill formations punctuated by a few kicks.

It wasn't until after the start of the new year that Lavinia and Florrie got more than an occasional postcard from Mayme, but, through the postmarks, her sisters followed Mayme's travels as the troupe toured the Middle Atlantic States and into the Midwest. When finally a letter arrived, it was postmarked Chicago and bore the news that Mayme had become a featured performer in the number two company of M. L. Leavitt's celebrated burlesque troupe, "Mme Rentz' Female Minstrels," based out of Chicago.

Mayme danced as well as any young woman in the chorus, but it was her lusty mezzo soprano and her winking, impish personality that set her apart and brought her downstage center. Her strong, low voice made her perfect for trouser roles, and she cut a fine figure in the breeches and skintight body stockings that only enhanced her feminine allure.

Abner never fully reconciled to his youngest daughter's decision to leave home unmarried and embark on a career in show business, but when, two years after leaving, Mayme's bookings took her to Boston, her father welcomed her and accepted her decision but remained unaware that Mayme had performed in burlesque. Although she continued in the employ of Mike Leavitt, he had branched out from his minstrel show style of burlesque and was producing four companies he advertised as "vaudeville." It was in Leavitt's Gigantic Vaudeville Stars company that Mayme first played Boston, and her father and sisters went to the Howard Athenaeum several times during that week to see her perform. They were impressed and proud.

Such an adventure, and the talent, will and skill to brave it, were beyond Florrie's dreams. Pinched souls predicted that Mayme Miller (for so she had renamed herself) would come a-cropper for her willful independence and scandalous choice of profession. On the wintry afternoon of 8 February 1904, a telegram addressed to Lavinia Portridge arrived to notify the family in Atlantic that Mayme had perished in a Baltimore hotel the previous day, along with other performers trapped in what came to be known as the Great Fire.

Lavinia and Florrie were shocked, grief-stricken and furious that unsafe hotels were allowed to operate and fire departments were inadequately equipped. Abner, their father, was crushed. Upon his death one year later and the receipt of their inheritance, Lavinia suggested that they sell their Boston rooming houses and invest the proceeds for income. Florrie knew nothing of investments, and Lavinia admitted she understood very little more. Both had been aware of last year's financial panic and those of the 1890s, so Lavinia agreed to Florrie's counter proposition: sell their jointly-owned property in Atlantic, move to the Boston property and gradually change their rooming houses into a safe and well-run boarding house for theatricals, a memorial of sorts to their baby sister.

Lavinia recognized that managing the rooming houses or converting them into a boarding house offered the hope of steady income, and they would have the proceeds from the sale of the Newbury Avenue house to sustain them while they built up their boardinghouse business. Unsaid was that Lavinia was not unhappy to leave a town saturated with sad memories.

CHAPTER 4

Saturday, Narragansett Hotel, Providence, Rhode Island

The light, rapid rap on the door didn't quite penetrate Rosetta Rice's preoccupation. She was sitting at the piano, flirting with the keys, limbering her vocal chords by running the scales and singing snatches of songs she might use for her Boston engagement next week.

When she retired several years earlier, she carefully pinned her fine fabric costumes onto padded hangers but didn't pack them away with her magnificent beaded cape and accessories. Occasionally, she tried on her stage dresses, primarily to assure herself that leisure had not added excess and unwanted flesh, but, as she looked in the mirror, each gown brought a memory of glory, glamour and beaux.

She would not have accepted Nate Furst's offer unless she knew her wardrobe would stand her well again. She was less certain about the particulars of her act. Certainly, the audience would welcome and expect to hear one or two of the songs for which she was remembered. Ideally, the choruses of several of those songs would have been deftly woven into a medley that provided her act with a rousing finish, but there was no time for an arranger now, at least for one in whom she had confidence to do justice to the material. Even if one could be found in Providence, there was insufficient time for him to copy by hand all the individual sides required by the pianist, drummer, violinist, trumpeter, trombonist, clarinetist and heaven knows how many other pieces were in the Tremont's current pit band.

No, she had decided earlier that morning, she'd just have to rummage through her trunks and see for which songs in her old repertoire she still had complete sets of instrumental charts on hand. From that selection she would choose those songs that seemed suitable.

A louder rap of knuckles on her door startled her. She wasn't expecting anyone.

"Who is it?"

"Bellhop, Ma'am. Telegram for Miss Rice."

"Just a minute."

On her way, she grabbed two dimes from her dresser. By the time she reached the door she had decided to give the boy only one. After all, he could have slid the message under her door. Teach him not to overplay his hand.

Sending him on his way and closing the door, she read "CAN YOU MEET ME YOUR HOTEL TEAROOM 4 PM TODAY STOP INTERESTING OFFER TO YOUR GAIN STOP SEND WORD BY RETURN WIRE." Rosetta realized she shouldn't have dismissed the bellhop so precipitously. Now she'd have to dress and go down to the lobby to send her acceptance. An invitation to meet from her attorney was never to be refused, especially a tête-à-tête that promised to be to her benefit. Dudley Pierce was as able, smart and honest as any lawyer in the city of Providence. It had been he who had guided her financial affairs since she had accumulated enough money to invest.

Palpably alert, even considered so among others in Providence who made it their business to spot those who were important, the maitre d' of the Narragansett Hotel Tearoom spied W. Dudley Pierce II as the lawyer was crossing the lobby, heading for the tearoom entrance. Welcoming the attorney by name (the maitre d' knew that "Pierce" was pronounced, in old Yankee fashion, more nearly as "purse"), he led Mr Pierce to a table set in the small bay window in full view of all who entered or left the hotel. That arrangement may have suited the management, but it did not suit Mr Pierce. He indicated a table off to the side and away from idle glances of those in the lobby as well as the hotel entrance. There, cosseted by drapery and potted palms, he awaited his guest.

Rosetta Rice arrived no more than a few minutes after four. Dudley rose, greeted her and signaled the waiter to bring the tea and sweets he had ordered upon arrival. Beyond simple pleasantries, he wasted no time explaining the proposition he had received through another attorney who represented a client he was bound not to name. It was a straightforward offer to purchase Rosetta's common stock in Ira Wood's Enterprises, a small chain of neighborhood vaudeville houses just outside Boston.

As Pierce outlined the deal, Rosetta grasped that the offer was a straight-forward cash deal and enough in excess of the original cost of her investment that it was only sensible to accept it, considering her holdings in Wood's theatre chain had not paid a dividend during the past few years. Well, that would be the new owner's problem.

"I've examined the offer thoroughly, and there are no qualifiers to consider. Also, I thought it wise to consult a few brokers I consider sharp. None of them has any knowledge of deals in the offing that might, in the foreseeable short-term future, increase the value of your Wood holdings."

"Any idea who the other lawyer represents?"

"No idea. A New York attorney with a reputable firm. That's all that was disclosed to me."

"Just curious." Rosetta paused for a moment. "He could be fronting Erlanger and Shubert. They're trying to buck Keith and Albee, and if that's true, I'll bet mine isn't the only block of Ira Wood stock they're going after. If it is them, and they pull it off, that will infuriate Keith and Albee."

"But aren't most of Wood's theatres small-time?"

"True, but they're right in Keith's backyard—in which case my stock is worth every penny they're offering. Probably more."

"Rosetta... Miss Rice, speculation isn't what I would advise..."

"Oh, don't worry. I'm not about to look a gift horse in the mouth. By all means, sell. Old Abe Erlanger is a better swindler than I could ever hope to be. I'm lucky he offered to pay." She paused for a moment. "Perhaps we should extend a formal right of first refusal to Ira Wood. After all, it was out of friendship that he advised me to purchase my ownership shares originally—just before the company went public. What do you think?"

"We can, if you wish, but I suggest that we give him not more than five business days to accept. We don't want to lose the other buyers. As you say, yours may not be only block of stock they are negotiating for—if it is Erlanger or Shubert—and once the bidder has a majority holding in the company, they won't need to purchase more.

"Yes, of course. Will you take care of notifying Mr Wood or shall I?"

"I'll do it. Let's keep it strictly business."

Dudley liked her ability to recognize her best interests and act decisively. As their business was settled, he relaxed, as much as he was accustomed, into affability. A widower for four years, in good health physically as well as financially and still trim and erect in his early sixties, he managed the estates of many widows, quite a number of whom had set their preposterously over-decorated bonnets for him. Rosetta Rice was different. She was never coy or giddy or played helpless as many older women did in the mistaken impression that what men found alluring in maidens was still attractive in supposedly mature women. Perhaps it was her years in show business that separated her from others. He enjoyed her pithy humor, her confidence in her own judgment and her ease among people of either gender and all classes. Not lost upon him was that, for a women he knew to be in her late forties, she was still handsome of face and figure, dressed with style rather than fashion, spoke in mellow tones and moved with grace. He was ever on the verge of inviting her to dine with him, in a public place of course, but that conflicted with what he saw was his primary duty to a client: to work dispassionately in her best interests.

"May I ask how you acquired the Wood stock?"

"Hard work." She let her answer hang in the air for a few seconds to see his reaction. As she had been in show business and not without admirers, most men, she expected, would assume the stock to have been a gift. "Hard work," she repeated after his expression failed to register any discernible judgment. "While others spent, I saved and invested, a few shares at a time. Oh, there were gentlemen who advised me—steered me in directions that proved profitable. They seemed content to tutor me." Such frankness was calculated to exact embarrassment—which it did, given Dudley Pearce's high color—and perhaps to tease and probably to put an end to such questions.

"I regret my unintended impertinence."

Rosetta softened; "Not at all. Your questions and advice have always been directed toward my best interests, and I appreciate that."

Over the last of their tea and pastries they chatted briefly about those prominent in local politics and society, and Rosetta told Pierce about the offer to play the Tremont Theatre and her acceptance. He asked where she would be staying while in Boston, and they parted with the promise that, as soon as he received a formal offer for her holdings, he would ensure that he had negotiated all provisions to her advantage and send the appropriate legal documents to Boston for her signature.

Rosetta bid good afternoon to him, and he stood as she left the table and stared after her for a few moments. In all their meetings over the past few years, she seemed invariably candid in conversation, even for a client, yet remained guarded at her core. Never once had he perceived a hint of intimacy to encourage him.

CHAPTER 5

Saturday: Out with the Old at Portridge Arms, Boston

For her week in Boston, Rosetta Rice made reservations at the Hotel Touraine, one of Boston's more notable establishments for both permanent and temporary residencies. Located at the corner of Tremont and Boylston Streets, the Touraine was less than a block away from the Tremont Theatre. From the time she could first afford it, she sought the formality and privacy of better hotels in place of theatrical lodgings that encouraged the chatty conviviality of show folk and their exclusive preoccupation with show business.

Rosetta thought of herself as reserved rather than snobbish; she made an effort to treat everyone with courtesy so as to deflect any jealousy or disaffection that could breed gossip. Lodging in theatrical boarding houses did not insulate against gossip, but attractive actors and performers who chose the seclusion of hotels were oftentimes assumed to be conducting affairs. This was acceptable to many in a profession in which it was difficult to maintain romantic relationships when the couple was separated for most of the year unless they managed to form an acceptable act that allowed them to tour together. But if a performer or actor were disliked for other behavior, his or her romantic affair or sexual liaisons were fair game for denigrating conjecture.

Rosetta carefully monitored and controlled her actions and responses toward other theatricals. Most performers took her as she represented herself: quiet and well-mannered, and for the most part she was spared whispered speculations. Certainly there were people, probably less parochial than most, whose company she enjoyed, along with others she arranged to meet outside the confines of the theatrical world. Among those in Boston was Lavinia Portridge. Four years ago, in 1904, Rosetta had starred in the ill-fated show that played Baltimore where Mayme and other cast members perished in a hotel fire. Although Rosetta had not lodged with the other performers, she had several scenes with Mayme and came to appreciate the girl for her no-nonsense professionalism.

The next time she played Boston, Rosetta arranged to meet the Portridge Sisters to give them several personal items that Rosetta had retrieved from Mayme's dressing room. She took a liking to Lavinia, whose direct but measured manner seemed quite in concert with her own personality and circumscribed behavior.

Once Rosetta was settled in her routine at the Tremont Theatre, she planned to contact Lavinia and invite her to lunch at the Touraine—or perhaps Schrafft's or Filene's. That arrangement, reasoned Rosetta, would make it difficult for Flora to attend as she would likely have to remain in charge at their boarding house. Rosetta admired the sincerity and intelligence of both Portridge sisters, but Flora's bizarre attire invited curious stares, and her lack of reserve and bubbling talkativeness quickly exhausted Rosetta. She hoped that neither sister was aware of her preference.

The majority of vaudevillians and actors working in Boston, less well-paid than Rosetta, found lodgings in the modest boarding houses scattered within walking distance, and usually south of the theatre district. Portridge Arms was among the closer and more commodious of such establishments.

The two South End buildings had been designed and erected in tandem, so the floors met at each level. Lavinia had engaged and overseen the local laborers she hired to renovate the two buildings. New boilers and furnaces were installed. Windows had to be replaced. Kitchens and bathrooms were enlarged and modernized. Walls separating the two buildings were broken through in two places on all five floors. As the houses had been designed identically and built at the same time, the floors in one building were as nearly on level as possible with the floors in the other. Thus, at the head and foot of the stairways at either end of the central halls, there were 'pass-throughs' that connected each floor of 146 Castle Street with its mate at 144.

This reconfiguration of the buildings' interiors and other improvements substantially diminished the cash they had received from the sale of the Atlantic house, but made the process of servicing and cleaning rooms simpler. No longer did Lavinia, Florrie or cleaning women have to climb and descend two sets of stairs to service or clean all the rooms on each level, and with two bathrooms on each floor available to the residents on both sides, long waits and frayed nerves proved less usual.

As the basements to both buildings sat only one half flight below street level at Castle Street and had been erected on building lots that sloped down to the basement entry level at the rear of the houses where the kitchen and storeroom were located, there were small windows running much of the way along the two sides. Large windows at the rear of the basement level made the remodeled kitchen bright as well as spacious.

Other amenities added during the renovations were two gas cooking stoves in the kitchen at 146 and a dumbwaiter, dubbed the 'bump-up' for its lurching progress as it serviced the upper floors. Pick-ups and deliveries of clean laundry, canned food stuffs and other supplies were made to the rear basement door on Paul Street.

Equal in size and shape to the large kitchen beside it, the storage room accommodated a cold storage room, two ice-boxes, shelves of canned and boxed goods, a rotating inventory of soaps, mops, brooms and clean linens for the changing of rooms and provisions for the kitchen. Near the rear door, soiled linens awaited pick-up by the laundry service. As needed, fresh linens and cleaning supplies were hoisted by the 'bump-up' to the second floor, then carried up by hand to linen closets situated on each of the upper three storeys where the lodgers' rooms were located.

Meals were sent upstairs to the second-floor dining room from the kitchen by the same hand-powered, counter-weight conveyance. Dishes and the rare leftovers from the dining room went back to the kitchen the same way.

In addition to two new gas cook stoves, there was also an oversized black iron and chrome coal stove known as 'the dragon' for the belches of flame that spewed when a burner lid was lifted and because of the vast quantities of range oil it consumed. The dragon's oven was used for all the baking that was done on premise while its hot, horizontal surface accommodated large pots of soups, chowders, tomatoes sauces and other concoctions that needed a long, slow simmer. Opposite was a large soapstone double sink with brass pipes and faucets kept gleaming through Florrie's industry. Cabinets and shelves for storage lined the walls, and two, large, free-standing counters topped with mortised maple wood planks were placed parallel in the center of the room: one, with polished pots hanging over it, close to the stoves, the other, with a marble slab at one end for making pastry, handy to the sinks.

It was a cheerful, efficient kitchen to work in, but Agnes' Friday evening sulk had prevailed throughout the following morning. The sisters surmised that it was more than the rushed preparations for Friday's meal and had no intention of inquiring beyond the state of her family's health and her own. Saturday was

26

a comparatively easy day at the boarding house. The performers had grown accustomed to their engagements by Tuesday and had struck up among their fellow boarders a few new acquaintances with whom they spent off-hours.

This particular Saturday had dawned brightly and the sun shone into the south-facing kitchen. Agnes had realized by bedtime Friday that no one was likely to take further notice of her distress. Over the course of the next day, while Lavinia straightened up the public rooms, thus sparing Agnes that chore, Florrie joined Agnes in the kitchen to prepare meals. File cards with ingredients were thumb-tacked to the wall beside the cupboards, but, after years of preparing meals, Lavinia and Florrie seldom had to resort to the cards for ingredients or their measurements. Cups of this and tablespoons of that were cues for Agnes. Florrie, in particular, seldom measured beyond a pinch, a shake or a fistful of one thing and another.

What remained of Agnes' pique gradually yielded to the rhythm of two sets of experienced hands that brought breakfast and dinner to the ready. Dishes found their way through the 'bump-up' to the long, oak dining table that Mr Boniface had set with his usual care.

Although there would be coffee, tea and plates of sandwiches left in the dining room for a small, late supper after the last show on Saturday night, and a largely cold buffet set out for departing guests on Sunday morning, the Saturday evening dinner was the last full meal of the lodgers' week at Portridge Arms. It was also payday, and the performers were buoyed at prospect of replenished purses and an audience filled with folks out on the town, looking to be entertained after suffering through their dull work weeks.

Two acts left town immediately after the evening performance Saturday night. Both had to catch overnight trains. One act grabbed a hansom cab roaming the theatre district for fares, arriving at North Union Station just in time to catch the Boston & Maine passenger train to Portland, Maine, to connect with an infrequently scheduled Sunday coach to the town of Camden where, on Monday, they were to begin a full week's engagement followed by five, split-week engagements in lesser theatres scattered along as many small coastal towns.

The other act, a mixed-double, raced for South Union Station in time to make the midnight train to Albany, New York, the nearest depot to the wife's family farm twenty miles northeast in Brunswick. They looked forward to a day-long visit with her father and mother before they showed up at ten the next morning for band call at Proctor's Theatre, nearby in Troy.

Such long jumps were not uncommon, and acts that had to suffer them took all their belongings to the theatre with them on Saturday in time for first show of the last day, one that might begin as early as 10 or 11 in the morning. As soon as the evening performance had ended between 10 and 11, the acts rubbed off their makeup, changed into civilian clothes, summoned hackneys and sped with their trunks and valises to the railway stations to catch the last train out of town going in their direction.

Of those who could wait until Sunday to travel, some who could afford it treated themselves to a midnight supper at Jacob Wirth's, the Adams House or Marliave's, perhaps dining with folks they knew in Boston. A few of the young single men, pay packets in pocket and an address or phone number in hand, preferred other closing-night arrangements that lasted into early Sunday morning. Long-married acts or older singles retired to the Portridge Arms where a late supper was spread out in the dining room, and comfort and good fellowship awaited in the adjoining front sitting room. Settled into comfy wing-back chairs, actors and performers swapped lies and anecdotes.

Whenever the sociability grew too loud and reached Florrie in her room below, part of which was situated beneath the guests' sitting room, she would wrap a kimono around her, ascend the stairs to remind the guests that other folks were sleeping and end up staying with them an hour or so to share stories. Florrie was as enthusiastic a raconteur as most of her professional guests and loved collecting stories and bits of gossip.

CHAPTER 6

What's What and Who's Who at Portridge Arms, Boston

Incoming guests trickled into Portridge Arms all day long on Sundays, the first sometimes arriving before noon. At the top of the front steps, under the curved stone archway were oak double doors that were usually unlocked on Sundays so that new arrivals could shelter inside the vestibule if the weather were unpleasant. After someone admitted them through the corresponding set of locked interior double doors, visitors found themselves in the main hall that led to the office and stairway to the upper floors. Whoever had answered the doorbell ushered guests to the small, formal drawing room, immediately off the hall to the right, where they awaited whomever they had asked to meet. Lodgers were directed toward a sign that indicated the business office at the rear end of the hall where Lavinia checked in new arrivals, kept meticulous records, prepared guests' bills and promptly paid vendors' invoices.

If the assigned rooms were not ready, Lavinia invited the guests to wait in the office, a portion of which still resembled the library it once was. A quartet of upholstered chairs welcomed the guests, and there were day-old and sometimes fresh editions of the *Boston Transcript*, the *Boston Record* and the *Christian Science Monitor*—when it could be found on sale—along with less recent editions of the *Police Gazette* and *Atlantic Monthly* to help pass the time. Despite the range of those daily options, the weekly theatrical trade papers were the first choice of actors and performers who passed over the latest *Transcript* in favor of a week-old *New York Clipper*, *Billboard* or *Variety*.

Other than the office-library and common areas, most of the first floor was given over to the sisters' living quarters. Between the front drawing room and the office was a large room that ran the length of the hall and served as the sisters' parlor for the rare times that they were not engaged by household duties.

The sister's private quarters consisted of a combination sitting room and bedroom. Florrie's rooms extended from the front of 144 halfway back along the hall. Lavinia's occupied the rear of 144, corresponding in location and size to the Portridge Arms office at 146. Between the sisters' individual bed-sitting-rooms was their shared bathroom.

Occasionally, while waiting, an inquisitive first-time guest might wander up to the floor above. Lavinia viewed such intrusions with suspicion until she had registered the guest. To Florrie it was completely understandable; she expected people to be as curious as she. Newcomers had been led to Portridge Arms because it offered amenities not found elsewhere. Lodgers in most theatrical boarding houses found access only to a dreary bedroom; the common dining room was usually locked between mealtimes.

The second floor of Portridge Arms held its public rooms, a bathroom and three guest rooms. A large dining room commanded the entire front width of 146 Castle. Made bright by three large front windows and a narrower one to the side, the room was dominated by a long table seating ten, there was just enough space for sideboards along the long interior walls and two smaller dining tables with four chairs apiece placed at the far end of the room where they faced Albion Street.

After mealtimes, if the performers had time to socialize before getting to their theatres, they met in the large sitting room next to the dining room. Corresponding in size to the dining room, it occupied the entire second floor front of number 144 and afforded a view of Castle Street. Book cases lined the long inside wall, while the other surfaces were adorned with groupings of framed photographs and cabinet cards of many actors from the legit, variety and burlesque stages—previous guests testifying to the Portridge Sisters' hospitality and friendship.

On the other side of the dining room, running the length of number 146 between the central hallway and Albion Street, was a large, music room with a player piano, always tuned, a book case with piano rolls and stacks of sheet music, and plenty of chairs and music stands for impromptu performances. Sharing pride of place with the piano was a tall, polished wood cabinet with a hand crank sticking out on one side, external evidence that it represented the latest advance in phonographs, a Victor Talking Machine *Electrola*—a name that advertising men soon contracted into *Victrola*. It played disks instead of cylinders, and its speaker horn was concealed within the cabinet rather than mounted on top. When guests used the music room to rehearse; the small ladderback chairs were pushed to the rear, and draperies along the inside wall were pulled back to expose a very large mirror.

Had a guest ventured beyond those three large rooms, perhaps to find a bathroom, he might have noticed that the single

30

bath on the second floor was located next to a simple guest bedroom ($8 weekly for one person, $12 for a couple) along the side of number 144 that faced the empty lot, and that there were two large bed-sitting rooms ($10/$15), next to each other that occupied the entire rear spaces of both houses.

Few actors wandered to the floors above unless and until they had been assigned to rooms there. Both the third floor and the fourth floor attic were devoted solely to guest rooms and baths. Like the rear rooms on the second floor, those on the third offered space and comfort. There were four bed-sitting room combinations—two across the rear and two across the front of the houses. Room and board in all four was $10 for a single person, $15 for a double and $18 for three. Between the front and rear bed-sits, were smaller side rooms, available at $8/$12, that lacked the amenity of a sitting room. Two bathrooms, one on either side of the building, served the tenants of all six rooms.

The third and final flight of stairs led to the less expensive guest rooms and those reserved for live-in help. Two bathrooms, side by side at the rear of 146 and 144, serviced all eight rooms. At the front end were two very small rooms next to each other, each with a single small window and just enough space to accommodate a single bed, a small wardrobe, a smaller dresser and a wooden chair. At $6 per week, both of these rooms were let only to single occupants, unless they were booked to house two children, in which case the chair was removed, the dresser and wardrobe crammed together to make room for a second cot, and the price rose to $9 for both.

The other six rooms in the attic floor rented at $7.50 as a single and $10.50 as a double. A window on each outside wall of the four corner rooms provided cross-ventilation. The two side rooms had two windows on the same wall but the rooms were a trifle larger and accommodated a day bed in addition to the double bed, two easy chairs and the wardrobe that furnished the corner rooms as well. The side attic room at 146 faced Albion Street; the other at 144 opened on the empty lot at 142 Castle. Even the most modest rooms were tastefully furnished.

Currently, two of the attic rooms were not available to guests. Agnes Rigney, assistant cook and general dogsbody, was installed in the front corner room at 144; room and board constituted part of her salary. Mr Boniface's room was diagonally opposite, in the rear corner of 146. The sisters had inherited Sidney Austin Boniface along with their buildings, and he held a position in the household that blended the role of a guest with that of staff. Over the course of their first year as proprietors of the newly established Portridge Arms, Lodgings for Theatricals, Mr Boniface had proven his usefulness, dependability and honesty so surely that even Lavinia trusted him, and he resided in his room rent-free and received a small weekly stipend for his services.

CHAPTER 7

Sunday: Dawn Patrol, Portridge Arms, Boston

It was still dark and many hours before the arrival of the first of the Portridge Arms' incoming guests when Sydney Boniface crept out of his attic room at 4 o'clock on Sunday morning. Quietly as Hamlet's Ghost, he visited the bathroom at the end of the hall and then descended the four flights into the cellars. Over his day clothes he wore a dark, worn, heavy bathrobe against the lingering frost of early morning.

Both furnaces were needed to heat all five floors. Before retiring each night, Sidney banked each—shaking the grates until only glowing embers remained, then loading the furnaces with coal and covering it with a layer of ash. He turned down the dampers and grates as far as he dared to restrict the passage of air. The trick was to pack in just enough coal to burn slowly all night without smothering the fire or letting it burn out.

This morning, as he did every morning, Sidney heaped a half dozen shovels-full of coal onto the fading embers. Once the fire began to awake, he shook the grate until the first tiny orange drops of hot coal sifted through, a sign that most if not all the ash had been dropped from the fire onto the bottom of the furnace. Despite his gangly frame and his sixty-four years, Sidney performed each part of the process efficiently, prodding one furnace into renewed life, then the other, and removing the spent ash from the bottoms of both.

In an hour's time, the morning chill would be banished and enough water heated in the boilers to serve the household. If the day grew sunny and the wind didn't kick in from the bay, to save fuel Sidney would bank the furnaces again in late morning and not fire them up again until mid afternoon.

When he heard Agnes coming down the stairs from her room, Sidney stayed put until she passed into the kitchen, and then he slipped out of the cellar and returned noiselessly to his room. He was not a mysterious man, nor unfriendly, but social contact was not easy for him unless there were a specific reason or occasion. When meeting people at mealtime or at the theatre, he felt guided by some unseen but familiar script. Even with Lavinia and Florrie or old comrades from his years as a leading man in stock theatre he hewed to formality in address until, in the process, his conversation grew more relaxed and unguarded.

Agnes moved around the kitchen methodically, still sleepy but following the prescribed path. She heated water on one of the gas cookers for coffee, tea and porridge. As she intermittently sipped her first cup of coffee, Agnes gradually emerged from her dawn trance and sped up her work. By eight o'clock she had to have set out the fixings and utensils for the morning buffet for the few performers who were early-risers or restless sleepers and those who had an early train to catch. Unless she maintained efficiency and kept to schedule, she'd not have time to bathe, dress herself in her Sunday best and get to nine o'clock Mass, the latest one that respectable Catholics could attend.

In Agnes' eyes, those who attended later Masses were either lazy or wastrels whose Saturday night revelries left them weak and ill. She allowed that those who attended High Mass at eleven were different but little better because they fancied pomp and ceremony and the chance to show off their finery. At least, thought she, they paid the penalty by having to endure St. Pat's boys choir.

Agnes went to church several times weekly, sometimes to perform the Stations of the Cross or, more often, a shorter visit to light candles and pray to the Sacred Heart for her family's well-being and to the Virgin Mary to grant her a husband who was kind and responsible. Whichever the occasion, young Miss Rigney dressed neatly and modestly.

Nine o'clock Sunday Mass at St. Patrick's Church was a Rigney family affair. After a week of cooking and cleaning for theatricals, she looked forward to joining her mother, father, two sisters and younger brother in the same pew and then returning with them to her parents' house for a mid-day meal of corned beef, cabbage and boiled potatoes or a smoked shoulder with *champ* or *culcannon*. On special occasions, such as a birthday or the breaking of a fast, her Ma prepared a couple of rasher and egg pies, and her Da brought a few bottles of red ale to the table.

Agnes shook her sleepy head free of anticipation of her day off at church and a proper Irish dinner with her family. She reminded herself that there was still the dining room to set for breakfast. Once she loaded plates, bowls, cups, saucers and flatware into the 'bump-up,' Agnes raced up the stairs to the second floor dining room and yanked the chords. Though balanced with counterweights, the dumbwaiter still took a sure grip and a strong back and arms to hoist the trolley to the upper level, drinking glasses jiggling and clinking all the way.

Clean tablecloths and napkins were stored in the dining room sideboard. Within a few minutes she had set out everything for the buffet except the food. By the time she got back to the kitchen, Florrie was there, pulling already-prepared dishes of food out of one of the two ice boxes and getting them ready to be sent up to the dining room.

"Good morning, Agnes, everything on the go?"

"Morning, Miss Flora. Just finished. If all is right with you in here, I'd better be readying myself for Mass."

"Fine. Just load the bump-up with these cold dishes and the pots of hot tea and coffee and then set it out for the early risers. Cora and Ida will be here soon to give a hand. Give our best to your mother and father."

"Yes, Ma'am." Always able to work faster when watched than when alone with her daydreams, Agnes quickly re-loaded the dumbwaiter, fairly skipped up the stairs and brought the food and beverages into the dining room, where she set out the morning spread. She had doffed her apron and her hair net and was about to sprint up the top two flights of stairs to her attic room, hoping to avoid Lavinia who was sure to have noticed something that Agnes had failed to do properly, when she rounded the corner into Lavinia.

"Good morning, Miss Lavinia."

"Good morning, Agnes. All your work done?"

"Yes, Ma'am."

"Is the buffet set out?"

"Yes, Ma'am."

"Well, don't let me keep you then. Give our regards to your family."

"Yes Ma'am," and off went Agnes like a shot.

The stove was hot enough to bake, and sitting on top were a pot of oatmeal with raisins and walnuts and a large cauldron that had been filled by Agnes with enough water to brew a second round of coffee and tea. Florrie had wrapped the forearms of her dress in pastry paper, each held in place with rubber bands, and was mixing the biscuit dough when Lavinia came into the kitchen.

"Off to Mass she goes, and the porridge hasn't even been set out. I checked. Seems a bit on the chilly side," added Lavinia in way of greeting.

"So I noticed. Porridge is ready; it's on 'the dragon.' " Florrie dumped the biscuit dough onto floured bread board. "I'll have these biscuits in the oven in a jiffy, and they'll be ready in ten minutes. No one's down to breakfast yet, are they?"

"Not yet, but soon I expect." Lavinia allowed, as she carried the lidded pot of oatmeal to the dumbwaiter.

CHAPTER 8

Sunday Morning: Busy Hands Make Busy

A few minutes later, as Lavinia was coming back down to the kitchen, there were two raps at the back door, one echoing the other.

"Cora and Ida are here," called Florrie, stirring a second pot of porridge that had just come to a boil on the gas stove before carrying it to the dragon to simmer. Lavinia left off her work to admit them. When she was available, it fell to Lavinia to deal with hired help, delivery and repair men. Florrie admitted she never really understood where to draw the line between business and sociability. She could drive a bargain outside the house, but once someone entered her home, even to work, Florrie tended to sidetrack them and confuse purpose with inquiries about their health, families and politics.

Cora had begun working for Lavinia and Florence soon after they opened for business and discovered they needed help with daily chores. First it was only on Sundays, turn-over day, but as business picked up they persuaded Cora to come in Tuesday and Thursday afternoons as well and to engage a helper for Sundays. Cora chose Ida.

Cora in particular simply wished to get her work done, get paid and go home. Ida, a goodly number of years younger, perhaps two generations, was more open to chatting, but Cora stifled that. Both women always arrived on Sundays at the same time together, yet each knocked on the door. The sisters suspected that Cora's was the first knock and that Ida added hers as evidence that she was not merely Cora's helper.

Both women arrived by streetcar from Roxbury, where an enclave of Negro families had begun to establish itself in recent years. Greetings were seldom more extended than a comment about the weather, but even Cora would not refuse a warming cup of tea offered on a chilly morn.

"Agnes gone off to church already?" Only after they completed their work at Portridge Arms, did Cora and Ida go home to clean up, prepare their families' meals, dine and then dress in their finest for the evening service conducted at the Ruggles Street Baptist Mission for those of its flock who had to work Sunday mornings.

"No-o-o," reposted Florrie, "she's still upstairs getting ready, so you will have a chance to say hello. And she'll be so pleased not to have missed you, Cora." Florrie and Lavinia allowed themselves a quick smile at each other. Whether the dislike between Cora and Agnes was strictly personal friction or there was some tribal bias at the root of it, only Lavinia's and Flora's refusal to tolerate that nonsense kept a lid on the animosity. To keep them apart as much as possible, when Cora was due to clean rooms, Agnes was assigned to kitchen work.

"Here's the list of the rooms that were occupied this week and those that are rented for this coming week. Two acts left early, so you can start on those. Cora, will you take number one? And Ida, number eleven on the top floor is ready for you." Lavinia always tried to give Cora fewer stairs to climb despite the older woman's frequently sour disposition. Ida certainly didn't object; she preferred being on her own to clean rather than take instruction from Cora on every matter from the correct way to fold towels to securing sheets under the mattress. But until Ida was out of her sight, Cora still pulled rank. "Don't forget to air the rooms, Ida."

Once inside the newly vacated rooms, they opened the windows to air the rooms as much as weather permitted, stripped the bed, bagged the dirty bed linen, towels and washcloths and set the bag out in the hall. Then upholstery and mattresses were brushed vigorously, everything from window ledges to furniture was dusted, the washbowl set scrubbed, clean towels placed on the washstand, the beds made with fresh linens and, finally, the carpet swept. Just before leaving the room, each woman closed the windows. Mr Boniface locked the doors of each of the clean rooms after he drew the shades.

That was the routine when a room was being rented again right away. If a room did not need to be cleaned immediately for the imminent arrival of a new guest, it was locked after the linens and rubbish were removed and washstands emptied. Those newly-vacated rooms that were not booked during the forthcoming week were given a more painstaking cleaning after change-over day on those Tuesday and Thursday afternoons that Cora was again due. If it were not raining or snowing, drapes and carpets were hauled out to the side yard of 144 where Agnes and Florrie administered a thorough beating, shaking and airing. Every month or so, the windows would be washed, and the woodwork and furniture in the room were treated to an application of lemon oil.

One by one, floor by floor, Cora and Ida cleaned the designated rooms and dragged the dirty linens down to the second floor bump-up to be sent to the basement where they awaited the weekly visit of the laundryman. When they met at the dumbwaiter, they gossiped about any tell-tale evidence left behind and lied to each other about how few or many coins had been left as tips.

For all they had to do, they worked quietly, efficiently and quickly, yet before they had finished the first rooms, guests often began stirring. Some greeted the cleaning women heartily. Ida smiled and returned the greeting; Cora regarded such exuberance with a fish eye and nodded perfunctorily. Other guests tried to slip by unnoticed and unengaged until a morning coffee restored to them the power of speech.

After 9 o'clock, Cora ceased to be quiet. It was her opinion, in which she put great trust, that laying about was not to be encouraged. Bad enough that stage people were godless and traveled on the Lord's Day instead of going to church; it wouldn't hurt them to rise in time to attend services before they had to catch their trains.

If Cora failed to comprehend the trials of actors' lives, theatre folk probably did not appreciate her or Ida's. Cora cleaned houses seven days a week to support an ill husband and two increasingly restive teenaged grandchildren. Her family had lived as freemen in Riverside, Cambridge, since before the American Revolution, but generation by generation, misfortune by misfortune, they had lost their purchase on middleclass life, and Cora, nearing seventy, was fighting to hold together what was left of her family.

Ida was single, although closing in on thirty, and had moved a few years earlier on her own to Boston from a small farm town outside Athens, Georgia. During the week Ida worked at Hinds Hand Laundry where she earned barely enough for her weekly room rate.

If the vaudevillians and actors filling up on coffee, tea, warm rolls, fruit preserves, and porridge knew nothing of the lives of the cleaning women, Lavinia and Florrie knew little more about either of them. Cora was too proud to discuss her troubles, and Ida, not much given to complaint.

By the time all the vacated rooms had been cleaned, it was lunchtime, and Florrie, as always, had set out some of the buffet on the kitchen table for Cora, Ida, Lavinia and herself. Lavinia usually fixed a plate to bring to her office where she worked while she ate. Florrie made it a point to sit with Cora and Ida, but gifted as she was in ferreting out bits of personal history in others, Florrie had made little headway with either Cora or Ida during the past three years. Mr Boniface always arrived just as the others were finishing. After a small snack, he put away the leftover food and washed up.

After lunch, Cora and Ida cleaned the first floor rooms, the hallways and stairs. By the time they finished, most of the departing lodgers had left the building, and Cora and Ida turned their hands to bathrooms and the dining, sitting and music rooms.

As the last of the departing boarders left for the next engagements, new lodgers began to show up, most arriving by late afternoon. Lavinia, by then clear of her weekly bookkeeping and account reconciliation, registered each act, and Mr Boniface helped them with their hand luggage as he escorted them to their assigned rooms on the upper floors. Once situated and unpacked, the actors and performers usually came down to the sitting room where an afternoon tea awaited them. It was a chance for performers and actors to renew acquaintance and swap the stories that were exaggerated only to make a point and earn a laugh.

CHAPTER 9

Sunday Morning: In with the New at Portridge Arms

The Hennigan Brothers were already settled in the second-floor sitting room when Victor Greeley & Company arrived. Mr Greeley, a bit past fifty, was expansive in all dimensions of the word. He laughed heartily, even in small gatherings, as though he needed to be sure his joviality reached and warmed the second balcony. The evidence of his appetite was well tailored with quality tweed and broadcloth. "& Company" referred to his wife, Doris. Equally well upholstered, Mrs Greeley was nearly mute in social situations. Perhaps she held back in relief that there were others present to absorb her husband's clubby garrulity.

Onstage, she was as active and vocal as her husband in their comedy sketch, "Shopping for Shoes." She played a demanding and clumsy customer; he was the salesman juggling piles of shoe boxes while trying to remain polite. No disrespect toward Doris Greeley was intended in the billing. Victor had played this act for nearly ten years, and his was a relatively well-known and well-paid act usually slotted in the coveted fourth or fifth spots on bill in the better small-time houses. Victor had hired Doris seven years ago to replace the female member of the three-person troupe. By the time they married a few years later (both for a second time), to change billing to include the new Mrs Greeley was to risk losing the reputation and good will the act had built up under its original name.

To increase their profit, they had dispensed with a third member of the act, reduced that role to a walk-on and hired a different person in each town to play the part. Usually someone from another act had time, before or after he performed in his own act, to make the brief appearance onstage that the Greeley's act required. If no professional were available, a stage hand was usually willing for the promise of a few extra dollars at the end of the week's engagement. No lines were required and the actor's own street clothes were sufficient wardrobe to play a delivery man who arrives with a truckload of shoes just before the blackout.

The Hennigan Brothers, Ned and Mike, were just beginning their first season as a double act in vaudeville, and, unless some young attractive females happened into the scene, the boys were happy to pick up tips from an old pro, and Victor Greeley relished the role. Lavinia, who had already met Ned and Mike, entered the room with an acknowledging nod and a fresh pitcher of coffee to re-fill the urn. Florrie followed behind with a bowl-shaped basket in her hands.

"Hello Victor, how are you. And Doris, lovely to see you, my dear. I'm so glad you two are staying with us again." Next to a stack of small plates, Florrie set down the basket of fresh sweet biscuits plump with raisins and kept warm by a large cotton cloth wrapped under and over them. "Where are you playing this week?"

"Closing the first half at the Tremont, happy to say. The good citizens of Boston are still welcoming our act enthusiastically."

"And why shouldn't they, Victor? I never tire of seeing it." Turning to the young men at her left, "I'm Flora Portridge. My sister Lavinia and I are happy to have you as guests. You haven't stayed with us before, have you?"

"No, Ma'am. First time," reported Ned, the self-appointed spokesman for the act. "I'm Ned and he's Mike. We're the Hennigan Brothers, 'Feet that Speak.' Only we're not real brothers."

"Not all are." Florrie spoke more enigmatically than she intended. "And it's good to meet you, too, Mike." Mike smiled and nodded as he rose from his seat, grateful for the acknowledgement. "We're on the bill at the National this week. Number two spot."

As soon as Mike said it, Ned squelched his partner: "That's just while we break in the new routine." All present except his new partner understood that the number two act on any bill held a position of little prestige. "After we set it, we'll add a little flash and get a better spot."

"I have every confidence that you will, Mr Hennigan," said Greeley reaching toward the platter. The biscuits were gone within minutes of Florrie's departure.

"Say, Mr Greeley, what did the old girl call herself?"

"Flora Portridge. Her sister is Miss Lavinia."

"The fellow in Providence who gave us this address called them the Porridge Sisters; said it was the cheapest clean digs in town."

"Ah, yes," chortled Victor Greeley, "the Porridge Sisters, as they are known to all and sundry who tour the provinces..."

"What?"

"Young fellow, were you not told about the food?" for once lowering his voice.

"What about the food?"

"The good sisters eschew all manner of butchered flesh."

"Say, talk in a plain way a feller can understand, will ya?"

"The sisters are vegetarian, and so must we be whilst at their table. They do not serve meat at any of their meals."

"Geez, I never heard of that. You mean we get no beef or ham?" asked Mike.

"Nor fish, nor fowl. A few years back, soon after the dear sisters first opened this establishment, some wag corrupted their name to Porridge, a symbol in his simple mind of their culinary limitations. But my wife and I—both of us committed omnivores, by the way—can assure that you will partake of some of the tastiest recipes you'll ever encounter in a theatrical boarding house. And the portions are copious."

Mrs Greeley nodded.

"That's why we patronize the Porridge Sisters. Clean, pleasant rooms, plenty of hot water, wholesome and plentiful food and superior company. Isn't that right, my dear?"

Mrs Greeley nodded again and added a smile.

"What the hell," muttered Ned.

"Do what others do. Order your roasted flesh for lunch between shows but save room for the evening repast. You won't be disappointed."

"And don't let them hear you call them the Porridge Sisters," stage-whispered Mrs Greeley.

She needn't have spoken sotto voce. The clatter from the floor below, made by the new arrivals and their luggage stopped conversation short and brought Florrie to the front hall to see if anything were the matter. Mr Boniface held open the front door to admit a grim, squat woman, portmanteau in either hand, surging through into the hall followed by three children, each banging their luggage across the polished oak floor. The woman hurried them along with a breathless stream of chatter until she reached Lavinia standing midway in the hall.

"Good afternoon, I'm Mrs Renée Cormier and this is my daughter, Dainty Alice, and we're appearing at the Tremont Theatre. You'll find our reservation for two rooms under my name." We are "Dainty Alice and Her Chums," and, indicating with a backhand wave two dispirited-looking lads, she added "these young lads assist her."

In a measured tone Lavinia uttered a "Good afternoon," and directed the new arrivals to the office. For their Boston engagement, the act's first trip East after several years playing small-time circuits in the South, Southwest and Midwest, Mrs Cormier had selected the Portridge Arms because she had been told the price was right and the food plentiful enough, if meatless, to satisfy the youngsters without additional expenditures on her part to augment their diets with lunches purchased elsewhere. She had also been told that children under seven were accepted without charge provided they stayed in the same room as the parents.

Mrs Cormier hadn't stopped chattering since she had barged through the front door, except to catch her breath and put her hand to her heart, a bit of poorly-calculated drama that failed to represent her as flustered or frail. She continued to bubble and spout as she was led into the office. No sooner inside and seated in a chair facing Lavinia, who had taken her proprietary place behind her desk, Mrs Cormier informed her landlady that all three children were under seven. Lavinia looked pointedly at the children. The boys might pass for eight, but Dainty Alice likely wouldn't see ten again, unless in another lifetime.

"You reserved two double rooms, our least expensive, correct?" And without a pause and as though she hadn't heard her new guest, Lavinia informed her "That will be ten dollars and fifty cents for each room, double occupancy. Departure time is eleven on Sunday morning."

"But I just told you that these children are under seven," protested Mrs Cormier.

"Ah, well, if that's the case, I doubt that the Gerry Society will allow those children to fulfill their contract here in Boston," countered Lavinia.

The mention of the Gerry Society felt like a punch to Mrs Cormier. Down South and in the Midwest there had been little evidence of the Society for the Prevention of Cruelty to Children, but she had heard stories about those busybodies who dragged children off the stage and their guardians into court. Of course, it mattered little to the SPCC whether the children were seven, eight, ten or twelve, and Mrs Cormier interpreted Lavinia's comment as a threat to notify the Gerry Society.

44

"My heavens, you're asking for twenty-one dollars! I can't afford that. I'm a widow…"

"You're appearing at the Tremont?," cut in Lavinia.

"Yes …"

"What spot on the bill?"

"Fourth… " No sooner said than regretted. Any act appearing fourth on the bill was receiving a decent salary, no less than $75 for the week and probably more.

Lavinia had no wish to prolong the encounter. "I'm assuming that you will share your room with your daughter, so that will be ten dollars and fifty cents, but I'll only charge you seven-fifty for the two boys to share the other double."

A resolute woman herself, Mrs Cormier recognized that quality in another person.

"That will be satisfactory."

Lavinia continued to look directly at Mrs Cormier.

"Thank you," added Mrs Cormier. Lavinia turned the registration book toward her new boarder and handed her a pen.

"Mr Boniface," Lavinia called, and he, just outside the door awaiting his cue like any conscientious actor, appeared immediately. "Would you help Mrs Cormier and her children with their luggage? Rooms ten and eleven." He gave a small bow and led the way up to the attic floor trailed by Cormier and company.

At the front of the hall, Florrie was greeting several new arrivals. Seeing that her sister was free, she escorted two young ladies to the office. "Lavinia, I'm sure you remember Marla and Paula." Several years had passed since the Franklin Sisters had played Boston, but old acquaintance is quickly renewed in show business, and Lavinia and the young women quickly and pleasantly concluded their business with a promise to meet in the sitting room later for tea and biscuits.

Another half dozen or so guests were expected, and they would arrive throughout the afternoon and into the evening. After each act was settled into its room, they were invited to join those below in the second-floor sitting room for light refreshments and to meet other boarders before dinner was served. Well after dinner time, sandwiches and coffee were left in the sitting room for those who arrived at night. If Lavinia were not available, Florrie or Mr Boniface registered the latecomers and showed them to their rooms.

CHAPTER 10

Monday Morning: Band Call at the Tremont

Monday mornings were the worst of the week, and Portridge Arms, like every other theatrical boarding house, was a madhouse. Vaudevillians had to arrive at their respective theatres earlier on Mondays than during the rest of the week. Some were preoccupied, others distracted, as they gathered in the dining room one by one or in pairs to partake of the morning buffet. Although their contracts specified the terms of their engagement—salary, dates of employment and description of their acts (performers could not change their acts without permission because the contract read "act as known")—the managers of each local theatre could change the order of bills or even fire an act after the Monday matinee.

The Portridge Arms' boarders included actors as well as variety performers. Several of the actors stayed beyond the single week, as their plays ran as long as audiences were willing to attend in sufficient numbers, rather than the single week usual for most vaudeville dates. Those actors who were to report to a new company and theatre in Boston were just as nervous as the variety acts. Some of the new actors were replacements and had to learn scripts and stage business that others in the cast already knew; others would be attending the first read-through and subsequent rehearsal of a play they had little time to study.

Vaudevillians, burlesquers or actors, all but the most robust personalities were muted due to the morning hour and lack of acquaintance among all but a few old friends and those they had met briefly on Sunday. Camaraderie blossomed quickly, commencing with the shared evening meal, provided that the day's work had gone well. By the end of the week, unless a rivalry or a grievance had been sparked, they considered themselves, one and all, dear friends for life, although it might be years before they met again.

Among the actors were two long-time acquaintances of Mr Boniface's—an older husband and wife who, after a long spell of being at liberty, had been engaged for some small parts at Castle Square for the remainder of the season. The old friends were delighted to be in each other's company again and to share the good news that too seldom blessed actors of their years. Mr

Boniface, too, has been an irregular in the Castle Square stock company for the better part of the past decade, essaying small roles and sometimes helping in the box office when there were no parts for him. Other theatres, when shorthanded because one of their employees was out sick, had quit or been fired, called upon Mr Boniface's temporary services because of his reliability and familiarity with business both backstage and at the front of the house.

The few actors present in the room tended to brood or to be quietly running lines in their heads, and they followed, as much as purse allowed, Polonius' sartorial advice. The vaudevillians were more animated and their clothes sportier than the garb of their thespian brethren. They had a long day ahead beginning with the Monday morning band call. Some were too keyed to ingest anything other than coffee. Others, especially the physical acts like the tumblers and dancers, loaded their plates at the buffet table several times. Wiser heads partook moderately: they ate enough to sustain themselves until dinner, but not so much that they felt bloated or sluggish and lost their edge during band call or the matinee performance.

As they arrived at their respective vaudeville houses, each act placed the folders containing its music downstage along the apron. The first to arrive put his pile in the center and each succeeding act added its charts to the right of the previous pile. That let the pit band leader know the order in which the acts had shown up at the call. Theoretically, the pit band leader handled the acts in that order, but headlining acts sometimes took advantage of their value to the bill by pleading an appointment with a reporter, a music publisher or a hairdresser that required them to leave as early as possible. Headliners also had the proprietary call on music. If an act lower on the bill sang, danced or played to the same music as the headliner, the star invariably claimed privilege, and the act on the undercard had to scramble for another tune to replace one he had expected to use.

Pit band leaders sometimes juggled the order of acts to be called regardless of who arrived before whom, choosing to deal with singers and dancers first because their orchestral accompaniments were more complicated. A monologist, however, might be dismissed earliest because he confirmed that all he needed was some upbeat music to cue him on and off stage and a few rim shots on the drum or a couple of wah-wahs on a trombone to drive home the jokes.

Sitting in on the call, off to one side, was the electrician who made note of requests for special lighting effects. Blackouts were needed to punch the closing lines of a comedy sketch, but appeals from acts on the undercard for a spotlight were often refused because more established acts demanded a spotlight, and the electrician and the theatre manager did not wish to overuse the effect. Also on stage sat the stage manager who determined what each act needed in the way of a drop. Only the more successful acts could afford to purchase and transport a custom-made drop curtain. Most acts simply hoped the theatre had on hand some painted scene, interior or exterior, appropriate to their acts.

For those acts that were neither preferred for the musical content of their act nor handled quickly for their minimal requirements, energy quickly ebbed at the call. If the call proved complicated and long, the last few performers, such as an acrobatic or bicycling act, might not get a chance to slip out of the theatre to grab a bite to eat before they had to be costumed, made up and ready to open the bill for the Monday matinee.

Wherever there were theatres, there were restaurants. Tea rooms like Schrafft's offered dainty sandwiches, pastries and ice cream and catered to women shoppers and matinee-goers. Mahogany enclaves with gleaming brass fixtures like Jacob Wirth's attracted successful businessmen and sporting types. Entertainers, unless they were stars, passed up atmosphere for small prices and large portions. Many male actors and variety performers sought out taverns where a five-cent beer bought access to a free lunch counter of pigs' knuckles, sausages, pickled eggs, cheeses, crackers and pumpernickel bread. Unless escorted by a male or extraordinarily immune to hard glances and whispered rude remarks, female entertainers usually patronized cafeterias instead or arranged for food to be brought into the theatre between shows.

The theatre district marked the crossroads between the Downtown shopping district of Lower Washington Street, the South End and Chinatown. A motley district, Chinatown was still home to a few Syrian and Jewish families and businesses that, prior to the arrival of the ever gathering Chinese, were tucked into warrens of two- and three-storey bricks houses surrounded by tall warehouses accommodating Boston's garment trade. To the east, just beyond those warehouses and tenements, lay South Union Railway Station and the wharfs of Boston's waterfront.

Between a Monday morning call and matinee, a performer who knew her or his way around Chinatown could shop for fabric, take it to a Jewish tailor or a Chinese seamstress with a sketch of what was desired, get measured and still have time to step into one of the tiny Chinese eateries for a fast, noodle-based lunch that was less expensive than anything in Downtown or the theatre district except the free lunch counter of a tavern. Almost as speedy as the cooks were the needle wizards who produced made-to-order garments in two days.

CHAPTER 11

Monday Matinee: Tremont Theatre

Lavinia and Florence customarily "showed the flag" at those theatres that booked their boarders. The sisters started this particular week by heading to the Monday matinee at the Tremont Theatre, where several of their boarders were playing. The following evening, they'd try to catch the bill at the Gaiety or the Globe, both on Lower Washington Street and, later in the week, they'd squeeze in a matinee at the National, a neighborhood theatre located a few long blocks south of the Portridge Arms. As Mr Boniface's friends' engagement at Castle Square was expected to last through the year's end, Lavinia and Florrie gave them time to settle into their parts and planned to attend an evening performance sometime during the second or third week.

Heretofore, Agnes has refused to attend any shows, even though the sisters had offered to pay for her ticket. This Monday, Lavinia insisted. "Consider it not a sin, but a duty to our customers. Besides, the Catholic Church isn't against vaudeville. Who do you think financed Keith's New Theatre up on Washington Street? Your own Cardinal O'Connell and the Boston archdiocese. Are you putting yourself above a Cardinal?"

The Tremont Theatre, opposite the lower end of the Boston Common and situated on Tremont Street a few buildings north of Boylston Street, was a ten-minute stroll up Tremont Street from Portridge Arms. Never before had Agnes set foot in a theatre; she had been brought up by her family to regard such entertainments as inappropriate for salt-of-the-earth, hard-working and God-fearing folks. Father O'Brien at St. Pat's went one better, deeming all public performance except Mass an occasion for sin.

Agnes had little idea what to expect, but Lavinia and Florrie noted that she was clearly impressed with the lobby, the colorfully executed murals that adorned the vaulted ceiling above the auditorium and the red, plush house curtain framed by a gilded proscenium. After she had taken in the wonders of design, Agnes occasionally lifted the programme to hide her face and turned around in her seat to peer at the hundreds of people who were filing in to take their seats. There seemed many more people than ever attended Mass at Saint Pat's—and some of the same. When she thought she spotted someone she knew, she quickly slumped down in her seat and directed her attention to her programme until the pit band launched into a medley of march music, ragtime ditties and parlor songs as the house lights dimmed.

Folks were still sauntering down the aisles to their seats when the curtain parted to reveal the full stage onto which ran three jugglers, Indian clubs flying back and forth among them. According to the card cradled on the easel next to the proscenium at the audience's left, the act was called The Kratoc Trio. Lavinia and Florrie noticed that Agnes was momentarily startled by their swift limber movements and, perhaps, by the red leotards that hugged their finely muscled physiques and the short, sequined trunks that adorned their nether regions. Clearly, after a few minutes into the acrobatic act, Agnes was oblivious of all but the entertainment before her.

As the front curtain descended and the applause receded, the bandleader signaled his musicians to quit the jugglers' exit music and strike up the entrance music for the next act. An usher stepped on stage from the space between the proscenium and the house curtain and slipped the Kratoc card behind the others resting on the easel. The usher was gone in a second, leaving exposed a new card that read "The Taylor Twins: Tunes & Trills," as two young women walked on from the opposite end of the stage whistling to their accompaniment.

For the next eight minutes, the Taylor girls dispatched three songs indistinguishable by pace or delivery, while standing nearly stock still down center in front of the house curtain—known as playing *in one*. Later, Agnes, when asked, couldn't remember a thing about their act except their gowns, which she had studied with such admiring intensity that she could have duplicated them from memory on the family sewing machine. Perfunctory applause barely lingered until the Taylors curtsied and ran offstage.

The audience was pepped up by a black-face comedian, Pearlie Williams. The curtain parted as Pearlie entered *in two* singing "Little 'Liza Jennie" and added quick eccentric steps between each couplet. "I've got a house in Baltimore, Little 'Liza Jennie," was punctuated by finger snaps and heel slaps. "Lots of chillum 'round de door, Little 'Liza Jennie," ended with a double spin and an abrupt stop facing the audience. By then downstage center, Pearlie, "The Ragtime Rascal," stood still as he sang a variant of the well-known chorus: "Oh, Eliza, Little 'Liza Jennie.

Oh, Eliza, Little 'Liza Jennie, Come my love and be with me, Little 'Liza Jennie."

Thankful to him for rescuing the bill, the audience interrupted (as Pearlie intended) with applause. As he stepped forward to acknowledge their appreciation, the front curtain closed behind him, leaving him playing *in one.* and Pearlie raised his white-gloved hand to stem the applause. He began telling how he met Little 'Liza, her Mama and then her entire county-wide family including her shot-gun-toting Daddy. The audience laughed heartily and frequently, and Pearlie finished his ten-minute spot with an eccentric dance. His legs flew in every direction and, too soon for the audience, he scampered offstage. The folks brought him back for two more calls, and he rewarded them by dancing offstage each time. With a matinee, dinner show and evening show scheduled with little time in between, theatre managers grew nervous when acts added minutes to their allotted times, so Pearlie bowed briefly each time, careful not to milk applause, and quickly danced off stage into the wing space.

What the audience didn't realize was that underneath the dark brown greasepaint was dark brown skin. Pearlie White, long successful in *colored* revues and burlesques, was among the few African Americans playing white vaudeville in 1908, and he was proving a hard act to follow. That could generate resentment among acts less talented or successful, so, when backstage, Pearlie White greeted everyone softly and formally and kept to himself as much as possible.

To the accompaniment of tinkling, nursery-rhyme music, the front curtain parted on "Dainty Alice & Her Chums" and the Tremont Theatre's stock drop curtain for rural settings. Alice, dressed as Little Bo Peep, stood downstage center. Her act also played *in two,* which was the front half of the stage, an area that included *in one,* the stage apron in front of the house curtain. Off to the rear and one side, Her Chums, tucked into bib overalls and flannel shirts, intoned the familiar lyrics: "Little Bo Peep has lost her sheep, and doesn't know where to find them," while Alice made the expected gestures such as shielding her eyes and looking to the stage wings on her right and then her left. The boys soprano voices reached "Leave them alone, and they'll come home, wagging their tails behind them" as Dainty Alice rose to the tips of her dainty toe shoes and lifted her arms and chin to the heavens in supplication before she began twirling in a series of pirouettes that circled the stage until she stepped between Her Chums and the three of them segued into a basic box step while they sang "Ida, Sweet as Apple Cider," with little concern that they had conferred upon Dainty Alice yet another alias.

If the audience had wondered about such matters or why Dainty Alice was a head taller than her chums or why she and the sheep were in a forest glade rather than a pasture or if the sheep would, indeed, find their way back, the audience—man, woman and child—had lost interest by the time the trio donned papier mâché derbies and piped and strutted to "Hunky Dory Cake Walk," ending with cartwheels into the wings by the boys and a last balletic fling on her toes by Dainty Alice.

Mrs Cormier, stationed in the wing space down left, immediately pushed Alice back on stage to prolong the applause. As the girl twirled, then scurried back into the wing space, Mrs Cormier hissed at the boys to cartwheel back on, but the applause had already diminished and the orchestra leader had signaled the downbeat for the next act's music as the lads backed off stage.

Only a few bars of exit music covered their retreat into the wings before the band ushered Victor Greeley & Company on stage. As it had in seasons past and in front of every type of audience, "Shopping for Shoes," with its blend of witty repartee and physical comedy, roused the audience again and successfully closed out the first half of the bill. The plush house curtain traveled in from both sides of the stage even as the exit music and applause continued. Curtain closed, several calls were taken by Victor and Doris Greeley before the house lights were turned up and the music ceased. Florrie, never reticent about such matters, suggested to Agnes that they visit the Ladies Lounge, knowing that Agnes would be embarrassed to mention a need.

CHAPTER 12

Monday Afternoon: Backstage Tempest, Tremont Theatre

Lavinia, Florrie and Agnes returned to their seats just before the
second half of the show opened with the County Cork Cloggers, a
lively and personable six person step-dancing ensemble performing
in three. They, in turn, were followed by El Barto, a close up, card-
manipulating magician who worked *in one* while the full stage
behind him was readied for the headliners. Each canvas drop,
when lowered, butted against a *teaser,* one of the short black
curtains that ran horizontally across and above the stage like a
window valance, and the corresponding vertical black wings that
jutted out a bit from the sides of the stage. If the proscenium were
the frame and the painted drop and actors comprised the picture,
the teasers and wings were the matting that brought frame and
picture neatly together, and blocked any light that might have
peeked through as the crew behind the drop assembled and
dressed the set for the next act.

Both the clog dancers and the magician had pleased the public
and put them in receptive mood for The Manners-Halsey Musical
Ensemble, a flash act that carried their own backdrop, one
featuring a *center stage fancy* opening. As the ensemble awaited
their entrance music, lined up in the narrow space between the
painted center stage fancy and the dusty brick wall that marked the
rear exterior of the theatre, they tried to keep their full dress suits
and gowns from getting soiled. Then, on cue, they popped through
what seemed to the audience to be an arched entrance and down
three 'marble' steps into a grand salon the exact size of the full
stage. As soon as the ladies and gentlemen entered the scene, they
paired off to dance decorously to the waltz music produced by the
pit band and a tuxedoed gent seated at an onstage piano. Several
potted plants and tapestries helped suggest a posh parlor
appearance appropriate to the name of the act, "Life of the Party."

When the music changed to ragtime, the young ladies and
gentlemen clustered around the grand piano mid-stage right,
quietly harmonizing in a medley of tunes and swaying in place as
each member, in turn, was urged to step downstage center left to
perform their specialty. All the turns were short and lively: two
couples sharing the floor as they performed a cakewalk, a romantic
duet in song, a brief comic solo dance by Bert Halsey, and another

medley, this one of sentimental minstrel songs by the entire ensemble, tambourines materializing from a table behind the piano.

Just as the ensemble singing momentarily ebbed, Maud Manners entered the scene through the upstage center door fancy. Stunningly dressed in a deep emerald-green gown and silver satin cape, she immediately caught everyone's eye, especially that of Bert Halsey, sharply turned-out in white tie and tails.

Manners and Halsey had been small-time headliners as long as anyone, especially they, could recall. They looked fit although they were well into their fifties yet were wise enough to let the younger members of their troupe perform the song and dance specialties that built up to the spot where Maud's and Bert's characters discovered each other at the party, engaged in flirtatious repartee and sang a ragtime duet.

As the music segued to Spanish march music, Manners & Halsey danced a *paso doble* while the rest of the company clustered admiringly in a semi-circle behind them and clacked castanets, also hitherto hidden. The *paso doble* was a dramatic dance, one that required control and audacity but did not demand great agility or speed. The act was smartly paced, fashionably dressed and offered a variety of dancing and singing along with clever dialogue. Despite those qualities, it remained an abbreviated and gussied up minstrel show shorn of its black greasepaint and corny jokes. At 18 minutes, it was a bit long and elicited nostalgic affection more than enthusiasm from 1908 audiences.

As the ensemble was taking its second call, Lavinia hustled Florrie and Agnes out of their seats and down an aisle to the side door that led to backstage. By the time they reached the end of the passageway, the curtain has reopened on the closing act, a solo musician playing a contraption that appeared to be, as much as they could see as they passed quickly through the wing space, a combination of a marimba, drums and chimes. The fervid racket did little to hold the audience to its chairs, and the theatre was half empty by the time the poor chap had finished flaying his invention, two mallets in each hand.

Florrie and Lavinia always went backstage to congratulate their boarders on their performances; the Porridge Sisters' compliments were no less sincere than others' but attending performances was also a good way to drum up business for their boarding house. Other performers noted that Lavinia and Florrie were alone among boardinghouse owners to show such support for their guests.

That afternoon, however, the theatre manager, Laurence Simpson, had preceded them backstage with a set of photographs under his arm. In vaudeville theatres across the land, there were signs in dressing rooms to warn acts not to send out their laundry until after the Monday performances, and a set of publicity photos tucked under a manager's arm meant that at least one act was getting the boot. In this case it was the Taylor Twins. The girls, sobbing, ran off to their dressing room.

Simpson then sought out Mrs Cormier and informed her that he was moving her daughter's act to the second spot—quite a comedown for an act originally booked into the number four spot, and that another act was being brought in from Providence to take over the fourth spot from that evening's show forward for the remainder of the week. Enraged, Mrs Cormier began berating the manager until he threatened to dismiss her act as well as the Taylor Twins. Renée Cormier shifted tactics immediately to pleading and crying.

Most theatre managers in vaudeville didn't enjoy firing an act or lowering its position on the bill, but his customers were his first priority, for without their patronage there would be no income to pay anyone. Simpson, General Manager of Ira Wood Enterprises as well as the Tremont's manager, displayed neither remorse nor obvious cruelty. Over the years he had heard every ploy for pity and every plea to reverse his decision, yet he always remained unswayed.

Discretion was merited amid the commotion, so Lavinia and Florrie pulled a goggle-eyed Agnes with them as they slipped behind a lowered drop and slinked to the stage door. Agnes was at least as fascinated with the backstage contretemps as she had been by the show. As they reached the exit, old Petey Martin, the stage-door tender, gave them a high sign and began to approach them, hoping to gossip, but Lavinia, who had no wish to be seen or to witness Mrs Cormier's ranting threats, stayed Petey with her upraised hand. Florrie caught his glance and mouthed a single word: "Later."

Unlike most stage-door tenders, old Petey was neither a retired performer nor a policeman. He had been a stage hand and over the years had seen too many displays of temper and temperament to sympathize with the insecurities, fears and high hopes of stage folk. Lavinia and Florrie knew that Petey would do his best to conceal his amusement or satisfaction, but Lavinia didn't wish to hear more than they had, and, as it involved one of their boarders, she was anxious that they leave before there was any chance of their lodger, Mrs Cormier dragging them into the skirmish.

At the moment, Lavinia was determined to get home as fast as possible. She and Florrie had to discuss how to handle matters at Portridge Arms before all their boarders arrived and gossip ensued when they met for dinner. Unless Lavinia and Flora could curtail the spread of tittle-tattle, it would prove a difficult week and create disharmony among the boarders, especially if Mrs Cormier didn't reconcile herself to events. As they closed the stage door behind them and picked their way down the steps into the alley leading to Beach Street, thence to Washington Street, Lavinia halted and looked at Agnes. "Agnes, not a word to anyone back at the house. Do you understand me?" Even in the half-light, Agnes knew Lavinia meant business, and she nodded her assent.

CHAPTER 13

Monday: A Quiet Dinner for Twenty Odd

The Taylor Twins, still in tears, had fled to the dressing rooms, stuffed their few belongings into their cardboard suitcases and rushed out of the theatre. The girls halted in the Tremont's back alley; they had not thought of anything except to flee the scene of their shame. Not only had they no place to go and only a few coins to get there, they had left their music behind with the conductor. Neither was willing just then to return to retrieve their music charts. They would wait until the other performers had left the theatre.

They ducked around a corner as Mrs Cormier, still railing against management and the rotten hand fate had dealt her, banged out the stage door, prodding the children ahead down the grated metal stairs and through the narrow alleyways of Haymarket Place and Bumstead Court onto Boylston Street. Once lost in the anonymity of other passersby, Cormier and her three charges slowed to a dispirited walk—her charges confused and she unaware of anyone or any misery except her own. They turned left onto Tremont Street and walked the rest of the way back to Portridge Arms in glum silence.

The rest of the acts, anxious to avoid embarrassment and troubled to think up something reassuring to say to two punk acts, stalled before they departed the theatre. Petey Martin found delight where others felt discomfit.

If Agnes didn't delight in others' misfortune, she certainly thrilled at the events of an afternoon unlike any other she had experienced. The vaudeville display of music, color, fancy clothes and attractive men may have been the devil's doing, but it had entranced. Then, imagine!, she had been one of the select who was allowed to go backstage where they were privy to a burst of excitement of another kind.

A niggling thought wormed its way into Agnes' recollection of events: perhaps the show and its aftermath were both occasions for sin. Well that was something that could be settled with Father Quinn the next time she went to confession. Meantime, oh, she had some story for her Ma and Da when she went home for Sunday dinner.

Lavinia's and Florrie's individual recollections were more sober. During their walk home, and even as they made ready tonight's dinner for their guests, they continued to dwell on the unhappy events they had witnessed. As she worked, Agnes watched vainly for a sign that some discussion was permitted about what they had seen backstage, but only a few questions and replies about food interrupted the near-silent bustle.

Lavinia knew that soon enough the squabble at the Tremont would become known to all the performers in Boston, and its aftermath would seep into Portridge Arms. Mrs Cormier was unpleasant enough in the best of circumstances; thwarted, she promised to be disruptive.

Florrie's thoughts flew back to the theatre. She felt sorry for those two girls who called themselves the Taylor Twins. Their singing was passable enough, but they seemed to have no inkling of what it took to build an act that found favor with audiences. It was as though they had never performed on a stage before. How on earth did they get a booking at the Tremont without some needed experience at smaller-time vaudeville houses to teach them what the public expected?

Although Florrie had prepared some dishes that morning, getting dinner ready was always a more rushed affair whenever Lavinia and Florrie also attended a vaudeville matinee. Portridge Arms was host to seventeen boarders that week, and they, along with Mr Boniface, Agnes, Lavinia and Florrie totaled 21 people to feed—never a simple task, and one that required all hands on board.

Florrie had made her decision well before dinner was cooked, the upstairs dining room table set or the food sent up in the dumbwaiter and served to a houseful of hungry vaudevillians. She gobbled her own dinner quickly and quietly and then immediately set about scrubbing pots and cleaning the kitchen's preparation tables while Lavinia, Agnes and Mr Boniface were still supping at the kitchen table.

Lavinia knew something was afoot, so it was not unexpected when Florrie announced that she had to go out and visit poor Mrs Woodhull up the street. It was useless to try to deter Florrie when she had a bee in her bonnet.

"I won't be long, Lavinia. No more than an hour. Just a quick visit and maybe run an errand for her. And I'll finish whatever cleaning still needs to be done when I get back."

Mrs Woodhull was likely on Florrie's agenda for that evening, but merely as a stop on the way to listen to Petey Martin's gossip. And both sisters knew that.

CHAPTER 14

Monday Evening Replacement Act: Tremont Theatre

As Miss Rice alit from the hackney in front of the Tremont Theatre, Laurence Simpson, on watch from within the interior lobby, came forward to greet her. Miss Rice had agreed to meet the manager precisely at 5 pm, and she was only a few minutes tardy. Simpson, a stickler for punctuality, for once wished she had been a few minutes later still. The contretemps backstage had ruffled him, and he wished he had more time to collect himself before Rosetta's arrival.

Nevertheless, he greeted Rosetta Rice cordially and calmly and, instead of accompanying her to the stage entrance as was customary for performers, he guided her into the Tremont through its lobby and asked her to wait in his private office while he attended to her luggage. As she glided forward with Simpson, Rosetta noticed with satisfaction but no outward sign that a sandwich board, placed in the inner lobby only minutes before she arrived, displayed her photograph and hailed "Rosetta Rice" as a "Special Attraction." Along with her purse, Rosetta carried a folio case containing her music charts. Simpson had tipped the driver generously to deliver her luggage backstage where a stage hand had been ordered to keep his ear cocked for a delivery at the stage door. In Simpson's private office, a tray awaited with a pot of steaming tea, cream, sugar and two sets of cups and saucers.

They exchanged a few formal pleasantries about the Tremont Theatre, barely touched their tea, before Rosetta suggested that they not keep the band from their dinner break longer than necessary.

Mr Simpson led Miss Rice down a side aisle and called to Earl Findley who, knowing Miss Rice was due for a quick cue-to-cue music and light check, had instructed his band members to wait after the matinee. "Earl, I know you remember Rosetta Rice. I expect all you fellows to be on your toes and do everything you can for her."

"Of course. It's our pleasure, Mr Simpson." Turning with a smile to Rosetta, he added "The boys know you're a top performer, Miss Rice. We won't let you down."

"Thank you, Earl," she couldn't recall his last name or even place his face, "you've always came through for me before, and I know you and your fine musicians will make me sound my best."

"Well, you don't need me, Earl. I'll be in the office, Rosetta, if there is anything I can do..." Simpson stopped mid-sentence. "Where's the stage manager—the new man, Ed Gilly?" The query was met with shrugs, and Simpson turned and went up the aisle to the front of the house. Rosetta called after him, "Thanks, Laurence, it's good to be back at the Tremont." She turned back and smiled at a man in work clothes sitting off to the side. Experience told her that he was the electrician who'd have to forego his dinner tonight in order to rearrange his lighting cues to accommodate the new act.

"Earl, please introduce me to this gentleman. Resident master magician of lighting?" she queried cheerily.

"Miss Rosetta Rice. Ned Geer, house electrician." Geer, who considered himself inured to show folks' charm, nonetheless found himself rising to acknowledge the introduction and to return the handsome woman's smile.

"Happy to meet you, Ned. And these gentlemen?," indicating the band. Earl Findley ticked off their names and each musician half rose or saluted with a smile as his name was called.

"Now, gentlemen, let's get on with it so you all can get to dinner and I can put my feet up in the dressing room until tonight's performance."

In less than the anticipated half-hour, the music and lights were set. Right after the brief rehearsal, Rosetta slipped twenty dollars to Earl Findley to conduct the pit band from the onstage piano. Later in her dressing room, she put a ten-dollar bill in an envelope marked for Ned Geer, the electrician and lighting man, and addressed another ten dollars to the stage manager, Ed Gilly, with a short note asking him to have the backstage baby grand piano polished and have his assistants push it on and off each show for her act.

The routine Rosetta and Earl worked out began with the band playing the first few bars of the chorus to the well-known "The Band Played On." The front curtains were to part and Rosetta would be found standing *in two,* dead center, as Earl sat at the baby grand on stage to her right and a foot or two up stage of her. After the lively opening chorus, the band was instructed to slip into pianissimo as Rosetta performed, parlando-style, the lyrics to the verse that began:

"Matt Casey formed a social club
That beat the town for style,
And hired for a meeting place a hall.
When pay day came around each week
They greased the floor with wax.
And danced with noise and vigor at the ball."

After completing half the first verse, the band was to pick up the pace and the volume, and Rosetta would swirl about the stage as she sang:

"Casey would waltz with a strawberry blonde,
And the band played on.
He'd glide 'cross the floor with the girl he adored,
And the band played on.
But his brain was so loaded it nearly exploded,
The poor girl would shake with alarm.
He'd ne'er leave the girl with the strawberry curls,
And the band played on."

Sheet music to the song had been published more than a decade earlier, so the audience was sure to know the words and sing along. One version or another had been around for decades, ever since Tony Pastor had made it a favorite back in the 1880s.

After some brief patter in which she would tell the audience how delightful it was to be back in Boston, Rosetta scheduled a comedy number, "Everybody Works but Father," that had been published the previous year.

To change pace for her third number and to show off her lyrical voice, Rosetta, accompanied only by Earl Findley at the baby grand, chose to sing "Will You Love Me In December." She moved next to the grand piano, nestled into its curve, and sang in an intimate fashion to Earl while the spotlight narrowed the audience's focus to just singer and accompanist.

To close her four song set, Rosetta selected the well-known "Has Anyone Here Seen Kelly?" with the original British lyrics that included "Kelly from the Isle of Man." Two hearty-voiced musicians in the pit band were deputized to call out "K-E-Double L-Y" when and where the lyrics indicated. Then, on the second chorus, Rosetta would encourage the audience to take up the refrain and join her in the choruses for a rousing finish to her act.

Lights and music settled, Rosetta thanked everyone and slipped out the stage door, picked her way down Haymarket Place to Avery Street and turned east to Washington Street. She was surprised how much change had come to Boston's rialto in the few years since she last visited as she walked the few blocks north to Filene's, the toney specialty store that provided much that anyone needed from clothing and accessories to home furnishings to personal services. Rosetta Rice was going to put her feet up, but not in some dreary dressing room when she could luxuriate in Filene's salon, get a facial, her hair dressed and nibble on tiny watercress sandwiches and dessert biscuits to stave off hunger until after the show, when she could treat herself to a proper dinner.

Rice had no intention of making a comeback, she enjoyed her current life of ease and occasional travel to Manhattan, but if she had to appear in public, even for a week, she'd be darn sure she looked and felt her best. At $750 for the week, she could afford to be pampered, and she'd be a proper fool not to savor it.

Dusk had settled. Washington Street blazed with artificial lighting. Rosetta stepped outside Filene's, and felt the damp air and promised rain. Once settled into a hackney for the drive back to her hotel, she noted a profusion of electric light that illuminated the shops and restaurants, crammed cheek by jowl along the cross streets of Boston's premier shopping district. It had been several years since she visited Boston. What earlier had struck her as an amusing novelty now seemed excessive—its incandescence garish compared to the warm, gentler glow of the old gas street lights.

CHAPTER 15

Monday Night: Florrie Sallies Forth

Florrie knew that Lavinia hadn't believed her. She didn't mind that her sister hadn't accepted Mrs Woodhull as the excuse; however, she disliked fibbing to her sister almost as much as she herself disliked being lied to, so Florrie was determined to stop in at the old lady's flat, nearby on Albion Street, for a quick visit. Better she do it first as 8:30 was rather late at night to visit an old person who lived alone. Florrie found Mrs Woodhull in considerable discomfit and without aspirin, so she agreed to pick up some, along with a few other items, on her way back from the Tremont Theatre.

Like most stage-door tenders, Petey Martin's job was to admit the performers and the theatre's staff, both front- and back-of-the-house employees, as they showed up for work in the morning and as they came and went during the day and night. Equally important was to keep out everyone who had no business there. Florrie had timed her visit to arrive after the conclusion of the first half of the evening bill, a time when Petey would have little to do but monitor the stage door. Almost as soon as Florrie rapped, he opened it and slipped outside.

He did his best not to appear cheerful or amused as he gave Florrie an earful about Mrs Cormier's tantrum when Dainty Alice was bumped from the number four spot and stuck into the number two spot—all of which Florrie had heard enough that afternoon after the matinee. Much as Florrie enjoyed a tale well told, it was a chilly October evening and they were standing in an alley seemingly angled to catch every gust of damp, cold wind whipping up the narrow streets from the Fort Point Channel a half mile away.

Florrie handled Petey like a straightman, asking leading questions and steering him back to the subject when he digressed. After recounting the events that Florrie had already witnessed, Petey swore that Mrs Cormier had raged later that evening, a half hour before that evening's show, when Rosetta Rice "walked in like the queen of the May dance"—Mrs Cormier's words, according to Petey.

After waiting for Florrie to appreciate that nugget of nasty gossip, Petey offered his topper—before all the show folk headed out of the theatre for dinner, and the band ran through Rosetta's cues. Then, after everyone had left, Mrs Cormier worked her revenge: she took Rosetta's charts for each instrument and scrambled them before the band returned for the start of the evening show. So said Petey Martin, correctly or wrongly, but there was no disputing the consequences. Although Earl Findley still had the correct sides for his onstage piano, the parts for trumpet, trombone, violins, clarinet and drums had been shuffled into each others' folders.

The overture for the start of the evening performance went well: the music was well-known to each band member and kept in a separate folder, as were the arrangements for each of the first three acts, and the scores for those acts were played properly.

But from the moment of Rosetta Rice's entrance music, which was the intro for her first song, there had been cacophony from the pit. The band was flustered, and the leader—stuck on stage—was at a momentary loss to know what to do. While it seemed much longer to all concerned, the confusion lasted only a matter of seconds until the musicians realized they had the wrong sides for their instruments. But before the band could resume, laughter spread through the theatre and a nervous stage hand unnecessarily closed the front curtain as a chagrined Rosetta Rice stood center stage. The stage manager hissed to immediately raise it. Earl, alone at the piano, immediately repeated the opening bars of "The Band Played On," and Rosetta sang as planned. The drummer had the sense to provide an impromptu beat while the rest of the pit band scrambled to exchange charts so that each musician had the correct charts for his instrument before the next number.

Wisely, Rosetta had planned a simple routine, so her act wasn't critically sabotaged. The audience admired her grace under pressure as Rosetta made light of the momentary confusion, and, as expected, the audience lustily joined in singing the choruses and gave Rosetta more than enough applause to call her back three times—the last for a brief encore of "Kelly." The experience had not been the tight, faultless routine Rosetta had intended, yet she displayed only good humor toward the audience, and, after her act, toward the band, the other acts waiting backstage, the stage manager and even the crew member who had closed the curtains in panic. It wasn't simply a matter of self-control. Rice believed that scores were often better settled later than sooner, and, as in all matters, she never inclined to behave in a manner that did not advance her interests.

Not so Mrs Cormier. Much to the embarrassment of other performers within earshot, she could be heard cackling from an upper level dressing room, "That'll teach the old has-been: taking spots that belong to young talent like my Alice." Either she was unaware or did not care, but with her outburst Mrs Cormier lost any sympathy that some of the other acts on the bill might have felt toward Alice.

It was trouble and scandal that engaged Petey, not solutions. Usually, as best he could, Petey concealed his glee as he spun his tale, but this latest transgression by Mrs Cormier had happened only twenty minutes before Florrie knocked on the stage door, so Petey, whose greatest delight was found in others' misfortune, had been thrilled when Florrie showed up at the stage door. He now had someone with whom he could share the scandal. "The old battleaxe really give it good to Miss High-and-Mighty. Neither one is no good. Didn't even tip me!"

Later that week, Petey would hold court at Kelly's Shamrock in South Boston and entertain the lads with his story of the shenanigans of show folks. His chance to report the night's disturbance to Florrie was only the first step in fashioning a few facts and a heavy dose of speculation and bias into an amusing story, but, to his annoyance, Florrie kept interrupting to ask questions that pointed more to fact than gossip, and that crimped Petey's act. Florrie's questions were direct, but she softened them with cluckings and wide-eyed looks of surprise to cadge more information from him.

"Oh, dear. Didn't the conductor check the chart folders before the show?"

"Guess not. They didn't have much time to go out and eat between the matinee and evening show what with having to rehearse Rosetta between the shows."

"Of course. You're right, Petey. But didn't anyone try to stop her? Mrs Cormier? Surely, someone must have noticed her fiddling with the charts."

"Dunno. Maybe they thought she was just handling her own act's sides."

"So, who caught her?"

"I dunno."

"Surely someone must have seen her. ... Petey?"

"Most everyone was out getting something to eat."

"Even you didn't see her?

"Nope."

"Then how did you find out she messed up Miss Rice's charts?"

"Well, Lord's sakes, Florrie, who else?"

"How about the sister act that was fired?"

"Nah. They left the theatre quick as they could. Right after the others. They was bawling their eyes out," he noted with ill-concealed satisfaction.

"Does the manager suspect Mrs Cormier?"

"No one else"—the first reply Petey was able to make with certainty. "He'll probably boot her kids off the bill."

"Perhaps so. But perhaps not; he'd have to locate a decent replacement..."

"They weren't so hot..."

"... And once he calms down he may realize that if Mrs Cormier makes a complaint to the United Booking Office, he'll need proof to back it up."

"Maybe so, but I'll bet it was her. A mother lion, she was. You seen her. A wonder she didn't claw him." Petey held up his hand, cracked open the stage door and cocked an ear. "It's the break; I gotta go." Quickly, Florrie thanked him for his news, handed him a bag containing one of the walnut and current tea breads left over from Sunday and bid him goodbye.

Sifting Petey's gossip for a dram of truth and hoping to get home before the rain began, Florrie had forgotten about Mrs Woodhull's sundries until she caught sight of the new Liggett's Drug Store diagonally across Tremont Street on the corner of Boylston. By the time Florrie had made her purchases and exited the store, it was raining. Caught without an umbrella, she pulled her hat down, stuffed her scarf inside her cloak, gathered it around her and scuttled homeward as fast as she could. By the time she delivered the goods to Mrs Woodhull, Florrie's outerwear was soaked and she chilled to the bone. Pleading the soggy condition of her garments, Florrie cut short her visit, promising Mrs Woodhull to come by again soon.

Thoroughly drenched by the time she reached home, Florrie entered by way of the basement, hung her wet clothes near a furnace, donned a warm, cotton, terrycloth robe she kept in the hall and joined her sister who was getting a head start on the following morning's breakfast preparations.

How is Mrs Woodhull?," asked Lavinia, never one to let anybody slide off her hook. "Well as can be expected at her age, I suppose?"

Florrie shucked her wet shoes and slid them under one of the kitchen stoves. "I went to the new Liggett's for her."

"And what did Petey have to report?"

"Not much," replied Florrie without embarrassment. She pulled on a pair of toasty warm carpet slippers that she kept tucked behind the stove. Florrie always preferred the loose comfort of slippers to laced-up shoes.

"After all that fuss this afternoon?"

"And more trouble this evening," Florrie added while tying on her apron "but Petey didn't seem to know much about it." Florrie moved to the sink to wash her hands.

"More trouble? What happened?" Lavinia was now more clearly interested. Florrie, noting what Lavinia was making, began lending a hand.

"Where's Agnes?"

"Doing something or other upstairs."

"Good." Lowering her voice, Florrie continued her report. "According to Petey, our Mrs Cormier sabotaged Rosetta Rice's act sometime between the matinee and evening shows."

"Good heavens! What did she do?"

While they kneaded bread dough for morning biscuits, covered it to rise in the barely warm ovens of the "dragon" and cleaned up the kitchen, Florrie related her conversation with Petey, almost word for word. Lavinia formed the same conclusion as she listened to Florrie's account of Petey's suspicions: it was all speculation without proof. "Still, I wouldn't put it past the old gorgon."

That night, Florrie, distressed by the gossip about their lodger, Mrs Cormier, didn't fall into a deep sleep until the early hours of the morning.

CHAPTER 16

Early Tuesday: Breakfast with an Unbidden Guest

Up before dawn, as usual, Mr Boniface padded noiselessly from the top floor down to the cellars to rouse the furnaces. He was shaking the grate in number 146 when a large cinder got stuck. Yanking the hand lever back and forth didn't dislodge it, so he looked around the boiler room for the long iron rod he used to poke free recalcitrant cinders.

A single, yellow-glowing, electric light in the boiler room hung between the furnace and coal bin. Its dim light barely illuminated much beyond, but Boniface spotted the rod hanging from a hook in the wall. As he grabbed It, a scuffling noise and motion from a far, darkened corner made him spin around in time to block the exit path of an intruder.

"Halt!" In his many years upon the stage, S. A. Boniface had played many characters—clerks, professors, artists, dukes, servants, undertakers and clergymen—especially servants and clergymen, but he had never had to assume the forceful presence of a hero. This was his chance and he was delighted that he had risen to it instinctually.

"What have we here!?" he bellowed in stentorian tones, holding his iron rod like a lance. There was no response, except for a pair of eyes darting about, searching for escape. "Who are you? Take two steps forward, into the light, so I can see you."

The shape complied. What Boniface saw standing a few feet in front of him was a slight boy. The vision nearly disarmed him; he burbled "Sorry, if I startled you."

"I'm okay." The lad was still wary but no longer afraid. In his experience, if a grown-up was going to hit him, he did it sooner as well as later.

Any competent actor can read his audience, and Boniface sensed that the boy was no longer in awe of him, yet neither did he seem intent on harm. "You startled me, too, you know." He had wanted only to put the lad at some ease, but as soon as the words were out of his mouth, he knew he had lost his command of the situation. Boniface, reverted to his previous tone: "Who are you, and what are you doing here."

"I'm Tommy. I help the ladies who live here. They let me sleep here when it's cold."

For a few moments Boniface mulled over the boy's explanation and realized that it couldn't be true. Lavinia and Florrie would certainly have let him know, given his early morning furnace duties. Further, had they permitted the boy to sleep there, they would have provided him with a cot and blankets at the least. Hearing Agnes shuffling down to the kitchen, Boniface, rod extended in hand, backed to the door of the boiler room and called out.

"Miss Agnes?! Good morning. Agnes? Can you hear me?"

"Yes, Mr. Boniface, and so can all the saints in heaven. Folks are still sleeping."

"Sorry, Miss Agnes, but I must ask you to find Miss Flora and ask her to come to the boiler room right away."

"Are you all right, Mr Boniface. Can I help?"

"No, Miss Agnes, please do as I ask and send Miss Flora to me. Ask her to hurry." Agnes didn't answer him, but he could hear her mumbling to herself as she plodded back up the stairs. Agnes had worked at Portridge Arms little more than half a year, and the theatrical, somewhat bohemian atmosphere unsettled her. Still, the job was a marked improvement over her previous ones. Miss Lavinia seemed saner than the rest and was fair in her dealings. As to the others, Agnes was able to keep a certain distance between her and them—inmates in a madhouse. Work was a trial anywhere, and Agnes had ordered a litany of woes that she muttered as she went about her work. It was a comfort.

Fully five minutes had elapsed before Boniface and Tommy heard Agnes' return accompanied by Florrie. In that time, Tommy tensed once and seemed about to bolt, but Boniface lifted his lance and blocked escape. Otherwise they remained as they had been, figures in a tableau. Agnes positioned herself safely outside the door as Florrie entered.

"Mr Boniface, what is… Oh, my, what have we …"

"Miss Flora, please." Boniface put his finger to his lips and whispered. "Please ask Agnes to go back to the kitchen. We don't wish to alarm her, do we?"

"Quite right, Mr Boniface. Agnes dear, everything's all right. Please return to the kitchen; the guests will be wanting breakfast." A few moments of uncertainty were followed by Agnes' grumbling as she clomped off to the kitchen.

"His name is Tommy. He says that you know him."

"Good morning. Tommy Shields, isn't it?" Turning back to Mr Boniface, Florrie explained matter-of-factly "This lad sells newspapers. He helped us home with our groceries Friday evening."

"He said you gave him permission to sleep here."

"I think not. No. And I'm sure Lavinia did not. What are you doing here, Tommy? How did you get in? How long have you been here?"

Tommy chose the most recent question. "I slept here last night, but I didn't do nothing wrong."

"As to that, we'll see. Why didn't you sleep in your own home?"

There was no answer.

"Have you been here every night since Friday? Please answer me, Tommy. If you don't answer my questions, and answer truthfully, you may be in more trouble than you think."

"Only last night. It got cold and started to rain."

"If I remember correctly, Tommy, you said you didn't live far away. Somewhere off Northampton Street, I think. With your mother."

"Yes Ma'am."

"Is that not true?"

"No, Ma'am."

"Come now, Tommy, I want proper answers; where do you live?"

"At the Burrough's. Sometimes. When they have room."

"What or who are the Burroughs?"

"Miss Flora, I believe he means the Burrough's Newsboys Foundation up in Pemberton Square. Is that right?"

"Yessir."

"But where is your mother?"

"She's gone."

"Gone?"

"Yes, Ma'am. She died last winter."

"Oh, dear. What about your father?"

"He went out West when I was a kid."

"Do you have grandparents or an aunt or uncle?"

"No, Ma'am."

"An older brother or sisters?"

"I think I had a sister once. She was younger than me. My Ma wouldn't talk about it."

"I'm sorry to hear that, Tommy. If it's true. Mr Boniface, we need to get to the bottom of this, and my sister will have to know. Do you believe him?"

"He seems sincere, Miss Flora."

"Yes, he does, but he may be a better actor than we credit him. How do we know you aren't lying, Tommy?"

"I didn't take nothing. I didn't hurt nothing. There wasn't any room at the Burrough's and it was too cold to sleep outdoors."

"What are we to do Mr Boniface?"

"Give him some breakfast, Miss Flora? He's probably hungry, and trip to the water closet may be in order."

"Clear thinking, Mr Boniface. Do you need to use the water closet, young man?

"Yes, Ma'am."

"Mr Boniface, will you kindly escort Tommy there and then bring him to the kitchen? Hands and face clean, young man. I'll have to talk to Agnes. I'm sure she's beside herself with curiosity by now. By the way, Tommy, how did you get in?"

"Through the coal chute."

"Oh, my. I never think to check to see if it's secured. Quite ingenious of you."

"Quite," chimed in Boniface. "No evidence of breaking in...,"

"No jimmied door locks..."

"No forced windows..."

"You're a resourceful lad. I spotted that the first time we met. Newsboy. Young gallant to aging damsels in distress. And, now, burglar?" This last Florrie threw out in a long, dramatic exhalation.

"Burglar!? Hey lady, I ain't no burglar. I didn't burgle nothing."

"That remains to be seen, and my sister will no doubt be the judge of that. I suspect that the worst of your sins is the habitual use of double negatives, but my sister is a keener judge of character than I. In the meantime, do not say "ain't." As to 'didn't burgle nothing,' we shall attend to your double negatives later. Mr Boniface, will you be good enough to accompany Tommy to the water closet while I speak with Agnes? I'll see you both in the kitchen"

"Certainly, Miss Flora."

CHAPTER 17

A Bit Later Tuesday Morning: an Interrogation

In less than ten minutes Boniface brought Tommy, somewhat cleaned up and relieved of any physical strain, back into the kitchen. Florrie was grateful for their reappearance as it cut off Agnes' complaints. As soon as Florrie had assured her on one point, such as the unlikelihood of being slashed to death in her bed, Agnes was ready with another worry. Florrie gently reminded Agnes that Tommy was her problem and a decision for her and Lavinia to make, and that Agnes was being informed of a situation, not asked for advice.

"Now, Tommy, may I assume you have not yet had your breakfast?" Without waiting for a reply, she turned to Mr Boniface, "He's washed his hands? Good." Florrie pointed to the long preparation table and invited Tommy to sit down. "The porridge isn't ready yet, but I have some cracked wheat bread left over from last night and some apple butter. That'll do for now. What do you usually drink?"

Tommy hadn't detected any sure means of escape, and the old lady's unique take on his intrusion was unlike anything he had experienced or expected. Curious to see where all this palaver was leading, Tommy complied with her directions and decided to answer her questions. At least he'd get something to eat before they called the coppers.

"Coffee." Quickly he remembered to add, "please."

"Coffee!" At your age? It'll stunt your growth. Tea or cocoa. Which will it be?"

"Cocoa, please."

"Not as good for you as tea, but delicious. I'll make some for us both. Real Dutch cocoa, not that pallid powder from Mr Hershey. Agnes, dear, I'll take care of the cocoa. Will you be so kind as to start breakfast?" Before Agnes had time to utter a word Florrie thanked her.

"Mr Boniface, I'd appreciate it if you would fetch my sister. And then, please set up the dining room for breakfast. Agnes will have her hands full until Lavinia and I are free." Wordlessly, Boniface immediately set off in search of Lavinia.

"Hmmpf!" It was the first sound from Agnes who, despite Florrie's admonition to keep her counsel to herself, could no longer hold back her skepticism about Florrie's handling of the situation and the soiled ragamuffin who had claimed center stage in what Agnes considered her kitchen. Since "hmmpf" occasioned no response, Agnes began making a bit more noise than necessary.

"Agnes, you need to help me now, not make things more difficult."

"It's nearly breakfast time," Agnes pouted, "and I can't get the food ready by myself."

"Do the best that you can, dear."

Florrie had her back to Tommy while making the cocoa, but she could see a reflection of him in the glass fronted cabinet doors over the cupboard. He betrayed no sign of looking to leave. Indeed, Tommie was enjoying the rare comfort of a warm room and had decided to stay and watch events play out. Florrie was of the same mind.

Just as they heard Lavinia and Boniface descending the stairs, Florrie placed in front of Tommy a mug of cocoa and a plate with two thick slices of bread liberally laden with apple butter. With Florrie's eyes diverted to Lavinia's approach, the boy slapped the two pieces of bread together and stuffed the sloppy sandwich into a pocket. Lavinia entered the kitchen with Mr Boniface behind her, and stood wordlessly, looking first at the boy and then at her sister, who broke several seconds silence.

"Lavinia. You remember Tommy, don't you?"

"Mr Boniface informs me that he was our unbidden guest last night," a declaration that Lavinia's tone turned into a question, looking for confirmation and further explanation.

"You know how cold it was last night, Lavinia..."

Lavinia turned to the boy and cut her sister short. "Perhaps you, boy, can tell me why you are here. My sister seems unable to come to the point."

"I got in through the coal chute."

"Wasn't that enterprising of him, Lavinia?"

"Unsettlingly so. Now, boy, putting aside my sister's misplaced admiration for your sly skills, let's deal with the facts. You are aware that you have committed criminal trespass?"

"What?"

"You broke into a house that isn't yours."

"Yeah, but I didn't do nothing."

"Tommy, we must do something about your double negatives," admonished Florrie.

"Flora, may we please stick to the matter at hand? This boy broke into our home. He could have pilfered any number of things, pawned them, and we'd never see them again. And what about our guests? Thievery could cost us our reputation, and how could we make good on their losses? Have you given a single thought to that, Flora? No! Instead you give him cocoa!"

"It better than coffee; that's what he usually drinks."

"Do you both want me to telephone the police?"

"Please, Ma'am, I didn't do nothing. Don't ..."

"No, Lavinia, we shan't telephone the police. Not yet, anyway. Tommy, tell my sister why you broke in last night. Go ahead. Don't be afraid. But if you aren't truthful, dear, she'll know it."

Agnes was starring goggle-eyed. "Agnes, Flora and I will be back in a few minutes to give you a hand. Young man, you come with Miss Flora and me to my office. Florrie, you lead the way, and I'll follow the boy." Florrie picked up his mug of hot cocoa and complied.

It is doubtful, unless indeed he were a burglar, that Tommy had ever seen the interior of a dwelling other than a humble tenement or a bleak institution. As he walked into the office, he took note of drapes and curtains, paintings and photographs on the walls, Lavinia's oak desk and chair and several stuffed chairs. To his surprise, Florrie invited him to sit on one of the upholstered chairs but, before he did, Lavinia grabbed one of Florrie's shawls, which could be found abandoned in almost any room, and covered the seat and back of the chair to spare it from the boy's soiled clothing.

"Now, then, why did you break into our house last night?"

"I didn't break in, Ma'am, I slid down the coal chute."

Florrie placed his cocoa on a side table next to his chair.

"Young man, it is definitely in your best interest to answer my questions honestly."Lavinia's tone was all the more persuasive because it was even. "Why did you break in."

"I didn't want to sleep out. It started to rain, and it was cold."

"Why didn't you go home to your mother?"

"He hasn't got a mother..." interjected Florrie.

"Flora, my questions are for the boy to answer."

"... And he doesn't have a father, either."

"No, family at all, boy?"

"No, Ma'am."

"How do you support yourself?"

"I sell papers. Do errands."

"Don't you have a home?"

"After my Ma died, the landlord wouldn't let me stay by myself"

"Where do you sleep?"

"Sometimes at the Burroughs, if I get there early enough for a bed. Sometimes in the park or the subway until the coppers kick us out.

"You sleep outdoors in this weather?"

"It ain't bad if you can get a spot next to a heating grate."

"Where do you eat?"

"I work," Tommy said proudly. "I pay for my food when I have money."

"And if you don't?"

"I go to the mission."

"Ever been in trouble with the police?"

"Not for stealing."

"For what, then?"

"Just sleeping out and fighting."

"Fighting?!" Florrie was horrified. She had taken a liking to the boy and admired his gumption and enterprise, but she had no wish to harbor a brawler.

Lavinia disliked fighting just as much, but she reasoned that a boy Tommy's size was unlikely to be the initiator. "What do you fight about?"

"You gotta fight to keep your spot."

"What spot?"

"My place to sell papers. Bigger guys try to take it away from you if you got a good one."

"Oh, my," sighed Florrie. Lavinia didn't say a word for a few moments, then asked quietly, "What's that in your pocket?"

Tommy withdrew the uncovered mess of bread and apple butter from his pocket.

"He needed something to eat, Lavinia."

"It's a mess. Throw it out for the birds. If what he says is true, we'll get him a proper sandwich before he leaves." This was the first indication Tommy had that they were likely to let him go without calling in the police or juvenile authorities.

Lavinia looked to the door just as Mr Boniface came into view.

"Everything is laid out in the dining room for breakfast, ladies."

"Thank you, Mr Boniface. Please take the boy downstairs and tell Agnes to give him some porridge," said Lavinia. "It must be ready by now. Oh, and ask her to wrap a sandwich for him. My sister and I need to discuss this matter, and you, young man, no doubt have papers to pick up and sell. I don't know if you are telling us the whole truth, but you can come by after six tonight and there'll be some dinner for you."

"The porridge is oatmeal with currants and crushed walnuts," put in Florrie. "Nutritious. Just what a young lad like you needs to build himself up on a cold morning to fend off those ruffians."

CHAPTER 18

Early Tuesday Afternoon: The Inspector Is Called

It was a bit before noontime and Inspector Malachi Brody's thoughts were turning toward lunch when he received a summons from Assistant Chief Inspector Joe Dugan.

Less than an hour earlier, word had worked its way up from Patrolman Moore to the Division Four Station House captain to the office of Chief Inspector William Watts at police headquarters in Pemberton Square. Watts charged Dugan with the investigation; Dugan in turn notified the coroner's office to send a man to the Tremont Theatre and assigned the investigation to Malachi Brody, the first available inspector.

The information passed on to Brody was slim; it seemed that Morris Weiss, the assistant theatre manager, had either discovered or learned from someone else at the theatre that there was a dead body in one of the dressing rooms. Weiss had been about to phone the local station house when the day-shift beat cop, Frankie Moore, passed by on his morning rounds.

Patrolman Moore verified that there was a dead body and used the theatre's box office phone to call a Division Four desk sergeant who relayed to Stationhouse Four's Captain Walsh the preliminary report by Moore that violence seemed certain and murder, most likely.

Most of the daily newspapers detailed one police reporter to each downtown station house. As soon as Captain Walsh dispatched Lieutenant Culhoon and Sergeant Crowder to follow up on Moore's report, the reporters assigned daily to Division Four, hoping for some news to break the monotony of arrests for public intoxication, fights and petty thievery, followed in the officers' wake.

A cluster of hastily dispatched newsmen from the *Post, Transcript, Herald, Globe, Traveler, Record* and *American* had gathered in front of the Tremont Theatre. Even two weeklies, the *Times* and the *Courier,* sent men. All were forbidden to enter the theatre. Crowded on the sidewalk, they waited for Brody—indeed for anyone from whom they hoped to cadge a statement. Several additional patrolmen had been detailed to guard the theatre's front entrance and limit access. At least, thought Brody, Captain Walsh had the sense to detail a few cops to keep the vultures at bay.

Brody nodded to the uniformed policemen on guard and bulled his way through the pack of yapping reporters flinging questions at him. Once inside the lobby, he marched to the ticket box. "Inspector Malachi Brody to see Laurence Simpson."

"I'm sorry, but Mr Simpson isn't here yet. Generally he doesn't show up until an hour before the matinee."

"Who are you?"

"Mo Weiss, Mr Simpson's assistant and box office manager. Inspector, can't you do something about those newsmen out there on the sidewalk?"

"Nothing. It's a free country."

"They'll drive our customers away."

"You cancelled the matinee, didn't you?"

"Yes..."

"Then you'll probably sell out tonight. Especially with those guys outside attracting attention. You may not get the kind of audience you hope for, but a full till is a full till, right?"

"I suppose so, but..."

"That is, *if* the captain and me give the go-ahead for tonight's show. By the way, why isn't Simpson here?"

"Mr Simpson has been in Lowell today, looking after one of our other theatres. He should be here soon."

"Doesn't he know there's been a murder?"

"A murder?! Oh, don't say that ..."

"Okay, maybe she did it herself. Let's go see. You got anybody working back there in the office?"

"Only Miss Stropell. She's my box office assistant."

"Call her out, Mr Weiss."

"Miss Stropell? Emily? The police inspector's here and he wants to ask you some questions."

"Questions? Oh, gracious, I didn't see anything. I'm not even sure I know what really happened." The small voice grew nearer as it was followed by a smaller person entering the box office. She stood partly behind Weiss. Well into her seventies, Brody guessed, one of those thousands of ancient maiden ladies who had to keep working as long as they could for a pittance to pay rent in some decrepit rooming house in the South End.

Brody had few soft spots, but one harbored the Miss Stropells of the world. He had seen dozens of them. Some dead from starvation, others willingly succumbed to fumes from the gas jets in their rooms. More barely kept alive sleeping on benches at night.

During the day they filled the warm reading rooms of the Public Library in Copley Square or nursed a pot of tea and toast at the nearby Hayes-Bickford, where the day and night managers, both kindly souls, played host to a fair measure of Boston's flotsam and jetsam. Emily Stropell was one of the fortunate ones; she had a job, however lowly, and Brody knew she wasn't likely to volunteer any information in the presence of her boss.

While Brody mused, Miss Stropell stood slightly behind Weiss, with hands clasped, one trying to steady a tremor in the other. "That's okay, Ma'am. Just wanted to meet you. But if you think of anything, let me know. I'm Inspector Brody. Now, Mr Weiss, let's you and me go to the dressing rooms and have a good look. And while we're walking, you can tell me everything you know. Let's start with who discovered the body."

"I—I did."

"You? And you don't know she was murdered?"

All Brody knew about show business was what he occasionally witnessed from a seat in an auditorium. The only actors he met offstage were the few that drank more than they could handle on a Saturday night, got into a fight with one of the locals or were mugged or arrested along with the prostitute they were soliciting. Still, Brody was curious to know why a box office man, even if he were the manager's assistant, would be visiting the dressing rooms. Weiss anticipated his question.

"I just delivered a box to Miss Rice."

"Don't the doormen usually handle the actors' mail and packages?"

"Yes, of course, but this wasn't mail. It was a package. A corsage in a box, as it turned out. And it was hand-delivered. At least, I supposed so."

"Meaning?"

"When Petey—he's our stage door tender—let me in this morning, I went directly to the front offices, of course."

"Of course." Brody found it useful and, truth be admitted, rather enjoyed keeping on edge those he was interrogating. "Go on."

"It wasn't until I came out into the lobby—an hour or so later, I guess—that I noticed the box hanging outside on the outer lobby door handle."

"It can't have been there long, or someone would have nicked it."

"No, I suppose not, now that you mention it."

"What time was that, you say?"

"Well I can't be sure, but, let's see, I got in a bit before ten. Went to the office, unlocked the safe. Checked last night's figures. Did a few other things—I hung up my hat and coat before all that. Oh, and I made tea for myself and Miss Stropell..."

"You make the tea?"

"Well, I'm the first to arrive in the morning—the first of the front of the house staff, I mean. And then I went into the lobby to put out the sandwich board and pick up some rubbish—discarded programmes and such." Weiss realized that he was rattling but couldn't stop himself. "Oh!, and I picked up the morning mail that the postman pushes through the slot. I do that every morning before I unlock the lobby doors and open up the box office. That's when I saw the flower box hanging outside—from the door handle—while I was in the lobby."

"Yeah, good. But about what time was that?"

"Shortly after Miss Stropell arrived, I guess."

"And that was...?"

"Oh, she always arrives on time, so it must have been just before 11 o'clock."

"What did you do then?"

"Well, I brought the box upstairs, just as we're doing now, and I knocked on her door. Miss Rice has one of the second floor rooms reserved for our headliners."

"And?...

"And—well, there was no answer. I didn't expect there would be. The performers usually arrive about an hour before showtime, and our matinee isn't until two o'clock. I imagine I was in a bit of a hurry, and there was still a lot to do before customers arrived for the matinee, and Miss Stropell was alone downstairs, and Mr Simpson told us all to show Miss Rice every courtesy, so I wanted to be sure she got the corsage as soon she got here. I tried to hook the box on the door handle, but the door pushed open. It shouldn't have been unlocked; the performers usually keep their dressing rooms locked. They have their trunks there—their costumes—props and personal items they don't want disturbed or stolen..." Weiss realized he was rattling again. He stopped, uncertain what else to say or do.

"But it *was* unlocked?"

"Yes sir, so I slipped in to put the box on her dresser, and...."

"And?..."

"She was sitting at the dresser. I called her name. Then I saw—in the mirror—blood all over her front."

CHAPTER 19

Tuesday Afternoon: Scene of the Crime, Tremont Theatre

They had arrived on the second floor backstage landing where Brody paused until Weiss finished his account. Ahead he glimpsed two men in overcoats, backing in and out of a dressing room. Although they weren't in uniform, Brody guessed they were Division Four police.

Guiding a reluctant Mo Weiss by the arm, Brody headed down the hall toward the open dressing room. Just inside, a third man, in shirtsleeves, had set up a tripod and was taking photographs of the late Miss Rice, still slumped back in her chair, her gown and peignoir caked with dried brown-red stains. The coroner stood off to one side.

Brody was always amazed anew by how much blood bodies held. Weiss looked as if he were going to faint. Seeing the horror the first time must have been a shock. Having to see it again nearly made Weiss sick, but Brody wanted to witness the reaction.

"Then what did you do?"

"Do!?" Weiss fumbled for control of his thought. "I'm not sure exactly. I must have gone right back to my office. I didn't know what to do. I was about to send Petey to the police station when I saw the street patrolman walk by, so I called him in. Then I took him to the dressing room... I couldn't go in again... Then he took me back to the office ..."

"Okay, Mr Weiss, you can return to your office. I'll see you on my way out. Have a list ready for me of the people you know were in the theatre this morning and those who should have been but weren't."

Brody turned back to the room and squeezed in past the exiting photographer. The coroner recognized and acknowledged the inspector by name, "Brody, we meet again."

"That we do, Evans. Always the same circumstances. Let me know when you're finished in here."

"Not more than a few minutes, Inspector. Looks like the beat cop's report was on the mark. I'll have to do a work-up, but right now I'd be hard pressed to call it anything but murder."

Brody stepped backed into the hall and nodded to the two uniformed officers. The lieutenant extended his hand, "I'm Lieutenant Culhoon. This is Crowder." Brody shook hands. "We've met before. Seen you men down at headquarters a few times. Pretty crowded in there."

"Yeah, I thought stars had fancy dressing rooms. And that shoebox, so they tell me, is for one of the stars."

"Any question about what happened?"

"The coroner got here almost as soon as Crowder and me did, so we didn't check it thorough-like, but it looks simple enough. She got her throat cut. Messy job. Not professional."

"Any weapon?"

"Nope. Nothing."

"Money or jewelry?"

"There's $72 bucks and change in her purse, and there's some jewelry stuff in the box on the dresser. Maybe some's gone. Maybe not."

Evans stepped out into the hall and spoke to Brody as he pulled on his coat. "She's been dead a while. Can't say for certain much more than someone slit her throat. Get back to you later today. So long."

"We'll shove off, too; I'll file a report at the stationhouse."

Brody stepped back into the room and looked for himself: cash along with a lace handkerchief and a vial of perfume in a small purse. The neckpieces, bracelets, earrings in the jewelry case didn't look like the real thing. Brody was no expert but he'd arrested enough burglars to see what quality gems and jewelry looked like; the stones seemed too large and bright and the settings were clunky. Probably made a lot of flash to the audience. The corsage lay in its open box, but there was no card to be found.

He looked around the small room for a minute or two, rummaged through the pockets of the costumes on hangers and the contents of a trunk, a couple of valises and dresser drawers that proved empty save for undergarments. Brody noted the make-up kit and open cold cream jar. He'd have to wait for the coroner's report, but for now it seemed the victim had been dead quite a while. Likely she had been cleaning up after last night's show.

On his way out, Brody stopped at the box office lobby window where Miss Stropell was seated. "Thought of anything you want to tell me, Miss Stropell?," he said quietly. "Did I get your name right?"

"Oh, yes. That's my name. But I can't think of anything that you'd wish to know. I'm sorry, officer."

"Inspector. Inspector Brody. Just in case you remember something."

"Certainly, Inspector, of course."

"By the way, Miss Stropell, what time did you come to work today?"

"Oh, I was on time. I always arrive before 11 o'clock—at least ten minutes early. I'm never late."

"Thanks. See you did tell me something I wanted to know." Brody offered a smile that was gratefully received.

"Thank you, Inspector Brody."

"Hey, there, Mr Weiss," Brody called into the room behind the box office. Mr Weiss appeared holding a piece of paper that he handed to Brody. "You're an efficient man, Mr Weiss."

"Thank you, sir."

As he walked toward the front lobby doors, Brody called over his shoulder. "You must be a great help to Mr Simpson." It never hurt to keep even the most unlikely of suspects a bit on edge with an ambiguous comment. Brody sailed out the door and headed to the local station house to meet Patrolman Frankie Moore.

CHAPTER 20

Tuesday Afternoon: News at the National Theatre, Boston

At the least, Agnes decided, she was entitled to some explanation for all the hushed goings-on of the morning. She had prepared a short speech to deliver to Lavinia and Flora: she was a loyal employee, and she lived here in this house and was entitled to feel safe from marauders, no matter how small or young.

At the sound of feet coming down the stairs, she turned, ready to confront her employers. But rather than the sisters, it was Mr Boniface who arrived at the kitchen, with the ragamuffin in tow, to convey the sisters' decision that Agnes was to give the boy a hot breakfast and send him on his way with a sandwich! It was almost too much to contend with: she, an honest, hard-working, respectable, daughter of the Church ordered to *serve* a rascally, grimy, wet-nosed sneak-thief!

Fueled by her anger and protestations, Agnes plopped a bowl of oatmeal in front of the lad along with a half pitcher of milk, a spoon, sugar and a napkin.

She barely acknowledged his "thank you, Miss Agnes," and turned back to the sink and had finished the pot scrubbing by the time Florrie and Lavinia returned to the kitchen. Agnes' pique deepened when the sisters failed to talk in her presence about the morning's discovery or even note how industrious she had been. Instead, Lavinia and Florrie discussed whether they could afford the time to attend the matinee bill at the National, as had been planned, or if it were better for one them, accompanied by Mr Boniface, to attend.

"I'm sorry we can't ask you, Agnes, but maybe later this week. There's the mid-week cleaning to be done as well as dinner to prepare." Lavinia added "I'm sure you understand. Cora will be here soon to clean. Dumbfounded, Agnes could do nothing but stare at the pot she was scrubbing as hot tears welled in her eyes. Last night she had pressed her best dress in anticipation of attending the vaudeville matinee, and now these two 'Porridge Sisters' (yes, she knew what folks called the sisters behind their backs) had added insult to her injury!

Unaware that Agnes' peevishness was soaring toward a record high, Florrie volunteered, "Lavinia, why don't you go without me? See if Mr Boniface is free to accompany you. I'll work with you today, Agnes. Cora can clean the common areas upstairs. You and I will clean the kitchen and you can help me with the marketing—we'll shop locally today. I hope we can get by until Lavinia and I do our big shopping at Haymarket on Friday."

Though she wouldn't have admitted it to anyone in the household, Agnes had been looking forward to the vaudeville at the National, especially as those two good-looking Irish lads, the Hennigan Brothers, were on the bill. Her sulk deepened, and if it was not noticeable to the others, it was because her petulance was not unusual. Lavinia went back upstairs to find Mr Boniface. The day had begun on a sour note, and Lavinia doubted the bill at the small-time National would improve her spirits.

Lavinia and Boniface had no time to spare by the time they left for the theatre. Under her black cape, Lavinia wore one of her black dresses and, except for a cameo, no jewelry. Mr Boniface wore, as he did in all seasons, a vintage charcoal-colored twill serge suit, his long black cloak and his wide-brimmed, black parson's hat. Had any performer seen the black-cloaked pair enter the auditorium, they might have thought they were agents from a funeral parlor, come to take bookings from those acts that failed to amuse.

The National scheduled their matinees at 2:30. Boniface and Lavinia arrived a bit later than either felt was respectful to the performers but managed to get seated before the end of the overture. Mr Boniface lacked the snobbery toward vaudeville and variety performers that infected too many of his fellow thespians. True, it wasn't Shakespeare or even Sheridan, but Boniface always marveled at graceful and deft physical feats.

However, in place of a live acrobatic act or its like, the show opened with newsreel film of President Teddy Roosevelt's adventures. It was a pastiche of various travels by the peripatetic president. Lavinia and Boniface enjoyed the scenes in the West, promoting conservation but were appalled when the film shifted to one of Teddy's hunting safaris. Lavinia allowed herself to remark in a clear voice that "I don't see how anyone can be in favor of the conservation of nature yet slaughter animals wholesale in the wild." Performers on the bill might have envied her ability to project.

Their mood gradually lightened through a procession of acts including a troupe of Burmese contortionists and aerialists; their boarders, the dancing Hennigan Brothers; a dramatic sketch; and a female Irish character singer much applauded by an audience dominated by her countrymen. Mr Boniface was disappointed that so little time in the dramatic sketch had been given to character development and that the plot raced to a contrived, melodramatic denouement, but he had seen enough vaudeville to know that subtlety and shadings of emotion were sacrificed to vaudeville audiences' preference for the high color and clear motives of whiz-bang storytelling. Two of the actors in the sketch were old acquaintances of Mr Boniface's. If he ran into them in the theatre district, he would have to resort to a few of those all-purpose remarks that are accepted as compliments by those eager to receive them.

Closing the first half of the bill was an act billed as "Plantation Party." Four black-faced couples in 1890s formal dress sang harmony and danced a lively cakewalk. It was a pleasant period piece and nicely done, but like an increasing number of folks, Lavinia and Boniface didn't see the need for white people to pretend to be black just so that they could perform uninhibitedly.

As Florrie and Agnes would probably need help with the finishing touches to dinner, Lavinia and Boniface had agreed to leave at intermission, after seeing their lodgers. Fortunately, the Hennigan Brothers had been slotted in the first half of the bill. Lavinia was surprised that the lads were quite good dancers and they showed more energy, personality and poise over the footlights than had been on display at Portridge Arms. As she and Mr Boniface joined other theatre-goers headed to the lobby and rest lounges, one of the ushers spotted Boniface and stopped him. He urged them to a corner of the lobby, out of sight of the box-office, wherein the manager and ticket seller were reconciling ticket stubs with cash receipts.

"Hello Miss Portridge; good to see you Mr Boniface; did you hear what happened at the Tremont this morning." At last a fluttered breath. "Terrible wasn't it?"

"What happened?", asked Boniface.

"You haven't heard?"

"No." Lavinia almost snapped, expecting some silly gossip, and she in a hurry to get home. "Now what terrible tragedy has befallen the Tremont?"

"They found Rosetta Rice murdered in her dressing room! And her in nothing but her dressing gown! Her throat slashed. Ear to ear, it was! Blood everywhere."

Lavinia was too stunned to curtail the gratuitous and gory details. Three years ago, during the Great Fire in Baltimore, her sister Mayme had died in the hotel that housed and then trapped her and dozens of other show folk. It had been Rosetta Rice who had collected Mayme Miller's personal effects from the theatre (those few items untouched by the fire), and brought them to Lavinia and Florrie. Mayme's death in an unsafe hotel and Rosetta's kindness had fostered the Portridge sisters' intent to revamp into a safe and hospitable theatrical boarding house the twin South End buildings they had inherited from their father.

Dazed, but with a subdued word of thanks to the young usher, the two worked their way through the intermission crowd clustered in the lobby. Once out on the street, they hurried the half-dozen blocks back home. Rosetta Rice was not their guest, but Mrs Cormier was. Her resentment of Miss Rice had to be common knowledge among show people in town, and reckless conjecture was sure to bring discord into the Portridge Arms.

Although he had not met Rosetta Rice nor knew of Lavinia's and Florrie's gratitude to her, Mr Boniface, pale and silent, was no less troubled. Murder in a theatre was desecration of a shrine. Neither spoke on the way, but Mr Boniface thought he heard Lavinia mutter something about the day bringing across their doorstep a second uninvited guest—insinuations of murder.

CHAPTER 21

Tuesday Mid-Afternoon: Ira Wood Journeys to Boston

Ira Wood was one of the first generation of Mike Leavitt's many protégées who permeated all ranks in corporate show business during the late nineteenth century. A man who tempered his ambition with caution, Ira had been content to assemble a modest but profitable chain of six theatres that he acquired, one by one, along the route of the Fitchburg Railroad. By the time the larger Boston & Maine railroad took over the Fitchburg line in 1900, Wood had built or bought a controlling interest in theatres in several of the towns along the rail route: Cambridge, Waltham, Ayer, Fitchburg and Lowell in Massachusetts, and Ira had recently concluded negotiations to acquire an existing theatre in Nashua, New Hampshire, the town where he recently had established a residence to which he expected soon to retire. The flagship of his modest circuit was the Tremont Theatre at the corner of Tremont and Avery Streets and across from the Boston Common.

Ira Wood Enterprises was among the many theatrical ventures that gravitated to the prestigious Colonial Building after the Colonial Theatre and the nine floors of offices above it were erected in 1900. Located on Boylston Street adjacent to the Little Building that anchored the southeast corner lot at Tremont Street, the handsome Colonial Building faced north across the expanse of the Boston Common and, beyond it, the slope of Beacon Hill crowned by the State House. A look out the Colonial's front windows also afforded, a bit to the east, a view of older commercial buildings, many quite charming, aligned along Tremont Street and facing west across the Common. Prominent among those edifices, due more to its marquee than its architecture, was the Tremont Theatre.

Ira Wood's aspiration for status stopped with the address and lobby of 100 Boylston Street. He selected one of the less expensive suites toward the rear of the building, on one of the lower floors. Except for the infrequent refurbishment of his better theatres, the move to the Colonial Building marked his last inclination to spend money on things that did not yield a quick return on his investment.

Ira's only son, Joshua, was vice president of the Wood's circuit and nominally in charge of the enterprise's business. Joshua rented an apartment at the Hotel Touraine, on the southwest corner of Boylston and Tremont, thus only a few minutes' walk from either the Tremont Theatre or his Colonial Building office.

Rather than the bustle one might expect at the headquarters of a theatrical venture, the atmosphere that suffused Ira Wood Enterprises was akin to a research library. The walls were lined with oak file cabinets filled with contracts, route sheets and other records. Other than the requisite portrait of Ira Wood and framed photographs of the various Wood theatres, the pale olive green walls of the outer office were bare. The windows, unadorned except for utilitarian shades looked into an airshaft and across to the windows of similar interior offices. A wool runner ran the length of the floor from entrance to reception door, not to welcome visitors so much as to efficiently direct them.

Although Ira took the train into Boston from Nashua no more than once a week, the interior office he shared with his son boasted fine appointments. Walnut desks for both Ira and Joshua Wood and padded chairs for them and their guests shared floor space with a well-chosen Anatolian carpet of silk and wool. Several paintings that mimicked the Hudson River School were impressively framed against paneled walls, and drapes and curtains screened the bleak view from windows looking out to an airshaft.

Unless a visitor arrived at Ira Wood Enterprises between 10 o'clock and noon, Joshua Wood was unlikely to be present. Even if someone arrived within that two-hour period, his chances of talking with the younger Wood were slim; Joshua usually met with those he wished to see and seldom with those who wished to see him.

A visitor had to explain his business twice, first to old Miss Jane Markey, who served as receptionist, secretary and file clerk, and then to old Mr Owen Yates, office manager and bookkeeper.

Any initial anticipation of excitement or glamour that long ago had lured Mr Yates or Miss Markey to seek positions with Ira Wood's theatrical enterprise had been smothered by unvarying routine, endless columns of numbers and sepulchral mood of the establishment. It had been a quarter of a century earlier when Ira Wood felt his growing success entitled him to hire his first assistant, Mr Yates. Several years later, he engaged Miss Markey. Both Yates and Markey had proved ideal employees for Ira Woods. Rare requests by either of them for increases in their wages had been even more rarely granted in all that time, yet so pinched in spirit were Yates and Markey that they quaked at the prospect of seeking other employment.

During the two decades that his son worked in the family business, Ira Wood repeatedly rejected Joshua's pleas to spiff up the premises. (Unspoken was the son's eventual plan to jettison Miss Markey and Mr Yates along with outer office furniture—originally inexpensive and since worn into decrepitude.) Joshua longed for theatrical trappings, high style and a comely and compliant receptionist. Unswayed by proposals that did not enhance the balance sheet, Ira remained committed to the lean operation that for decades had produced reliably increasing margins of profit.

Ira had hoped that as Joshua matured in years he would begin to display evidence of the mettle necessary to keep the business thriving. During the past few years, however, Ira had inclined to the opinion that, upon inheriting the company, Joshua would leech its resources at the same time he mismanaged. Affection did not always accompany kinship, and that was true of father and son in this case. Ira's dreams were bedeviled by the spectre of a bankrupt legacy. Perhaps it would be wiser if Joshua drew an annual income from a conservatively-invested irrevocable trust.

As the enterprise grew profitable, Ira grew elderly, Joshua passed from youth into middle age never in the employ of anyone but his father, and an ever-increasing burden of tiresome business details was shunted to Mr Yates. Joshua pursued more agreeable tasks of the enterprise, like entertaining and negotiating. Cannier than he was industrious, an acceptable percentage of Joshua's deals contributed to the company coffers, and the senior Mr Wood grudgingly and gradually ceded the day-to-day business operations to his son who, in turn, made decisions but passed on many of the attendant responsibilities to Mr Yates.

The office hummed in anticipation when the senior Mr Wood was scheduled to visit. On those days, Miss Markey dusted everything in sight, Mr Yates laid out ledgers for inspection, and Joshua managed to arrive earlier than his father and cancelled his luncheon appointments for those afternoons. Generally Ira spent the better part of the mornings reviewing financial recordkeeping with Mr Yates and then discussing particulars with his son for an hour before meeting some of his retired cronies at Jacob Wirth's for lunch prior to catching an afternoon train home to Nashua.

Ira Wood's venture into Boston on this particular day, however, was not his usual. Just before noon, he had received a phone call from the Boston Police's Chief Inspector. The conversation with Chief Inspector Watts concluded with Ira's agreement to visit Pemberton Square headquarters as early that afternoon as the Fitchburg branch train schedule allowed. Before leaving for Boston, Ira telephoned the Governor's office, the Tremont Theatre and his own office. Thus prepared, Ira Wood took the next train in from Nashua and arrived at police headquarters before 2 o'clock. That meeting had been short and to the point, after which Ira walked the four blocks to the Parker House where he quickly ordered and ate a late light lunch.

CHAPTER 22

Tuesday: Father and Son Tete-a-Tete, Colonial Building

Still dwelling on the disconcerting interview at police headquarters, Ira again chose to walk to his office rather than hail a hackney. Though the sky was dull, rain did not seem to be in the immediate offing. He crossed over Tremont for a brief visit to the Granary Burial Grounds. Some old people shied away from the evidence of mortality, but Ira, like a few others of his age wandering through the graveyard, took an odd comfort in the granite memorials that guarded their claim to space on earth for the deceased.

Leaving the burial grounds, Ira headed down the Great Mall to his office. Running alongside Tremont Street on the eastern border of the Boston Common, the mall treated strollers to an arboreal display. Most of the colorful and crackling leaves of autumn had fallen and drifted into clusters on the ground, yet the midday temperature tempted casual visitors along angled pathways amid stately if nearly bare trees and wrought iron fountains.

Wood had nearly yielded to the Common's charms when, catching sight of his Tremont Theatre on the opposite side of the street, his mind reverted to the matter at hand. He picked up his pace and headed straight for his office; he had no wish to visit his theatre today. Five men in overcoats were standing in the outer lobby—newsmen, no doubt, lying in wait to cadge a comment that might pump new interest into yesterday's news.

Ira Wood had alerted his son and staff to expect him. Instead of getting down to business with Mr Yates, as was usual after his customary terse greeting, old Mr Wood marched directly into the inner office. That formalities between father and son were soon concluded was evident by a rise in their voices. The thick wooden door between outer and inner compartments didn't bar entirely their conversation as it escalated into a quarrel.

Miss Markey and Mister Yates were drawn to the file cabinets nearest the connecting door. For as long as they dared, each rifled purposelessly through papers, each hoping the other didn't notice the subterfuge. After a shout from Joshua, the two dropped their pretence and edged toward the door.

"Inspector Brody told me that you didn't bother getting in touch with the police? Why not, Joshua?!"

"Why should I? I didn't discover the body. Mr Simpson seems to have handled it well enough."

"It's one of our theatres. You're *supposed* to be in charge!

"What would you have had me say? My manager tells me there's been a murder. I know nothing about it, but my pa*pa* thinks I should come and talk to you?"

"Sarcasm is your defense? For your information, Mr Simpson wasn't at the theatre. He didn't contact the police or you ..."

"Well someone called the police, didn't they? Probably Mo Weiss...

"... so I get called into police headquarters because you don't pay attention to business..."

"Really? Am I supposed to be the night watchman at the Tremont?"

"Rosetta Rice was a star. Her murder was bound to cause headlines, and headlines mean unfavorable publicity for our business."

Joshua's voice quieted. "Oh, so it was only a matter of business to you...?"

Ira stared at his son and replied coldly, "You better not mean what I think you're insinuating. I've always been faithful to your dear mother."

"Yeah, sure, Pop. Whatever you say. But I know damn well that in the old days...

"Miss Rice and I were once good friends. No more than that. Not that it's any of your business."

"It's only my business when it's business, not pleasure." Joshua was deliberately trying to goad his father into losing his temper. He may have to take the old man's scolding, but Joshua would be damned before he would let his father enjoy it. "So, not one of your old doxies, then?"

"You impertinent...!"

"Those two antiques in the outer office can probably hear you yelling..."

Ira lowered his voice and turned from scorn to ask his son what he considered a reasonable question: "Night or day, Joshua when was the last time you visited your own theatre?"

"Oh, so it's mine, now, is it?"

"Tell me!," Ira, newly exasperated, demanded: "When was the last time?!"

"Sometime last week, I suppose. What of it? I'm busy making deals..."

"You're busy spending money all over town!"

"And you've lost touch with the business! D'you know that?! It isn't the 1890s anymore. Bennie Keith and Ned Albee have been cutting off my access to good acts. And now Erlanger and Shubert are crowding us out. Have you even heard—way up there in your Nashua museum—about the United Booking Office or the United States Amusement Company?"

"Yes. I've heard, young man. I've heard a lot more than you guess. This isn't the first time I've had to ride out competition. You win by husbanding your resources, not getting into a spending war with men with bigger purses."

"Is that so? Why don't you try booking the acts again?"

"That's your job. One of the damn few things you do for your salary."

"The only reason we get decent acts at a discount is because I wine and dine some of the bookers and agents. How the hell do you think I get name acts to go to Ayer and Fitchburg for half their asking price?"

"Don't use that language with me. Don't forget..."

"I get them cheap because I nose around over lunch and a few drinks and find out which acts have an open week they want to fill."

"Bookers are businessmen, not like your easy women that you ply with presents."

"All right, I'll do it your way. You're the master. Yeah, now that I think about it, it's a brilliant idea to turn our theatres into third-rate houses...."

"Sarcasm..."

"And maybe I can get you Jojo the Dog-Faced Boy and we can drop our prices..."

"Shut up! I won't be spoken to that way. Not by you. Not by any employee."

"Employee? Is that what I am to you. One of your employees?!"

"You don't see your name on the door, yet, do you? Keep up the smart talk and maybe you never will."

The following pause was not one of calm.

When Joshua spoke, it was with controlled seething. "Like it or not, I am your only heir and you are an old, old man. I don't think mother would permit you to..."

Ira's reply was cruelly measured. "You think your mother is your champion, do you? Just like when you were a spoiled little boy? And I'm an old, old man, eh? Well, I may be that, but it's a long time since you were a boy. You're well into middle age, unmarried, without career prospects—except those I provide—and with few left of the qualities that stirred your mother's love." Ira's voice was rising again. "What makes you think she has any better opinion of you than I do? When was the last time you visited her? Even thought about her?! Anything I choose to do will have her support. Good Lord, man, see yourself for what you are! An ungrateful, selfish profligate!"

Miss Markey and Mr Yates skittered back to their desks as they heard a chair scrape against the floor. Ira Wood opened the connecting door between the offices, but Joshua brushed past him, hat and coat in hand, and marched out the office without a further word.

Ira Wood closed the connecting door and turned to his employees whose faces were tilted downward as their hands shuffled through papers.

"Mr Yates? You have the books ready? Let's get to it, shall we?"

CHAPTER 23

Tuesday Afternoon: Lawyer and Booker in Stand-off

While Ira Wood was reviewing accounts with Owen Yates, the afternoon train from Providence pulled into South Union Station. Dudley Pierce's last-minute trip to Boston had been prompted by his morning telephone call to the Hotel Touraine where the desk clerk informed him that Miss Rice was no longer a guest. Upon pressing, the Touraine's manager was brought to the phone. Mr Pierce told the manager that he was Miss Rice's attorney and suggested that if the manager would check Miss Rice's registration he would likely see that Pierce was listed as the person to notify in any emergency. This proved so, but the Touraine's manager limited himself to the news that Miss Rice was dead and referred Attorney Pierce to the police department for further details.

As well-connected as he was prominent, Dudley Pierce telephoned the Providence, Rhode Island, chief of police who was able to get the information from Chief Inspector Watt's office in Boston that Rosetta Rice had been murdered sometime during Monday night. Once possessed of that distressing information, Pierce lost no time in getting to Boston.

Wearing a homburg and a chesterfield coat, and carrying a tightly-furled umbrella in one hand and a worn but well-made portmanteau in the other, Dudley Pierce strode through the concourse and hailed one of the hackneys arrayed alongside the sidewalk outside.

"Keith's New Theatre on Washington Street."

The hackney driver acknowledged the instruction with no more than a nod and directed his horse into the Atlantic Avenue traffic, then turned west on Summer Street toward Washington. Despite the uneasy combination of motored and horse-drawn traffic, the half-mile was covered quickly, and Mr Pierce alit in front of the building that housed Keith's New Theatre and the Boston branch of the United Booking Offices.

Apprised by another booker in the U.B.O. office that Nathan Furst more frequently did business at his Chauncy Street office, little more than two blocks away, Pierce arrived there a few minutes later and climbed the three steep flights of stairs. His knock on the door was answered in person.

"Mr Nathan Furst?"

"Yes?"

"My name is Dudley Pierce," a response accompanied by a proffered business card. "I am—was Miss Rosetta Rice's attorney and now represent her estate."

Furst took a moment to gather himself and try to blend cordiality with sympathy. A wan attempt at a smile resulted. "Please, come in." He indicated a chair facing his and, now recovered, added, "I was devastated to hear of Rosetta's—Miss Rice's death. Please accept my condolences."

"You knew Rosetta—Miss Rice, well, did you?"

Nathan recognized a lawyerly query; "Strictly business, Mr ..." Despite hearing the lawyer pronounce his name in the old Yankee manner of "purse," Nathan glanced at the card still in his hand and mispronounced it "pierce." Attorney Pierce didn't bother to correct Furst and allowed the booker to continue. "Much to my regret it was me who booked Miss Rice into the Tremont this week. Who could have known? Believe me, now I wish I had never gone to Providence."

"Miss Rice had retired, Mr Furst. What made you think of booking her?"

"The Tremont canceled an act; they needed a replacement."

"Yes, I understand that. But surely there were other acts at liberty?"

"Not a draw like her." Furst knew he was fencing with Pierce, but he hoped to give away as little as possible until he better understood Pierce's purpose in coming to him instead of the police. "Can I get you some coffee, Mr Pierce?"

"No, thank you." Pierce sensed Furst's reluctance. "Miss Rice was not only a valued client, Mr Furst, she had become, over the years, a family friend, one whose interests I did my best to protect and nurture."

Furst's initial reaction was that Pierce, in spite of his gentlemanly manner must be a tough customer, indeed, if he were able to "protect and nurture" Rosetta's interests better than the old bird did for herself. To break the pause and try to reverse what he felt was becoming a defensive position, Nathan asked "What exactly, Mr Pierce, can I do for you?"

"Thank you, Mr Furst. You can tell me why Rosetta Rice, rather than another performer, perhaps one who lived here in Boston, was booked at the Tremont."

"We knew she was available."

"Who is we?"

"The United Booking Office."

"Come, now, Mr Furst. Corporations don't book. People do. Was it you who offered what I believe is an extraordinary salary to entice her to Boston?"

Pierce meant to sting, but rather than upset the booking agent, the lawyer's thrust gave Furst the opportunity to deflect the offense: "I am strictly an agent. As you are an attorney, you must understand that I am not authorized to discuss with you the particulars of the United Booking Office's business or its clients."

For a few seconds, the two men regarded each other across Furst's desk.

"Do I understand correctly that you are unwilling to discuss this matter with her attorney, one who represents her estate?"

"If your questions are about her estate, I would be happy to answer them, but I don't know anything about her financial affairs. If your questions are about the murder, that is a police matter."

"Then you have talked with the police?"

"They haven't contacted me as yet. When they do—if they do, I'll do exactly what they tell me."

Pierce rose and moved toward the door. He stifled the urge to warn that he would pursue his inquiries elsewhere. Instead he chose to give no more than he got and leave the interview unresolved in Furst's mind as well as his own.

Pierce had noticed the telephone in Furst's office, so he paused for a half minute outside the door in the hope he might overhear a phone call. Inside, Furst stood at the window overlooking the Chauncy Street entrance. He would place his phone calls only after he saw Attorney Pierce leave the building.

The interview had been brief but the sun was low on the horizon as Dudley Pierce walked the three short blocks from Chauncy to Essex to Boylston Streets. Rosetta Rice had taken apartments at the Hotel Touraine, and Pierce had thought it wise that he do the same as he anticipated being in Boston at least overnight. From Providence he had wired to reserve a bed-sitting chamber with private bath, and was fortunate that one was available on short notice. Upon reflection, he had been a bit disconcerted to grasp that the availability could be due solely to Rosetta's murder and yet equally intrigued that he might be inhabiting a space recently occupied by her.

Five minutes behind Pierce and unintentionally following in his footsteps—but only to the point where Essex met Washington Street—Nathan was about to round the corner and head south toward Eliot Street when he stopped short to consider more carefully a destination. He didn't fancy trotting all over town searching for someone he should have been able to contact by phone. A few minutes earlier, when he had dialed Ira Wood Enterprises, Nathan had hoped against probability that Joshua Wood would be at his office. Predictably, Mr Yates had informed Nathan when he called that Mr Joshua Wood had departed the premises before 3 o'clock. Unexpectedly, Mr Yates added that Mr Ira Wood had left just a few minutes ago, about 4 o'clock, after one of his rare unscheduled visits.

Nathan figured that Ira's visit was not simply coincidental to Rosetta Rice's murder in their flagship theatre. As he knew both men and was aware of some antagonism between senior and junior Wood, Nathan guessed that while Joshua might trade barbs with his father, he would not chance alienating Wood senior and would now be licking his wounds either alone in a hotel bar or, more likely, seeking jovial company and an ample supply of spirits.

Nathan's first guess had been that Joshua would be holding forth at Jacob Wirth's, a frequent haunt, but then he recalled Ira Wood was in town and often met his old associates there as well. Joshua would be sure to avoid a second confrontation that day with his father. That left about fifty other taverns in downtown Boston. Upon reflecting while standing at the corner, Nathan decided that Joshua would probably race to a nearby watering hole, probably an inconspicuous saloon where he was unlikely to meet people he knew through business and where overindulgence was tolerated. That thought led to Lagrange Street, diagonally across from where Nathan was standing. The narrow Lagrange Street did not attract casual traffic but housed several small taverns behind the Hotel Touraine—convenient refuges for Joshua that required only a brief stagger home through a discreet service entrance into the Touraine.

Joshua spotted Nathan enter the small establishment at 98 Lagrange, and motioned him to join him. Two other men were already seated at the table, but perhaps Joshua was tiring of them. Joshua introduced his "good friend, Nate" to the others. Nathan knew better than try to sequester his quarry while the man was seeking comfort in easy fellowship, so Nathan ordered a mug of Berliner-Weiss, a brew with rich color yet low in alcohol.

As the only fully sober man seated at the table, Nathan knew the others would soon tire of his somber presence. Joshua's two companions could excuse themselves and leave, but Joshua, because it had been he who invited Nathan to join the table, would not have that option. Nathan had patience, and when it came time to leave nearly an hour later, Joshua Wood seemed sufficiently boiled to be less guarded than when sober but not yet befuddled. Genially, Joshua invited Nathan to accompany him back to his suite at the Touraine. A shoulder to lean on would steady Joshua's gait and save him from possible embarrassment. Nor was it lost on Nathan that this occasion would be the first and only time such an invitation would be extended.

CHAPTER 24

Late Tuesday Afternoon: Bringing Bad Tidings Home

As calmly as possible, Lavinia and Mr Boniface doffed their outer garments and entered the kitchen where Florrie and Agnes had begun to fix dinner. Lavinia nodded a greeting, walked directly to the sink to wash her hands. Mr Boniface followed suit. Florrie and Agnes, each with a nose for drama, ceased work, anticipated some announcement. Lavinia had intended not to mention their news in front of Agnes; she hadn't even discussed it with Mr Boniface on their way home, but faced with the expectant expressions of her sister and Agnes, Lavinia spoke.

"I think we should sit down and talk for a few minutes before our lodgers return. Mr Boniface and I have heard some distressing news." Noticing Agnes standing apart, Lavinia added, "Agnes, I think you had better join us, but I am sorry to have to drag you into this mess." Agnes could not have been more pleased. "Rosetta Rice was murdered. It happened at the Tremont Theatre. In her dressing room." A momentary silence was succeeded by an excited jumble of astonished gasps, exclamations and questions.

"Please!" Lavinia held up her hands, and Florrie and Agnes drew breaths and took turns.

"When?" asked Florrie.

"How?" asked Agnes, quickly crossing herself.

"All we know is what we heard from a young usher at the National. Just the basic fact that she was killed. Bad news travels fast among show folk, so the usher probably heard about it just minutes before he told us. As to the who, why—and yes, Agnes, how of the matter—we know nothing. It must have happened sometime between last night's show and today's matinee. Now you know as much as we do. Meanwhile the question at hand is how we handle our guests this evening. They'll be coming back for dinner in about an hour, I expect, and you can be sure they'll have heard at least as much about what happened as we have. We mustn't allow gossip to run..."

"Vinnie, you can't expect actors not to talk..."

"Florrie, have you forgotten that Mrs Cormier is lodging under our roof? You think our guests won't have heard about the trouble between her and Miss Rice? Cormier's an unpleasant woman, but that doesn't make her a murderer. Even if she has brought the

104

gossip on herself, we should protect her daughter and the boys from hearing it. Now, let's decide what we need to do so we can be ready before everyone arrives."

Mr Boniface, who had seemed to drift into the ether during the discussion, surprised all when he spoke first. "Why don't I serve them dinner here in the kitchen? Then Mrs Cormier and the youngsters can leave by the kitchen door for the theatre this evening. Or perhaps Mrs Cormier would prefer taking her meal in her room, alone, rather than with the children in the kitchen?"

In the short silence that followed these suggestions, no one could think better.

"Good thinking, Mr Boniface," congratulated Florrie. "And not a moment too soon. I think I hear Victor Greeley upstairs."

"Oh, bother!" Lavinia had hoped to have a strategy in place before their lodgers returned for dinner. "Why are they back here so early? Dinner's not for nearly an hour yet."

Indeed, Mr Greeley had been alone in the sitting room for almost an hour, waiting for someone with whom to gossip about Rosetta Rice's murder. Doris Greeley had endured all she could stand of her husband's oscillation between anger and conjecture after they discovered their matinee had been cancelled and why. Even the walk home from the Tremont had not drained him of his fervor for the topic. Doris had only met Miss Rice once or twice several years ago, but news of her murder had upset her, so she left her husband in the sitting room while she repaired upstairs. She had no intention of returning until dinner was served.

The Hennigan Brothers, whose number two spot at the nearby National allowed them to leave after intermission, were the first of the other lodgers to make it back to Portridge Arms. When they walked into the sitting room, Mr Greeley had his audience. His resounding baritone alerted those in the kitchen they were not alone and neither was Victor Greeley.

"Oh, good heavens! Victor is just the one to spread gossip. Lavinia, don't you think we'd better talk to our guests first—but what can we say? What do we really know?"

"Once the rest of them have gathered and start swapping gossip, I imagine they will be telling us more than we can tell them. We can think about it while we get on with making dinner. What still needs to be done? Everyone will be so preoccupied that I think we can dispense with frills. Let's keep dinner simple but ample."

"I just put four nut loaves and six cheese, potato and cauliflower casseroles in the ovens, and Agnes has water heating in the cauldron to boil corn on the cob. That should be ready in about 30 minutes or so. And there's some dinner buns from yesterday. Agnes, will you pull them out of the cold storage? We'll pop the buns in the oven to warm just before we serve dinner. Meanwhile, I'd better get a wiggle on; I need to whip up a savory sauce for the nut loaf, but there isn't anything made for dessert yet, Lavinia."

"Agnes, after you get the buns, you can help me peel and chop up some apples. What other fruit is there, Flora?'

"The fruit at the market down the street was dreadful except for their apples. I doubt we have anything else but raisins."

"That would make for an odd combination."

"Not if we drown it in a cinnamon custard sauce and crumble in some cookies," offered Florrie.

"That'll have to do. Mr Boniface, will you bring some crackers and herb dip up to whomever is in the sitting room? Perhaps full mouths will plug wagging tongues." Despite saying it, Lavinia kept to herself the contrary thought that it was unlikely that any quantity of food would long stem Victor's appetite for speculation.

For the next half hour, three sets of hands busily put the finishing touches to the night's meal. After he had set the tables, Boniface came back down to the kitchen. "I think most of our guests have arrived. Everyone seems to be in the sitting room, except Mrs Cormier and the youngsters. I haven't seen them."

"Thank you, Mr Boniface," said Lavinia. "We'll all go up together in a minute. As soon as you spot the children and Mrs Cormier, will you bring them down to the kitchen—or take them up to their rooms? Whichever they prefer? At least the children. Who knows, perhaps Mrs Cormier will brazen it out and sit at table with the other lodgers. In any case, you, Florrie, should make an announcement."

"I? But they've probably heard more about it than I."

"Yes, and likely a lot of things that are mere guesswork. They'll all be looking to you, expecting that you will have ferreted out all that can be known thus far."

"Lavinia, that's not kind."

"But it is true, Florrie, don't you think so? If I were to speak to them, they'd be sure I was withholding something important."

"I suppose you're right," admitted Florrie. "I'll make it short and simple."

"I hope so," countered Lavinia. "Now, Agnes, this is a very serious matter—one that can ruin reputations and get people, even those children, into great trouble, so, unless you can refrain from talking about this tragedy to the lodgers, you may stay in the kitchen while we serve."

"I promise, Miss Lavinia. Not a word."

"Not even if they ask you?"

"No, Ma'am, I promise!" Agnes was almost willing to forego confession to be allowed to hear the gossip.

"All right then. Now let's serve them dinner."

CHAPTER 25

Tuesday Evening: Dinner Table Talk at Portridge Arms

Agnes shoved the steaming covered dishes into the dumbwaiter and sent the dumbwaiter on its way with several vigorous pulls. Boniface, Lavinia and Florrie toted baskets of bread rolls and trays with containers of margarine, condiments and sauces as they climbed up the stairs to serve dinner and face a barrage of questions. Lavinia muttered, ""This is not going to go well, I can feel it."

The last of the several loads of food sent up in the dumbwaiter, Agnes raced up the stairs so as not to miss any of the unfolding drama.

Never were actors so helpful with chores. Several sidled up to Florrie at the dumb-waiter to ask if they might help carry the dishes into the dining room; this followed by a quick, hushed question?: "Was it a heart attack?" "Is she dead?" and "Did you hear it was foul play," With so many willing hands, it only took a few minutes to lay out the meal.

"Ladies and gentlemen," intoned Florrie, "please sit down. Thank you. We, like you, have just learned that Miss Rosetta Rice—I'm sure some of you knew her—was stricken, fatally, I'm sorry to say, at the Tremont Theatre. We have been told it was after her evening performance. Beyond that, I assure you, we know no more than any of you."

It was a mistake to have made her announcement so short. A longer speech might have dissipated some of the pent-up excitement; instead, Florrie was besieged with questions.

Above the ensuing hubbub, could be heard, "Well, I know for a fact that someone—another act on the bill—deliberately sabotaged her act, and heaven knows what else!"

It was unlikely that Mrs Cormier's arrival at that very moment had been cue for Greeley's remark, or the remark unintentionally announced her arrival. What was clear was that she was stopped short at the doorway into the dining room. The cynosure of all, her abrupt halt at the entrance produced an expectant hush throughout the room. Had any of the performers present had time to think about it, they would have envied the rapt attention focused on Mrs Cormier and Mr Greeley, for it had been he who uttered the accusation.

For once at a loss for a retort, Mrs Cormier stood as if frozen at the doorway, then turned and abruptly left the room. Flora sped after her, catching her by the elbow part way up the stairs. "I'm sorry, dear, about the careless chatter, but you know how actors are. Let me send a few trays of dinner up to your rooms for you and the children. Or, if you like, we can serve you in the kitchen." Mrs Cormier simply stared at Florrie white-faced and blank of expression before fleeing upstairs. Florrie called after her: "Please, at least send the children down to dine with my sister and me."

Back in the dining room, the hubbub had subdued to murmurs when Florrie re-entered to quietly ask Mr Boniface and Agnes to prepare four trays of food and deliver them to Mrs Cormier's rooms. Without a further word or glance, Florrie left the room and Lavinia followed her down the stairs. "You did the best you could, Flora, given Mr Greeley's unfortunate remark."

"I should have sorted him out, guest or not, right then and there. What an awful thing to say! That was akin to an accusation of murder. I expected better of him."

"Well, the cat's out of the bag, now. They'll soon find out she was stabbed to death."

"Stabbed?!" Florrie stopped stock-still midway down to the basement. "Oh, Lavinia, you didn't tell me that!"

"Not while Agnes was present. It's even worse. Her throat was slit."

Florrie stopped abruptly on the stairs. Her left hand clasped her breast and her right flung itself upward to her brow and slid down to cover her mouth. Although her reaction resembled stock physical expressions rife in melodrama, Florrie's emotion was sincere; at her core, she had never accepted that cruelty and violence were part of human nature—any nature.

"It happened in Rosetta's dressing room," continued Lavinia, "and she not fully dressed at best. So it may, indeed, have been someone connected to the theatre."

"Heaven forbid."

"It had to be someone who had the right to roam about backstage."

Recovered from the shock, Florrie's thoughts turned to the immediate and practical: "Not one of our lodgers, I hope."

"I've been thinking about that. Mr and Mrs Greeley and Dainty Alice, her chums and her mum make up about one-fourth of the performers on the Tremont's bill."

"I think we may discount Alice and the two lads. If nothing else, I doubt they have the interest or energy to murder…"

"Unless it were their gorgon of a stage mother," cut in Lavinia.

Florrie thought for a moment. "How did you mean that?"

"Either way." deadpanned Lavinia.

"Indeed. Those poor children. Getting dragged around town to town, without any playmates or schooling, experiencing nothing but dreary small-time theatres and unfriendly audiences. Anyway, discounting the children, the list of murder suspects under our roof declines to about ten percent, although that's little consolation."

"Rather less if you factor in the men backstage and In front of the house."

"Small comfort that is, Lavinia. It could still be someone we more or less know."

"Like Petey Martin? It would have to be someone with little compunction about slitting a woman's throat."

"Petey…!"

Further dismay was interrupted by a tentative knocking at the Castle Street basement door. Lavinia stepped past Florrie, who had grasped a banister and slumped down on the stairs muttering "oh dear, oh dear."

Lavinia opened the door to a raggedy-dressed young boy. She looked at him uncomprehendingly.

CHAPTER 26

Tuesday Evening: Look to the Children

"Ma'am—Miss Lavinia, you told me to come by tonight?" Realizing that Lavinia was uncertain, his explanation had risen into a question.

"Did we? Oh, yes, we did. Come in. Flora, the boy is here."

Quickly jettisoning one problem for another more pleasant and easier to solve, Florrie scuttled down the remaining steps to welcome him. She had to stifle a need to hug him.

"Tommy, my sister and I are so glad you took us at our word. Come inside. We have some lovely hot food for you."

Lavinia was almost as relieved as Florrie to be diverted from what had transpired upstairs among the guests. Florrie was setting the kettle to boil for tea and cocoa when she remembered "I asked Agnes and Mr Boniface to make up trays and bring them up to Mrs Cormier in her room. I hope the children are with her. I wouldn't want them to hear any of the loose talk...."

"I'll find out where they are. You stay here with the boy, Florrie," called Lavinia as she went up the stairs. "And I'll send Agnes down here. I don't want her around the guests any longer than need be."

If Tommy noted that anything unusual was transpiring, he didn't show it as he watched Florrie hand him a mug of cocoa and a warm roll spread with peanut butter. He looked at it oddly.

"That's what they call peanut butter, Tommy. It's made with roasted nuts. I think it's a great improvement on the paste they make with steamed nuts. We'll have a hot, nutritious meal as soon as we're all seated for dinner. Tell me about your day." Florrie was as eager for something other than the murder to discuss as Tommy was to make fast his friendship with this odd but probably kind woman.

"I made 78 cents selling papers and 15 cents more in tips running errands."

"That's very good, Tommy. Or I imagine so. Is it?" Florrie had little idea of the measure for success in Tommy's world.

"Pretty good in this weather. But you need to hustle."

"Yes, I should think so." She was about to say more when she heard Lavinia and Agnes talking at the top of the stairs.

"Mr Boniface can look after things upstairs by himself, Agnes. We don't need you standing around eavesdropping. I'm disappointed in you. My sister directed you and Mr Boniface to bring up trays of food to the children and Mrs Cormier in their rooms, and you refused..."

"I couldn't..."

"Of course you could! You've got two legs. Instead you made poor Mr Boniface carry all those trays up two flights of stairs each time. Next time we send food up to Mrs Cormier in her room you alone will take up all the trays."

"Me!?"

"And why not?"

"She's a murderer!"

"Agnes!" snapped Lavinia, "You know nothing about it. That's sheer nonsense!"

"I heard them talking..."

"You heard them gossiping! And I don't want to add to that by discussing the matter with you up here." They began descending the stairs into the kitchen, and Lavinia remembered that Tommy was there. "Now, hold your tongue. We have a guest," nodding in Tommy's direction.

"Him, a guest!? That ragamuffin."

"Yes, Agnes, *him*. It is a matter for my sister and I to decide and for you to accept. If you cannot....," Lavinia wished to brook no more argument, but she softened her tone to temper the threat, "then maybe you'd better look elsewhere for more agreeable employment. Tommy has been invited to share dinner with us every night, and you will welcome him with as generous amount of Christian charity as your church would wish and you can muster."

Flummoxed whenever anyone played the 'good Christian' card against her, Agnes' eyes began to smart with tears. She knew she had little choice to say anything but "Yes, Ma'am," but where in her catechism did it say to wait on raggedy, dirty boys?

Had Agnes not objected to him, Lavinia would hardly have been as staunch a defender of "the ragamuffin." It usually fell to Lavinia to remind Agnes, gently or firmly, that she was to do as she was told when given a reasonable order. It remained to be seen whether Agnes was worth the trouble. Part of the problem was that Flora's familiarity with staff had to be kept in check, else everyone would think herself entitled to a voice in the affairs of the house.

Lavinia noticed that Florrie had seated Tommy at the table although his hands were filthy and his face smudged.

"Young man, Mr Boniface showed you the way to the water closet yesterday. Do you think you can find it on your own tonight?"

"Yes Miss Lavinia." Off he went around the corner to the other side of the building. Lavinia had to admit that he seemed a quick lad who needed little more than a hint. Perhaps he'd prove too quick. Sometimes Lavinia wished she had some small share of her sister's optimism.

Tommy returned, face washed and hair combed. He showed the sisters his hands—clean to the wrists, but his fingernails, Lavinia noted, seemed resistant to a cursory soaping.

The sound of lurching gears and rattling crockery signaled that Mr Boniface was sending down the dumbwaiter with its first after-dinner cargo of empty serving dishes and left-overs. The warming oven still held two casseroles and three nut loaves. While Lavinia finished setting table and Agnes added a few ears of corn to a small pot of water on the boil, Mr Boniface came downstairs.

"How are things upstairs?," asked Florrie.

"A bit more calm, I think. Mr Greeley's comment may have dampened some of the urge to talk. At table, at least. I expect there will be more said in smaller groups in the sitting room." Florrie and Lavinia were nearly open-mouthed. It had been a while since either of them had heard Boniface utter a string of sentences and make bold with an opinion. "I think the children sense something is quite wrong. Mrs Cormier does not hide her distress well. Do you think a few extra dishes of pudding might be in order?"

"Good idea, Mr Boniface," offered Florrie.

Lavinia looked to Agnes, "Please put up a few dishes of pudding and a pot of tea and I'll take them up," Lavinia.

"I'll help you carry them," volunteered Agnes quietly.

Florrie and Lavinia needed to do no more than glance at each other.

"Why don't the rest of you begin eating," offered Lavinia. "Agnes and I will be back in a few minutes."

Florrie barely heard her..

CHAPTER 27

Late Tuesday afternoon: The Latest News

Florrie felt she should explain some of what Tommy must have heard. So, while they ate, she turned to Tommy. "I expect you already know something from the afternoon papers about what happened at the Tremont Theatre."

"Yeah," he managed between chews and gulps, "I heard 'bout it."

"The woman who died, Miss Rice, was an acquaintance of ours and some of our lodgers, so they are a bit upset. None of us, including the newspapers, I expect, really knows what happened..."

"Her throat was cut. Sometime around midnight." Tommy didn't miss a beat with his fork and spoon.

"Tommy!" Florrie took a second to recover. "How do you know this. Was it in the Record? Already?"

"Nope, I heard it from the cops."

Florrie looked at Boniface and wondered why he didn't appear as astonished as she felt.

"Surely, they didn't tell you all this?"

"Naw, I heard them talking at the stationhouse on Lagrange. If I get there early enough and they ain't got their papers yet, they let me go round the offices selling the *Record*."

"They just let you wander around Station Four?"

"I guess so. They never notice me. A lot of the other boys don't want to sell in the stations because some cops got a grudge on them, so I kinda got Station Four to myself."

Excited, Florrie was almost gobbling her meal. "What else did you hear?"

"Well, they don't think it was robbery."

"Why not?"

" 'Cause the killer left her money and jewels."

Mr Boniface had hardly touched his dinner, but Florrie, thrilled to be the recipient of inside information, and Tommy, driven by a growing boy's appetite, had picked their plates clean by the time Lavinia and Agnes returned. Mr Boniface's dinner remained uneaten.

Florrie burbled a rush of words as she rose from the table and grabbed her cloak and knitted cap that she kept by the back door.

"Mr Boniface, Lavinia, Agnes—will you spare me? I need to have a word with Mr Greeley before he leaves for the theatre tonight, and then I'm off to see Petey Martin. Don't forget to give Tommy some of the apple crumb pudding, Agnes, and thank you for your help this evening. Tommy, you're welcome to come by for dinner tomorrow night as well." With that she dashed upstairs, cloak and hat in hand. Lavinia had no option but to acquiesce.

Upstairs, standing just inside the doorway to the sitting room, Florrie caught Victor Greeley's eye. When he didn't respond to Florrie's subtle nod to the hall, she left her cloak and hat on a small hall table and walked into the room.

"Mr Greeley, will you kindly join me next door? I won't take but a minute of your time." Whether he understood before or not, he soon comprehended that Miss Flora wanted something other than a social chat. He rose and followed her out. Once inside the empty dining room next door, Florrie closed the door. "Mr Greeley—Victor, my sister and I feel privileged to have had you and Mrs Greeley as guests at Portridge Arms more than a few times. You were among our first clients, and I hope you will stay with us again when you are booked in Boston. You've both been pleasant and responsible. But what you did this evening, what you said at dinner was not responsible, was it Mr Greeley?" Florrie gently held up a finger to request that she be allowed to say her piece. "Regardless of what you—or Lavinia and I, for the matter, think about Mrs Cormier, we have a duty to act civilly, at the least, and not humiliate a fellow lodger, especially as there are children involved. Do you agree, Mr Greeley?"

"Yes, of course, Flora, and I do regret my outburst. But Rosetta was humiliated, too. Rosetta hadn't performed in several years; she was vulnerable. When someone destroys your act in front of hundreds of people—an audience of strangers, that is humiliation!" He paused. "That's why I was angry. It was an insult to her and our profession. And, then, the news of her death! It was all too much." He shifted his eyes from Florrie and stared out a window. "It's no excuse, but, long ago, Rosetta Rice was dear to me, though I doubt she ever felt the same way about me. But all these years later, I still admired her as a professional and as a woman. I regret that I let my anger get the better of me." He was silent for a few moments then looked back at Florrie. "I do truly regret my outburst tonight, Miss Portridge. It was uncharitable and truly unprofessional. I hope you'll forgive me."

"Only if you continue to call me Florrie. Let's speak no more about it, Victor, except for me to ask you to do your best to calm the other guests and discourage gossip."

They left the dining room together; Victor to return to the sitting room. Florrie began to descend the stairs when she remembered her pocketbook. She stopped in the front hall, turned down the hall to her room, retrieved her pocketbook, donned her cloak and hat and sped through the first floor entrance and onto the sidewalk.

Downstairs, Tommy had remembered to thank everyone for dinner. As he rose to leave, he pulled from his canvas newsboy bag two copies of *The Boston Evening Record*. He handed one to Lavinia and another to Agnes. Agnes accepted open-mouthed. Lavinia smiled and thought "This is one artful beggar."

116

CHAPTER 28

Tuesday Night: Two Sundaes

Tommy waited on the sidewalk for Florrie. Late October was when it grew noticeably dark early, and he was feeling the young gallant. In his mind, Florrie was an old lady, kind and friendly and likely too gullible and naïve to walk alone in the dark. He intended to walk her to the theatre.

"I hope you enjoyed dinner, Tommy."

"Yes, Ma'am."

"Are you headed to the Burrough's Foundation?"

"Yeah. Can I walk you to the theatre? It's on my way."

"How'd you know I was going there?"

"You said so—right after you talked to Mr Greeley first."

"My, you don't miss much, do you. Let's keep walking, shall we? The performers will be leaving any minute to get to their evening shows, and I'd prefer that we didn't have to meet up with any of them again this evening. But if I go to the Tremont now, I'll run into Mr Greeley again and Mrs Cormier and her children. Both acts are appearing at the Tremont. Do you know what an act is, Tommy?"

"Not really, 'cept it's part of a show."

"Are you interested in the theatre?"

"Don't know. I ain't never seen a show 'cept the freaks at the Grand Museum down Dover Street."

"Ain't never? Oh, dear. You and I shall have to work on your double negatives, Tommy, and sometime soon. As to gawking at poor unfortunates, well, I shall take you to proper theatre to see a vaudeville show. But for now why don't we go to the new Liggett's and talk about it over a couple of ice cream sundaes? You're not too full from dinner, are you?" Tommy's face lit up like a marquee. She had seen him smile before, usually a bit slyly, but now he wore a big grin, and Florrie made note that he would need to see a dentist soon.

Liggett's, still new, was bright and warm. Florrie and Tommy had ordered at the soda fountain and were seated at a small table near the windows when two sundaes arrived, each topped with a brightly-colored maraschino cherry and accompanied by spoons, napkins and glasses of water.

"You see that sign and all those lights across the street? Up a few buildings on Tremont?"

"You mean the Tremont Theatre? Where it says '9 Big Acts of Vaudeville'?"

"Good, you read well."

"My Ma taught me before... I ain't gone to school since then."

"I think you're a bright lad, Tommy, and there's a lot going on in the world that you will want to know about as you make your way." She instinctively understood that Tommy, at present, was primarily interested in the world immediately about him: newspapers, police, crime, baseball probably—most young men were—and possibly show business, at least the supposed glamour and riches associated with it. Of those, their only shared interests were likely to be show business and newspapers, and she doubted that Tommy was yet aware of the *Boston Transcript,* much less likely the *Christian Science Monitor.* Certainly, Tommy perceived some small connection with show business through the Portridge Arms, so vaudeville was as good a topic as any to begin his education.

"You said you weren't sure what an act is, right, Tommy? Well in most other kinds of stage shows there is a story and all the actors and performers play somebody in the story. In vaudeville, there is no story, no real story, although sometimes there is a short one as part of the bill. Each of the acts... Perhaps I should ask: do you know what a bill is?"

"Don't think so."

"A bill is what vaudevillians call the show, and each of those nine acts at the Tremont has its own place on the bill."

"Like innings at a baseball game? There's nine of them, too."

Florrie realized she had learned a valuable lesson in teaching: make connections with that which the student already knew. She recalled someone had called it 'the building blocks of knowledge.'

"Yes, Tommy, like innings at a baseball game. Anyway, each of the acts on stage is its own little show and very different from the others. Some acts sing, others dance or tell funny jokes or juggle or do tricks. Sometimes, there's more than one person in act."

"What's Mr Greeley's act?

"Oh, he and his wife, Doris, do a funny bit about a shoe store..."

"And what did Rosetta Rice do?"

"She was a singer, poor dear."

"Why was she murdered?"

"Heavens, Tommy! I have no idea."

"I think it was a crime of passion."

"Tommy! Whatever made you say that? Where did you ever hear such a thing?"

"*The Record*. They call a lot of murders 'crimes of passion.' Besides, the cops didn't find none of her stuff missing. ... Of course, whoever did it—killed Miss Rice—coulda taken some of the stuff and left the rest just to trick the cops."

Florrie stared at the boy in growing admiration. His was a canny mind. Now if it could just be harnessed to good purpose, he would turn out a fine young man.

"What time do you need to get to Burroughs to get a bed?" Florrie looked at the clock high up on the middle of the drug store wall. "It's 7:30."

"If I go now, I can pick up some copies of the late edition and sell them on my way. Thanks for the ice cream, Miss Flora."

"Don't forget to stop by tomorrow night for dinner."

She watched through the window as he waved, then held her breath as Tommy darted across the street through the traffic and sped toward Newspaper Row. Performers would still be showing up at the stage door for tonight's performance, so Florrie needed to wait at least another hour before bearding Petey Martin at the theatre. "Oh, bother!" The words were exclaimed aloud before she caught herself. She had forgotten to bring a bag of cookies for Petey, so she had better shop around for a little something. It was a wonder she had remembered to bring her purse. At least she had plenty of time. R. & J. Gilchrist's was only a few blocks north up Washington Street. A department store, it contained a bakery department renowned for its almond macaroons. She'd buy Petey some of those and maybe a few more for herself and Lavinia.

Florrie always enjoyed the nighttime walk up Washington Street. Marquees blazed their attractions across the front of the Park, the Globe, the Gayety, the Bijou and Keith's New Theatre. The whole of the street flaunted a festive air. Her hour of waiting passed buying macaroons, window shopping and watching people.

CHAPTER 29

Tuesday Night: A Backstage Visit

By the time Flora Portridge visited Petey Martin at the Tremont, the police had left the premises, except for an older policeman stationed in a chair along the corridor of the second floor dressings rooms where Rosetta's sealed room was located. The front- and back-of-the-house staff had been permitted to prepare for the evening performance, and the show had gotten underway.

To replace Miss Rice, Simpson, as General manager of the Wood circuit, had the authority to bring in a young rube comic named Chic Sale from the bill at their sister theatre in Lowell, where Chic had made a good hit even with their mill-worker audiences. The theatre manager at the Lowell house was then forced to find a local act to replace Mr Sale. Most theatre managers had a short list of replacement acts—usually "coast-defenders," those acts that didn't travel far afield because they had family responsibilities, were semi-retired or quite young and just breaking into vaudeville.

It might have seemed too obvious to present most people a box of cookies when one wanted information, but Petey Martin preferred gifts to subtlety and was as anxious to talk as Flora was to listen and question.

"You saw her, Petey?"

"Yep. A bloody mess it was. Blood all over her. Her sitting there in her dressing gown and dead as a doornail."

"How did you get in? Weren't the police on guard?"

"Naw, they didn't come yet. Except for Frankie Moore, he's the patrolman. He come backstage to get me to lock up the room until the officers come."

"So, that's when you saw her?"

"Dead with her throat cut ear to ear and blood all over her..."

Florrie was not squeamish; no detail was too gory if it were relevant, but she needed to keep Petey on track without stifling his willingness to tell all her knew. "Was the body cold?"

"How would I know? I didn't touch her!"

"Oh, no, Petey, I didn't mean that. But I'm wondering when the deed was done. You're an observant chap, you see everything that goes on. Did the blood look bright and fresh, or had it dried? Perhaps more dark brown than red"

"Well, it did look dark. Especially on the floor and the dresser."

"Oh, my! Blood everywhere, was there?"

"All over her dressing gown, on the dresser, on the floor. I could see her in the mirror. Officer Moore shooed me out before I could get a better look."

"What time was that?"

"Sometime around eleven this morning."

"Was anything stolen?"

"Don't know. Didn't ask."

"Did anyone hear a commotion last night or this morning?"

"I didn't hear nothing this morning, and I'm the first in."

"And last night?"

"Nothing I know of, and everybody leaves before I do."

"That may not have been the case, Petey."

"Hey, I'm pretty sure. I checked them all out. Them that leaves by the stage door, anyways. Then the stage manager goes and checks all the dressing rooms."

"I don't think I've ever met the stage manager, Petey. Who is he?"

"Ed Gilly. New here. Come about a month ago from one of the other theatres; Fitchburg, I think."

"Was anyone still in the dressing rooms?"

"Guess not. All Ed does is knock on the door; he ain't supposed to go in, especially not the women's rooms."

"You have a checklist for when performers arrive and leave, don't you?"

"Yeah. Here," Petey replied and handed the clipboard to Florrie. He was losing enthusiasm; it was the murder he wanted to gab about, not all this stuff about locking up or not.

"You're sure all the acts are listed?"

"Sure. Every week, everybody in the act. I check 'em as they come in the morning. I check 'em off when they go out at night."

"Maybe somebody came back later? Did you find any signs of a forced entry last night or this morning?"

"Nope."

"There are no checkmarks beside Rosetta's name, Petey."

"She come in the front way Monday."

"Can you take me up to her dressing room?"

"Not a chance. They closed off her room. Brody got a copper stationed up there, too."

"Who's Brody?"

"Inspector from police headquarters."

"Who called the police? Mr Simpson?"

"Naw. He weren't here. Up in one of our other houses. Lowell, maybe. Maybe Fitchburg."

"Then who found the body and called in the police?"

"Must have been Mo."

"Mo? Morris Weiss? The box office manager?"

"Yeah. When Simpson ain't here, Mo takes over. Covers for him."

Florrie decided she had gleaned as much solid information from Petey Martin as he had to yield. She promised to bring him some Irish soda bread and baked beans, and he promised to keep his eyes and ears open.

It had been an upsetting day. Nevertheless, Florrie felt she had assembled a few more pieces of the story. What Petey didn't tell her, Tommy did, and she was beginning to think that little Tommy was the more discerning, reliable and agreeable source. Tomorrow, she'd talk to Mr Weiss and Miss Stropell. The prospect exhilarated her: she began to feel like a detective. Good that she had bought extra macaroons, they'd be a treat tonight for the four of them: Lavinia, Agnes, Mr Boniface and herself. Part celebration and part peace offering to restore good will all around.

CHAPTER 30

Early Wednesday Morning: The Quest

Florrie took up detecting as she had her other enthusiasms like gardening, cooking and trying to figure what made people tick. Wednesday morning, Florrie awoke with a mission. She had learned enough about how and when Rosetta Rice was murdered to be curious to know why and by whom. Granted the matter was properly police business; but Florrie felt it was hers as well. She knew that she'd have to persuade Lavinia—at least toward acceptance if not acquiescence—that Rosetta's murder was also their business.

Florrie tried to marshal her motives as one prepares for cross-examination on a witness stand: murder was a barbarous assault on individual life, an affront to civilized society, and every citizen must do her duty. Rehearsing in front of her dresser mirror, she could not convince herself, and Lavinia was a far harder case.

Most mornings Lavinia and Florrie met in the kitchen within a few minutes of each other. This morning, Florrie, already dressed, knocked on the door of her sister's bed-sit. Florrie had practiced her revised pitch. "Rosetta Rice's murder has reached inside Portridge Arms. Our home. The police don't understand how vaudeville works. I do, and I think I can help them."

"Florrie! You are a 53-year-old innkeeper. A woman with absolutely no police training, not an inspector. You can't go meddling."

"Exactly why I can, Lavinia. Some people—probably the police, too—look at me and see a busybody who loves gossip. That's why neither the police nor the culprit will pay any heed to me until I come up with something."

"*If* you come up with something."

"As you say, but I'm determined to try."

Lavinia was not happy with Florrie's new-found obsession.

"Flora, has it occurred to you that you are far better at losing things than finding them? And what about all the daily work that needs to be done around the house, Florrie? You can't expect Agnes to do it all—or do it all well—just because you may be bored and want an adventure. I have my own work, you know: a household to oversee, accounts to reconcile and bills to pay. What would happen to this place and our business if *I* decided to abandon it for the thrill of sleuthing?" Left unsaid was that Lavinia feared that her sister's curiosity could lead to serious trouble.

Lavinia's several causes for concern were not lost on Florrie. Indeed, she understood that she inclined to recklessness and made herself rather too conspicuous in attire, manner and directness to prove a good detective. But she also knew that she was persistent and could dig out information better than most.

"I'm sorry, Lavinia, but I promise I shall make extra time at night to do as many of my chores as possible, but I feel that I must help find out the truth of what happened. Don't worry; I shan't put myself in harm's way, and as soon as I know anything I'll come to you. You've always had better judgment than I, so I'll rely on you to make sense of whatever I may find out." She paused. "If I don't discover anything by Friday night, I'll give it up." She waited for Lavinia's response and hoped for the best. "I promise."

"You give me no choice, Flora. If I say 'no,' you'll do it anyway. Go ahead but I'm going to hold you to your word: Friday night will be the end of it. Are we agreed?"

"Yes, Lavinia. Agreed. Thank you."

"For heaven's sake be careful, will you? You know how you get. Once you get a bee in your bonnet, you forget to pay attention to what's going on around you."

"Please don't worry Lavinia. After we serve breakfast to the guests, I'm simply going to pay a little visit to Station Four on Lagrange Street. That should be safe enough. I've been up since four o'clock. I woke up thinking about Rosetta, Mrs Cormier and the rest of our lodgers. I couldn't get back to sleep so I went down to kitchen and prepared some pot pies for dinner. Agnes and I already have breakfast well underway. If it's all right with you, I'll leave for the station house right after we serve. Mr Boniface said he'd help with clean-up."

"All right, Flora, all right. I'll see you downstairs."

By the time Lavinia joined Florrie and Agnes in the kitchen, Florrie was humming to herself and seemed absorbed by the tasks before her, but Lavinia knew Florrie's mind had raced ahead to Station Four.

"Good morning Agnes. Did you sleep well?"

"Yes. Miss Lavinia." Nothing further was forthcoming. Florrie was preoccupied; Agnes, for once, not inclined to chat. Both had breakfast well in hand, so Lavinia went back upstairs. In the dining room, Mr Boniface had almost finished setting tables. "Good morning, Mr Boniface." He looked up: "Good morning to you, Miss Lavinia." It was obvious to Lavinia that on this rare day her help wasn't required until breakfast was over and it was time to clean up, so she walked downstairs to her office.

A pile of unopened mail awaited her, and she sorted it. Invoices. Reservations. Advertisements. Lodgers' mail. Nothing personal for her or Florrie. Generally, keeping records straight and the house running smoothly provided a goodly measure of satisfaction to Lavinia, but this morning she caught herself a bit irked that she faced ledgers while Florrie pursued adventure.

Only heaven knew what trouble Florrie would bring on herself—and her—and the household. Yet that concern did not long engage her; the circumstances of crime captured her thoughts. Could the murder have been unpremeditated? Would a robber have stowed away and waited until Rosetta was alone and then forced his way into her dressing room? Perhaps she refused to give him her money and jewels, and he killed her in a struggle. But why wouldn't he have waited until she left the theatre and then robbed every dressing room as well as hers? And the box office, too— didn't they leave petty cash overnight for the following day?

Robbery faded as the motive for her murder. Rosetta's jewels and money—at least some of them—were still in the dressing room as were, presumably, everyone's else's valuables, or that would have made the news—at least the inside gossip.

Was the murder planned? Rosetta had only been in town for the evening show when she was murdered that night. There hadn't been time to advertise her. Whoever killed her must have known ahead of time that she was coming to Boston. Was it someone who followed her here from Providence so as to deflect suspicion? Or was she brought to Boston so that someone here could kill her? Lavinia sat very still at her desk. Before she knew who killed Rosetta Rice, she needed to know why. That realization jolted her. It was foolish enough that Florrie wanted to play detective. One of them needed to act sensibly. Still, a few inquiries in her spare hours might prove useful. A moving shape startled her. Mr Boniface was standing at the doorway. "Excuse me, Miss Lavinia. The guests have been served, and your breakfast is waiting downstairs."

CHAPTER 31

Wednesday Morning: Florrie Follows the Trail

Other than a couple of newshounds who eyed everyone who entered and departed, there wasn't as much activity at the station house as Florrie expected at ten in the morning, considering that there had so recently been a murder in the neighborhood. Most of the reporters assigned to Division Four were standing watch at the Tremont Theatre.

Inspector Brody had arrived at the station house a few minutes before Florrie. Immediately collared by reporters, he was doing his best to tell them nothing they didn't know already or anything that could produce more lurid headlines. Unnoticed except by one of the desk sergeants, Florrie slipped inside the station house and walked quietly to the front desk. She had known that Danny Riordan would be on day duty at Division Four, and, while he was not indiscreet, Officer Riordan was a friendly sort and might divulge a morsel or two of information.

"Hello, Sergeant Riordan."

"Miss Porridge---Portridge, ... er ..."

"That's quite all right, Officer, I don't mind a bit."

"How are things at the Portridge Arms? Is there something can we do for you"?

"Thank you for asking, and, yes, there is. You know that our clientele are of the theatre ..."

"The vo-de-villes, right?"

"Quite right, and this hideous murder at the Tremont has all our guests sick with worry. I'll have to tell them something when I get back, poor dears. Several of our lodgers are on the bill at the Tremont, and they knew Rosetta Rice very well. Some of them are frantic with fear. Especially the women. Those lovely, Franklin Sisters. Pretty young girls, so new to show business and so young. Franklin is just their stage name, you know; their manager made them change it from Shaunessey—can't understand why. Anyway, they're such sweet girls and so terrified about what happened to poor Rosetta Rice, and herself such a dear friend of Lavinia's and mine." Florrie had intended to whelm Riordan with her plaint and seemed to have succeeded, although she had barely skirted incredulity when she, an old Yankee, carried away by her own cant, had referred to Rice as "herself," an expression common only to the Irish.

Riordan had not seemed to notice or at least did not recognize it as parody and take offense.

Florrie quickly covered with a question, "Who's that man over here, talking to the reporters?"

"Inspector Brody? It's him that's been assigned to the case."

"Well, I don't wish to trouble him when he has so much to do, but when I go home I need to reassure my guests, especially Bridie and Katie Shaunessey, that there's nothing to fear." That Marla and Paula Franklin were their real names and they were on the bill at the Globe rather than the Tremont, were facts she was rather sure Officer Riordan never need know and was unlikely to find out. Florrie made a mental note to share her fib with Paula and Marla. She knew the girls would play along as innocents and in the matter of their names. If Sergeant Riordan found out the Franklin Sisters were playing the Globe instead of the Tremont Theatre, he'd likely ascribe that discrepancy to the meandering mind of a dotty old woman than to intentional deception.

"Miss Portridge, I'm the desk sergeant, so I'm not on the case. There's nothing I can tell you. Mind you, I was surprised as all get-out when headquarters let the show go on that very night and all day yesterday."

"Yes, we were surprised, too. As I said, several of our guests are appearing at the Tremont, and it was very hard for them to go on stage that night and entertain folks, as if nothing had happened."

"It certainly wasn't the way we did things in the old days." Riordan looked around, fearing he might have raised his voice. No one seemed to have taken notice, so he added in a lower voice: "Seems that the boss of the Tremont, Laurence Simpson, has drag. The District Attorney told us to seal the place up for a few days, but Simpson or someone higher up—maybe old man Wood—got to the Governor, and it's the Governor what appoints the commissioner of police. So they opened that very night."

"Do they know why dear Rosetta was killed or who did it?" Florrie knew she was rushing her inquiry, but she was afraid that her continued presence would soon catch Brody's attention. Riordan, thinking he saw Brody turn in his direction and feeling he had already told a bit too much, brought his voice back to a usual conversational level:

"Miss Portridge, Ma'am, I don't know a thing about the case. Even if I did, I couldn't speak about it."

"No, of course, Officer Riordan, I understand that." Taking her cue from the sergeant, Florrie raised her voice a bit. "You are to be commended for your adherence to duty as well as your courtesy to a distressed old lady." She turned to leave, but hesitated and turned back. In a lower voice she asked "By the way, I was told that the young policeman who was at the Tremont Theatre is also the beat patrolman for my neighborhood. Is Moore his name? Anyway, you might suggest to him that he visit the Portridge Arms to reassure our lodgers. Some of them might have a bit of useful knowledge Patrolmen Moore could pass on to the Inspector. One never knows." Florrie quickly left the building, paused on the sidewalk and swirled her cape about her with satisfaction.

Overeager to get on with her investigations, she had failed to consider what time Mr Weiss and Miss Stropell arrived at work. Florrie expected that they came in ahead of the manager, Laurence Simpson, so she had to time her visit after they came to work yet before Simpson did; Emily and Mo wouldn't talk to her if their boss were around. It would be difficult enough getting either to talk in the presence of the other—especially when the topic was murder. The only way she could find out a propitious time for her box office visit was to ask Petey. And then it dawned on her. This was the second time that she, a petitioner on a mission, had left Portridge Arms without a gift for Petey, and she had promised him Irish soda bread and baked beans on her next visit. "Goodness, I'm becoming a dotty old lady." A passerby glanced at her. She kept her next words to herself: "Good Lord, now I've taken to talking aloud to myself. I must keep my wits about me."

Florrie felt for her purse in her pocketbook. Only a few dollars remained after her extravagance last night at Gilchrest's. Perhaps she had something at home she could take to Petey. And to Emily and Mo. There was no alternative. She'd have to go home and make Petey some sandwiches and hope that there were cookies left to give Mo and Emily.

Florrie rushed back to Portridge Arms, arms and scarves flapping in the breeze. It was 10:30 when she entered the kitchen. She could hear Agnes upstairs running the carpet sweeper over the rugs. Mr Boniface was probably out, perhaps tending box office at one of the theatres. She hoped Lavinia was similarly occupied;

Florrie had no wish to give her sister further reason to think her scattered.

Quickly she assembled slices of cracked wheat bread, lettuce and cheese into two large sandwiches spread with mayonnaise and mustard sauce. She wrapped them in waxed paper and went in search of cookies or some other sweets for Emily and Mo. The cookies had been used up for last night's desert, but there was an unopened tin of English toffee. Perfect! Prettily packaged but not too extravagant a gift. Her treats bundled, Florrie slipped out of the house confident that no one, not even Lavinia, had been the wiser.

Florrie would not have been quite so pleased with herself had she known that while she was surreptitiously making sandwiches in the kitchen, Attorney Dudley Pierce was closeted with Lavinia in her office as they tried to put together pieces of the puzzle that surrounded Rosetta Rice's murder.

CHAPTER 32

Wednesday Morning: Mr Pierce Visits Portridge Arms

Rosetta's attorney had phoned Portridge Arms only minutes after Florrie had left earlier that morning. Lavinia took the call and agreed to 10 o'clock that morning for what Mr Pierce assured her would be a brief appointment. On the dot of that hour, while Florrie was at the local police station, Pierce arrived at Portridge Arms. He presented himself to Mr Boniface with a calling card. Ushered into Lavinia's office, Pierce produced a power-of-attorney document given him by Rosetta Rice and explained the purpose of his visit.

"Thank you for consenting to see me on short notice, Mrs Salter, but I only learned of Miss Rice's death from a news story in yesterday morning's *Journal.* As her executor, there's much to do, and frankly I hadn't a clear enough mind to plan much of an avenue of inquiry into the circumstances of her ... until I was riding the train up to Boston last night. By the way, I'm staying at the Hotel Touraine for the next few days."

"I'm glad you telephoned me, Mr Pierce, my sister and I knew and admired Rosetta. Her murder is a shocking obscenity.

"Indeed it is, Mrs Salter...."

"Excuse me, Mr Pierce, I reverted to my maiden name of Portridge after the death of my husband and my sister Flora and I started our lodging house business. Portridge became what one may call a professional name as well."

"Miss Portridge it is, then. Like you, I am motivated by my personal regard for Rosetta as well as my professional obligation. I can't say we were friends in the accepted sense. I think her friends were few. She maintained a cordial reserve, even during her years when she was active on the stage—at least late in her career when she became my client. Perhaps her restraint was a reaction to the careless familiarity she found common among show people. Rosetta spoke of a false bonhomie that seemed to her more intrusive than welcoming."

Lavinia noted that Pierce had used Rosetta's given name twice rather than her surname, and she suspected that his feelings ran deeper than what was usually true of a casual acquaintance or professional duty. "My point is, Miss Portridge, that not only had she, to my knowledge, few close friends, but none of them had any association with the stage. You and your sister seem to have been the only connection she maintained with her performing past. At least you were the only stage people she ever mentioned to me. I thought if we could talk, you might be able to help me in my inquiries."

"Like you, Mr Pierce, I wouldn't have thought that Rosetta considered us intimate friends. She visited us whenever she played Boston, but we hadn't seen her since she left the business. We met eight or nine years ago when she was booked in town here, and she brought us some personal belongings of our sister who died in Baltimore ten years ago. It was very kind of her. Next year, when she was again playing in Boston, she invited Flora and me to lunch. She accepted our invitation to lunch here at Portridge Arms once or twice, but I don't think she relished the company of most show folks, and preferred to meet at one of the quieter restaurants. I always enjoyed our talks—she was well-informed, but never much inclined to talk about personal matters or show business—which suited me rather more than it did my sister. It's often like that for people in theatre—if you work a particular city only once a year, it's hard to maintain real friendships. You stay in touch by letters and Christmas cards."

"Ah." Pierce had not expected that the Porridge's sisters acquaintance with Rosetta Rice was more limited than his own—yet neither was he surprised. "I had hoped that you would be able to tell me whom she might have met in Boston or where she went. I don't think the police have much to go on, and I thought I might be of some use."

"As to that, Mr Pierce, my sister Flora has taken it upon herself to make some inquiries. In fact, she's out and about as we speak, talking to the local police and probably people at the Tremont Theatre. Frankly, it isn't something I feel she should be doing. People willingly talk to her, but Florrie is, I'm afraid, not always subtle. I fear she could get into trouble, yet, I must admit, I find myself drawn into this as well. Terrible as Rosetta's murder is, there's something else: her death has reached inside our house. Several other performers on the Tremont bill are staying with us this week, and there's been some careless speculation growing within the theatrical community."

"So there are some suspects?"

"I hope it hasn't reached that stage yet. But one of our lodgers, Mrs Cormier—her little children perform in an act at the

Tremont—created quite a fuss when their act was bumped from a rather prestigious spot on the bill to one much lower. Then, when Rosetta was brought up to Boston and put in the Cormiers' old spot, Mrs Cormier was livid. She raised a hullabaloo backstage, and later, when someone tried to spoil Rosetta's act, suspicion fell on Mrs Cormier."

"What's your impression of Mrs Cormier?"

"Unpleasant. Venal."

"Capable of murder had she the motive and opportunity?"

"I can't say; I've disliked her from the start." Lavinia caught herself. "Show business is a discouraging profession. For many at some point, it becomes little more than a battle for survival, so who can say?"

"Still she had the motive and the opportunity. No?"

"The Cormier act was only shifted to a lesser spot. Another act, the Taylor Twins, was fired to make room on the bill for Rosetta. Neither occurrence is uncommon in vaudeville, I'm afraid, yet, never to my knowledge, have they been the cause for murder.

"But, as another act on the bill, Mrs Cormier must have had access to the theatre during hours it was closed to the public. Didn't that provide her with an opportunity?"

"Opportunity? Perhaps; perhaps not. Mrs Cormier seldom lets her daughter or the two boys in the act out of her sight. Unless I'm mistaken, Rosetta was murdered late at night—sometime after the evening show. Here at Portridge Arms we lock our doors after midnight, so latecomers have to ring, and that wasn't the case with Mrs Cormier—or any other lodger—Monday night."

"Can you think of anyone else who might have had a motive?"

Lavinia thought carefully, and it didn't seem necessary to mention Victor Greeley's vague accusation against Mrs Cormier.

"That's the question I've been asking myself. But instead of answers, all I come up with are more questions. Did she have any visitors at the Touraine? Someone we don't know about. Or was it a robbery gone viciously wrong? If so, why weren't other dressing rooms and the box office broken into? I don't know whether her door was forced or whether Rosetta let the murderer in—perhaps, Mr Pierce, you could find some answers? If the lock wasn't forced, it must have been someone Rosetta knew and felt comfortable with because she was wearing a dressing gown, not proper clothes."

Mr Pierce caught his breath and stared at Lavinia.

"Someone she was intimate with?"

"A crime of passion, as the yellow journalists say? I wouldn't know. As her attorney and adviser, were you aware of frequent trips to Boston?"

"No. None to anywhere, I should think. Rosetta seldom traveled. She always said she was sick of it after all those years on the road."

"Then, if the murderer were someone with whom she had a special relationship, that person must have followed her from Providence..."

"...And he would have had to know about her appearance at the Tremont..." Dudley Pierce almost startled himself. If that were the case, it pointed to him among others. "That, I suppose, makes me a suspect."

"I doubt that, Mr Pierce. And I doubt it was a passionate act. I've come to think it was planned. The murderer expected her in Boston, and she had no qualm about allowing him into her dressing room. That doesn't mean he—or she—was an intimate. Actors and performers follow far more casual standards of dress and behavior inside the theatre than outside. Whatever stage of undress she might be in, she would just put on her dressing gown before admitting another performer, the stage manager or anyone else connected with the theatre."

"How many people work at the theatre who might be there after the last show?"

"I've thought about that. Most likely the manager, a few ushers, stage manager, his crew, the electrician, door tender, janitor, other acts—a couple of dozen people in all, I guess. One of them might have hidden until after the rest left, but I doubt any of the other acts or the back- or front-of-the-house employees knew Rosetta was booked at the Tremont until she arrived after the matinee. So, if Rosetta's murder was not a botched robbery, it does seem it was premeditated, don't you think?"

"I take your point. But I've never practiced criminal law, so I'm a bit out of my depth. However, my position as a lawyer does give me access to people in the criminal justice system. One thing I have discovered is that Nathan Furst of the United Booking Office in Boston was the man who engaged Rosetta Rice. He offered her an exorbitant salary to get her to agree to come to Boston. I'll be grateful if you and your sister are willing to share your findings with me. Please believe me, I'm determined to see Rosetta's murder solved and the culprit prosecuted."

"Do you know when Rosetta arrived in Boston, Mr Pierce?"

"Late Sunday afternoon or early evening. She checked in at seven. Perhaps she made a train reservation, but I doubt it for such a short trip. If so, she probably would have had a return ticket as well. The police have impounded her belongings—her baggage. I've made an official request for access to her things. I expect to be granted that permission tomorrow morning."

"Well, Mr Pierce, if you have time, why don't you join us for lunch tomorrow? Perhaps you will know more by then, and my sister may have discovered something. In either event, I know she'll be most anxious to meet you. In fact, I warn you, my sister will interrogate you relentlessly."

"It will be my pleasure. Thank you, Miss Portridge. And, now, I've taken quite enough of your time. Until tomorrow, then?"

"Does one o'clock suit you?" Dudley Pierce offered a courtly and consenting bow. Lavinia showed him to the door. "I'm glad that Rosetta had a caring friend."

Pierce looked as though he might blush, then smiled gratefully as he donned his overcoat, gloves and hat, picked up his umbrella and left.

CHAPTER 33

Early Wednesday Morning: Greeley Explains the Game

As Florrie was leaving Portridge Arms by the basement's front entrance, Doris and Victor Greeley were descending the upper level front steps down to the sidewalk. "Good morning," called Florrie. "You two are out and about early this morning."

"Good morning, Florrie," replied Doris Greeley. "It was such a lovely morning, we decided to visit the Museum of Fine Arts and have lunch in Copley Square before our matinee." That Doris offered more than a greeting indicated she was clearly happy to be doing something other than going back and forth to the theatre.

"May I walk with you both part way?"

"Certainly, dear lady. Indeed, Doris and I would be delighted if you would join us for lunch at the Hotel Brunswick. Their food is humble, but we always hope we'll catch sight of either Lotta Crabtree or Mrs Fiske there."

"That sounds delightful, Victor, but I have a full day of errands ahead of me."

"Our loss, dear Florrie. Perhaps another day? Anyway, it is a lovely morning no matter what one's destination. A blessed change after the last few grey and rainy days. We're anxious to pay one last visit to the Museum before it departs that glorious gothic gingerbread palace for its new digs on the Fenway. So many things are changing so fast. It seems civilization has adopted the motto of out with the old and in with the new. Change permeates our society. Even vaudeville."

Even during a short walk, Victor Greeley was not without a topic on which to hold forth. "The motion picture may be a tiresome novelty to some, but that fellow Porter, who works for Edison, he's begun to create stories for the camera rather than simply record events. And there's that Frenchman, Georges Méliès, or something like that. Have you seen their films, Miss Flora? No? Do try. I think you'd be surprised. Those men are offering the public stories filled with action, adventure. Pretty soon the public won't be satisfied with the confines of the stage and amusing patter. Anyway, whether the flickers prove a fad or not, vaudeville is changing, and not for the better. Ned Albee's nefarious project, the United Booking Office is turning vaudeville into a monopoly. The U.B.O. has a stranglehold on all the good vaudeville houses—

at least here in the East, and, if you don't do what they want and act like good little boys and girls, you can be blackballed. One can't even trust one's agent anymore. I swear most of them are working for the bookers and theatre managers."

"Now, Victor, there's no use getting upset. We've not had any trouble ourselves."

"No, not yet, Doris. But we may. There's turmoil ahead. The vaudevillians have formed a union! We're artistes, not laborers! Mere cogs in an industry! Much as I sympathize with their aims, I shall *not* join a union. What would do us more good is some *real* competition for Albee and his U.B.O."

"I thought the United States Amusement Company was beginning to provide that, Victor. Especially with William Morris leading the effort. Everyone I know thinks highly of him."

"A good man, indeed, Miss Flora, but he's a dupe swimming with sharks."

"What do you mean?"

"Abraham Lincoln Erlanger—what a sadly ironic name that is for a villain. He and his partners have already monopolized the legitimate theatre, and now he has allied himself with his former enemy, Lee Shubert, to sabotage the vaudeville business. Benny Keith and Ned Albee may be refugees from the flim-flam of the carnival world, but Erlanger and Shubert are more than their match at pulling a con. The United States Amusement Company has been making a public play at acquiring theatres floating on Erlanger's money and Shubert's empty theatres, but it's going to sink William Morris and all those acts he's enticed—admittedly in good faith— to leave Keith and the U.B.O. for the United States Amusement con. Once Abe and Lee fold their tent, Morris and all those vaudeville acts will be left out in the cold and Albee won't take them back until each one has bowed, kissed his ring and taken a cut in salary."

"But why should they fold, Victor? Are they losing money?"

"They're all losing money, Miss Flora—all of them. It's a farce on a grand scale. Each one trying to outlast the other. Erlanger and Shubert have no intention of staying in vaudeville once they force Keith and Albee to buy them off."

"But, Victor, what about all the theatres they've acquired?"

"Those they've bought, they'll keep, I suppose. Those that they leased or are negotiating for, they'll drop like hotcakes. I heard they were trying to buy a chain of theatres just outside of

Boston to go up against Keith's houses, but I don't know if the deal went through. Anyway, from what I hear, it'll all be over in a few weeks. It's not public knowledge yet—not even in the trades, but people who should know have assured me that Albee's agreed to pay an extortionate amount of cash to Erlanger and Shubert. In turn, Lee and Abe have agreed to retire from the fray. That will leave the corpses of William Morris and thousands of acts littering the battlefield.

"Good heavens. As bad as that?" Florrie came to a halt at the corner of Tremont and Eliot Streets. "Fascinating. You are undoubtedly the most reliably-informed man I know. Thank you for confiding in me, Victor. Now, it seems you and Doris will be heading uptown to Copley while I go downtown. Goodbye, Doris. See you at dinner."

"Always our pleasure Miss Flora."

Florrie saw no reason to tell Victor she was heading for the Tremont Theatre. By the time Florrie pushed the stage door bell it was 11:30. The door was quickly answered. "I know I promised you some Irish soda bread and baked beans, dear," Florrie burbled, "but I shan't be making them until Saturday. So I brought you a couple of cheddar cheese and lettuce sandwiches. I hope you like them. As she carefully withdrew them from her woven sisal bag, Petey bent over to see what else was in the bag but not destined for him. "Just a tin of something I'm returning today." Because Petey Martin was so blatantly nosey, Florrie had no compunction about lying to him. She was sure he didn't actually spot the canned toffee, so if he spied it in the box office he wouldn't know it came from her.

"Petey? When does Mr Simpson come to work?"

"Never can tell. Sometimes as early as noon; most of the time he come in between one and two to make sure everything's okay for the matinee. He likes to surprise people. Keep Mo and Emily on their toes."

"Oh, must they always be at work before him?"

"Yep. Both comes in early so as Simpson ain't got nothing to squawk about. Mo comes in before 10 o'clock, so he's been here for a couple of hours, I expect. Emily gets here before 11."

"Hey! Petey, get over here." The harsh voice belonged to a tall burly man in shirtsleeves that Florrie had never seen at the Tremont. Just before Petey closed the door on her, Florrie managed to whisper "Who's he?" Petey hissed "New stage

137

manager" and shut the door. As she walked around the building to the box office, her fleeting impression that Petey was intimidated was immediately overshadowed by the realization that she had timed her visit just right: Simpson wasn't expected for at least an hour, and both Morris Weiss and Emily Stropell should be present in the front office.

CHAPTER 34

Wednesday Morning: Box Office, Tremont Theatre

Florrie had known Mo and Emily since she and Lavinia had moved to Boston, but their relationship was little more than that of theatre patrons and theatre employees. The transaction of buying tickets did not admit much more than brief courtesy. Though neither Mr Weiss nor Miss Stropell displayed any inclination to progress too far beyond greetings, Florrie was sure it was their natural reserve or timidity and a fear of losing their jobs that prevented more affability. That, she decided, must change today.

Florrie believed that people seldom failed to respond to friendly overtures. On the few occasions when she had been rebuffed dismissively, she felt well-served by the encounter. It reminded her to observe people more carefully before extending herself—a lesson she ignored with each new introduction. When an approach fared poorly, Florrie's comfort was that she had been spared the company of unpleasant people. She was sure that would not be the unhappy outcome with Mo Weiss or Emily Stropell.

The doors to the Tremont's inner lobby were kept locked until one p.m. when the box office opened, an obstruction to her investigation that she had failed to take into account. Faced with the locked door, Florrie realized that she had gone off this morning half-cocked. Her enthusiasm for the chase was not enough; she must think ahead and prepare herself more thoroughly tomorrow.

But chance was her ally. At that moment, while Florrie was searching for an outdoor bell or buzzer, Mo Weiss emerged from the office with a small broom and dust pan and began to pick up scraps of paper discarded the previous evening by departing customers. They caught sight of each other through the glass doors.

"Good morning, Mr Weiss," called out Florrie brightly. Mr Weiss' eyesight was better suited for bookkeeping than distance, and he failed to recognize his greeter until he reached the door.

"Oh!, Miss Porridge. Good morning to you," he called though the locked door. "I'm sorry, but the office isn't open yet." Preoccupied with his chores, Mo Weiss had no idea that he had addressed Florrie by her soubriquet. Florrie let it pass, as she always did.

"Aha, I've come too early, have I? What is your usual time?"

"One o'clock."

"I've gotten a bit chilled, Mr Weiss. May I step inside for just a moment?"

"Oh, yes, of course. But Mr Simpson should be here any moment, and he doesn't allow us to admit anyone before one o'clock."

"I shan't take but a moment of your time. Is dear Miss Stropell here, as well?"

"Yes, she's in the office."

"Please tell her I was asking for her. By the way, I thought you both might enjoy this small tin of toffee."

"Oh, my... well, thank you, Miss Flora..."

"Not at all. But I do need to talk to you, Mr Weiss. And perhaps Emily, too. You may know that a number of the performers playing here at the Tremont are staying with my sister and me at Portridge Arms. Everyone is very upset, and Lavinia and I are trying to calm matters. Is there any time today you could spare me a few minutes?"

"I'm afraid I'm on duty until the box office closes at nine at night, and then Mr Simpson takes over."

"Dear heavens! You come in at ten, don't you? That's eleven hours a day."

"Well, I do get time off for supper at four. Provided that Mr Simpson is here to take over."

"And you said he is expected today?"

Mr Weiss quickly pulled out a watch from his vest pocket. "Good gracious! Any minute now." Though his pocket watch was an inexpensive Waltham model, it reminded him that his station in life was not all that mean. "Usually Mr Simpson comes in afternoons between one and two o'clock, but he phoned to say that he was coming in this morning to talk to the police."

"Did he come in early yesterday?"

"Tuesday? Oh, no. Mr Simpson had to be in Lowell all day, at one of our theatres. He's the General Manager of all seven of the Wood theatres."

"And Monday? The day Rosetta ..."

"Oh, yes. Mr Simpson was here Monday. He met Miss Rice in person right here. Brought her into his office until the theatre crowd cleared out. Then took her through the theatre to meet the orchestra. Very cordial."

"Oh? Were they friends?"

"I couldn't speak to that, Miss Flora. None of my business. Just very cordial, as I said. Miss Flora, I really have to get back to my duties..."

"It must have been very hard on you, finding the body and notifying the police...."

"Dreadful! That poor woman. And alone there, suffering. Who knows how long?"

"How awful for you, Mr Weiss."

"I was setting up the lobby—just about this time of day—just as I was doing when I saw you at the door. There was a box of flowers hooked on the handle outdoors. They were for Miss Rice, so I brought them up to her dressing room..."

"How did you know the flowers were for her?"

"The card. Her name was on the card attached to the box."

"Of course. And you brought the flowers to her room?"

"Yes." He shivered slightly. "I knocked on the door, but there was no answer. I don't know why I tried the door. It was supposed to be locked. But it was open.... And I saw her."

"Dead?"

"What?! Yes, of course. Oh, dear, perhaps I've said too much, Miss Flora..."

"What you've told me, Mr Weiss, was in confidence. It shall go no further. I understand it was you who called the police; did Mr Simpson contact the office?"

"Mr Simpson! Oh, dear, he'll be here at noon. Any minute now..."

"I shan't keep you but a moment longer, Mr Weiss. You see, I'm looking for Miss Rice's address in Providence. As we were her closest friends in Boston, my sister Lavinia and I feel it is our duty to contact her relatives."

"I'm sorry, Miss Flora, but I don't have that kind of information. Why don't you go to our office in the Colonial Building and ask Mr Yates. He might have that information. Good day, Miss Porridge." Florrie edged outside but kept her hand on the open door between them.

"Thank you, Mr Weiss; but what is the name of your office in the Colonial?"

"Ira Wood Enterprises... Oh, Lord! Here comes Mr Simpson. Please...."

CHAPTER 35

Wednesday Noon: Police Come to Call at Portridge Arms

It hadn't been half an hour since Dudley Pierce's departure when another caller asked for Lavinia. She had struggled during the intervening time to divert her thoughts from Rosetta's murder to the urgent matter of paying bills. She had begun to immerse herself in the chore when the insistent ring of the doorbell shattered Lavinia's fragile concentration. A morning of interruptions did not conduce to the successful tallying of columns of figures and reconciling totals.

She figured that Agnes and Mr Boniface must be out of range of the bell while Florrie was out playing bloodhound. Reluctantly, Lavinia rose from her chair to answer the bell. Just as she opened her office door, she saw Agnes dashing down the stairs and opening the front door. Lavinia returned to work. If it were important, Agnes could fetch her from the office.

"Is either of the Misses Portridges at home?" Inspector Brody offered his calling card in one hand and flashed his badge with the other. Behind him stood a uniformed policeman. As soon as she spotted him, Agnes recognized him as the handsome young beat cop for the neighborhood. She whipped off her hair net and put on her most gracious manner. "Miss Lavinia is in, but Miss Flora is out right now."

"Then will you tell Miss *Lavinia* Portridge that Inspector Brody from homicide is here to see her?" Agnes stifled a gasp.

"Yes, please come in, and I'll get her." Agnes admitted both policemen into the house and directed them to the small front drawing room to the right just inside. She then raced down the hall to Lavinia's office and knocked.

"Come in."

Agnes half-opened the door and hissed in a stage whisper, "Miss Lavinia, the murder police are here asking for you and Miss Florrie. I put them in the drawing room."

"It's all right, Agnes. We were expecting them—but stop whispering, you sound like a stage prompter." Lavinia stacked her paperwork and weighted it down with an inkwell. "They might have telephoned first, but I suppose we can't tell them to come back at a more convenient time. Oh, well, nothing to be done about it now. Bring them here to my office."

Agnes ushered herself along with the policemen into the office.

"Good afternoon, Ma'am, I'm Inspector Brody: this is Patrolman Moore. We're investigating the death of Rosetta Rice an actress at the Tremont Theatre. This is just routine visit, but I'm told you knew Miss Rice so you may be able to give us some useful information."

"Please make yourselves comfortable, Inspector—and you, too, young man."

"Thanks." Brody sat in the nearest armchair as Moore silently demurred.

"My sister and I met Miss Rice several years ago when we first moved to Boston and opened Portridge Arms as a lodging house for theatricals. I don't think I can tell you anything you don't know or that hasn't appeared in the newspapers, but I'll do what I can. Agnes, would you make us all some tea and bring it into my office? Inspector...?"

"Brody, Ma'am."

"Sorry. Thank you, Inspector Brody. Perhaps you will permit the patrolman to accompany Agnes to the kitchen?" Lavinia made the request looking directly at Brody, and he understood that Lavinia wished to send Agnes from the room and that the company of a good-looking young policeman wouldn't hasten her return.

"Patrolman Moore, you go help her." Brody waited until he and Lavinia were alone and the office door again closed. "How much have you heard about what happened at the Tremont Theatre on Monday, Miss Portridge."

"I know that Rosetta was murdered. That it happened sometime after the evening show, Monday night, and that it was particularly gruesome."

"Got any idea who might have wanted to kill her?"

"None."

"They tell me there was a dust-up at the theatre between her and one of the other performers. A woman named Cormier, and that she's staying here in your boardinghouse."

"That's correct. She and her children. Is Mrs Cormier a suspect?"

"Shouldn't she be?"

"Inspector, I imagine it must have taken you years to achieve your rank in the police department. Am I correct? And you don't expect to be demoted in the ordinary course of events after you have attained a new and higher rank?"

"Right, as you say. But help me here; I'm not seeing your point..."

"The point, Inspector, is that vaudevillians hope for promotion every week, and fear demotion. Year after year, they work hard to perfect their act and win a better spot on the bill at better theatres for a better salary. That's what keeps them going from one town to the next. Even when they're sick. Or in bad weather. Or playing to rude audiences. Their performance reviews don't occur once a year, as I expect yours does. Every week at every new theatre there's the chance that a vaudeville act will get demoted, and that's what happened to Mrs Cormier and her children this week."

"You're telling me that, in your opinion, Mrs Cormier didn't murder Miss Rice?"

"How could I possibly know that, one way or the other. I hoped I was being clear when I explained that what went on at the theatre after the Monday matinee was not necessarily a motive for murder. My sister and I have made it a practice to attend bills that include our lodgers. Afterwards, we go backstage and congratulate them—whether we feel they deserve it or not. Last Monday, my sister Flora and I took Agnes—our maid whom you've just met—to the matinee at the Tremont. As usual, we went backstage, we overheard some of the contretemps. We didn't want to get involved or have our lodgers, Mrs Cormier and her children, be embarrassed in our presence, so we scooted out as inconspicuously and quickly as possible."

Contretemps was an unfamiliar word to the Inspector, but once again Lavinia had provided context rather than answers, and he sensed her meaning.

"Worse than being moved to an inferior spot on the bill, Inspector, is that an act can get fired. Perhaps you know that also happened at the Tremont this week?" Brody didn't indicate either way, so Lavinia continued. "The theatre manager fired The Taylor Twins. Right after the Monday matinee—the first show of the week. Those two young women were told to get out—collect their costumes, their sheet music, their photos and get out. As I said, my sister and I were there at the matinee, and I'll admit the Taylor Twins weren't good, but just think how they felt. Fired and without the week's pay they were counting on and no other job to go to."

"Are you saying the Taylor Twins are more likely suspects?"

144

"Not at all. The point I'm trying to make, Inspector, is that when an act is fired or demoted to a lower position on the bill, it lets loose all sorts of emotion: anger, fear, shame. Not the sort of public display a killer is liable to make if he has decided upon murder. I wonder if such a spontaneous passionate outburst could be sustained with sufficient heat to lead to murder seven or eight or however many hours later—especially if there was no chance the manager would reverse his decision and had already engaged a replacement act. Unless, of course, the murder was coldly premeditated." Lavinia paused, reluctant to say more. "Sorry, Inspector, I didn't mean to rattle on, but I want you to understand that if being cancelled or slotted lower on the bill was a cause for murder, you'd have murders every Monday, given all the theatres we have in Boston."

Inspector Brody looked steadily at Lavinia while he digested what she said. Lavinia hadn't directly responded to his suggestion that Mrs Cormier might be a murder suspect, but neither did she waste his time with irrelevant jabber or unreasoned opinion. All too often he had to sift for small useful facts among a welter of dissembling and reckless supposition.

"What did you mean about there being no chance the manager would change his mind about firing the girl act and demoting Mrs Cormier's?"

"I've been thinking about that since this morning. Rosetta Rice lived in Providence. She was retired. That means she didn't have an act already to perform. To accept an engagement to go back on the stage, she would need to decide on her music, get her wardrobe ready, pack, make reservations in a hotel and take a train to Boston. Yet she arrived at the Tremont within an hour or two after the manager fired the Taylor Twins and switched Cormier's children's act from the fourth to the second spot. No, Rosetta must have agreed at least a day or two earlier to replace an act at the Tremont."

"So why didn't the manager simply hire Rice in the first place instead of going with a couple of acts he didn't like?

"I think, Inspector, we both agree that is a good question."

CHAPTER 36

Wednesday Afternoon: Tea for Two—and Two

Whatever deprivation Agnes felt at being dismissed from the interrogation had been made up by a handsome, young Irish policeman escorting her to the kitchen. Normally, Agnes would have burbled like a spring stream, offering every morsel of speculation and accusation she had overheard the past couple of days, but her desire to charm the patrolman checked her impulse to chatter about the murder. Instead, she concentrated on the personal.

"Are you the beat patrolman?"

"Daytime shift. Frankie Moore's the name. And you're Agnes Rigney."

She brought the kettle to the sink and filled it with tap water. With her back to the patrolman she asked, "And how do you know that?"

"I'd be a fine policeman if I didn't know that." Agnes allowed herself to hope that he had seen her previously and made inquiries to find out her name. Instead, he added "Miss Porridge said your name."

"Oh ... But not my last name." She turned with a challenging smile and put the full kettle on the gas stove.

"Not a bad policeman yourself. I also know that you go to nine o'clock Mass at Saint Pat's every Sunday and sit with your family."

"And does a beat patrolman check up on everyone in the neighborhood?"

"It's my job. And a pleasure, too, to look at a pretty young lady dressed in her best."

"You should be a detective." Agnes managed to suppress her delight with a coy air as she filled the creamer with milk from the cold chest and added sugar to the bowl. She set out a tray with three cups and saucers, several teaspoons, napkins, milk, sugar and a plate of biscuits.

"No detective, Miss Rigney. Someday, I hope. Speaking of some days, perhaps some Sunday after Mass, I could walk you home?" He didn't wait for the only answer a proper girl could make—a demurral. "But right now, as you see, I'm on duty, and we have a murder to solve. Did you know Miss Rosetta Rice?"

"No. Wouldn't recognize her if I fell over her. But horrible wasn't it?" The chance to talk about the murder nudged aside her curiosity as to how Patrolman Moore learned her last name was Rigney. Certainly not from Miss Lavinia who never called her anything but 'Agnes.'

"Then Miss Rice wasn't boarding here?"

"No. But some others on the bill were," she added as she pulled a tin of tea and a ceramic teapot out of a cupboard. "The bill—that's what the people in the *vo-de-villes* call their show." The kettle had started to boil.

"Really? Know a lot about show business, do you?"

"I keep my eyes open. Like I said, some of our lodgers are on the bill at the Tremont Theatre." She swirled hot water in the teapot, dumped it into the sink, measured four heaped teaspoons of tea leaves into the pot, filled it with boiled water and fitted a quilted cozy over it. "Victor Greeley and his wife; they've got a funny act. And there's Mrs Cormier—she's a harpy, if ever there was one, and her kids—well, only the girl is her own, but there's also two little boys in the act. The whole crew is a sorry lot if you ask me. Anyway, I've promised not to say a thing, but there's little love lost between Victor Greeley and Mrs Cormier."

"What happened?"

"I'll never tell. You're the policeman." She lifted the tray and started for the stairs but Patrolman played the gallant and took the tray from her hands. "I'll tell you this, though, about show folk," as she led the way upstairs, "they spend all their time, eating, gossiping and laughing."

"Been on the stage yourself?"

"Holy Mother!," Agnes stopped and turned so suddenly on the stairway that she nearly upset the tray that Frankie Moore was carrying. "Never! Is that what you think of me?"

"You're pretty enough ..."

Agnes turned away to hide her blush and resumed climbing. "Well, I'll not be showing off myself to a bunch of gawkers."

"You don't approve of the show business, then?"

"Not honest, respectable work, is it, now? Not for a girl brought up proper."

"Have you ever seen a vaudeville show, Miss Agnes?"

"Of course. The two old sisters who run this place took me just last week."

"And you didn't like it?"

"It was all right."

"But you have to work around show folks, don't you? Don't you like them? Or do some of them get fresh with you?" They had reached the first floor and Agnes stopped.

"Certainly not! Miss Lavinia would never allow it. And neither would I! This is a respectable place I'll have you know." Agnes caught herself, paused in the hallway and lowered her voice. "I've been here six months and these actors behave a sight lot better than some of the people I've worked for. They're interesting and decent enough for what they are. But I'll tell you, for all that, they don't go to church on the Lord's Day."

"Let me see if I've got this right, Miss Agnes. You've worked here six months; your boss, Miss Lavinia Portridge runs a tight ship. No hanky-panky as far as you know. The actors are an okay lot, but Mr Greeley and Mrs Cormier didn't like each other, and Rosetta Rice didn't lodge here. Have I got all that right?"

"That's what I said," replied Agnes, a bit let down that their conversation had shifted from the personal to the official.

"Do you know if Miss Rice ever visited anybody here?"

"No. I don't think so. No, I would have known."

"You live here, do you?" Agnes nodded. "Any other permanent residents beside you and Miss Porridge... Portridge?" Agnes stifled a giggle and led the way back to Lavinia's office.

"There's the other Miss Portridge. Flora is her name. And Mr Boniface. ... Oh, and now they've taken in this newsboy. He's a sly one, I'll tell you." She knocked on the door.

Inspector Brody had reached an impasse with Lavinia. He had requested that Lavinia show him to Mrs Cormier's rooms so he could look around, but Lavinia had refused. If he wished to search any part of Portridge Arms, she informed him, he had to produce a warrant.

"Come in, Agnes."

CHAPTER 37

Wednesday Afternoon: Florrie, Onward and Over Some

Florrie yielded her grip on the outside lobby door and quickly walked away as Weiss closed it. But Mr Simpson, having punctually reached the Tremont, turned to stare after her as Mr Weiss admitted him. "What did that woman want, Mr Weiss?"

"She was a friend of Miss Rice. She wanted her address in Providence."

"If she was a friend of Miss Rice, it would seem, Mr Weiss, that she would know the address. Why did you let her in? We're not open yet."

"She was very insistent, and I thought it better to avoid a fuss..."

"Policy is policy, Mr Weiss. We keep our doors locked for safety. There's money in the box office—not so?"

"Yes, sir."

"And there was a murder here on Monday, was there not?"

"Yes, sir."

"And somehow the killer found his way into this theatre. How do you think he did that, Mr Weiss?"

Weiss couldn't articulate beyond a stuttered "I-I... d-d-don't know. I-I ..."

"Unless it was someone who worked here. Do you think that, Mr Weiss?"

Words failed Mr Weiss.

"Has the inspector arrived yet?"

"No, n-n-not yet, sir."

"Stop stuttering, man. He's due here at noon. I'll be in my office, Mr Weiss. Show him in when he gets here."

Florrie had noticed the tall, smartly-tailored man striding toward the theatre and staring at her as she left the Tremont. Instead of cutting across the corner of the Common to the Colonial Building, as she normally would have, chancing the on-coming traffic, she walked toward the corner of Tremont and Boylston, stopping in front of the first shop window to catch a sidelong glance at the tall man. He was not in sight. He must have turned into the theatre. Doubtless, Mr Simpson, Florrie decided, and hoped she had not been the cause of trouble for Mr Weiss. As she turned to continue toward Ira Woods Enterprises, she nearly collided with Inspector Brody accompanied by a young uniformed officer. Several seconds later, Florrie recalled that Mo Weiss had told her that Laurence Simpson was to meet with the police this morning, so Florrie lingered at the corner, as though waiting for a break in the vehicular traffic, and indeed, the uniformed officer and the other man, whom she realized must be an inspector, entered the Tremont Theatre.

A few minutes later, a doorman admitted Florrie into the lobby of the Colonial Building, and she proceeded to the reception desk to ask for Ira Wood Enterprises. Advised that the office was located on the third floor rear, Florrie was disappointed that her ride in the elevator was to be brief. The contraption still delighted her, and she wondered how expensive it would be to motorize the dumbwaiter at home. With that thought, she found herself directed off the elevator and down a dim corridor toward the rear of the building.

She knocked on the door but heard no response. Then she spotted a small tin plate on the door that read "knock and enter." She rapped louder the second time and pushed the door open. There at the back of a long room stood two somber, elderly people. Not at all the sort she expected to staff a theatrical office.

"Good afternoon. I'm Flora Portridge of Portridge Arms, and I'm trying to locate the relatives of dear Miss Rosetta Rice—a very old friend of ours—who was on the bill at your Tremont Theatre before…" Looking expectantly at the waxworks, Florrie left the sentence unfinished. Miss Markey left the file cabinets and stepped to the reception desk.

"Do you have an appointment?"

"No, I'm sorry. I just wish to obtain Miss Rice's Providence address from you."

"Perhaps Mr Yates can help you. Although he was not four feet away, Miss Markey turned to him and repeated, "This lady is looking for information about Miss Rice."

"Yes?" That was all from him, and he didn't deign to turn in Florrie's direction. Unless he were deaf, he must certainly have heard her initial request. Florrie raised her voice. "I'm Flora Portridge. My sister and I are the proprietresses of Portridge Arms, a theatrical…"

"Mr Wood is out."

"All I want is an address for Miss Rice. After all she was appearing at your…"

"We don't keep such information. Perhaps the booker can help you. Good day."

"May I inquire as to *which* booker?" Florrie was beginning to get annoyed. Rather than discourage her, resistance stimulated her persistence.

"Don't know."

"Well, if you can't help me, perhaps I'd better wait for Mr Wood to return." And with that Florrie moved to a bench that lined the wall.

"Mr Wood doesn't see people without an appointment."

"Do you think he might if I show up with my nephew, Police Sergeant Daniel Riordan from Station Four? It was Danny who suggested I see you. I don't think Mr Wood will...."

"United Booking Office in the Keith Theatre Building. You can ask there."

"Thank you Mr ...?"

"Yates."

"Much better, Mr Yates." Florrie nodded in their direction before turning to the exit. Miss Markey, staring at Florrie, certainly took note of Florrie's triumphal smile, and Florrie had little doubt that Mr Yates felt bested.

As she was leaving the Colonial Building, the lobby clock chimed 12:30, and Florrie realized she was a bit peckish and growing tired. Just a few doors away, Schrafft's offered a pot of tea and an oatmeal cookie that would hit the spot. She had neglected to replenish the cash in her purse when she had gone home, but she knew she had enough for a snack and her subway ride back to Portridge Arms.

Inside the fashionable tearoom, Florrie waited to be seated in a crush of ladies in town for lunch, perhaps a theatre matinee and a bit of shopping. Women in twos and threes were shown to tables, but the hostess was reluctant to use even a table for two for a single customer at the height of the luncheon rush. Miffed after standing around far too long on her sore feet, Florrie departed the too popular purveyor of nibbly sandwiches and pretty confections. She had a mind to stop at the corner Liggett's Drug Store, but good as their peanut butter and jam sandwiches were, their tea was harsh, obviously boiled from crumbled leavings, bought for a penny for a pound at wholesale tea marts.

Florrie stopped abruptly at Liggett's entrance and caused a minor chain collision among the pedestrians on the busy corner.

After all, her next destination was the United Booking Office a few blocks up on Washington Street where, a few blocks further, Gilchrist's beckoned with the promise of her favorite almond macaroons and a decent, though not superior, pot of tea. Besides she needed to plan her next moves somewhere less hectic than a corner lunch counter where careless or rude people bumped into each other.

Usually, the sun warmed the air, and the brick and granite buildings absorbed a bit of the heat by midday, but this Wednesday had begun grey and the granite sky didn't promise to let through the sun anytime soon. When she reached the U.B.O.'s suite in Keith's New Theatre building, she had a chance to sit down—and for quite a bit longer than she wished or had anticipated. Even after the receptionist was free of a seemingly endless series of incoming calls and Florrie managed to voice her inquiry, it took at least a half hour before someone from an inner office came out to speak briefly to her. Florrie learned exactly what Attorney Pierce had discovered a day earlier. The booker who engaged Miss Rice was likely to be at his Chauncy Street office a short walk away.

On the sidewalk outside Keith's and U.B.O., Florrie vacillated: tea and a macaroon at Gilchrist's, three blocks north, or the office of Mr Furst, two blocks southeast. This was the day she was supposed to sort things out concerning Rosetta Rice's murder. Instead, hours were slipping by with little accomplished, so Florrie, in a combination of her usual determination and a rare instance of self-control, forewent tea to seek booker Nathan Furst at his Chauncy Street address.

When Florrie reached Mr Furst's office and looked at the building directory, her heart sunk, and she wished she had decided on Gilchrist's and a rest: Mr Furst's office was on the third floor. The stairs in the high-ceilinged building were steep, and there was no elevator to be found. Florrie trudged up the cast-iron plate steps, and by the time she had reached the next to last landing, her feet stung and her knees ached.

Buoyed by the knowledge she would finally meet the man who had engaged Rosetta Rice for the Tremont, she made it to the third floor where a sign informed her that Mr Furst occupied the corner office near the stairway. She knocked. And knocked again. Florrie called out "Mr Furst!" Still no answer. A peek through the

152

brass letter slot in the door showed windows with half-drawn shades and no evidence of Mr Furst.

"Oh, bother!" Fired with determination since before dawn and now drained and discouraged, Florrie realized she had nothing to show for her first day of investigation. It was best that she head home. With luck, she might have time to put her feet up for an hour before she had to prepare supper.

Tired further by the ten-minute walk to Castle Street, Florrie's spirits sagged along with her energy. Maybe Lavinia was right. Maybe she lacked the perception and ability to formulate a plan needed be a detective. Certainly she was not observant enough to notice that a tall, brawny, stubble-faced redhead about 40 years old had been following her at least since she left the U.B.O. office. He continued to trail her long enough to watch her enter Portridge Arms.

CHAPTER 38

Wednesday Evening: Cooking and Carping

Lavinia, Mr Boniface and Agnes were busy in the kitchen. Though they didn't lift their eyes as Florrie entered, she felt tension in the room. Florrie looked to the clock. Quarter to four. Methodically she removed her cape, shawls and hat, shed her shoes, stuffed her aching feet into her slippers kept warm beneath the stove and wrapped an apron around herself as she stepped up to the work table.

"May I assume that you have solved the crime?"

"Ah, Lavinia. What is my trespass on this occasion?"

"It's 4 o'clock..."

"Not quite."

"...And well past time to start preparing dinner."

"Have you checked the larder? I left a half-dozen vegetable pot pies cooling in there. Did you forget I told you I prepared them this morning? All you and Agnes need do is to pop them in the oven for an hour before mealtime. In the meantime, I'll make a side dish of whipped squash, and Agnes can get the broccoli ready. As I recall, Lavinia, you were going to make Indian Pudding for tonight?"

"As *I* recall, Flora, though perhaps you have forgotten, we were to make a decision tonight?

"A decision?"

"About your Tommy. The boy you and Mr Boniface seem so eager to adopt."

"Ah, as to that, I stopped by the police station and talked to Officer Riordan today." And there Florrie stopped. Best to pick her way carefully through her sister's questions and not be caught in an outright lie. "It was difficult to get anyone to discuss anything but Rosetta Rice's murder. I expect that's all our lodgers will be talking about, too." Florrie set a pot in the sink, filled it with several inches of water and toted it to the gas stove. Agnes began cutting the broccoli into florets, peeling and chopping the stems, while Lavinia put a pan of milk and margarine on the fire to scald and began blending cornmeal, salt and a bit of flour before trickling in the molasses.

"Quite so, but the immediate problem is what to do about Tommy. You've let him think he's welcomed here, and we know nothing about him. So, let's get to the point. Has he been in trouble with the police?"

"Not that I found out." Florrie talked as she brought three large butternut squashes from the vegetable bins, rinsed them in the sink and selected a paring knife. "You know as well as I, Lavinia, that the police don't trifle with scraps between newsboys or run after a boy who's snatched an apple from a fruit stand." Long, sure strokes pared the squashes. "Besides, Patrolman Moore will be by—tomorrow, I expect. You can ask him yourself, Lavinia, about Tommy. As a beat patrolman, I expect he is more familiar with the doings of street boys than a desk sergeant."

"Officer Moore was here today," snapped Lavinia.

"So soon?"

"And he brought Inspector Brody with him. What on earth did you tell the police, Flora? That we were harboring criminals?"

A series of quicksilver thrusts with a french knife sliced the peeled butternut squashes into cubes. "Nothing of the kind, Vinny. I simply let it slip that several of our lodgers were on the bill with Rosetta, and they might be able to add to what the police already know about the murder."

"Mother of God..." gurgled Agnes as her knife clattered to the floor, reversing the sequence in the old superstition that a dropped knife signaled an impending visit. Lavinia and Florrie had forgotten Agnes was there with them, taking in all they said.

"Agnes," warned Lavinia, "We know as little about it as you do, and I suspect that none of our lodgers knows any more. Did Patrolman Moore ask you anything this morning?"

"No, Ma'am. Nothing about the murder or the lodgers."

"Well if he or any other policeman asks you any questions just remember that you know as little as we do. Just because you overhear someone say something doesn't mean it is a fact to be repeated to the police. Whatever you hear transpiring in Portridge Arms will remain locked in Portridge Arms. Is that clear?"

"Yes, Ma'am, but.."

"There are no 'buts,' Agnes."

Agnes didn't know what 'transpiring' meant, but she took Lavinia's meaning well enough.

"You needn't be afraid, Agnes," added Florrie; "besides, young Patrolman Moore is rather a handsome Irish lad, isn't he? I expect, if he calls again, it won't be to talk to you about the murder." Three squashes, each pared and cubed, filled a large steel bowl.

"For heaven sakes, Florrie, stick to the subject," snapped Lavinia. "You were supposed to ask them about Tommy, not involve us in a murder investigation."

"True, Vinnie, and since I usually disappoint you, I'm sure you had the foresight to ask the police about Tommy. What did they tell you?"

"The inspector was from headquarters, Flora, not the local stationhouse. What would he know about a newsboy?"

"I have no idea, Lavinia. Did you ask him?"

"Of course not! I was confronted with an investigation; Inspector Brody wanted to search the house! What did you tell them at Station Four? That we had information about Rosetta's murder?! Thank heavens our guests had left for the day. Your impulsive behavior could damage our reputation with other theatricals!"

"Lavinia, you forget that Mrs Cormier is likely to be on their list of suspects."

"I'm not likely to forget that! It was her room that the inspector wanted to search..."

"And think for a moment, Lavinia. It's not what I've said or shall say that will cause trouble. It's what old Petey Martin is sure to have said. All that fuss Mrs Cormier raised backstage and more. Petey is positive, although he shouldn't be, that it was Mrs Cormier who messed up Rosetta's music. Inspector Brody will soon hear about that if he hasn't already. Better I told Riordan that all of us here were grieving and upset about Rosetta's death..."

"Which, indeed, we are..."

"... and we were willing to share whatever information we had. And that's *all* I said." Florrie placed a mesh colander into the pot of heated water and then dumped in the cubed squash, covered the pot and turned down the heat half way. There was a pensive silence for a few minutes while the three women completed preparations.

"I knew that woman would be trouble."

"Yes, Lavinia, you did."

"But, a murderer? I can't believe that. Well, there's nothing for it but to hope that the police discover the killer before they drag all our lodgers into the mess."

156

"It's 4:30," observed Florrie, "I don't hear anything upstairs. I thought most of the performers from the first half of the bills would be back by now."

"Some are, but they seem to be keeping to themselves today. I don't think anyone—including Victor Greeley—is in the mood to play the raconteur.

"Mrs Cormier?..."

"She went directly up to her room with her daughter."

"And the little boys?"

"I don't know, Flora. I've enough to do here without playing governess while you're out gossiping..." Mr Boniface had materialized in the kitchen.

Florrie rallied. "Mr Boniface, would you look in on the Cormier lads? They must be rather confused with all that's going on. And take some raisin cookies with you, please." Anticipating a rote objection from her sister, Florrie added, "I don't think we need worry about ruining their appetites at a time like this."

Lavinia was not about to object. Instead, she felt a bit spent by jousting with her sister, but drew a breath, fixed her sister in the eye, and asked, "Since you are so interested in the well-being of children, Flora, would you mind telling me what you intend to do about Tommy? It looks as if it might rain again tonight. Are you going to permit him to stay in this house tonight?"

"Lavinia, that's not my decision to make."

"No, it isn't; but you'll end up getting your way, and I want you to think this out carefully. Even if he is honest—although a clever rascal seems more like it to me—you must realize that we'll become responsible for him. And that's no small task or expense: school, doctors, clothes, food..."

"I'd expect him to continue selling papers—after school, that is, and doing chores in turn for his keep..."

"And what about discipline? Are you going to see that he goes to school? A boy like that is used to going his own way..."

"He's independent, of course. He's had to be. Like all those lads and girls on the street. With a bit of loving guidance, I'm sure he'll find his way to his better interests in time."

"Hmmph!" The snort was a reminder that Agnes was present.

"Have you something to say, Agnes"

Seeing Lavinia's expression, Agnes chose the only possible response: "No, Ma'am."

"Then please turn off the squash that my sister seems willing to let burn. And if you've done preparing the broccoli, leave it for me to cook before you go upstairs and set the dining room. I expect Mr Boniface will be there shortly to help. And absolutely no talking about any of this with lodgers. Understood?"

"Yes, Miss Lavinia."

CHAPTER 39

Wednesday Dinnertime: A Sober Occasion

For the next few minutes, Florrie and Lavinia redirected their attention to the final preparations of dinner. Wordlessly, squash was mashed, seasoned with nutmeg and a dash of clove and then whisked into a puree with brown sugar, salt, black pepper and margarine. Pot pies were pulled from the oven, browned and bubbling, and the contents of stove pans were emptied into covered serving dishes, while beverages, rolls and condiments were retrieved from ice-boxes, bread tins, shelves and drawers then piled into the dumbwaiter. Lavinia gave a series of sharp yanks on the chord to send it up to the second floor.

Florrie followed Lavinia up the stairs, and the two of them joined Agnes and Mr Boniface to set out dinner for their guests. As they entered the dining room and found their seats, the lodgers were subdued in their greetings, each a bit distracted by his own thoughts but likely thinking about the same thing. Even Victor Greeley's customary hearty volubility was tempered. His "compliments to the chef" for the pot pies elicited no more than assenting murmurs, and he made no further effort at sociability. At the sideboard, Florrie and Lavinia assembled several trays of food for the Cormier crew. Lavinia was about to ask Mr Boniface to carry up a tray, but he was already standing at the ready.

"Go ahead, please, Mr Boniface. We'll be right up. Agnes, we're taking the Cormiers their dinners. After the guests are finished, get started cleaning up, will you? As soon as we're free we'll give you a hand.

It was hard to read Mrs Cormier. She admitted the sisters and Mr Boniface to her small room, displaying neither gratitude nor condescension for the room service. If being consigned to Coventry by the other performers had embarrassed her, there was no sign from her other than anxiety. Her eyes darted about, glancing only for a moment at a time at the visitors, at the food, out the window or at her own fidgety hands.

She seemed consumed by the need to figure out some escape. Doubtless the urge was to be elsewhere, away from unspoken accusations of sabotage or murder and whispered disparagements about the children's act, but, unsettling as the present engagement

159

was proving, the compensation was the best salary the act had earned since Alice had outgrown her "dainty" billing.

Next week and the future beyond held little hope or comfort. The remainder of their U. B. O. bookings in the East had been cancelled, and Mrs Cormler could see no attractive alternative to a return to the poor-paying, spirit-numbing grind of low-level vaudeville, farm fairs and medicine wagon shows from which she had connived and bullied her way up to the Keith circuit.

Mrs Cormier barely took in the departure and soft words of Flora, Lavinia and Mr Boniface. She hated these Boston audiences—phony sophisticates with cool manners and superior attitudes. She seethed when her mind turned to Laurence Simpson, one more in an endless string of heartless theatre managers who enjoyed beating down women trying to make their way in the world. If a woman wasn't attractive, she had no place in a man's world except in his kitchen. Well, damn them all! She had as little use for men as they had for her.

Renée Cormier left one lout after four years of drudgery and abuse. All he ever provided her with was a child. When it turned out to be a girl... Well, she showed him; she took Alice, their clothes and every penny she could find—what little money there was left after his boozing and buying drinks for those floozies at the road house. "Yeah, I showed him!—set fire to the house and grabbed the first bus out of town. Damn men! Damn booze! And damn those women! The ones who weren't even loyal to their own kind. The ones who were pretty and didn't have to take the abuse men handed out to the rest! Damn Rosetta Rice!" She and Laurence Simpson had killed Renée's big chance. Well, she was glad that Rosetta was dead. Simpson deserved the same. "Damn him, too!"

This last was uttered aloud and Renée Cormier snapped out of her trance to see her daughter staring at her. Alice had finished eating. "Ma? You want I should take the boys their tray?" Mrs Cormier looked at her daughter sadly. Nothing seemed to touch her child. Not anger, excitement or joy—what little there had been of the last. Sometimes she wished she could be as accepting as her daughter seemed to be, but then she envisioned Alice's future. "Yeah. Take them a tray. No! Wait a minute. Tell them to come here and get it. You're a star, baby, not a waitress." And with that, Mrs Cormier picked up a fork and began to eat.

CHAPTER 40

Wednesday Evening: A New Lodger

After Florrie, Mr Boniface and she left Mrs Cormier's room, Lavinia halted them on the third floor landing. "Before we join Agnes in the kitchen, Mr Boniface, I'd like your advice on a matter. My sister is determined to add to our household…" Florrie was about to protest, but a warning glance from Lavinia suggested that if Florrie was going to get her way in the matter, it was best that she not interrupt. "… and I don't want Agnes sticking in her two cents' worth. We need to fashion some sort of sleeping accommodation for our new boarder in the basement. Something temporary for now. Perhaps there's a space for Tommy in the large storage room?"

"Can't we put him on the top floor with Mr Boniface and Agnes?" asked Florrie.

"Oh, no." countered Lavinia. "I expect Agnes would resent that, and I think it better, for sake of harmony in this house, to limit their contact for the present. Also, our small rooms are almost always rented; we can't afford to give one up. I doubt that Tommy has lately enjoyed any accommodations superior to the storage room, once it's cleaned up."

Warming to the prospect, Florrie added, "There's a water closet nearby. We'll figure out somewhere he can bathe…"

"If we can get him to bathe…"

"… and I'll clean up in the storage room, Lavinia, and help Mr Boniface set up one of the extra camp cots. Perhaps, Lavinia, you can bring some blankets and a pillow. A bridge lamp, too, if you can find one."

"I think a swept corner, blankets, pillow and a cot to sleep on will be enough for now, Flora. But, Mr Boniface, it is you who attend to the furnaces. Will he be in your way?"

"Not that I can imagine, Miss Lavinia."

"Thank you, Mr Boniface." Turning to Flora, Lavinia added, "You and I had better help Agnes in the kitchen before there's an insurrection. I have no wish to train another housemaid, probably one surlier than she. As to cleaning up a space for Tommy in the storeroom, Mr Boniface, you can put him to that chore, if you will—but under your supervision. He'd better start out learning he has to pull his weight if he's going to bed and board here."

When Agnes heard Lavinia, Florrie and Mr Boniface reach the stairs down to the kitchen, Agnes bellowed from below. "He's here." Florrie fairly dashed down the steps. A resigned Lavinia, with Mr Boniface following, assumed a more moderate pace.

Florrie hung Tommy's cap and coat on a peg and seated him at the table. On the opposite side of the table, Agnes stood with arms crossed glaring at Tommy. As Lavinia and Boniface stepped into the room, Tommy jumped up from his seat and turned toward the sister he knew was the one to win over.

"Good evening, Ma'am."

"Good evening Tommy. I'll get to the point immediately, before you have dinner. My sister Flora and I have agreed to let you sleep here nights and to provide you with a breakfast and a dinner, *but,*" Lavinia emphasized, "we shall not brook any betrayal of our trust or any misbehavior on your part. Is that understood.?"

"I... yes, Ma'am."

"In return, young man, you are expected to *behave* like a young man. The money you earn selling newspapers will be yours to keep. Save or spend as you may. But you will also help around this house, doing chores and running errands. We also expect you to keep your person and your room clean. Is that understood? Good. If things work out satisfactorily for you and us, we shall then provide you with a key. But, for now, one of us will let you in. We must consider your schooling, but that will come later. I think you're a smart young lad, so I shall offer this advice only once. If you wish shelter and food under our roof, do not betray our trust or you are out! Now, do you have any questions?"

"No, Ma'am. Thank you Ma'am."

"Now, Tommy," piped in Florrie, seeking to end the interview on a softer note. "You'd best call us by our names. I'm Miss Flora, and my sister is Miss Lavinia Portridge. You know Mr Boniface's and Agnes' names, of course. After Agnes and I have given you dinner, you will help Mr Boniface clean out part of the storeroom, and we'll set up a cot for you."

"Thank you, Ma'am—Miss Lavinia. Miss Florrie—Flora!"

" 'Miss Florrie' will do fine, Tommy. Have we any pot pie left, Agnes? Good. Put a couple of pieces into the oven to warm up, will you? And some squash and broccoli. There are rolls and oleo to start."

"But, first, young man," spoke Mr Boniface, "perhaps you would like to repair to the water closet to clean up?"

Tommy picked up his cue immediately.

"Flora, I think Agnes can manage without you for a few minutes. By the way, Agnes, we'll have a guest tomorrow for lunch, an old family friend. Perhaps if you do the clean-up tonight, my sister and I can take care of lunch ourselves and you can have a couple of hours to yourself—from noon to... shall we say 3 o'clock? "Flora?, "there's something I need you to help me with upstairs." Lavinia's stern countenance cautioned Flora not to ask questions yet, and they went up to Lavinia's office and didn't speak further until Lavinia shut the door.

"I'm sorry I snapped at you, Florrie. I completely forgot that you had prepared pot pies this morning. It's been a busy day, and I thought it best to forestall any discussion until we were alone. The police came—that you know already, but early this morning, just after you left the house, Rosetta's lawyer called..."

"What did he want?"

"He wanted to come here and talk. So I invited him..."

"Does he know something about her murder?"

"Pity sakes!, Flora, give me a chance."

"I'm sorry, dear. It's just that I had such a fruitless day, and I was hoping that someone had discovered something."

"What happened?"

"Never mind. We can talk about that later. First, tell me about the lawyer—and the police."

"Well, as I said, he called just after you left—Dudley Pierce is his name, just like the food shops—"

"Do you think he's related to S. S. Pierce?"

"I have no idea, Flora, and I didn't ask."

"Go on."

"I'll try. He telephoned right after you left. I hadn't really dug into my work yet, so I invited him to come here as soon as he was free. He arrived on the dot of ten." For once, Florrie didn't interrupt. She was silently chiding herself for slipping in and out of the kitchen at that very hour. One more failure as a detective. "He had some business to discuss with Rosetta, but when he telephoned her hotel, he found out she was dead."

"Poor man."

"Yes. He even admitted that his decision to come to Boston and look into matters personally was motivated by—in his words, if I recall correctly—admiration as much as professional duty. I think he said he took the afternoon train from Providence yesterday. He's staying at the Touraine."

"That's where Rosetta had rooms."

"That's the point. I suggested to Mr Pierce that he look into whether Rosetta had any visitors at the hotel—someone we don't yet know about. Someone who would have had to know she was coming to Boston."

There was a pause before Florrie admitted "It seems you discovered more sitting at home than I did walking my feet off all day. I think the only thing I discovered was that Rosetta was booked into the Tremont by an agent named Nathan Furst."

"Yes, dear, that's quite right. Indeed, Mr Pierce informed me that Mr Furst had to offer Rosetta an unheard of amount of money to convince her to come to Boston."

"Oh, bother! My entire day wasted."

"I'm sorry, Florrie. But don't think of it that way. Perhaps something will come of your adventures today. One never knows. Anyway, you looked tired. I'll help Agnes finish the clean-up. You go lie down." Florrie nodded gratefully. Only the prospect of an even more comfortable rest in her bed induced Florrie to hoist up herself from the easy chair and head to the door.

"Oh, I nearly forgot. I've invited Mr Pierce for lunch tomorrow at one. You and I shall have to pull together a decent lunch by ourselves because I've given Agnes the early afternoon off. I don't want her around while the three of us exchange information."

"Well, since I shan't have much to bring to the table, the least I can do is make lunch. Cora is due tomorrow; I don't know whether she'll be pleased or peeved that Agnes won't be around. Goodnight Lavinia."

CHAPTER 41

Wednesday: Night Visitors

After performing her nightly toilet, Florrie fell asleep within minutes of getting into bed. Lavinia helped Agnes in the kitchen, while Mr Boniface and Tommy, swept out a bin in the storage room. As they were setting up a camp cot and assembled bedding and a pillow, Tommy asked "You been living here long, Mr Boniface?"

"Oh, yes. Many years."

"You known Miss Lavinia and Miss Florrie long?"

"Ever since they moved into this house."

Tommy waited a bit before he ventured further. "They seem kinda different."

"Different? Perhaps... Yes, I suppose they may seem that way to some."

Edging around the topic was not getting Tommy the answers he wanted, so he put his question straight out: "Why don't they eat no meat?"

"Ah, as to that, I suggest you ask Miss Flora."

"Don't you know?"

"Oh, yes, Certainly. But...". Mr Boniface was unsure how to continue.

Tommy was not. "Don't they like meat?"

That seemed to provide Mr Boniface with the cue he required. "Miss Flora and Miss Lavinia like animals, Tommy. They believe that all the earth's creatures have the right to live in peace, and that people don't have the right to eat them."

His explanation clearly provided Tommy with something to think about, and, much to Mr Boniface's relief, there were no further questions as they busied themselves pulling together some manner of accommodation for Tommy. To provide some semblance of privacy and separate the lad's sleeping quarters from the shelves and piles of storage, Mr Boniface surrounded two sides of the cot with an old but still lovely three-section mahogany screen from Malay—one of Captain Portridge's imports that had failed to find a permanent place in the sisters' current abode.

Previously, Mr Boniface had arrayed towels, washcloths, soap, tooth powder and toothbrush and a fingernail file in the water closet. When all was in place, Mr Boniface suggested to Tommy that he volunteer to dispose of the garbage.

Mr Boniface accompanied him to the outside garbage pail a few feet from the rear corner of the kitchen. Sunken garbage pails were nearly universal in Greater Boston. Food scraps were dumped into deep removable pails that fit into equally deep concrete cylinders sunk into the ground. Their only evidence was a cast iron collar and lid that poked up several inches above ground.

Twice a week horse-drawn garbage wagons arrived. House by house, the men lifted out the pails, dumped the already fermenting leavings into their often uncovered trucks and, eventually, sold the maggot-infested slop to middlemen who, in turn, retailed the reeking mess to pig farmers. By the day of collection, especially in warmer weather, the stench had begun to spread throughout the neighborhood, and flies could lead a first-timer to every sunken pail in town.

Each evening, Tommy was accustomed to heading downtown to the Boston Record's plant, picking up a bundle of the late edition and selling them to theatergoers on their way home. He did so his first night as a resident of Portridge Arms. Meanwhile, Florrie slept well, awaking only when the front doorbell rang and Lavinia let in several groups of their lodgers who were returning after appearing in the last half of their respective bills. Tommy straggled in with the last of them.

Downstairs, he was tempted to forego washing up, but he wanted to make a good faith effort to conform to the Porridge Sisters' expectations, so he washed his hands, face and neck and made a few passes with the new toothbrush. He found it brought back comforting memories of living with his mother. As he fell asleep, Tommy listened to the usual household noises he had all but forgotten: the flush of a toilet, the rattle of pipes, the pop of embers, the plunk of a cinder.

A few hours later, Tommy awoke to a rustling sound. At first he merely kicked at his covers, expecting to send a rat scuttling away, but after a second such noise he snapped alert, quickly realizing he was indoors at the Portridge Arms, not curled up in an alleyway or sleeping under a bridge.

Accustomed to sleeping in unsafe places, he had become a wary sleeper. Now, bolt upright on his cot near a rear window, he strained to identify the rustling. Someone was walking close to the house, crunching the dry fallen leaves of autumn. Did he imagine he heard voices? Probably a couple of drunks had ducked into the back yard to relieve themselves. Tommy rose to look through the window. It was not the brightest of nights, but it looked as though two human shapes were moving away from the rear of Portridge Arms toward Paul Street.

Tommy had settled back into bed when he heard a clang of metal. He jumped to window again and saw the two shapes heading back toward the house. As they came nearer, Tommy saw that they carried rubbish barrels: the shorter shape carried one while the taller one was trying to tote two. Both seemed a bit unsteady on their feet, and, whether it was because of drink or their burden, they failed to prevent the barrels from clinking against each other.

When they reached the rear of the house, they seemed to be headed to the exterior door of the kitchen, but at the same time that their nearness began to afford Tommy a clearer look, they stepped out of his angle of vision. Even as he pressed his face against the window, Tommy could no longer see them.

Afraid to turn on any lights, he felt his way into the kitchen. The shades were drawn against the large, ground-level rear windows. Creeping to the rear wall, Tommy crouched and raised a window shade little more than an inch; he saw the two men upend the contents of a barrel against the rear wall.

Tommy heard "Jeez, Buddy, watch it!" just before a blaze of light flared. The men grinned for a few moments as the flames rose and illuminated their faces, then Tommy heard the taller of the two men hiss, "Let's get outta here, Pop." Castle Street provided the nearer exit route, but the short, slower man managed to trip over the protruding garbage pail lid and fell, smashing his lantern, which set the dry autumn weeds afire.

Tommy ran up the stairs and rapped as hard as he could on the door to Lavinia's office. After what was less than what seemed to be several minutes, Lavinia poked her head out her bedroom door down the rear hall.

"What's all the banging? Tommy, what's...."

"Fire, Miss Lavinia: back of the house." With that he ran back downstairs and opened the kitchen exit, but the swoosh of air from the opening door pulled several burning newspapers and cartons onto the kitchen floor. Tommy grabbed a broom and pushed the fiery mess back outside, then closed the door as Lavinia came downstairs.

Tommy yelled "Don't open the kitchen door!" and bolted outside through the lower Castle Street entrance and around the side of the house to the fire.

CHAPTER 42

Midnight Wednesday: All Hands Turn to It

Lavinia saw the flames through the kitchen windows and watched in horror as the barefooted boy turned the three barrels over the burning pile, smothering the worst of the blaze. She ran back upstairs to her office to telephone the fire department. By then, lodgers were starting to cluster about the third-floor landing. A few, still groggy, numbly watched the scramble below. Others, growing alert, called down to ask what was happening. A few ventured downstairs to the second- and first-floor landings.

In slippers and pulling an old kimona around her nightgown, Florrie repeated "I don't know, I don't know," as she worked her way downstairs through the growing knot of lodgers in the stairwell. As Florrie and Lavinia passed each other, Lavinia huffed one word, "Fire!"

Mr Boniface and Agnes were not far behind by the time Florrie reached the kitchen. Florrie immediately grabbed several buckets out of the storage room and began filling them at the sink.

"Here! Take these. Perhaps we can quench the fire before it spreads."

Mr Boniface was the first to jump forward and Agnes followed. Boniface grabbed one partially-filled bucket and headed for the rear door. He singed his hand on the door knob. Agnes grabbed a pot holder, and, between them, they tugged open the scorched but still intact outside kitchen door. Agnes went back to the sink for pail of water.

"Be careful you two, you've only got your slippers on." As soon as a third bucket filled, Florrie brought it out herself. There stood Tommy, bare-foot in his union suit, beating out the flames near the door with the broad side of the broom. "Tommy, come inside. We'll get it under control. Lavinia's telephoned the fire department. Tommy, please! You can help me fill the buckets." Tommy let Florrie lead him into the kitchen where the Hennigan Brothers and Mr Boniface were waiting for Agnes to refill pails. "Good heavens, Tommy, you've gashed your foot! How did that happen?

Lavinia clambered down the stairs into the kitchen. "The fire department should be here any minute."

"One of the firebugs dropped his lantern. The glass musta broke."

"Never mind, Tommy. You can tell us later. Lavinia would you ..."

"Oh, Lord," Lavinia spotted the blood on the floor and Tommy's foot. "Mr Hennigan, will you help me get Tommy up to my bathroom?" For a moment Ned and Mike looked at each other. "You go Mike. I got my shoes on."

Florrie returned to the sink. Lavinia grabbed the dishtowel from the rack by the sink and wrapped it around Tommy's foot. Mike lifted Tommy in his arms, and Lavinia led them upstairs to the bathroom she shared with her sister.

Meanwhile, Agnes and Florrie continued to re-fill pails, and Mr Boniface and Ned Hennigan took turns pouring the water on the burning rubbish. Within minutes, Victor Greeley, the Franklin Sisters and the Vetter Trio lined up for pails of water. Mike Hennigan soon returned to the kitchen and joined them. Enough people were lending a hand so that Mr Boniface slipped away to the water closet to run cold water over his stinging hand and apply some of the salve that Florrie concocted out of flowers and aloe leaves to treat burns incurred during cooking.

Acrobats performing at the Globe Theatre, the Vetters spoke what Mr Boniface determined was a polyglot of German, Czech and French with no more than a few English words and phrases. Except at mealtimes, they had kept to themselves—practicing tumbling exercises in the backyard on warm mornings or, when the day was chilly or drizzling, performing calisthenics in the music/practice room.

That night it was clear that the Vetter Trio welcomed the opportunity to join their performing fellows. By gestures the acrobats organized the bucket brigade into an efficient line so that filled pails were passed outdoors from one person to the next and empty ones returned to the sink at the same orderly pace. Communication was limited to smiles, hand motions and the occasional *"ja," "nein"* or *"pardon moi"* that the others soon adopted in good humor.

Rubbish burned fast and bright, but quickly consumed itself before the flames could do more than char the wood trim and kitchen door. When the flames were pretty well doused, Ned Hennigan asked Mr Boniface where he could find a rake and shovel. Mr Boniface returned from the storage room with two rakes, while Ned grabbed both shovels from the coal bins. Outdoors, where Mike and the Vetter Brothers were stomping on persistent embers, Ned distributed the implements. While the others were raking over glowing bits of trash and weeds, Ned brought them barrels into which they could shovel the burnt bits and went to the shed at the back of the yard to locate the discarded covers for the barrels.

The clanging bell of the fire wagon could be heard in the distance as the performers filled and covered the last barrel. Everything under control, Mr Boniface again discretely repaired to apply more of Florrie's burn salve and bandage his hand properly.

When the firemen arrived, Florrie stood, hands on hips, facing their captain. Given the moment to think, she thought better of lacing into him for time it had taken for his company to arrive at the scene and relaxed her posture.

"We seem to have it under control, Captain, but I'd appreciate it if your men would give the back of the house and the yard a thorough soaking." The captain didn't expect to be told what to do by a civilian, and a woman to boot; nonetheless it was obvious that she was right. The captain gave his men the order, and two firemen ran a hose down the side of the house to the rear as the others pumped the wagon. Soon a stream of water sprayed along the side and back of the house and over the ground to drench remaining embers.

Upstairs, Lavinia had washed Tommy's cut foot with her own face soap, then flushed the cut with witch hazel. "Tommy, what happened?" She asked as much to distract him while she next swabbed the wound with iodine. He didn't allow himself more than a shudder and a grunt. The cut probably wasn't long or deep enough to require stitching, but Tommy wouldn't be hustling around town hawking his newspapers for a week or two.

"I heard some noise outside and saw two guys dumping the trash out of the barrels. They started the fire right up against the kitchen door—I guess 'cause it's wood and the wall is brick? Then they ran away, and I tried to put it out."

"Do you know who they were?" asked Lavinia, wondering if it were one of the local gangs who prowled about. Or maybe they were boys who knew Tommy and had followed him home.

"Nope. But I kinda got a look at 'em when the fire lit up. One guy was old. The other guy called him 'Pop'. The old guy called him Buddy."

Lavinia stared at the boy. "My sister said you were a smart boy. Remember what you saw, Tommy. I'll have the police here in the morning." Lavinia finished binding his foot with gauze and secured it in place with adhesive tape. "And you're a brave lad to boot." She put away the iodine, scissors and bandaging, drew a tumbler of water and handed it along with two aspirin to Tommy and went into her bedroom. She returned with a pair of her slippers and a bathrobe. Both items were plain and sensible looking, so Tommy wasn't embarrassed about wearing them. "Now, let's see if you can hop on one foot while I help you downstairs. We'll take it slowly. If you put any pressure on that foot, the cut will reopen and won't heal properly."

By the time Lavinia and Tommy arrived back downstairs, the firemen were spraying the grounds. The captain knocked at the kitchen's rear door as Lavinia helped Tommy to an end seat at the kitchen table and propped his leg on a cushion atop a nail keg from the storage room. Lavinia then attended to the waiting captain. Displeased by the fire crew's tardiness, Lavinia did not invite in the captain, but mindful of possible future need for his services, she managed a civil tone of appreciation and intimated that the police had been contacted and would arrive in the morning for a report when she was refreshed by a few hours sleep and able to recall more accurately what led to the fire. The captain, thus dismissed, reluctantly said good night and led his firefighters back to their fire station.

So as not to disturb lodgers who had gone back to bed, a few extra chairs were requisitioned from the dining room and brought down to the kitchen to accommodate Victor Greeley, Marla and Paula Franklin, Ned and Mike Hennigan and Andras, Karel and Dietmar Vetter as they gathered around the large work table to relax in the afterglow of their adventure.

As Florrie set out dishes of ice cream, she noticed Marla Franklin place her hand on Mike Hennigan's knee. Florrie kept her smile to herself and averted her eyes. Well, it wouldn't do to mention that to Lavinia. Agnes foraged for biscuits while the tea she made was steeping, and Mr Boniface, gauze wrapped around the hand singed by the kitchen doorknob, placed cups and saucers on the table.

Lavinia had disappeared. When she returned she had a bottle of Cockburn's Ruby Port. Florrie immediately set out small juice glasses all around. Once the celebratory snack was laid, Lavinia invited Agnes and Mr Boniface to sit down. Agnes was delighted to be included, but Mr Boniface begged off to retreat to his room. It was well after 2 AM, and he dearly needed rest before he had to rise in a few hours to stoke the furnaces into life.

After a half-hour of camaraderie, conversation calmed, and sleep was reclaiming the celebrants. Mr Greeley was the first to repair to bed and Florrie followed him upstairs. "Victor, thank you for your help this evening. You're a good friend."

CHAPTER 43

Thursday Morning: The Inspector Calls Again

Reports of suspected arson in the South End were frequent but seldom led to arrests and convictions. Station Four routinely dispatched a sergeant to look into the accusations, but most subsequent action didn't progress beyond a statement of particulars, including "perpetrator or perpetrators unknown," that were filed, seldom to be exhumed.

When Lavinia awoke the next morning a bit before 8 AM— much later than was usual—she placed a telephone call directly to Inspector Brody's office at Pemberton Square. Brody jettisoned his schedule for the day to hasten to Portridge Arms. It wasn't only Lavinia's assertion of arson that claimed his immediate attention; he had received a message that the petition he had filed yesterday for a search warrant to inspect Mrs Cormier's rooms had just been granted by Magistrate Billy Dyer. To pick it up Brody only had to cross the street from police headquarters at 37 Pemberton Square to the massive granite Suffolk County Court House that also housed the Massachusetts Supreme Judicial and Boston Municipal Courts.

The day was starting well, and Brody liked good omens. Indeed, upon examining the warrant, the Inspector noted that Billy Dyer had expanded its scope to cover the entire premises at 146 and 144 Castle Street as a favor to his good friend and brother-in-law, Malachi Brody. Before leaving Police Headquarters, Brody had phoned Station Four to alert them that he wanted Patrolman Moore waiting at 146 Castle Street in no more than 30 minutes. Brody liked having a neighborhood beat officer accompany him on investigations. It freed Brody to concentrate on the principals in an investigation and saved him from the tedious, dead-end and often wholly speculative blathering of people who imagined they saw more than they had or bent the facts to settle old but still vexing scores. Brody stepped into one of the hackneys that lined up outside the Court House and directed its driver to Portridge Arms.

Brody intended to detail Patrolman Moore to the surrounding houses to locate possible witnesses. Residents of more troubled neighborhoods were often uncooperative, even hostile, to police inquires unless the beat patrolman had cultivated their trust and goodwill. From what Brody had heard and seen, Patrolman Frankie Moore seemed accepted by most households on his beat.

As Brody was ringing the Portridge Arms doorbell at 8:45 Thursday morning, Frankie Moore was rounding the corner from Albion Street at full gallop. When Lavinia opened the door she saw a smiling Inspector Brody and a panting Patrolman Moore. Lavinia admitted both officers just as Agnes was reaching the foyer. When she caught a glimpse of Frankie Moore, Agnes ducked back down the stairs. Out of sight, she quickly removed her hair net and was running a brush over her hair when she heard Lavinia and the police coming downstairs.

"Good morning, Agnes. I trust you slept well."

"Yes, Miss Lavinia."

"You look quite refreshed despite all our excitement." Only Agnes was in position to spot Lavinia's slight smile. "I'm sure you remember Inspector Brody and Patrolman Moore. Ah, I smell coffee. Is it ready?"

"Yes, Ma'am."

"I know I could use a cup. Perhaps the officers will join me. That's all right, Agnes. I can take care of it. Will you rouse my sister and tell her we're waiting in the kitchen?"

Nothing invigorated Florrie like the excitement of unexpected events in life. When Agnes rapped on her door, Florrie, already washed and dressed, was just short of ready when Agnes informed her that the police were waiting with Lavinia in the kitchen. Garbed sensibly in an old sweater and bloomers for a day of cleaning up the yard after breakfast, Florrie decided that a meeting with the police required a more professional appearance, so she cloaked her work clothes with a kimona and chose a particularly vivid one. As pleased as surprised that the police had arrived early, Florrie eagerly clumped downstairs with Agnes in tow.

"Inspector Brody, I believe? I'm Flora Portridge. And you must be Patrolman Moore. Aren't you the handsome fellow? I see my sister has served you coffee. How about some bread and marmalade?

"No thanks, Miss Portridge. We're fine." Brody spoke only for himself. That Frankie Moore had been about to assent to a serving was not lost on Agnes. With as little fuss as possible, Agnes sliced off a couple of pieces from a loaf of graham bread, slid them onto a plate with dollops of butter and marmalade and added a table knife and napkin—all of which she quietly placed at the patrolman's elbow.

"You'll forgive me, officers, if I start making breakfast—Agnes, you give me a hand, won't you? Any minute now we'll have a dozen lodgers up and about and hungry."

"Quite all right Ma'am. I'm sure Miss Lavinia can help me," said Brady, "but if you think of anything additional, just..."

"Oh, dear me!" Florrie was looking at the breakfast menu for the day while she tied on an apron. "Potatoes O'Brien, fruit compote and cinnamon rolls; well, that's too ambitious for a morning like this, Agnes. We'll have to improvise. Make up a large batch of porridge. Two pots. Plenty of raisins and walnuts but a bit thinner gruel than usual. Don't overcook; I'll turn it into pancakes. Then all we'll need to do is peel and cut up some fruit."

Brody decided that he'd better ignore Flora who was bustling about and direct his questions solely to Lavinia. "The message I got this morning was that somebody tried to set fire to your house last night?"

"I'm not sure, Inspector, they intended to burn our house down" interjected Florrie as she vigorously cracked walnuts on the work table. "After all, it is brick except for doors and trim. I suspect their purpose was to frighten us."

"Why would someone want to frighten you?"

"I think that's plain enough, Inspector: to deter my inquiries. Agnes, bring us a dozen apples, a couple of tins of pineapple and whatever else you can find in cold storage that will mix well for a fruit bowl." Florrie put the stopper in the sink and ran cold water.

The inspector resumed directing his questions to Lavinia: "Are you sure the fire wasn't an accident?"

"Quite sure, inspector." Florrie pulled both boiling pots of porridge off the stove and set them into the sinks to cool. "We have a witness."

"Someone who saw the firebug?"

"Firebugs. Two of them." Into the oatmeal Florrie stirred several splashes of apple cider, some margarine, shelled walnuts and raisins and a few dashes of cinnamon.

"If they *were* firebugs," countered Lavinia. "I thought firebugs were people who felt compelled to start fires—just to watch the blaze. Arsonists, as I understand it, use fire to perpetrate a crime such as collecting insurance, intimidating witnesses or..."

"Technically, of course, you're right..."

176

"Or murder?," finished Lavinia.

"Hasn't my sister explained to you about last night's—or rather this morning's adventure?" interjected Florrie.

"Not yet, Ma'am. I was just asking Miss Portridge…"

"As there are two Miss Portridges," put in Lavinia, thoroughly enjoying watching the inspector trying to cope with Florrie as well herself, "may I suggest that you refer to me as Miss Lavinia and my sister as Miss Flora? Neither of us likes being 'ma'am-ed.' It rather makes me feel I'm in a barnyard."

"Yes, Ma'am… Miss Lavinia."

Agnes reentered the kitchen carrying a basket of apples and two cans of pineapples. To make room for Agnes to rinse the fruit, Florrie quickly removed the porridge pots from the sink. The oatmeal, raisin and nut mixture was not quite as cooled as she would have liked; nevertheless Florrie chanced it and added flour, baking powder and baking soda to the first pot of oatmeal.

Lavinia asked "Is there anything I can do to help, Florrie?"

"Everything's coming along; I'm about to take a breather myself." Florrie poured herself another cup of tea and sat for a moment with Lavinia and the policemen while she waited for the pancake batter to bubble and rise a bit. At that moment, Tommy limped into the room and stood at the table, uncertain whether he should sit without an invitation.

CHAPTER 44

Thursday Morning: Thrust and Parry

"Good morning, my young hero." Florrie jumped up and poured a glass of apple cider for Tommy, then looked at the kitchen wall clock; "I haven't heard Mr Boniface upstairs, Lavinia. Have you? Perhaps you'd better peel and chop the fruit while Agnes sets out things in the dining room if he isn't there. And don't forget to bring up lots of maple syrup for the pancakes," called Florrie as she ladled batter onto a large cast iron griddle atop 'the dragon' where it sizzled to her satisfaction. Turning her attention to the police, Florrie added "By the way Inspector, let me introduce you to Tommy. He's our young friend who witnessed last night's arson. Tommy, this is Inspector Brody and that is Patrolman Moore."

Before Brody could utter a word, Lavinia whispered to Tommy and he left the room.

Tommy exited the kitchen just as Agnes came back downstairs. "Mr Boniface already had everything all laid out. He did it early this morning after the furnaces. Now he's gone back to bed if you don't mind. The dining room's half full already."

"Miss Lavinia, I want to talk to that lad."

"I'm sure you do, Inspector, but I suggested to him that he wash up and get dressed before coming to table. I didn't wish to embarrass him by saying it aloud in front of you gentlemen."

Florrie called to Agnes before Brody could reply. "You can take up the first batch of pancakes to our guests. Tell them there'll be more to come.

"And who is Mr Boni..."

"How thoughtful of him. Poor man probably slept only a few hours before he had to wake up the furnaces," marveled Lavinia. "Agnes, will you take over the fruit again? I'm sure the Inspector has questions he wants to ask. Just chop the fruit into bite-sized chunks and dribble the juice from the pineapple cans over it. While you're at it, why don't you look and see if we have a jar of maraschino cherries to toss in for color?

Brody felt he was losing control of the situation. "Is he the janitor?"

"Who?"

"That Mr Bonyface or whatever his name is."

"Goodness, no, Inspector," chimed in Florrie, ladling a second pot of pancake batter onto the griddle. "Mr Boniface is a guest—and an actor of some note. Ah, our brave lad is back. I'll bring you some pancakes."

"Thanks, Miss Florrie."

"Mr A. S. Boniface," Florrie continued, "was one of the more distinguished actors at the Boston Museum during its heyday. May I get either of you officers more coffee?"

Brody's "no, thanks" was gruffer than he intended. "Miss Lavinia..."

"Tea, perhaps? Or some apple cider?" Patrolman Moore, who had done his best not to smile during the verbal tennis match with Brody, caught Agnes' eye and winked. She blushed a smile in return, pleased that he was keeping an eye on her.

Brody decided the boy would not be so apt at parrying his questions. "Say, Tommy..." Brody got no further.

Florrie interrupted. "And how's your foot, Tommy. Did you soak it yet?"

"Not yet."

"Young fella..."

"As soon as you've had breakfast, young man," cautioned Lavinia, "I want to see how that foot looks."

"Agnes," called Florrie, I've got another batch of pancakes ready."

"And, now, Inspector," asked Lavinia as she rose from the table, "I believe you're here to inspect the vandalism?"

After the verbal volleys of the past quarter hour, Lavinia's attention to him was unexpected, but Brody rallied, stood up and handed his warrant to Lavinia. She glanced at it for a moment, laid it on the table and headed for the outside door at the rear of the kitchen. "Since you gentlemen are already downstairs, why don't we start with the damage?" As Lavinia stood there waiting with the door open, Brody had little choice but to comply. "Come, Inspector; we don't want to let all our heat out. You, too, Patrolman. The taxpayers don't pay for our coal."

"Can I go look?" Tommy asked Florrie.

"I don't see why not." Tommy made as much haste as he could while favoring his foot. Florrie wished she had gone out herself to inspect before she started breakfast, but she reminded herself that is was good discipline for her to complete the task at hand before getting sidetracked as she was wont to do. She called after Tommy, "Be careful of your foot." Lavinia had enjoyed jousting with Brody, but the sight that greeted her in the morning light sobered her. "Oh, dear Lord..." The outside surface of the door looked like charcoal, but what stunned her most was the crudely painted warning on the brick wall: "NOSEY BIDDYS GET HURT."

At the rear of the yard, a few residents of Paul Street were standing about, hoping for an invitation to gawk more closely. Brody dispatched Moore to keep them away as well as determine whether any of them could claim to be legitimate witnesses or were simply curious idlers with nothing better to do.

Tommy followed Brody and Lavinia round to the side of the house. Brody spotted the kerosene lantern lying on its side with its glass globe shattered and the shards scattered about.

"There was two of 'em."

"Two what?"

"Two men. Two lanterns, too. The old guy tripped and broke that one."

Brody turned around toward Tommy. "You saw them?"

"That must have been what you cut your foot on, Tommy. The poor boy was out here all by himself in his underwear and without shoes on battling the fire."

"So, you're the only one in the house who saw what there was to see?"

"I guess so."

"Okay, son. Tell me about it."

"Why don't we go back inside. Neither Tommy nor I are dressed properly and I'm getting chilled."

"Go ahead. I'll be right in." Brody thrust two fingers in his mouth and whistled for Moore who came trotting back.

Just as Lavinia and Tommy reentered the kitchen, Florrie was on her way out, having passed the last batch of pancakes to Agnes to bring to the dining room.

Lavinia had been stunned at the sight. Florrie was disheartened. She felt like sitting on the ground and crying, but then she realized that the damage had not been prompted by hate. She and her sister were not targeted for vandalism because of who they were but because of what someone thought they knew or might yet find out. That made her angry. Brody took Florrie by the arm and guided her back into the kitchen. Moore remained outside to make notes as Brody had directed.

Inside, Lavinia and Tommy sat in silence at the table. Agnes came down the stairs as Florrie and Brody reentered.

"Agnes, will you make another pot of coffee?," asked Lavinia. "When it's ready, please join us. You probably know as much about what went on last night—this morning—as any of us except Tommy.

"I'll do it, Agnes," offered Florrie, happy to have a chore to turn her hands and mind to. "If you haven't seen to the children yet, I'll appreciate it if you bring them some breakfast." Agnes seemed to pick up that Florrie didn't want any mention of Mrs Cormier's name. "Cora should be here at ten. She can clean up while we are questioned by the Inspector." Agnes noted there was neither porridge nor pancakes left, so she assembled a tray of Mr Kellogg's brand new Toasted Corn Flakes, five bananas, a pitcher of milk, some sugar, bowls, spoons and napkins and hurried to the top floor as fast as she could without spilling, anxious not to miss a minute more than necessary of the investigation.

CHAPTER 45

Thursday Morning: a Lead from the Lad

Brody sat dazed by the frenetic activity and nearly defeated by the verbal interplay, so Lavinia spoke up. "My sister and I want you to think carefully, Tommy. Remember every little thing you can from the moment you woke up and answer all of Inspector Brody's questions. All right?"

"Sure." There was an ensuing moment of silence as if Brody wasn't quite sure the crafty sisters had ceded control of the situation.

"Good boy, Tommy," began Brody. "Just like Miss Lavinia said, tell me everything that happened."

"I guess I thought it was just rats..."

"Rats!? ..."

"Permit me, Inspector. Tommy is a new member of our household. Ever since his mother died last year, he's been on the streets, sleeping where he can. Alleyways and such. He sells newspapers and does some errands for us, so we invited him to take his meals here. Yesterday we fixed up a spot down here in the basement, on the far side of the building, where he could sleep. Last night was his first night with us, and thank heavens he was here."

Brody stood up. "Tommy, show me where you slept last night. The rest of you can stay here, if you don't mind." As they walked through the passageway into number 144, Brody asked "How did you meet the sisters?"

"I helped them home with their groceries."

"That's it?

"Yup." Tommy knew how to answer questions without offering more than required. "Here's the toilet. I sleep over there." Tommy pointed to a cot separated from the rest of the storage room by the three-piece screen.

"So, if it wasn't rats, what woke you up?"

"Talking, maybe. I figured it was some drunks come behind the house to take a piss, so I didn't get up. Anyway, not until I heard some barrels."

"Barrels?"

"Yeah, banging. So I looked out the window. It was dark so I couldn't see too much at first, but there was two guys walking from the shed out back up to the house. They was probably drunk, because one of them banged his barrels. Anyway, I just watched them until I couldn't see them no more."

"Why not? Did they leave?"

"No. They was outside the kitchen. You can't see that from this angle. Don't know why nobody else woke up. They made noise."

"How?"

"Banging the barrels."

"What were they doing? Banging on them like drums?"

"Naw. Turning 'em upside down and shaking all the shi... stuff outta them. I couldn't get a good look so I goes into the kitchen to see what they was doing"

"And?," Brody encouraged.

"Like I said. Shaking all the stuff outta the barrels and kicking it up against the back door."

"Why didn't they run away when they saw you?"

" 'Cause they didn't see me."

"If you could see them, why..."

" 'Cause I didn't turn no lights on and the shades was down. I didn't have my shoes on so I didn't make no noise. Anyway, I got under a window and peeked out just when they lit the whole pile of stuff on fire. I seen 'em.

"You saw their faces?"

"Yup."

"Would you recognize those guys if you saw them again?"

"I guess so."

"You gotta do better than guess, Tommy."

"Yeah. Sure. One guy was old and short. The other guy was taller. The tall guy was younger. He called the old guy "Pop.""

"Well. That's something to go on."

The old guy called the other one "Buddy."

"Great!"

"They musta had trouble lighting the lantern 'cause the old guy says to the tall one, something like 'Watch it, Buddy.' After they got the fire going, they stood around for a minute, then the tall guy called the old one 'Pop,' and they started to run away, but the old guy tripped and broke his lantern. They ran up the side to Castle Street."

"See which way they went?"

"Nope."

"Great, kid. Let's get back to the kitchen."

By then, Agnes had rejoined Lavinia, Florrie and Frankie Moore. A tea pot, coffee urn, bananas, bread, fruit preserves, peanut butter, plates, mugs and flatware were spread about the table. Without a word, Moore quietly got up and went out to the yard.

"Inspector, Tommy. Please help yourselves. No need to be too formal now that we're all acquainted."

Lavinia got down to business. "Did you find out what you needed to know, Inspector?"

"The young lad, he kept his wits about him. Says he could identify the men if we find them."

"Excellent," cheered Florrie.

"*If* we can find them, Miss Flora."

"But you said Tommy could recognize..."

"Only *if* we know where to find them, Miss Flora. Even if we knew where to look, chances are they'd be long gone. Professional arsonists don't hang around waiting to be caught."

"They wasn't no pros," opined Tommy

"Watch your double negatives, Tommy..."

"If they was real pros, they would'na been drinking, I would'na heard them, and they would'na shown their faces."

"There's something to that" admitted Brody.

"Inspector?" Frankie Moore had reentered the kitchen.

"Yeah, Patrolman?"

"I was outside, having a look around. That's a railway lantern lying on the ground."

"How d'you figure that?"

"My Da is a brakeman for the Old Colony down at South Union. He uses those kind of lanterns."

"Any chance your father's at work now, Frankie?"

"Maybe. He's on days. If he wasn't scheduled for a run, he's probably working at the maintenance shed."

"We may have something here. If Frankie's father knows a couple of workers named Pop and Buddy, we'll have solid lead, and I don't want to lose any time following up on it. Miss Lavinia: two things. I'd like Tommy to come along with us to South Union Station. We'll take a hackney, so he won't have to walk much, but maybe you want to change his bandage first? Maybe if it doesn't look so good, I can bring him to City Hospital and they can patch it up. I mean, if it's all right with you and Miss Florrie? Okay with you Tommy?

"Sure!" The boy had never ridden in a hackney.

"What do you think, Lavinia?" deferred Florrie.

"He's probably as safe with the police as he is here, Florrie. Inspector, will you help me get him upstairs? Then you can use the telephone in my office."

Lavinia headed into the bathroom she shared with her sister, drew several inches of warm water in the tub, told Tommy to undress and give himself a quick wash. She then led Brody into her office, pointed to the telephone and left him, closing the door behind her.

Tommy's clothes, never clean, were now filthy. Lavinia, wondering if Mr Boniface had something Tommy could wear, climbed up to his room and rapped gently.

"I'm sorry to disturb you, Mr Boniface, but might you have some garments that Tommy can wear until we get him some clothing? His own look to be beyond cleaning or repair?"

"Please come in, Miss Lavinia. We'll see if we can find something." As Mr Boniface was quite thin, a shirt, sweater and socks presented little problem, but trousers were another matter: Boniface was more than a foot taller than Tommy. Rummaging through his trunk, Mr Boniface withdrew a pair of knickers and some knee-length hose; "I think these are the best we can do for now."

"We'll get him some new clothes this afternoon, but one more thing, Mr Boniface: can you spare him a union suit? I'll get you a new set when we take Tommy shopping." Even to his underwear, Mr Boniface was forthcoming; but embarrassed to be exposing Lavinia to such a personal and threadbare article, he folded it several times. Thoughtfully, Lavinia lifted the sweater off the pile so that Mr Boniface could hide the donated union suit midway in the pile of clothes she was holding.

CHAPTER 46

Thursday Morning: Clothes Makes the Lad

By the time Lavinia returned to her quarters, Tommy had washed, presumably rinsed, and stood shivering with naught but a towel around him. Lavinia handed him one of her cotton bathrobes and then inspected his foot. It didn't seem infected, but she doused it with witch hazel and swabbed on another coating of iodine. Tommy did no more than flinch. After bandaging his foot, she left him to dress himself in Mr Boniface's loaned clothes, gathered Tommy's old garments and took them downstairs to the furnace room.

Florrie was chattering away to Patrolman Moore who was smiling at Agnes who was furtive stealing glances at him. That Agnes blushed repeatedly amused the young policeman.

Lavinia marched past them into the furnace room. When she marched back into the kitchen, it was to the sink where she washed her hands thoroughly.

Inspector Brody returned from his telephone call. "Patrolman Moore? I've arranged with your station house to have someone take over your beat for the rest of the week. You've been assigned to me through Saturday. Okay?"

"Yessir!"

"That's settled. Where's Tommy?"

"Upstairs. He's probably dressed by now. I think we can forgo bringing Tommy to the hospital; I've cleaned and bound his cut. Why don't we all go up to the first floor," suggested Lavinia. "It'll be easier on Tommy if he has only to walk down the front stairs to the cab." All traipsed upstairs.

"Agnes? Please see if the guests need anything else? We'll give you a hand with the clean-up in a few minutes."

Tommy hobbled down the hallway as the others climbed upstairs. Suddenly two thoughts came to Florrie. She tugged on Patrolman Moore's sleeve to hold him back and whispered, "I'll be right back. I want you to buy him some clothes while you're out. I'll bring you money." Before Moore could say a thing, Florrie dashed back downstairs and into the storage room. On the way back, she stopped in the kitchen, opened a spice drawer and extracted a ten dollar bill.

Brody turned to Lavinia: "By the way..."

"Yes, Inspector?"

"I haven't forgotten our little trip to Mrs Cormier's room." He smiled not in an unfriendly way, but to show that he had not been completely put off course by Lavinia and Florrie. "I'll be back this afternoon."

"Perfect, Inspector. By that time, Mrs Cormier and her children will be playing the matinee." Lavinia thrust her hand forward. "Don't forget your warrant."

Florrie burst on the scene with a red, white and blue cane in her right hand. As she brushed by Patrolman Moore, her left hand pressed the ten dollar bill into his palm. "It's a song-and-dance man's cane, Tommy, not too substantial but you can lean on it a bit. It belonged to Red Norris, a dear old minstrel man."

Lavinia spotted the cab as it pulled in front of the house.

"Do try to get back here in time to meet Dudley Pierce," Lavinia reminded Brody. "He was Rosetta Rice's attorney, and he's a very resourceful man. Well connected, too. He's coming for lunch and you're welcomed to join us. I think you'll find it worth your time. No doubt you'll both have information to share. Lunch is at one o'clock."

Patrolman Moore helped Tommy clamber into the hackney

"Where to?," asked the cabman.

"South Union Station. You know where the Old Colony maintenance shed is?"

"I'll find it."

"Well don't take me to Cape Cod while you do."

"Down Kneeland and 'round in back on Dot Ave, right?"

"Right," confirmed Officer Moore. "By the way, Inspector, one of the sisters slipped me a sawbuck to buy Tommy some clothes. We could stop at Mordecai's down on Dover near the elevated tracks. Cheap clothes. New and used."

"Okay. Hey, driver. Hang a right on Washington Street to Dover. We're stopping there first. Least we can do for our star witness, right, Tommy? Geez, kid, what've you got on? Looks like you crawled outta a rag bag."

"Then, from there, sir, we can head down Dover to Harrison Ave and go that way straight to the maintenance shed. Okay, Inspector?"

"Right. Tommy, you and Patrolman Moore do the shopping. Just pick up what you need for today and don't take too long."

"Hey, driver, stop at the corner of Dover Street."

Tommy had only a vague memory of shopping in a clothing store with his mother. Clearer memories were of stealing and being chased. Fortunately, this store was new to him. High rods from which were suspended hangers of suits and overcoats lined the two long sides of Mordecai's. At the center of the floor bins were stacked with piles of underwear, socks, flannel shirts, corduroy knickers and dungarees. Boxes of black navy shoes and brown work boots were stacked beside the cashier counter.

Moore held up a pair of knickers. "Know what size you take?"

Tommy shrugged, but asked, "Can I have these instead?" indicating bib overalls.

"Sure. Why not. How 'bout a flannel shirt and some long underwear? Winter's coming." Between the two, they assembled underwear, two pairs of socks, overalls, a shirt and a scully cap. It took a while to find shoes that fit, especially since Lavinia had padded one foot with bandages. While Tommy tried on a few pair, Moore called out to a salesman, "Got a pea coat to fit this fella?" Frankie Moore reminded Tommy that he needed room to grow, and they settled for size 6 brown workmen's boots. Tommy's heart thumped when he noticed the pea jacket that the salesman held in front of him. It was the smallest in the store but still several sizes larger than Tommy when he tried it on. No matter; Tommy wanted his pea coat.

"Jeez, this is a corker! How much?"

"Seven dollars."

"I'll give ya five."

"Seven bucks is the price. Where else you gonna find new for seven dollars?"

"It ain't new."

"Almost, $6.50 is the best I can do" Moore enjoyed watching the boy dicker.

"Make it six and you gotta deal." That the boy was accompanied by a police officer who seemed to be the kid's friend was not lost on the salesman.

At the cashier's desk, the total rang up to $13.75. Tommy pulled out three dollar bills and some coin from a pocket of his borrowed knickers.

"Put it away, kid. Miss Flora gave me money."

Tommy was about to protest, but the Patrolman smiled and tousled Tommy's hair. "Forget it. Go change."

"Thanks, officer." Tommy wouldn't forget it.

Brody was standing outside the cab when Patrolman Moore exited Mordecai's with Tommy clutching the brown paper parcel of his borrowed clothes.

"Fifteen minutes! What'ya do? Buy him a trousseau? Get in the cab. It's after ten, and I gotta be back at the Portridge house at one to meet that lawyer."

"Sorry, Inspector, but..."

"Never mind; just get in. My wife woulda taken all morning. You look good, kid."

Tommy was beaming. He'd forgotten the sense of well-being that being clean and wearing new clothes could bestow.

CHAPTER 47

Late Thursday Morning: Many Questions, Fewer Answers

Underway once again, Inspector Brody attempted to draw more out of the boy and asked Tommy to describe again what he had seen last night. The Inspector didn't interrupt except when he needed to elicit more than Tommy's bare bones account. Both officers noted to themselves that Tommy's account remained consistent without seeming rehearsed. Brody complimented Tommy for being an alert young fellow. "You oughta make a good detective some day." After a moment's pause, "So who else lives there?"

"The lodgers. People in show business."

"Yeah, but they come and go every week, right, Tommy?" A single nod confirmed that obvious fact. "Who else besides you lives there all the time?" The inspector's effort to probe was not lost on Tommy, but he decided there wasn't any harm in giving answers as long as he was careful not to betray Florrie's and Lavinia's trust. Anyway, how much did he know? He'd only met the Porridge sisters a week ago. "Besides Miss Florrie and Miss Lavinia, there's old Mr Boniface and Agnes. That's all."

"Miss Flora told me that Mr Boniface was a great actor."

"I guess so."

"What about Agnes?"

"She's okay." Young as he was, Tommy had picked up on the chumminess between Agnes and Patrolman Moore, so he caught himself before mentioning that Agnes sulked a lot and didn't take to him.

"You like the sisters?"

"Sure."

"You like one better over the other?"

"Naw. They're just different."

"How so?"

"Miss Florrie's real friendly. Miss Lavinia's real smart. Miss Florrie's smart, too. Both of them's real nice." Tommy thought for a few second but couldn't offer more than "Just different."

"Yeah, I can see Miss Lavinia's smart. Good head on her shoulders. Run's the business, I hear."

"I guess."

"Miss Florrie okay with that?"

"I guess. She runs the kitchen."

"She a good cook?"

"Yeah! Real good. Never know you ain't eating meat." Brody, focused on his line of inquiry, missed the significance of the last comment.

"Sounds like Miss Florrie's the creative one, eh, Tommy? Maybe artistic? A little eccentric?"

Tommy looked to the inspector for a clue. Seeing none he asked "What's eccentric?"

"Oh, you know, a little queer? Gets excited? Imagines things maybe?"

"Naaaw." Tommy's reply was as dismissive as it was long-drawn out.

Inspector Brody recognized a dead end when he ran smack into it. "Patrolman, swap seats with the kid." Tommy quickly complied and, once settled, pressed his head against the window as the cab sped past one long brick warehouse after another. What a great two days it had been for him: a new home, new clothes and two motherly women to care for him. He was determined to take care of them in turn. He hadn't felt this safe and happy since before his mother got ill. He hoped the priests were right: that she was up there somewhere, safe and happy for herself as well as him. As the cab rattled down the cobblestone streets, Brody and Moore plotted out their moves, while Tommy enjoyed the rare company of men who weren't about to hurt him. Frankie Moore was a good cop.

After the bustle of preparing and serving breakfast and the departure of Tommy and the police, Florrie's and Lavinia's spirits began to sink as they made their way back to the kitchen. Neither spoke, but their apprehension was similar; whoever set the fire was determined to scare them, and it could well be that their troubles were just starting.

At the bottom of the stairs, the sisters stopped and stared. Agnes, more chipper than they had ever seen her, sang to herself and buzzed about her chores. Then they heard the single loud knock on the kitchen's rear door. Cora had arrived.

"What happened?," demanded Cora without any greeting and pointing to the door.

Lavinia spoke up quickly. "Some tramps were drinking out back last night and got careless, it seems."

"You see them?"

"No, Cora, we didn't."

"Police catch them?" Cora had been on her way up the sidewalk when she spotted the uniformed patrolman leaving Portridge Arms. She had halted, several buildings down on Castle Street, until the patrolman left in a hackney with a man and a boy.

"No, Cora, not yet, as far we know. We only telephoned the police this morning."

"They sure come quick around here." Cora hung up her coat and hat, thinking that a call for police from her neighborhood wouldn't be answered for several days, if at all.

"The firemen were here last night. They probably filed a report."

"Hmmph!" Realizing that she'd squeeze no more information out of Lavinia, Cora went to fetch her pails, dust mop, the carpet sweeper and a jug of white vinegar. When she returned from the storage room she volunteered "I see you got someone sleeping in there."

"I just made a fresh pot of tea, Cora. Will you have a cup?" There was a silence of several seconds, for it had been Agnes who offered the tea—one of the rare civil exchanges between the two women.

"I best be getting on with my cleaning." Cora, as puzzled as Lavinia and Florrie by Agnes' courtesy—for the offer concealed no condescension, quickly stuffed her implements into the 'bump up,' gave the cords several sharp tugs and trudged up the stairs. The sisters shot a glance at each other, acknowledging that they had both witnessed a baffling episode, and then turned their hands to preparing lunch for Dudley Pierce, Inspector Brody and themselves. Later they would discuss whether Agnes' gesture was a manifestation of her newly-kindled good will, centered on Patrolman Moore but radiating toward all mankind, or simply a way of diverting Cora from asking further questions about the fire. In either case—as a demonstration of courtesy or one of loyalty and discretion, it was welcomed.

192

CHAPTER 48

Late Morning, Thursday: In Pursuit

The hackney took Brody, Moore and Tommy to the main gate to the rail yard. A few yards inside was a one-room metal shed marked OFFICE. After riding along streets lined with brick buildings five storeys high, the rail yard looked vast, and the office looked like a tiny dinghy anchored on the edge of a sea of railroad track. Spread ahead were rail cars looking much smaller than they were; some were stalled, others sailed slowly on rails toward the large islands of metal sheds.

Francis Moore, Senior, wasn't out on a train run that day. According to the attendant in the office shed, he was working in the roundhouse.

"Be a good lad, Tommy, and wait here." Brody indicated the wood bench outside the office. "We'll be wandering about. First we have to find his dad. No sense you traipsing with us on that foot. If we locate our suspect, Patrolman Moore will be back for you to identify him. Okay?"

"Sure." Tommy looked about him as he relaxed on the bench, content, thus far, with the events of the day. The sun was shining after a week of grey skies and intermittent rain, but the air was brisk, and that made his new coat all the more a treasure. All around him were freight cars and passenger coaches and miles of track as far as he could see. It wasn't Tommy's first visit to the rail yards, but this time he was here with the police and not being chased by them while trying to carry away an armful of scrap metal to sell.

Moore spotted his father about 30 yards in front of them and headed, as they themselves were, to the round house entrance. Jogging, the two policemen easily caught up with Mr Moore.

Francis Moore led his son and the inspector inside to introduce him and the inspector to the railway men who were testing brakes, cleaning fire boxes, readying the locomotives for the next haul and quite willing to stop work for a few of the old man's good-natured jokes about the son whose purpose, ambition and industry made him proud.

After several minutes, Inspector Brody drew Francis Moore off to the side and explained why they were there.

"Jeez, Inspector, half the men working here are called 'Pop' or 'Buddy.' "

"Da, we've got a bit of a description. This guy Buddy is younger and taller. The guy he called 'Pop' is shorter and older. And maybe he's Buddy's real father."

"They may have been drunk," added Brody.

"Let me tell, you, Inspector, that don't narrow it down none. Half of these boyos come in drunk and leave the same way. Hey! Kevvy, come 'ere, will ya?"

Kevvy sauntered over, detouring slightly to drop his wrench into a tool box.

"Yeah, Francis? What's up?"

"My boy, here, is working with the Inspector to find some firebugs that tried to burn down two ladies' house last night. He got their names. Seems a good chance they work here. Names 'Pop' and 'Buddy' mean anything to ya?"

"Cripes, half the guys in the yard ..."

"That's what I told them, Kevvy, but we think they may be a father and his son. That strike a bell?"

While Kevvy gave it some thought, Patrolman Moore added, "Not pros, though. Least, we don't think so. Just a couple of guys who aren't particular how they pick up a couple of extra bucks."

Kevvy spoke carefully; it wouldn't do to have word get about that he had put the finger on a co-worker. "Now, Francis, this ain't none of my business, but since you asked me as a favor like, and what I say don't go no further, there's a guy what works over in Shed Four that answers to 'Buddy.' His old man works somewhere around here, too. Don't really know neither of them, but word is neither of them's any better than they should be. That's all I'm going to say, Francis. I gotta get back to work."

Kevvy headed back to the engine he had been working on as Francis pointed the way to Shed Four. The Inspector thanked Mr Moore and turned to his son. "Frankie, you'd better get the kid. He'll have to hoof it, but he's the only one who can recognize the guy." Frankie had turned to leave when Brody had another thought. "When you get him, send Tommy over to Shed Four by himself, I'll be waiting inside. Keep as close as you can without anyone inside seeing you; I don't want this Buddy guy to spot a uniform. If he's our suspect, he might bolt on us."

Tommy spotted Frankie even before the patrolman directed a piercing, two-fingered whistle to get his attention. A hand wave followed and Tommy, minstrel cane in hand, picked his way as quickly as he could across the tracks.

Frankie relayed the Inspector's instructions. "Be careful..." Moore paused and looked at Tommy. This kid didn't survive a year on the streets minus his common sense. Moore pointed out where Shed Four was located: right in back of the one marked with a large "2" painted in white. "Inspector Brody'll be with you. Right? Good man." Tommy headed where he was directed. "I won't be far behind, Tommy," assured Patrolman Moore.

Brody waited until he saw Tommy round the corner of Shed Two, and gave the lad a small wave. The men working in Shed Four paid no apparent notice as Brody entered. He let his eyes wander to scout the exits as well clusters of workers and rail cars. When Tommy reached the opening, Brody nodded him toward the right-hand tracks, where two men were working under a coach.

"Hey, kid. Whad'ya doing? Get outta here."

"I'm looking for my uncle."

"Yeah? Who's that?" Tommy ignored them and moved on. Brody kept him in sight, walking parallel but two tracks over, as the boy moved further into the shed. A couple of sidelined rail cars blocked Brody's view of Tommy and he lost track of him. He pulled the .38 Smith & Wesson from his holster, dashed down the length of two cars and cut across several tracks. There Brody found Tommy sitting on the rear end hitch of a freight car, waiting for him.

"There's three guys in that car back there." Tommy jerked his thumb to indicate a gondola one track over where the men were wrenching levers and pulling at loading chutes. "See the one without a moustache? That's him, I think. 'Buddy.' "

"You sure?"

"I didn't get too close. But I'm pretty sure. He saw me looking at him."

"Okay, wait here." Brody holstered his pistol, and walked over to the gondola car.

"Hey, you," he called out to the man. "I'm Brody, I'm inspecting these cars for headquarters. Give a look over here. I think there's fluid leaking out." The man grumbled, pulled himself upright and followed Brody to where Tommy was concealed. As soon as they reached the boy, Brody had his right hand on his pistol, the other on the man's arm and his foot placed surreptitiously but squarely between the man's shoes. "This him?"

"Yah. That's him."

Buddy spun away and tried to run but Brody raised his leg instantly and caught him up just below the knees. Buddy spilled to the ground. Looking up, dazed, he saw Brody's drawn pistol and police badge flashing at him.

Brody had no wish to attract attention and alert Buddy's accomplices or even his co-workers. Seeing an exit at the rear of the shed, Brody led his captive outside to a fairly concealed spot between two passenger cars. "Get Patrolman Moore, will you?" Tommy hurried, as best as he was able, to where he was in sight of Frankie Moore. Tommy's whistle was nearly as sharp as Moore's own. The patrolman came on the run. Tommy hobbled back toward the Inspector, and Moore caught up with Tommy just before they reached Brody and his suspect.

CHAPTER 49

Noontime, Thursday: Like Father, Like Son

Buddy refused to answer any questions, even as to his surname, but demanded to know why he was under arrest.

Brody grinned. "You tell me; I'll tell you." After this exchange was repeated several times, their captive turned from defiant to sullenly silent as Brody and Moore marched him into the yard office. Tommy stayed outside.

Brody flashed his badge to remind the clerk that he was a police inspector.

"Know this guy? He's one of yours."

The clerk paused, warned by Buddy's expression. Only a few seconds elapsed before the clerk decided the inspector had the advantage, and identified Buddy as Declan Plunkett, Jr.

"Got any other Plunketts working the yards?"

"Declan Plunkett, Senior."

"This guy's father?"

"Not sure."

"They got the same name and you don't know if they're related?"

The clerk shrugged.

"Any way to find out?," pressed Brody.

"Check with the office in the terminal."

Brody turned to his subordinate, "Patrolman, take this guy outta here." To the clerk he demanded "Hand me your telephone."

But once Declan "Buddy" Plunckett was outside, the clerk was forthcoming. "His father should be in Shed 1, over there." Brody crossed to the one small window. The clerk was pointing at a shed they had just passed.

"Describe the father."

"Like what?"

"Tall or short for a start."

"I dunno. Prob'bly medium, you know?"

"No I don't. Is he taller or shorter than me?"

"Shorter, I guess."

"Fatter or thinner?"

"Fatter, I guess."

"Older or younger?"

"Older."

Brody picked up the telephone again. This time he put through his call. "This is Inspector Brody from Headquarters. Who's this? Sergeant Riordan? You're on desk patrol, right? Look, I'm with your Patrolman Moore down at the South Union car barns. How fast can you get me an officer here? I got a man in custody I want booked and Moore and I are after a second guy...." "Ten minutes? Send him to the little office building just inside the gate off Dot Ave. Tell him to be quiet; I don't want him to scare off my other guy."

Brody hung up the phone. "Stay in here until I get back." The clerk nodded. "And just to be sure you don't make any telephone calls, I'll be sending in Patrolman Moore to keep you company."

Outside, Brody told Patrolman Moore to move inside with "our new friend," indicating Buddy Plunkett, "while the kid and me take a look. You up to it, Tommy? How's the foot holding out?"

"Okay."

"Okay, then. Let's find him. Shed One. Same as we did last time, right?"

"Right."

Shed One was smaller than the ones built later; consequently it seemed more crowded and noisier. Again Tommy walked down the right side of the shed and Brody took the center route. They met at the back end of the shed. Tommy had seen no one that resembled the man called "Pop." They crossed the back of the shed and began walking, together this time, up the left aisle.

"That's him!" Tommy had tried to speak softly, but the man exiting the water closet ahead must have heard Tommy's exited whisper and, quickening his pace, hobbled across a couple of tracks and tried to lose himself in a cluster of cars. Brody bolted after him. Tommy knelt on the ground to peer beneath the intervening rail cars and follow their feet but soon lost sight of both men.

The man's route had taken him in the direction of two coaches. He could be inside or under either one. Brody circled and looked under both cars. That there were other men working under the coaches, didn't help his view, but Pop Plunkett appeared not to be among them. Brody stepped up into one of the passenger cars and sped down the aisle, stopping midway only to check both lavatories. As he exited the car, he spied his man running out of the shed's front opening.

When Brody reached the entrance, he saw the man ahead by 50 or more paces but starting to stumble whether from age, poor condition or drunkenness. Less than a minute later, Brody nabbed Plunkett well inside the gate just as the man fell panting stale alcohol fumes. A hackney pulled to a stop in front, and a policeman jumped onto the sidewalk. Seeing the uniform, Pop frantically tried to wrest free of Brody's grasp. Then, spotting his son emerge from the yard office in a patrolman's custody, Plunkett senior stopped struggling and dropped again to the ground. Sitting on the gravel, he looked confounded.

"Don't say nothin', Pop. They won't tell me the charge."

"Have you that many crimes to your discredit, Buddy," riposted Brody, "that you don't know which one caught you up? Handcuff his father, too, and we'll take 'em both in." Brody had deliberately called the older man Buddy's father and noted with satisfaction that neither suspect had denied the relationship. Indeed, Buddy had addressed Declan senior as "Pop."

Both suspects were handcuffs and pushed into the hackney that had brought the third policeman from Station Four. The driver's curiosity had trumped his desire to find another fare, and he had been transfixed by the struggle and arrest. The officer that Brody had requested for assistance hadn't really been needed, as it turned out, and five men and a boy made for a crowded trip back to the station house, but Brody like to have the odds on his side.

All-in-all, Brody felt buoyed. He was pretty sure the Plunketts, both father and son, were the culprits; the boy's identification of them had been certain.

The cab pulled up in front of 56 Lagrange Street, and Brody and the two patrolmen ushered their prisoners into the station house. Tommy was told to stay in the hackney as Brody would only be a few minutes.

Sergeant Riordan?" called Brody.

"Hello? Ah, Inspector Brody. Got a couple of guests for us?"

"They're yours 'till I get back here late afternoon. Hold 'em both on suspicion of grand larceny," Brody looked steadily at Moore, in effect telling the young patrolman not to question the booking. "Put them in separate cells. Far apart. I don't want them cooking up any stories together. Patrolman Moore, it's unpleasant duty to stick you with the company of these two hooligans for the afternoon. Are you up to it?"

"Absolutely, Inspector."

As Brody passed behind Frankie on his way out, he whispered, "When I return, you can sit in on the questioning. Maybe help."

"Thank you, sir."

Brody fairly skipped down the eight granite steps and across the sidewalk into the waiting cab. It was one o'clock already, but Portridge Arms was barely five minutes ride away. "Tommy, me boyo, I think we deserve our fine lunch today. Maybe some smoked shoulder or beef stew? Whad'd'ya say, lad. What're the chances?"

Tommy looked at the inspector for a moment. Calculating the advisability of winning a sure bet, he decided against it. "Nope. I don't think neither one."

"Well this lawyer fellow is coming, too, and your Miss Lavinia seems pretty impressed by him. I expect that'll be reason enough for the old girls to put on the dog."

'Nope. Won't be no dog neither," deadpanned Tommy. He had decided to string Brody along a bit."

The inspector eyed Tommy. "Clever one, aren't you."

Tommy decided a short chuckle would rescue him, and added "Sir, they don't eat meat."

"None at all? Never? How 'bout fish?" Chicken? Each question brought a shake of the head from Tommy. "Sweet Jesus! That's sad news, hungry as I am."

"The food's good, though—and lots of it," assured Tommy. By now the hackney was halting in front of 146 Castle Street a few minutes after one o'clock.

"Oh, yeah. You said something this morning about 'never knowing you weren't eating meat.' I didn't get what you meant. Well, there's always a first time for everything." Brody pushed the bell and reflexively brushed his hands over his suit. He saw that the seat and knees of Tommy's overalls had already picked up dirt and soot, and he took his hand to Tommy's backside just as Florrie opened the front door. Brody quickly doffed his hat.

"Inspector. Delighted you could make it. Come in please. My sister and Mr Pierce are in our dining room." She pronounced the attorney's name correctly as "purse" as a hint to the inspector. "We're just about ready to serve. And, you, Tommy? How's my hero. Ah, look at your new clothes. You look quite the handsome young fellow, if already a bit soiled." She had a hint for Tommy as well. "You can use the bathroom on the second floor, and then join us in the dining room."

CHAPTER 50

Thursday Noon: Food for Thought

Meals were planned in advance to develop the week's shopping list and ensure variety at table. Today's lunch with Attorney Pierce and Inspector Brody, with only a day's notice to prepare, had to be fitted into the normal schedule of cooking, cleaning and record-keeping. Fortunately, Cora was on hand Thursday mornings to clean and dust.

Earlier, Florrie had surveyed the contents of their ice boxes and cold storage. She decided that her version of dosas, a South Indian dish her father loved, was the most sensible choice for lunch. Cooked potatoes, cabbage and green peas left from previous meals gave her a head start on preparations. The cold leftovers were cut up and mashed into a mixture of hot, freshly chopped leeks sautéed in margarine with curry leaves, crushed cumin and cardamom seeds, powdered turmeric, chopped garlic and a hint of asafoetida. She placed the mixture in the 'dragon's' warming oven, where the spices could heat throughout the mash while she turned her hands to the dosas.

Because Lavinia had promised Agnes a few hours off starting at noon, Florrie thought it best to have Agnes, whose culinary skill had not yet progressed beyond boiling and frying, prepare the salad of lettuce, apples, walnuts, white mushrooms and cold string beans. "Best to start with the beans. After you blanch them—you know how, don't you?—then marinate them with several cloves of shaved garlic and olive oil. Use enough oil and herbs, and that'll be dressing enough. Do see if we have apples, dear? Oh, while you're there," called Florrie, "see if you can find a couple of plums." The cold storage bins yielded two of each fruit, and those proved enough in Florrie's estimation. "I'll take the plums; you leave the apples for the salad. I don't want them peeled or sliced until the last minute or they go brown on you." Agnes shot her a glance rather than say "Any fool knows that."

After she completed paying bills, Lavinia polished the dining room table and buffet and dressed both with delicately embroidered linens. The sisters had a trunk filled with similar treasures, all brought home from their father's various travels, but occasions to use such finery were infrequent. Mr Boniface came by in time to help Lavinia set the table and buffet. Once Lavinia was satisfied with the way things looked in the dining room, she helped Cora finish the usual midweek housework. By noon, Cora was done with her half day of cleaning and had left for home. Agnes, who had run upstairs to freshen up and change to her street clothes, wasn't far behind in leaving Portridge Arms.

Mr Boniface came downstairs to inquire whether there was something else he could do. "Ah!, Mr Boniface. Just in the nick of time. I neglected dessert. Would you go to the new Syrian bakery down the street? I think it's called Sami's." Florrie wiped her hands on her apron, extracted a five dollar bill from her cache of cash in the spice drawer and handed it to Mr Boniface. "Perhaps an assortment of baklava and almond cookies, do you think? Or whatever they have that looks good to you." Mr Boniface, minus his cloak, quickly left for Sami's.

Rather than the expected lentil or chutney dipping sauces for the dosas, Florrie whipped up a white sauce to which she added dried mustard, lime juice, brown sugar, raisins and a generous tablespoon of grated ginger. After the sauce had thickened and the flavors permeated, Florrie added thin slices of plum and poured the sauce into a covered bowl with a ladle so that each diner could serve himself.

Florrie always kept rice flour on hand; she liked the crispness it added to the usual white flour or oatmeal she used in pancakes. This time her pancake mixture was roughly half and half rice and wheat flours, with sufficient chick pea flour added for taste yet still keeping the batter more a thin gruel than a batter one would form for puffy pancakes. When it was almost time to serve dinner, Florrie would then quickly fry a large batch of good-sized dosa, which were very thin, nearly crisp pancakes, rather like eggless crepes.

Daily breakfasts and dinners were the usual order of the day and had their own timetables. Everyone knew exactly what to do. An unscheduled meal had less order to it. Florrie looked at the clock. "Oh, dear, its quarter to one. I'd better start the dosas." Fortunately, Mr Boniface had returned in time to help. So quietly had he had entered the kitchen from outdoors, a box of dessert in either hand, that Florrie hadn't heard him, but only spotted him out of the corner of her eye as he laid the two boxes of dessert from the bakery on the table. "Thank heavens you're back, Mr Boniface. Things are getting a bit out of my hands. Would you make tea and coffee?" Once he had set water to boil, he lifted a platter from a cupboard to arrange the cookies.

"We need fruit juice. Tommy shouldn't drink coffee or tea. I hope there's still some apple cider. Oh, but I'm putting sliced apple into the salad; now I don't know what to do."

"Shall I make some hot cocoa for the lad?"

"Mr Boniface, you unfailingly offer sensible solutions. Thank you. I'm quite in a dither. Where's my sister? Do you know?"

"Upstairs. We came home together. She was coming into the bakery just as I was leaving."

"Oh, bother! I'm getting so rattled. I forgot Lavinia told me she'd take care of dessert. Ah, Sami *did* have almond cookies today. Yummy. I always find the baklava too sweet, but most people seem to like it."

Mr Boniface opened the larger paper box. "Two spice cakes with walnuts. Miss Lavinia said it would save you the trouble of making something for tonight's dessert."

"How lovely. I hope I remember to thank Lavinia. Where's Agnes gone?"

"Upstairs or out, I believe. Miss Lavinia gave her a few hours off."

"Lordy, I'm getting rattled; I completely forgot." She glanced at the clock again. "Heavens, I need to get a wiggle on." Florrie managed to turn out two dozen small dosas from the griddle and two fry pans in quick succession. As each dosa browned, Florrie quickly removed it from the frying pan, spooned a thick ribbon of spiced potato, cabbage and pea filling across the dosa, rolled it up and arranged the lot into two large covered-baking dishes she had kept heated in the warming oven.

After Florrie had fried, stuffed and rolled the last dosa and placed it in a baking dish, Boniface took both covered dishes from the warming oven and loaded them into the dumb-waiter along with the pots of tea and coffee and a jug of hot cocoa and sent the 'bump-up' to the dining room. Florrie quickly peeled and sliced two apples into the salad, tossed the ingredients with a light oil and lime dressing and carried it upstairs. It was only a few minutes past one o'clock when Boniface and Florrie unloaded the dumbwaiter's contents onto the dining room buffet.

Gathered around the dining table were Mr Pierce, Inspector Brody, Lavinia Portridge, Mr Boniface and Tommy Shields. Dressed variously, they made for an odd assortment. Lavinia and Mr

Boniface wore their usual severe black; Tommy sported his new dungarees and flannel; the Inspector wore a dark blue serge suit, shiny in spots; and Mr Pierce had donned a sharply-creased grey-on-grey pinstriped worsted. Florrie, before she left the kitchen, had doffed her chef's apron and cooking gloves for a bright red and gold Chinese tunic over a long and full madras skirt that sported the remainder of the brighter colors in the spectrum.

Although the purpose was serious the mood was convivial. Boarding house rules were encouraged: the diners served themselves, reaching across the table, asking others to pass a particular dish or waiting as one dish was passed down the line and around to the other side.

Mr Boniface felt ill at ease among so many people placed so closely together. Twice he had tried to get up from the table to help with serving and to escape the chatter, but Florrie wouldn't hear of it. Tommy, for the first time, had not needed to be reminded to visit the water closet before sitting down to eat.

Inspector Brody noticed that several heads were bowed in what he assumed was a silent grace before the meal. As soon as their heads were lifted, he announced, "This morning, thanks to our young lad, here, we arrested the two men who tried to burn your house down. Tommy positively identified them. We're letting them stew in their cells over at the Fourth. It'll a be a while before a lawyer or anyone else knows where to find them. Give them time to contemplate their sins." Tommy blushed brightly as those at the table clapped and Brody extended his big paw to squeeze Tommy's shoulder.

Small talk between Brody and Pierce along with periodic compliments about the meal, interrupted or amended by Florrie, carried them through lunch. Lavinia had left the dining room door open and positioned herself at the table to give her a good view of the stairway.

When the diners finished eating, Lavinia rose to clear the table of some dishes and block Brody's view of Mrs Cormier hurrying Alice and the two boys down the stairs. "I believe all our lodgers have left for their matinees by now, so perhaps we should go downstairs and begin to share what information we have about the murder and the attempted arson. Not that I think they are linked necessarily, but perhaps as we piece things together some pattern may emerge."

Mr Boniface, anxious to leave the confines of a dinner table, volunteered to make fresh tea and coffee and bring it to the sisters' private parlor.

"Thank you, Mr Boniface. I'll give you a hand. Flora, will you bring the rest of the cookies?"

CHAPTER 51,

Thursday Afternoon: Pieces of the Puzzle

Florrie led the way downstairs, tray in hand until Mr Pierce gallantly relieved her of it, fearful she might trip on the hem of her long billowing skirt. Brody, Pierce, Tommy and Florrie were settled comfortably in arm chairs when Lavinia appeared holding a tray of fresh cups, saucers, spoons and napkins. Mr Boniface soon joined them with a tray containing a pot each of tea and coffee and servers of cream and sugar.

"Thank you both. Mr Boniface will you stay, please?" Lavinia continued: "Inspector, I doubt that you feel able to disclose what your investigation has uncovered, so may I suggest we tell you what we know? I'm sure we'll all try to avoid extraneous comments..." Lavinia directed a cautioning glance at Florrie, "...and be as straightforward as possible."

"Go right ahead, Ma'am—Miss Lavinia." In truth, Brody was relieved to conceal how little he actually had discovered about either incident.

"Thank you, Inspector. The number of people who may have had access to Miss Rice on Monday night includes, at the very least, everyone who worked at the Tremont—all the other acts, the backstage crew and front-of-the-house personnel. Far too many to sort through right now. And, unless anyone here has some inkling of a possible motive for revenge other than professional jealousy"—Lavinia scanned the faces of those at the table and settled on Brody's—"I think possible motives are as many or as unknown as there are suspects, so may I suggest we follow the events of the past week and see where they take us? As far as we know at present, Miss Rice was at home in Providence when she was first contacted about performing at the Tremont. Perhaps, Mr Pierce, might it not be sensible to start with what Miss Rice told you?"

A bit taken aback to discover that the inquiry would begin with him, Pierce coughed slightly and wiped his mouth with his napkin while he ordered his thoughts.

"Rosetta—Miss Rice didn't like to use the telephone, so on Saturday I sent her a telegram asking to meet to discuss business. We met for lunch in her hotel tearoom later that afternoon."

"Doing business on a Saturday? Isn't that unusual?"

"Perhaps for some, Inspector, but I have a limited client list, and I try to accommodate myself to their needs and schedules. Anyway, after we concluded our business, Miss Rice informed me that, on the previous day, Friday, a Mr Furst offered Miss Rice a contract to play the Tremont this week and that she had accepted."

"Who's Furst?" asked Brody.

"Nathan Furst," popped in Florrie, "an agent from the Boston branch of the United Booking Office."

"Yes, quite right," continued Pierce. "Anyway, from what she told me, Mr Furst took the train down from Boston to make the offer in person. I gather that is quite unusual."

"Quite!" Florrie ignored Lavinia's sharp stare.

"It seemed so," added Pierce. "Perhaps Mr Furst understood that Miss Rice had no intention of returning to the stage."

"So why did she accept?"

"Ah, well, Inspector, Miss Rice was an astute businesswoman, and he made her an offer she couldn't resist."

"How much?"

Pierce felt very uncomfortable revealing details of a client's business, even one gone to her reward, but he realized the amount could be germane to the investigation. His reply of "$750 plus all expenses" brought a gasp from everyone at the table.

"For a single week?" Florrie demanded.

"Yes. One week only, two shows a day starting Monday night."

"That's unheard of." Florrie was astounded. "Of course, headliners like May Irwin or Eddie Foy may command that, but Rosetta hadn't been active in several years, and she wasn't the headliner."

"It would seem that someone wanted Rosetta Rice to come to Boston very much." Lavinia's comment directed others at the table to the same conclusion, if they hadn't already reached it themselves.

"So this guy, Furst, offers her all this money to come to Boston for one ..." Brody didn't get to finish before Florrie explained. "Mr Furst worked for the United Booking Office, so any offer he made above the standard had to have been approved by the office. Unless he were willing to pay $750 dollars out of his own pocket, it was someone else who authorized him to meet her price."

"It's my understanding that Miss Rice and Mr Furst concluded their negotiations rather quickly," said Pierce. "Miss Rice was not one to dicker. She knew what she wanted in business matters, so Mr Furst must have been empowered to meet her price if he couldn't bargain with her."

"I think an act in the number four spot might earn as much as $175," Lavinia speculated, "possibly even $250, for a week's booking at the Tremont, but not more. After all, it's not as if the Tremont were Keith's New Theatre. I doubt the Tremont talent budget for a week is more than $2000. Florrie? You're the one who faithfully reads the *trades*."

"I'd say $2000 was about right," confirmed Florrie. "And I doubt that Bert and Maud, who are the headliners—with a large flash act—get less than $750. That plus Rosetta's salary would leave $500 to pay all the other seven acts. No, no. Not possible. A theatre manager would be hard pressed to justify exceeding his weekly talent budget. Only some extraordinary circumstance could persuade him to do that. He'd be operating in the red and have to answer to the owners."

Brody injected himself back into the discussion. "The way I see it, this manager guy..." Brody flipped through his notebook searching for the name.

"Laurence Simpson," supplied Florrie

"Simpson, yeah. Well anyway. My question is if he really wanted Rosetta Rice, why didn't he hire her in the first place."

Lavinia smiled. It was exactly the point she had made to the Inspector yesterday, but she held her tongue.

Pierce spoke up. "Perhaps he wanted to. Perhaps Miss Rice turned him down prior to Friday, and that could be why he sent the fellow from the booking office down ..." And here Pierce faltered. "...although I assume that's not usual for a booker...?"

"Not at *all* usual, Mr Pierce," advised Florrie. "It's the performer—or, more customarily, the performer's agent—who seeks out the booker."

"So it would seem, in my sister's words," chimed in Lavinia, "that an 'extraordinary circumstance' must have prevailed. The question then is what was that extraordinary circumstance."

There was a temporary silence while Florrie, Lavinia, Pierce and Brody considered the question. Dudley Pierce was the first to speak, and he did so carefully. "There was another matter. One of confidentiality that I've been hesitant to discuss for professional reasons. You see, I feel—I have felt—legally bound to honor my promise, but Miss Rice's murder seems to have rendered my obligation moot."

Brody cut in. "You're losing me, Mr Pierce."

"Sorry. I'll try to be clearer. My purpose in meeting Miss Rice on Saturday was not to discuss her engagement at the Tremont. In fact, I wasn't aware of that until she told me at lunch. I needed to talk to her about a proposal I had received..." Here Pierce paused. "I don't know who made the offer, but it was relayed to me through a reputable New York law firm—I'm honor-bound not to disclose the name of the firm. The offer was to purchase Rosetta Rice's stock in Ira Wood Enterprises."

It took everyone a few moments for the implications of that information to register and direct them toward a new avenue of inquiry. Florrie was first off the mark. "My question, Mr Pierce, is impertinent but, I think you'll agree, necessary. Did Rosetta own a substantial portion of Wood Enterprises?"

"Her holdings in Wood Enterprises represented a significant portion of her assets, but whether it amounted to a substantial portion of ownership of Wood Enterprises, I couldn't say."

"Secretary of State's office." Brody's comment was largely a note to himself. "I'll have someone in the Chief Inspector's office check on the filings. That should tell us what percentage..."

Mr Pierce interrupted: "I think that unlikely, Inspector. While the Secretary of State's office will have annual filings, those filings list only the officers of the corporation and its directors. Not stockholders."

Lavinia heard the telephone jangle in her office. "Excuse me. I'll see to that."

Brody raised his hands to command attention. "I think maybe we're getting off the track here. What does it matter how much her stock was worth unless someone was trying to steal it? And how do you steal stock? From what Mr Pierce says, somebody was wanting to buy it. No, I think we're looking at revenge or..."

"I'm sorry, Inspector," butt in Mr Pierce, but I can't accept that. Rosetta was never one to let personal or professional matters get out of hand. Perhaps it is mere coincidence—the offer to buy her Ira Wood stock and her being paid an exorbitant salary to play in one of Wood's theatres, but..."

"Maybe it's a coincidence or maybe there's a connection," continued the Inspector. "But if it isn't just a coincidence then explain to me what and where's the connection. How do you connect a legitimate offer to buy stock to a murder?" Brody sat back expectantly and not without satisfaction. He was willing to listen but, when all this palaver was over, he was going to Mrs Cormier's room and see what he could find there.

Lavinia reappeared at the door. "Inspector, it's for you. I'll show you the way."

Murmured questions from Florrie to Mr Pierce ceased when Lavinia returned a minute later to the drawing room. "I think it better that we suspend our discussion for the moment, until the Inspector returns. Please help yourself to dessert, Mr Pierce. More coffee or tea?"

CHAPTER 52

Thursday Mid-Afternoon: a New Angle

The phone connection was tenuous, even though Patrolman Moore was calling from the nearby Lagrange Street stationhouse. Most likely, the interference stemmed from telephone lineman laying more cable and hooking up more businesses and homes to telephone service. The telephone company was hard pressed to meet rapidly escalating customer demands.

"Your office is trying to contact you, Inspector. Some guy, a Mr Furst, wants to talk about Rosetta Rice. He's up at headquarters. What do you want me to tell them?"

"Tell them I'll be there in a half an hour or so. Meantime, you tell Riordan I said to have someone keep an eye on the two guys we brought in; he'll take care of it. I don't want those two knuckleheads to get the chance to cook their stories. Then you get a hackney and come get me at the Porridge Sisters."

Brody was back in the drawing room in a matter of minutes. He looked at Dudley Pierce. "That was my office. Patrolman Moore will be picking me up in about ten minutes, so I need to wrap this up for now. Where were we?," he asked as an invitation for Pierce to resume his narrative.

Pierce sipped his tea while he reclaimed his thoughts. "Well, when I told Miss Rice about the offer to purchase her stock, she mentioned that it hadn't paid a dividend in some time so she was quite willing to part with it, especially since the offer was above market value. However, she insisted that I notify Ira Wood that she was prepared to accept the offer yet willing to allow him five business days to match it. From what Rosetta said, I believe that the senior Mr Woods had made the stock available to her at a discount prior to going public with a common stock offering.

"So, maybe, some years ago, Rosetta Rice had an affair with the old man?"

Pierce's voice sharpened. "Inspector, that is unwarranted. Miss Rice *was* one of the stage beauties of her day, but she was as intelligent and level-headed as she was glamorous. Many successful men are attracted to those qualities in a woman." If Pierce had intended this last remark to be a slight to Brody, he didn't underscore it. Others at the table were likely more apt to have noted that Pierce had employed the present tense and, thus, revealed his own partiality to Rosetta Rice's charms. "It's true that more than a few men took an interest in her, but whatever may have prompted that interest, it soon turned paternal and protective. These were successful men who liked to be seen with her and appreciated her common sense and humor. They guided her to invest wisely for her future."

"Still..."

"Yesterday, my office left a message for me at the Touraine that Ira Wood had telegraphed them that morning. Although he offered his condolences and regretted such a thing could have happened to Miss Rice in one of his theatres, the point of his telegram was to state that whether Miss Rice's death had rendered her offer void or not, he was not interested in buying back her stock."

Pierce's tone had quieted when he returned to his account of his meeting with Rosetta the previous Saturday. "When I told Miss Rice last Saturday that I didn't know on whose behalf the offer had been made, I recall that she speculated that it might be a blind offer made on behalf of—let's see—Early and some other name.

"Erlanger?"

"Yes, that it."

"And Shubert?"

"I think so."

"Aha!" Florrie declaimed melodramatically. "Erlanger and Shubert! They've been trying to buy up theatres in cities where they could go toe-to-toe with Keith and Albee!" Florrie's voice shifted to a confidential tone. "Victor Greeley explained it all to me yesterday. He even knew they were negotiating for a chain of vaudeville theatres just outside Boston, but he couldn't say which one."

"Except for the Tremont, I believe all of Ira Wood's theatres are outside Boston, from Cambridge up to New Hampshire." It was Mr Boniface's first contribution to the discussion.

"Thank you, Mr Boniface. I think you've hit on it. Abe Erlanger and Lee Shubert could very well have been the ones to make the offer to Rosetta though their New York attorneys—or maybe someone acting on their behalf. The Tremont's only a couple of blocks away from Keith's New Theatre on Washington Street, and I'll bet that other of Woods theatres are located close to other Keith houses in Massachusetts." Given the looks on the faces around the table, it seemed only Lavinia grasped Florrie reasoning.

"Don't you see?," Florrie continued, "Abe Erlanger and Lee Shubert wanted to cut into vaudeville, so they'd have to take on Keith, Albee and their United Booking Office. Building new theatres would take too long and be far too expensive. What smarter way to challenge Keith than acquire a controlling interest in rival theatres at a fraction of the probable purchase price?" Florrie paused while her reasoning began to take hold among others at the table.

"According to Victor, the entire effort by the United States Amusement Company—that's what Erlanger and Shubert call their sham enterprise—is turning out to be a way of pressuring Keith and Albee to buy them off. I truly doubt that the offer you received, Mr Pierce, for Rosetta's stock, was bona fide. According to Victor Greeley, whose instincts, I must say, are as reliable as his information, both sets of scoundrels have already reached an agreement; one that will be announced within a few weeks."

"So, that's common knowledge?," asked Brody.

"Now it may be, I suppose. But not last week. Certainly not outside the profession."

"Not to lawyers?, suggested Pierce.

"Probably the law firm in New York was acting in good faith," Florrie assured him. "I doubt they'd be privy to all the behind-the-scenes machinations."

"Suppose someone had wished to block the sale?" All eyes turned to Lavinia. "Then we have a possible motive for her murder."

"Good heavens, Lavinia! I hadn't thought of that." Florrie's comment was lost in a jumble of murmurs.

"Hold on, folks," commanded Brody. "Let's not get ahead of ourselves. I can see your point, Miss Lavinia, but who would have a reason to stop it? I don't know Mr Keith or this Albee guy, but I've met Mrs Keith. She's a pillar of the Church, a good friend of Cardinal O'Connor. I don't figure any of the Keiths to be sneaking in some theatre and cutting Miss Rice's throat." His vivid description of the cause of Rosetta's death reminded everyone that her murder wasn't simply a ploy in some business shenanigans but a horrid act that required a killer who didn't shy from bloodying his hands.

"Of course not, Inspector," countered Lavinia, "but those who are squeamish about violence, if they have the means, can hire others to do their dirty work."

Although he had seemed to withdraw from the conversation, it was Mr Boniface who spoke up: "If Mr Keith and Mr Albee were negotiating with Mr Erlanger and Mr Shubert, none of them would have reason to prevent a sale of stock that was not destined to take place."

"Once again Mr Boniface," exulted Florrie, "you have put the matter squarely before us. So now the question is who else would have reason to prevent the sale of stock?"

"Or," Lavinia amended, "*why* would someone wish to prevent the sale?"

CHAPTER 53

Thursday Afternoon: Pemberton Square Police HQ

Nathan Furst had been waiting for an hour since his initial meeting with the Assistant Chief Inspector. Each time he rose from the hard wooden bench outside the Assistant Inspector's office to inquire how much longer he had to wait for Inspector Brody, the desk sergeant assured him it was only a matter of minutes. As each of those minutes ticked into the next, Furst's unease increased until he began to regret his decision to volunteer the little information he had concerning Rosetta Rice's murder.

The agent was gathering his hat, overcoat and briefcase, ready to depart, when the Inspector clumped down the hall with Patrolman Moore at his heels. Furst rose and walked toward the exit stairs as Brody sailed past Furst into the Assistant Chief Inspector's office. Halfway down the hall, Furst heard Brody call him back.

Brody directed Nathan Furst and Frankie Moore to his small office and sat Mr Furst in the only visitor's chair. At a nod from Brody, Patrolman Moore made a seat of sorts on the sill of the only window. Brody made an expansive gesture as he eased back in the chair behind his desk. "What can I do for you, Mr Furst?"

Somewhat taken aback at the Inspector's seeming lack of familiarity with his purpose in coming to the police, Furst's reply failed to hide a hint of irritation. "I'm here as a good citizen, Inspector. I took time out of my busy day to speak to the police about what little I know about the circumstances regarding Miss Rosetta Rice's death this past Monday. Your superior informed me that you were the inspector in charge of the case."

"That I am, Mr Furst." Brody did not go beyond that single statement. From the conversation at the Portridge Arms luncheon, he was mindful that Nathan Furst was an agent experienced in negotiation, and Furst's resentment at being kept waiting suggested that the agent was used to being in command of situations. If Brody pressed questions, Furst might turn defensive and withhold information. Brody decided to mute his obvious interest in the case and let agent Furst convince him of the importance and relevance of his part in the drama.

"Perhaps you don't understand, Inspector. I am a senior associate at the United Booking Office here in town. It was me who brought Rosetta Rice to Boston to play the Tremont."

"Go on, Mr Furst. How does that connect you to her murder?"

"Inspector!, I'm not connected to anybody's murder. All I did was go to Providence and make her an offer to play the Tremont."

"Sorry, Mr Furst. What I meant was that if hiring Miss Rice was your only role in this case, why did you come to the police?" Brody silently congratulated himself on using the word 'role.'

"Like I said, I'm a good citizen, and I wanted to make myself available in case I could help. Of course, all I know is Miss Rice agreed last Saturday to perform at the Tremont. We reached terms, and I came back to Boston."

"Sure. I understand." Brody rose from his chair as if to end the interview. "And I appreciate your public spirit, Mr Furst—that you took time out of a busy day to volunteer your assistance." Just as Furst began to rise from his chair. Brody slipped around his desk and sat on its front edge, his knees little more than a foot from the agent's chest. "You know, I'm a bit out of my field here; I don't know much about the show business, Mr Furst. Perhaps you could explain it some to me?"

Nathan regarded the question uncertainly and Brody's looming, uncomfortably close presence warily. "What can I tell you, Inspector?"

"Well, I'm a bit of a fan of the vaudevilles, and I always wonder how you find all those different actors—acts? That what you call 'em, right? Anyway, every week you offer a different show."

Furst nodded and casually rose from his chair to redress the subordinate physical position Brody had imposed upon him. "Variety is the game. You gotta put together a bill that has something for everyone." Furst moved to the window, ostensibly to look out upon the city, then turned to face Brody. "That's our job at the U.B.O.—that's the United Booking Office. We're the largest booking service for vaudeville theatres east of the Mississippi—probably in the whole U.S.A. I make it my business to know every good act in the business."

Brody had his opening. "So you knew Miss Rice personally?"

Furst pulled back. "No, not personally. Professionally. Only professionally. She was a famous act, you know."

"Like you said, Mr Furst, Rosetta Rice *was* a famous act." Brody circled in back of Furst's chair. "But she retired a few years ago, right? What made you think she wanted to come back into vaudeville?" He was facing Furst when he posed his next question. "Why did you choose to go to Providence and pay her a fortune to come to Boston for a single week?"

Furst hadn't seen it coming, but, instead of getting flustered, Furst calmly steeled himself. "We needed a top act—one that was available on short notice. Rosetta Rice lived in Providence, a quick and easy train ride from Boston, and I knew she was at liberty."

"At liberty?"

"Not currently working."

"That makes sense," allowed Brody, "but even if she was willing, how could she do it? She was retired, right? Hadn't performed in years—three or four years?"

Furst nodded.

"So what about costumes, music and a piano player?" Brody was glad of his lunch-time tutorial, but Furst was no pushover.

The agent smiled patronizingly. "Performers are like firehouse dogs, Inspector. They hear the bell, they come running. Show business is an exciting profession, and most performers cannot resist the thrill. Maybe Miss Rice wanted to see if she still had the magic. I was pretty sure she still had all her old costumes and music. They all do."

"Were you sure she still had the magic?"

"A talent like that? Sure she had it. And, when I met her. I saw she was still a looker with a fine figure."

"So, you just made an offer and she accepted? Just like that?"

"Like I said, she was a professional, and she knew her worth. She clipped me for a hefty fee. More than I usually offer, but I needed an act on short notice, so I had to pay a bit more than usual."

"Your idea of a bit more is $750 plus expenses?"

Realizing that Brody could know this figure only if he had talked with Dudley Pierce, Nathan paused before he spoke. "My instructions were to find a top talent on short notice. I was authorized to offer an unusually high fee to secure those services."

Brody wasn't satisfied. "Were you told specifically to engage Miss Rice?"

"That booking was recommended."

"By who?"

"I work for the United Booking Office and follow their directives."

"Are you telling me that the U.B.O., as you call it, directed you to engage Miss Rice and go as high as you went—$750 for one week's work? Before you answer, Mr Furst, let me tell you that we will check your story with your boss, Mr Hodgdon."

Nathan's eye muscles twitched slightly yet visibly, and he shifted in his seat. "My orders came from Ira Woods Enterprises, one of our U.B.O. clients. I assumed that they cleared it earlier with Mr Hodgdon. It was Joshua Wood who telegraphed me Friday evening at my home—after business hours. I had to leave for Providence the next morning. There wasn't time to check in with my office."

"A business call after hours to hire a retired singer at $750 for a week without any confirmation by your boss, and you go along with that?"

"I do what I'm told, Inspector. Show business is never usual. It's always unusual."

"And murder makes it more exciting?"

"I know nothing about that. I never saw Miss Rice after my meeting with her in Providence. Remember, Inspector, I came here like a good citizen and I've tried to be helpful. If you have any more of that type of question for me, I'll want my lawyer present. Now—can I go? I've lost a lot of time at work coming here today."

Brody nodded. Moore had slipped over to the door and opened it for a red-faced Mr Furst who quickly departed.

"Frankie, my lad, get us a cab and make it snappy. I'll see you down front." On his way out, Brody paused at the desk just outside his office and told the sergeant "Get the number for Ira Woods Enterprises in the Colonial building and telephone them. Right away. I don't care how you do it, but keep them on the line for ten minutes even if you have to keep calling every time they hang up." Brody dashed down the stairs and out the front door of police headquarters and found Patrolman Moore at the curb with a cab. Within minutes they were riding down Tremont Street to the Colonial Building. "Hurry it up," the Inspector called to the hackney driver. To Moore he added in a quiet tone, "I want to get to Joshua Wood before our friend Nathan does."

CHAPTER 54

Mid Afternoon, Thursday at Ira Wood Enterprises.

Instead of knocking first, Inspector Brody pushed open the door to Ira Wood Enterprises with a good deal of theatrical force, startling both Owen Yates and Jane Markey. When she saw the uniformed patrolman following Brody into the outer office, Miss Markey dropped the armful of files she had been carrying. Her supervisor was not as readily disarmed. "The sign says 'Knock Before Entering;' what do you want?," barked Yates.

"I'm here to see Joshua Wood." Brody and Moore had reached the front desk. "Tell him Inspector Brody is here."

"Not here." Yates turned his back on the police and resumed reviewing documents.

"Does that mean he's out?"

"Gone for the day."

"When do you expect him."

"Tomorrow. Maybe."

"Who are you?"

Yates pointed to the name plate on the edge of his desk.

"Okay, Mr Office Manager Owen Yates, put down those papers and talk to me. I'm not some hang-dog actor looking for a job; I'm Inspector Malachi Brody from Police Headquarters, and we can either talk here or up at Pemberton Square."

Jane Markey had picked up her fallen files and, quivering, retreated to the most distant file cabinet where she made busy pushing in and pulling out folders. Yates, on the other hand, regarded the inspector resignedly and without any sign of fear. "What do you want?"

"I want to see Joshua Wood." Brody struggled to control his exasperation.

"As I explained, Mr Wood, Junior, has left for the day."

"Where can I find Junior?"

"Mr Wood spends much of his day meeting with people in our business; that is all I can tell you. He doesn't inform us of his daily schedule."

"That his office?" Brody nodded to the only door other than the entrance.

"Yes."

"Let's see it."

"I'm not allowed in there; it is their private office."

"Joshua's and whose else?"

"Mr Wood, Senior's."

Brody tried the handle. It was locked. "You got the key?"

"We're not allowed in there unless asked."

"You haven't answered my question. You got a key?"

Owen Yates looked straight ahead without answering.

"Look, Yates, I'm investigating a murder at one of your theatres, as you probably figured out. Right now, there is nothing I'd like more than hauling you down to the station and holding you as an uncooperative witness. One of your company lawyers might bail you out, but believe me, it'll take a day or two, and the jail I'll park you in will be pretty rough on an old guy like you. So tell me: have you got the damn key!?"

Yates opened his desk drawer and extended the key to Brody.

"You open it."

"Miss Markey is my witness that I do so under duress."

"*Duress,* huh? That's pretty good. You some amateur lawyer? Open it!"

Brody stood at the doorway without entering and regarded the difference between the drab, utilitarian outer office and the well-appointed, wood-paneled inner office. Patrolman Moore looked over his shoulder. "Pretty fancy, eh?"

Brody didn't respond but turned to Yates. "That wasn't hard, was it? Your bosses, they come and go without you knowing?"

"During business hours, while I am here, they always enter and leave through this office."

"Maybe, when he heard me asking for him, your Mr Wood, Junior, slipped out his door?"

"He left nearly two hours ago. Around two o'clock."

"Where's the old man—Ira Wood?"

"At home, I would think. He usually comes in once a week."

"What's your name, Ma'am?" Brody had wheeled from Yates to Miss Markey.

Her mouth worked but no words came forth as she looked to Mr Yates.

Brody moved around her so that she had to turn her back to Yates to face the Inspector. "What's your name, Ma'am" Brody repeated, but in softer tones and with a smile he hoped appeared friendly.

"Miss Markey. Miss Jane Markey." Her voice was barely audible.

"And what is your position with Ira Wood Enterprises, Miss Markey?"

"I'm... I'm just the receptionist." Brody decided that this show business wasn't all that it was cracked up to be. He had expected a gorgeous Gibson girl as the receptionist and an atmosphere crackling with excitement. This joint was a dead as the police department records morgue. He pressed on.

"Surely there's more to your duties. You were filing when we came in."

"I try to help Mr Yates. Whatever he needs done."

"Tell me, Miss Markey, can you verify everything that your boss told us?"

"Oh, yes, sir."

"So, Mr Yates, as I understand it, the old man pops in once a week and the son comes in for a couple of hours most days. Have I got that right?"

"Both gentleman have responsibilities that often require their presence elsewhere."

"Well, I guess that leaves you pretty much in charge, right?"

"I do my best to carry out their instructions."

"But as you are the only one here all day, every day, you have to advise them what needs their attention, right?"

"Miss Markey and I each have worked for Mr Ira Wood for more than 20 years, Inspector. I believe we have his confidence and proved ourselves worthy of that. Much of our day-to-day work is record-keeping, handling correspondence and such. Both Mr Wood Senior and Junior prefer that we take care of those duties to allow them to focus on matters more important to the success of the company."

"Do they ever ask for your advice?"

"Rarely."

"Like when and what?"

"I'd have to think about that. As I said, 'rarely'...

If Mr Yates was about to amplify his answer it was interrupted by a knock on the door, and he called out in a harsh and surprisingly strong voice, "Come in."

Nathan Furst was unable to mask his surprise at finding Brody and Moore in the Wood Enterprises office.

"I thought we'd meet you here, Mr Furst." Brody's greeting was delivered with fake heartiness and welcome. "Glad you could make it. I guess you know Mr Yates and Miss Markey." There was a pause as no one seemed to know what to do. "No need to stand there. Come on in. I think we're both looking for the same person. He's not here; isn't that right Mr Yates?" Eliciting no response, Brody continued. "Unless you have business with Mr Owen Yates, here, why don't you and I hunt down Mr Joshua Wood? The sooner he confirms your story, the sooner you are off the hook—my hook—and the sooner you can get back to all your work that's piling up. Whad'd'ya say?"

Nathan managed to speak in a normal voice. "Mr Yates, do you have any idea where Joshua Wood might be?"

"No sir. He does not share his schedule with me."

"Ah. Well, that's all right. I'll try to find him. If I don't, tell him to contact me. Good afternoon Mr Yates. Miss Markey." Opening the door he turned to Inspector Brody. "I suppose, Inspector, that you and the officer are going to accompany me?"

"A night on the town? Wouldn't miss it."

CHAPTER 55

Thursday, Mid Afternoon: Assignments for Amateurs

Brody's abrupt departure had left Florrie, Lavinia, Mr Boniface and Mr Pierce with the feeling that little had been solved regarding the reason for killing Rosetta Rice or the identity of the murderer. True, they agreed, the matter was now firmly in the hands of the police, a matter for the Chief Inspector's department, but surely there was something they could do.

"The Inspector seems a sensible chap." As he intended, Pierce's apparently innocuous statement immediately reopened the discussion.

"But rather too wed to a particular motive," amended Lavinia.

"And doesn't understand 'the show business'," added Florrie, who considered herself a part of the profession. "He's quite off the track as to motive. I think we must look to profit rather than revenge. But who could possibly gain from Rosetta's death?"

"She had no kin. I'm sure of that. When I prepared her will, I advised her that it could be challenged by any legitimate claimants. Rosetta assured me that if she had any relatives, they were so distant as to be unknown to her." He paused for a moment. "She never spoke to me of her childhood. I suspect that she was an orphan—and she never married..."

"So, if there was no one to gain by her death, perhaps someone," suggested Florrie, "wanted to stop her from talking."

"About what, in heaven's name?," asked Lavinia.

"Wouldn't they have attempted blackmail first?," put in Mr Boniface.

"Good point, sir," acknowledged Pierce. "While Miss Rice was a most private person, I, out of necessity, handled most of her affairs, legal and financial. I'm sure I would have become aware of any unaccountable expenditures in any significant amounts."

Lavinia spoke up. "Which may bring us back to my earlier suggestion that someone may have wished to prevent the sale of her share of Ira Wood Enterprises. If that is possible, then how would someone gain from stopping Rosetta from selling?"

"Or," suggested Pierce, "if I may turn that question around a bit. How could someone *lose* if Miss Rice sold her share of the business?" The proposition prompted a thoughtful silence until Pierce resumed thinking aloud. "We've been considering the result rather than the process. The sale might or might not add to someone's wealth or threaten it. Clearly we don't know, except that several powerful men in show business were once interested in acquiring her shares. But the process of the sale may provide a motive for murder."

Lavinia was quick on the mark. "The buyers would examine the books to verify the value of the business."

"Of course!," agreed Florrie. "Just like buying peaches. Are they ripe or going mushy. I missed that entirely."

"That, Flora, is because you buy the peaches and I manage the books."

Florrie ignored Lavinia's gentle swipe. "Is there any way, Mr Pierce, that you can rightfully demand to see the books?"

"Probably. I do have Miss Rice's power of attorney and am her executor, but it could take weeks of work by an accountant to ferret out any improprieties. If there were embezzlement I expect it was done by a professional who could cover his tracks well..."

"Owen Yates!" Florrie beamed as if she had discovered the moon. "That sour old man looks just the type!"

Lavinia and Mr Pierce ignored Florrie's huffy judgment about Mr Yates but nodded in agreement with the probability that if there had been falsification of the books, then Mr Yates was either complicit or incompetent or had carelessly delegated his responsibility.

"I gather," confided Pierce, "that Wood Senior relies on Yates's bookkeeping to provide him with a weekly summary of income and expenditures, yet Ira doesn't check the accuracy of the entries themselves, and Joshua doesn't consult the books at all. That places Owen Yates in a perfect position to manipulate accounts. I don't know anything about his assistant, Miss Jane Markey."

"From what little I've seen, Mr Pierce, that timid little dormouse has neither the gumption or the guile for criminal adventure. I doubt the poor thing can do much more than file, fetch and carry for Mr Yates."

"Or—perhaps it's one of the managers or bookkeepers who work at one of the Wood's theatres who's doing the finagling," suggested Lavinia.

Pierce sighed. "Thoroughly checking one set of books is hard enough; checking six or seven component records would take more accountants, several weeks and a lot of money."

"May I ask you two questions, Mr Pierce? Does your role as executor and your power of attorney give you the authority to demand to have the books at Wood Enterprises examined?"

"It could, but I'd have to make my case for a court order."

"Thank you, Mr Pierce. Now, my sister Lavinia is far more knowledgeable than I in matters of business, so I am likely out of my depth with my second question, but could you not obtain an order to sequester—I think that's the term—the company's financial records pending an investigation of the books? Only we few know that the offer from Erlanger and Shubert is about to be withdrawn, so the offer to purchase is technically still legitimate."

"I'm afraid, Miss Flora, that you overestimate my influence. After all, I'm an interloper from Rhode Island in this affair. Ira Wood Enterprises is an important business in Massachusetts, and apparently Ira knows the governor quite well."

"Why assume that Ira Wood's interests are contrary to ours?" asked Lavinia. "If both Ira and Joshua are so removed from the details of their own business, wouldn't Ira, at least, be eager to prevent further embezzlement? Mr Pierce, perhaps if you and Ira Wood were to jointly petition to impound the books, you might make faster work of it."

"I suppose I could telephone..." Dudley Pierce got no further than that before Florrie interrupted.

"I'll bet Nathan Furst has his phone number. Or maybe the telephone operator. Ira lives in Nashua, New Hampshire. You can catch a Boston & Maine train at North Union Station and be there in a couple of hours..."

"Simmer down, Florrie. Let the man think."

"Perhaps a telephone call will prove to be all that is necessary. May I use your office, Miss Lavinia?" Lavinia ushered him to her office. When she returned, Florrie was already telling Mr Boniface that she was going to visit Mo Weiss and Petey Martin again.

"But not until after we have prepared dinner," cautioned Lavinia, who had just stepped back into the drawing room.

Florrie deflated. "Lavinia, you promised me until Friday for my investigations..."

"True, Flora, but we have a business to run, and dinner has yet to be cooked for our lodgers. We've been playing catch-as-catch-can with meals for the past two days, and it's time to present a proper meal." Lavinia forestalled a rejoinder from Florrie: "If you will take charge of dinner while I catch up on my office work, I'll work with Agnes and Tommy to clean up."

"All right. Just as long as I can get to the Tremont between the end of the matinee and before the performers return for the evening show."

"If we all get to work right away, that should work out fine. Or better yet—I shouldn't suggest this before I ask you, Mr Boniface—if you could accompany my sister—it's getting dark earlier each day—I would appreciate it. Tommy can help clean up so you can be free."

"Certainly, Miss Lavinia. I shall be pleased to accompany Miss Flora, if she will have it."

"Dear Mr Boniface, what lady in distress would not welcome such gallantry?"

Lavinia, Florrie and Mr Boniface were quitting the drawing room as Dudley Pierce walked toward them from Lavinia's office.

"Did you speak to Mr Wood, inquired Lavinia."

"Yes; I'm surprised I contacted him so easily. It occurs to me now that it was rather a bold intrusion on my part. Mr Wood was quite guarded, as any sensible person would be. I introduced myself, as well as one can by telephone, explained my professional responsibility to Miss Rice and her estate and voiced our suspicion about improprieties and the possibility of embezzlement. When I mentioned the need to quickly sequester his firm's books, he initially balked. However, if I can locate Inspector Brody and he can persuade the Assistant Chief Inspector, Joseph Dugan, then Ira Wood said he will consider it.

"That's a good start, Mr Pierce," congratulated Lavinia."

Graciousness trumped, as ever, by her enthusiasm, Florrie had already pulled Pierce's hat, overcoat and umbrella from the hall coat rack and extended them to him with the admonition, "If you hurry, you may be able to catch Inspector Brody at Station Four, on Lagrange Street, just behind the Touraine where you're staying. I hope he agrees to speak to the Chief Inspector. Shall I telephone for a hackney?"

"Thank you, no, Miss Flora. I expect I can walk there in about the same time as it would take a hackney to come here and go there. Good day ladies. Thank you for lunch. Delicious...and interesting. Good day to you, Mr Boniface."

CHAPTER 56,

Later Thursday Afternoon: Men about Town

Upon exiting the Colonial office building, Brody halted on the sidewalk and his two companions looked to him expectantly. "I think, Patrolman Moore, that you had better return to the station house. I'll see you there in a while. Better not to have a uniform around. Don't want to put the scare in young Mr Wood. Not yet anyway." Moore lost no time in following Brody's directive.

"Mr Furst, I leaned on you're a little hard today, but you have to realize I had to. You weren't giving me much. Anyway, I ask myself what have you got to gain by killing Rosetta Rice? A lost commission? It doesn't make sense for you, unless you're protecting somebody. So, until I find out more about what's been going on, I think you'd be smart to help me. You're an agent, right? Think of it as a good deal for us both, eh?"

"I got nothing to hide, Inspector. I'm not covering for anybody 'cause I don't know any more about this than you—maybe a lot less—and I sure don't need people in the business thinking I'm mixed up in this. Like you said, maybe we can help each other clear this up. But don't try to pressure me, right?"

"Right. You stay square with me and I'll do my best to keep you out of it. Now, where are we headed?"

"Joshua Wood likes to do his business informally—a little food, a few drinks and maybe a good looking working girl for dessert. Depending on who he's trying to do business with, he could be anywhere around here. Or maybe he's just boozing. One thing in our favor is he doesn't like to stray far from where he lives."

"Where's that?"

"The Touraine."

"Good. We're practically there."

"If he isn't home, we check out Jake Wirth's and then, who knows?"

"While we're looking, tell me about Wood Enterprises."

"Ira started it. Built it up from scratch. One little theatre out in the sticks. He's been grooming Joshua to take over." Nathan paused. "Anything I tell you, you don't repeat, okay? I got a reputation to keep. Businessmen gotta trust their booker. Okay?"

"Got it. So?"

"Anyway, father and son, best I can figure out, don't always agree. Hell, they don't often agree. Ira's conservative and close with the bucks; Joshua likes to flash it around."

"What about those two mummies in the office?"

"They've been there as long as I've been in show business. Yates was the old man's assistant. Then the son came into the business—sorta displaced Owen, I guess. The old gal is scared of her shadow. She does whatever Owen tells her."

"So now Yates is the son's assistant?"

"I'm not sure how it works now. Ira comes in once in a while and gets a run-down on the books, but Yates handles the finances. As far as I know, the managers of each of the Wood theatres report weekly to Yates: box office take, expenses, all that stuff. Between you and me, I doubt if Joshua can read a balance sheet."

"So the son is a dummy as well as an idler."

"No, no. Don't sell him short. The business is changing. The big boys are crowding out the small-time family operations like Wood's. Their outfit is small time. Good small time but small time. Ira probably won't admit it, even to himself, but Joshua has a good nose for what sells and how to sell it. Wood Enterprises might not still be in business without Joshua. But after he cuts a good deal, he figures he's done his job, and it's up to Owen or somebody else to wrap up the paperwork."

Brody and Furst had reached the concierge's desk in the Touraine lobby. Informed that Joshua Wood was not in, they headed out the side entrance to begin their tour of Joshua's oases with a visit to Jacob Wirth's restaurant. Nathan continued, "Yates is old—maybe as old as Ira. And Ira, I figure, is about 70. Old as he is, Owen Yates is sharp—possibly the only one who's up-to-date on all the details of the business, the accounts—all that stuff. Joshua, even Ira, they both rely on Owen."

"The guy looks ancient."

"But still sharp, Inspector, and given what I guess Ira pays Yates, I doubt the old fella has saved much. He'll work there until he keels over, or the business goes belly up."

There were few customers at Jacob Wirth's. The lunch-time crowd had returned to office desks, and those who usually gathered for a late afternoon bit of jollity before they headed homeward for the family dinner had not yet slipped out of work. A quick glance inside assured Brody and Furst that Nathan was elsewhere—somewhere livelier.

Nathan suggested they try the nearby Lagrange Street Tavern where he had found Joshua yesterday afternoon. Small, only a single room wide, the taproom occupied the first floor of a two-storey, eighteenth century brick building. Cafe curtains were drawn across the lower half of the front window, shielding its clientele from the prying eyes of passing wives or employers.

Joshua was in the rear room, flirting with a serving girl, offering her his boutonnière with one arm and trying to reach around her waist with his other. Given his conspicuous behavior and a half-empty bottle of cognac on the table, it seemed to Brody that Joshua was well on his way. "Best we walk by and let him call us to his table." Nathan nodded and led the way past.

"Nathan! Nathan Furst! Come over here. Join me." Brody and Furst waved their acceptance and took seats at his table. "Haven't seen you for weeks and now two days in a row. What'll you have, gentlemen?" To Joshua's disappointment, both men ordered coffee. Joshua extended his hand to the stranger; "I'm Joshua Wood. Nathan and I are in much the same business."

"Malachi Brody. Thanks for the invitation. Nathan and I are also involved in some business together. You own Wood Enterprises, right?"

Joshua temporarily deflected the question by refilling his glass. "My father and I do. You in the vaudeville business?"

"Not quite. I work for the city. Inspections, sort of."

"Uh, oh!" Joshua put his finger to his lips in mock horror. "Don't say *inspection* in this joint. Or better yet, do—we won't have to pay for a drink." Furst and Brody faked a semblance of laughter.

"I'm an inspector with the Police Department." Brody dropped the clarification like a bomb to see Joshua's reaction. "I'm investigating the murder of Rosetta Rice."

That information immediately put a damper on Joshua's ebullience. "Sad thing. Sad." Joshua stared at his drink. "Happened in one of *our* theatres. A *shame*." He looked up at Brody. "Don't know what else to say. Don't know much about it. My father told me yesterday—no, the day before. Your Chief Inspector telephoned him, Dad came down from Nashua yesterday—no, Tuesday—to meet with the Inspector—Chief Inspector. Even the Governor phoned Dad. They're old pals. Dad asks the Governor to allow the show to go on that night. It goes on! On the same damn day she's killed. Everybody phones my father. Nobody tells me anything. Not even the old guy in the box office who found her body. And Laurence Simpson! He's up in Lowell or Fitchburg when it happens. What the hell's he doing up there? He's supposed to be the manager of the damned Tremont!" Joshua emptied his glass.

Nathan saw his opening. "Well, at least you took care of business. You were right on it—told my office last Friday who you decided on as a replacement into the Tremont."

"Nope. Not me." Joshua poured himself another. "I wasn't even in town. Left Friday noon for Marblehead. Sailing. Visiting friends for the weekend." Joshua's attention slipped to the tawny cognac he was absently swirling in his glass snifter.

"Who did call my office, then?"

"I dunno. Maybe Father. Maybe Simpson. Maybe Yates. Maybe the Man In the Moon, for all I know." Joshua looked up smiling and softly singing a ditty from a few years past, "The Man in the Moon might tell, might tell; the...," and then his head dropped forward.

Nathan looked at Brody who nodded. Both men rose from their chairs. "Well, that caps it for me. We'd better get your friend home, Mr Furst."

Nathan plunked down a few dollars on the table and went around to Joshua. "Joshua? Joshua, come on. It's time to go. Get a little food. Come back later. Okay?"

"Okay."

Furst repeated the drill from the previous evening: into the Touraine through the service entrance and up the back stairway to Joshua's apartment.

Brody held open the barroom door. The cool autumn air seem to revive Joshua some, but not enough for him to cross the street on his own. "I'll take this side of him," volunteered Brody. "I'm headed up the street to Station Four. Gotta check on a couple of jugheads." Brody chuckled to himself: Jugheads in the jug. Not bad, or so he thought.

CHAPTER 57

Late Thursday Afternoon: Drink Does in Pop

Several hours had elapsed since Pop and Buddy Plunkett were booked, and Brody was anxious to question them. Perhaps one of them was ready to talk. He decided they could wait a few more minutes while he helped Nathan Furst steer Joshua Wood up several flights of back stairs to his apartment. Once they arrived at Joshua's door, Brody bid a quick goodbye and left Nathan to maneuver the sodden Joshua into bed. Although Brody and Furst went their separate ways, the same question nagged them both: if Joshua didn't telegram Furst to book Rosetta Rice, who did?

Dudley Pierce was waiting for the inspector at Station Four; so were Sergeant Riordan and Patrolman Moore. From the moment Brody entered the building he could hear wailing interrupted by cursing coming from the cell area. "Anyone I know?," asked Brody.

"The old boy wants a drink, and I think he's ready to sell his soul for one. We put him in the cell back there, and he was sleeping until ten minutes ago. Now he won't shut up until he gets a drink."

"What about the son? He back there, too?"

"Downstairs. In the tombs," smiled Riordan. I shoulda put the old man there instead. The son won't talk—be a nice change for us from that bellyaching."

"Okay, we'll see what we can do, but first, I guess, Mr Pierce and I have a little business?"

Pierce quickly explained that he needed Brody to contact Chief Inspector William Watts or—failing that—Assistant Chief Inspector Dugan and get either of them to back Pierce's request to examine the books at Ira Wood Enterprises.

"Oh, boy. Let me tell you, neither Watts or Dugan likes to stick his neck out…"

"I've already spoken to Ira Wood himself," added Pierce. He'll go along with the request to sequester the books if the Chief Inspector supports our theory that someone is embezzling from Ira Wood."

"Whose theory is that?"

Rather than respond directly, Pierce gently suggested to Brody that "the profitability and integrity of Ira Wood Enterprises is sure to become an issue; I think it wise to be prepared."

Brody was not convinced, but he could tell the Chief Inspector that both Rice's attorney and the owner himself wanted to sequester the books, and that, even if they didn't catch the killer, at least the police could prove they did everything they could to Investigate. He grumbled his assent and reached for the desk telephone. His first call was to Dugan; he left a message. His second call went to his friend, Magistrate Billy Dyer. Dyer was still in his office. Brody prepared him for whatever might be required in the way of a court order. "Glad to oblige, Malachi; that's two drinks now you owe me."

Brody replaced the receiver into the telephone's cradle. "I hope that does it for both our sakes, Mr Pierce. Now, if you'll excuse me, I've got to speak to Captain Walsh and deal with a couple of hooligans. Pierce and Brody shook hands goodbye. Pierce left for his rooms at the Touraine; Brody went upstairs to secure the cooperation of Captain Walsh to Brody's continued free hand in his investigations. Walsh willingly obliged. "I'm glad you're finding young Frankie Moore useful. He's a smart lad—and the sooner I can return him to his beat the better. If you need any more of my men for a detail, I'll do my level best but we're a small station, Inspector, and sometimes it gets pretty wild in this part of town—especially on a weekend night."

Brody thanked Captain Walsh, adding that he was sure that Assistant Chief Inspector Dugan would appreciate his cooperation, and headed back down to the main floor. "Okay, Sergeant let's go and give Pop Plunkett his drink." Riordan hesitated. "Sergeant, I've been in every station house in the City, and there isn't one that doesn't have a bottle of hootch somewhere—for a good purpose, no doubt—so just get it and bring a glass, and we'll go stop that caterwauling."

As soon as Brody headed into the rear quarters of the station house with the two uniforms, the old man grasping the bars of his cell yelled "I gotta piss!,"

"Okay, Patrolman Moore, you take him to the gents' before he stinks up the place." Riordan unlocked the cell and passed Pop Plunkett to Moore by the old man's coat collar. Moore hustled him down the hall to the nearest water closet. "We'll be back in a few minutes, Frankie. Put him back in his cell when he's done his business. Okay sergeant, let's visit the son."

A few hours in a basement cell had only fueled Declan "Buddy" Plunkett's insolence. "Where's my lawyer," he growled when he spotted Brody.

"Where, indeed?" countered the Inspector. Subtlety was lost on Buddy Plunkett as Brody had expected. Turning to Riordan, the Inspector directed him to "Make a note for the record that the prisoner, asked the whereabouts of his legal counsel, declined to respond." Brody spoke rapidly, sure that Buddy would have difficulty comprehending. Then, returning his attention to Buddy, the Inspector smiled and spoke in a friendly tone, "What reason did you and your old man have to try to burn down those ladies' house last night?"

"We didn't."

"You didn't have a reason?"

"N-no." Buddy took a moment to sort out the implication. "We didn't do it."

"Buddy, I got a dozen witnesses who saw you there: tossing the trash about, lighting the lanterns and you telling your Da to hurry up. He even tripped and broke his lantern."

Buddy instinctively understood he was liable to be trapped into saying more than was good for him and retreated into his dim interior muddle. A few more questions from Brody yielded nothing, so he and Riordan left young Plunkett to stew in his predicament with a parting thrust: "Okay, Buddy, it's your decision if you want to go to prison. Just remember, I got witnesses that any jury in Boston will believe, and when they ship you off to a cell in Char-les-town"—Brody pronounced it the fresh-off-the-boat-Irish way—"it will be for arson, destruction of property and attempted murder." For the first time, a momentary expression of fear displaced Buddy's dull, tough-guy pose. "And don't expect your Da will there with you. He's upstairs crying for a wee touch o' the creature. You know your father, Buddy. A few drinks in him, he'll tell us all about it. Then we won't need your help, and you'll be jailed for the maximum." Brody turned heel and, while still within Buddy's hearing, told Sergeant Riordan, "We're going to call on this unfortunate lad's unfortunate father," leaving Buddy to ponder his diminished options.

Moore had returned Pop Plunkett to his cell by the time the two policemen arrived back upstairs. Riordan went to fetch a bottle of whiskey while Brody joined Moore outside Pop's cell and regarded his prisoner in silence. A quick wink and nod at Moore brought the young patrolman to his side. Pop must have felt as hapless as an animal at a zoo: caged in grim surroundings and the object of scorn or amusement by gawkers.

When Riordan arrived with the bottle and a glass, Brody held them at chest level, tantalizing the thirsting, quivering man before him. Finally, Pop Plunkett could stand it no longer. "For Jesus' sake, man, give me a drink!"

"A drink? For the likes of you? You must know, Mr Declan Plunkett Senior, that I'm not supposed to give a prisoner a drink of whiskey, much less an old souse like you." Brody pretended to study the label. "And it's a jug of our finest—good Irish whiskey. Too bad it's against all the rules."

Pop whimpered intelligibly; Brody continued. "For me to break the rules, you'd have to give me a good reason. A very good reason."

"Sweet Mother of Jesus, I'm hurtin'."

"Ah, well, that's not a good enough reason. What do you say, gentlemen, shall we leave this sinner to his sorrows...?"

"Whad'd'ya want from me? "

"I want to know why you tried to kill those old ladies over on Castle Street."

"What!? No, no, no. I didn't kill no old ladies."

"You tried to. You tried to burn down their house with them and a lot of other people in it. You destroyed their property..."

"I want a lawyer!" Pop's panic broke through his hangover and overcame his self pity.

"Sure, Mr Plunkett. Tell me his name. I'll have the sergeant phone him for you. That is, if you got the money to pay him."

"I got the money." Brody looked sideways at Riordan who nodded. "Him and his son had nearly eighty bucks between them when I booked 'em."

"That's a lot of money, Mr Plunkett. Enough to get you a lawyer. Not a very good lawyer, though. And you'll need a very, very good lawyer to beat the charges. Let's see, sergeant, what did all those witnesses in the house see him doing? Ah, yes. Dumping trash up against their house. Setting the fire that burned down these poor old ladies' house and almost killed them and all their roomers. Anything else? Oh, yes, almost crippling a poor, young Irish newsboy. Yessir, Mr Plunkett, it going to take a very good, a very, very expensive lawyer to get you off the hook—maybe even out of the noose—with all the witnesses we got."

234

Brody changed his manner abruptly. "You stupid, drunken arse, you and your son made so much noise that half the neighborhood saw you. Watched you tripping over your own feet and breaking your lantern. Oh, yes, you two drunken jugheads put on quite a show."

CHAPTER 58

Thursday Afternoon: A Key to the Murder

As soon as Mr Pierce left, Lavinia, Florrie and Mr Boniface went down to the kitchen to clean up after lunch and get started on dinner. As it wasn't yet quite 3 PM, there was plenty of time, for once that week, to prepare the evening's dinner without rushing.

While checking the posted weekly menu, Florrie was reminded that tomorrow's dinner for their guests called for a main dish of baked beans. Rather than chance forgetting until it was too late to put the bean to soak overnight, Florrie roughly measured eight cups of kidney beans, spread them across a large bread board and picked out the tiny pebbles and bits of grit that were an inevitable find in dried beans. As she often did while in the kitchen, she talked to herself even though others were present. It helped her concentrate on the various steps of the chores before her and kept her mind from wandering away to things that had nothing to do with cooking. "We don't want any little stones to slip by. I don't see why most people insist on using pinto beans. The grit is apt to be nearly the same color as the pintos. Besides, dark red kidneys are much tastier." Satisfied the job was done, she swept the beans into a colander, rinsed them and then put them to soak in a large crockery pot of cold water until tomorrow morning.

That chore out of the way, Florrie turned her attention to the evening's menu: casseroles of brown rice, broccoli, onions and cheese with a side dish of boiled beets sautéed with carrots and tossed with a thin sauce of garlic, mustard, olive oil and white wine.

Just as Florrie realized she needed at least one more pair of hands, she looked up and was surprised that Lavinia and Mr Boniface were still in the kitchen. Seeing them quietly at work reminded Florrie that her sister had already taken care of dessert with the loaves of spice cake from Sami's Syrian bakery. One more chore out of the way.

"I'm doing the casseroles. When you have a few minutes, Lavinia, will you chop some onions and herbs?" Florrie went to the cold storage room to get the broccoli and cheeses. Not much left in the larder, she observed to herself; especially as they had done only a small, mid-week shopping locally. Tomorrow she'd have a larger than usual list of things to buy at Haymarket. Mr Boniface was a bit too old to help Lavinia and her carry large bundles, and Tommy, with a bum foot, couldn't help. Perhaps, if Mr Boniface cleaned up, with Tommy's help, after Friday morning's breakfast, Agnes would be free to accompany her and Lavinia on their weekly marketing expedition to Haymarket. Florrie resumed talking before she reentered the kitchen from cold storage. "Mr Boniface, have you time to grate some cheese for the casseroles?" Florrie spotted Tommy through the kitchen's rear windows. "What's Tommy doing?"

"Cleaning up the yard," replied Mr Boniface.

"Initiative. I told you he's a good lad, Lavinia."

"He shouldn't be hobbling about on that foot of his."

"Tommy's used to being active. A bit of exercise won't hurt his foot. You've done a fine job of bandaging it, Lavinia. I suspect that you're growing fond of the lad."

"He's our responsibility now, Flora."

For several minutes there was only the sound of Florrie humming to herself, accompanied by the clatter of dishes, pots and utensils. Lavinia and Boniface recognized that Florrie's mind was drifting elsewhere while her muscle memory guided her hands through rinsing, chopping and blending. Midway in her internal conversation, her thoughts became audible: "But even if it is a matter of embezzlement or misappropriation of funds or whatever the law calls it, we are still left with a goodly list of suspects. Joshua Wood, for one."

"We can't rule out Ira Wood..." added Lavinia.

"Or that waxworks in their office—Yates something or other..."

"Owen Yates," put in Boniface.

"That's him. What about the U.B.O. booker, Nathan Furst?" For a moment Florrie hoped it was he. She was resolutely on the side of the actors against the ever-more powerful forces of management and believed anything that could bring disrepute to the U.B.O. was fully deserved.

Lavinia asked "And what about the Tremont's employees? I know Laurence Simpson is the manager, but who else works front-of-the-house?"

"You mean Morris Weiss and Emily Stropell? Why, they wouldn't! Emily is as timid as a church mouse, and Mo, well, he's a dear, old soul. Isn't that so, Mr Boniface? You've worked with them on occasion."

"Oh, yes, Miss Flora. I've seen Mr Weiss and Miss Stropell spend hours to reconcile their accounts. Some employees in other box offices where I've assisted are less scrupulous."

"I'm not accusing them, Flora. I'm simply trying to think of all the people who handle money for Wood's."

"Well, Lavinia," challenged Florrie, "our suspect also needs the nerve to steal and murder. I think we can rule out Emily and Mo on both counts."

"Motive and temperament aside," cautioned Lavinia, "The killer also needed access to the theatre at night. And, as I understand it, only performers have keys to their dressing rooms."

"Stage managers, too."

Lavinia and Florrie stared at Boniface.

"Are you sure?," queried Florrie.

Mr Boniface nodded, "It isn't generally known because some actors or performers would be upset, but stage managers have keys to everything—at least back stage."

Who's the stage manager at the Tremont, Mr Boniface?"

"I don't know him, Miss Lavinia. "He's new."

"Oh, that's right," recalled Florrie. "Petey told me. Give me a minute. I'll think of it."

"What happened to old Bill Moxley?," asked Lavinia.

"I believe the work had become too strenuous for him."

"Or the booze too strong," muttered Florrie.

"At least we've narrowed down the list of possible murderers to a dozen or so," said Lavinia as she rose from her seat at the kitchen table and walked to a window. "But I doubt we'll ever discover who tried to burn us down."

Lavinia watched Tommy as he filled the last of three barrels with a shovelful of charred debris. When he began struggling to drag one barrel back down the length of the back yard, Lavinia stepped outside. "Tommy, just put the lids on and leave them. Thank you anyway but don't try to do more than you can. I want to see how your foot is healing, so why don't you go inside and give it a good washing. I'll be right in to dress it." Uncharacteristically, Lavinia patted the top of Tommy's head as he left.

Mr Boniface had followed Lavinia outside and was trying to drag one of the galvanized metal barrels to the shed; Lavinia grabbed the other handle. "Thank you Mr Boniface. Shall we give it a try?"

238

Inside, oblivious to the absence of Lavinia and Boniface, Florrie continued to talk. "Why wouldn't Petey have told me about Bill Moxley quitting the Tremont? If he *did* quit. Maybe he was dismissed. But if he were fired, surely Petey would have told me. All the gossipy details. And what is that new stage manager's name? Oh, bother. I must be getting dotty; I never used to forget things like that." It barely registered when Tommy entered and passed through the kitchen to the water closet. "I should also talk to Mo and Emily. Maybe Mo can tell me something about how the accounts at all the theatres are conveyed to the Wood's office That's what I'll do. I'll go talk to both Mo and Petey as soon as I'm finished. Perhaps, Mr Boniface, you will..." Florrie had turned around to discover her audience had vanished.

CHAPTER 59

Thursday Afternoon: Breeding Tells

Pop Plunkett began to sink into an immobilizing muddle after Brody recounted the mess he and Buddy had made of things last night and the number of witnesses ready to testIfy.

Time was pressing, so, after a minute or so of watching Pop stare off into space, Brody clinked the glass against the bottle to bring Pop back into the here and now.

When Pop spoke, it was huskily and wearily. "Give me a drink."

"Sergeant, pour our friend a drink. One finger only." As soon as it was extended between the bars, Pops staggered to his feet, grabbed the glass and downed it in a single gulp. He handed it back with a look that pleaded for more. Brody took the glass.

"You've got lots to tell me, Mr Plunkett. When I think you told me enough to earn another taste of this fine whiskey, I'll give it to you myself. The faster you answer my questions, the sooner you'll get another drink." Brody looked around for a chair and saw one outside another cell. He pulled the chair up to Pop's cell and sat facing him as the old man sank back onto his cot.

"I'll keep the bottle, Sergeant. You and Frankie can go back upstairs; I'll yell for you young hearties if this tough guy takes me on." Riordan left to resume his duties at the front desk and Moore accompanied him while Brody settled himself in the seat facing Plunkett. "And keep this in mind, Pop: some of what I'll be asking, is some of what I already know. So don't bother lying. If you do, me and this bottle will leave you. Ever have delirium tremens, Mr Plunkett?"

Pop looked blankly at Brody.

"The *shakes,* man! You know, when you start throwing up and your body starts to twitch and gets cold, then hot? And your head hurts like it's going to crack open? Lots of people die from that, you know. 'Specially when there's no doctor or hospital around." Pops had either witnessed someone in a state of delirium tremens or had some acquaintance with its symptoms himself. He drooped on his cot, back slumped against the wall, jaw slack and eyes cast down to his fingers massaging his knuckles. "Anyway," Brody continued, "as long as you answer my questions—and no lying—I won't let that happen to you. Now, tell me why you tried to kill those old ladies?"

"I didn't! We was told to scare them. That's all we did."

"Oh, no, Mr Plunkett, you did a lot more than that. Children injured, people nearly killed, destruction of property, arson—I already told you what I'm going to charge you with if you don't tell me everything. Listen good, now: who told you to burn down that house? Your son?"

"No!, not Buddy!"

"Who, then?"

"Some guy..."

Brody slowly poured another finger of whiskey into the glass. Pop reached for it. Brody drew back his hand. "Who? Who's this 'guy'?"

"I don't know!"

Brody carefully poured the whiskey back into the bottle. "You don't know this guy, but he gives you and Buddy a hundred bucks or so to burn down a building? You're wasting my time, Pop." Brody rose and recapped the bottle. "You may have time to waste, but it'll be over at Prison Point in Char-les-town. But get this good: unless I testify that you helped me with this investigation, your time to waste will be cut short with a hangman's noose. And I'll be there, waving goodbye." Brody was a few feet away when Plunkett called him back.

"A guy in a bar."

"What bar?"

"Molly's." Pop's voice had reduced to a mumble.

"Molly's? Where?"

"Molly's Cheap Lunch."

"On Washington Street? Near Garland?" Both questions elicited a nod from the old man. Brody knew the place. A hole-in-the-wall that started up about a decade earlier to provide lunch for the workers constructing the Boston Elevated Railway along and above Washington Street. Molly had married one of the construction workers, Denny Hare, whose sideline was selling tools and scrap metal that disappeared from a number of sites where he had been employed. The laborers moved on to their next jobs after they finished erecting the Elevated Railway, and Molly's fell into decline, Denny and Molly turned their back storage room into a blind pig and sold booze without a license and at all hours. It became a way station for alcoholics of all stripes and an employment exchange for recently released but unreformed felons and miscreants looking to reestablish or make new connections.

Many in the Boston Police Department found Molly's useful. Higher-ups like inspectors discovered that, in return for overlooking Molly's unorthodox business policy, arrangements could be made to leave messages there for those who peddled information. Policemen lower in rank found refuge in Molly's when bitter weather or an untimely thirst overtook them.

"When was this?"

"The other night."

"What other night?"

"Wednesday, I guess. Gimme a drink!"

"Who's the guy who hired you and Buddy?"

"A guy Buddy knows there brings him over."

"And who's this friend of Buddy's?"

"Some guy we do business with."

"A name, a full name gets you two fingers." Brody slowly starts to pour the drink.

"Nick."

"Come again?"

"Nick. That's all I know. He don't say more. He buys stuff, you know?"

"And you sell him stuff?" Brody's question was presented as a statement.

"How 'bout that drink?"

"One more question: stuff like copper, steel—other metal?"

"Yeh."

Brody handed him the drink. It was gone in two gulps.

"Stuff you and Buddy steal from the rail yards."

Pop knew there was nothing to say.

"So, this Nick guy, he brings this other guy—the one that pays you a hundred bucks…"

"No."

"No?"

"Forty bucks each."

"Okay, forty bucks…Nick brings the guy to you, right? And you don't know nothing about the guy, right?"

Pop nodded.

"So tell me about Nick."

"Don't know nothing."

"You been selling stolen goods to this guy for—what?—years, and you don't know anything about him? Where he lives? How do you get in touch with him? How does he find you?"

"Comes to the rail yard."

"That's it? How's he know where to find you?"

"Buddy."

"So, he's your son's friend. How's he get to know your son?" There was a long pause, so Brody poured a third drink but withheld it.

"They was in school together. At Shirley." Shirley, a town near Fitchburg, about 50 miles northwest of Boston, was the site of a boy's reform school. Both men knew that this was all Pop was going to give Brody, so the Inspector screwed the cap back on the bottle, passed the glass to Pop. Without a further word, Brody left the cell area. Pop held onto the glass, now empty of the amber liquid, as if it were the Holy Grail.

CHAPTER 60

Late Thursday Afternoon: Where the Discreet Meet

Brody decided he had enough to convince Buddy that his father was cooperating. Back downstairs, Brody came directly to the point. "Tell me about your buddy Nick."

Buddy eyes flashed alert, but he said nothing. Brody persisted. "Your father says Nick's your pal. You two met up in Shirley. He's your fence; you've been selling him stolen stuff."

Yeah? Prove it. What did I sell him?"

"Frankly, Buddy, I don't care about stolen goods 'cause I'm about ready to charge you with murder..."

"I ain't never murdered no one!"

"Maybe not. But right now you're my number one suspect. You see, Buddy boy, this is the way it works: the police department's got a murder to solve. The woman's dead so it doesn't matter much to her, I guess, but it does to me. I need to arrest somebody real fast or the Chief Inspector will get mad. I got you and Pop in jail already. No jury would believe that drunken old sot is capable of murder, so that leaves you all by your lonesome to go to trial—and the gallows. So unless you tell me what I want to know—and tell me straight and right away—I'm going upstairs and change the arrest order to murder. I got witnesses who will positively identify you. Or, on the other hand, Buddy, maybe I like what you tell me so much I reduce the charges to a couple of misdemeanors. You see, Buddy, you got choices— but very little time. Now, when can I find Nick at Molly's?"

All of Buddy's hesitancy dissipated when he heard Brody mention Molly's. Clearly the Inspector knew too much to take a chance on bluffing. "Nick comes and goes. Most days, usually after work. About now, maybe."

"Where does Nick work?"

"His ole man has a junk yard on Dot Ave."

"Not too far from the rail yards at Union South, right?

"Yeah." Buddy wondered how Brody knew this and how much more. Better to keep on giving straight answers.

"Who's the guy Nick introduces you to? The guy who pays you to burn the old ladies' house down?"

"We didn't try to burn it down. Pop and me just needed to put a scare into 'em."

"Arson, willful destruction of property, injuring a child, attempted murder..."

"We didn't attempt no murder!"

"Like you said to me, Buddy: prove it. At least convince me that it wasn't your idea. That you were working for somebody else.

"I ain't a fink."

"Fink or no fink, You'll go to jail wearing the reputation I pin on you. If you *don't* tell me this guy's name, then I let it be known you *did*. You tell me his name, *then* I keep it quiet. Like I said: it's your choice..."

"Okay. I got it. Only I don't know his name. Nobody uses names. If they do, they ain't right names, you know? But I think I hear Nick call him 'Ed,' maybe 'Ted'."

"Know where he lives. Where he works?"

"Nothing."

"If that's true, how were you and your Da going to get your money for doing the job? And don't tell me he paid you first and trusted you to do the job."

"He come to the rail yard yesterday morning. Little before eight. We met at the gate before work."

"Okay for now, sonny boy, but I'll be back. Meanwhile make yourself comfortable."

"Hey," Buddy called as Brody walked away, "How about some grub?"

"I'll take that up with the chef, Mr Plunkett. Don't go away." The Inspector took the stairs up two at a time.

"Frankie, get over to Molly's lunch on Washington Street between Garland and... and..."

"Waterford," supplied the Patrolman.

"That's it. I want you to pick up a fence named Nick. I don't know his last name..."

"Nikitin, maybe?" piped up Riordan. "Goes by the name of Nikitin. We've pulled him in more than a few times. I can look up his first name."

"Good, Sergeant. When you get his file, give me a shout. I want to know this guy's history. Patrolman, You got any civilian clothes here? Good. Best not to drop into Molly's in a uniform." Brody noticed Frankie Moore's unspoken question: "I know the regulations, Patrolman, but you're on loan to the Chief Inspector's office, and it's my orders—no uniform. When you get there, before you ask Molly or Denny to point out Nick, order a beer and pay for it with a sawbuck. Don't take the change. Push it back to them. You got a ten dollar bill? And give them a peek at your badge, but don't flash it. If they want to know who you are, tell 'em you work with me. Follow their eyes. If he's in the front room, they'll let you know. If he's most likely in back, they'll give you a nod in that direction. Got it?"

Riordan thumbed through the "N" files and found a folder marked "Nikitin, Vladimir." The folder was full enough to confirm the Vladimir "Nick" Nikitin was career criminal, but there was neither a photograph nor a sketch of him. Riordan brought the folder to Brody. "First name Vladimir."

"Thanks, Sergeant."

When Moore, dressed in his civilian attire, appeared before Brody for approval, the Inspector told him to doff the tie and turn up his coat collar. "Frankie, if our Mr Nikitin isn't at Molly's when you get there, buy yourself a beer and wait awhile. Molly or Denny'll give you a nod when he comes in. Just don't drink the house brew. Good luck."

It had taken Patrolman Moore little more than five minutes to change into his street clothes at the Station and about ten more to walk from Lagrange Street down Washington to Molly's, so he arrived well before 4 PM. The front room was empty except for Denny sitting behind his lunch counter.

"Ain't never seen you here before." It was not an affable greeting.

"I've seen you."

"That so? Where?"

Frankie opened his palm to reveal his badge. "Around with Malachi Brody. Good friend of yours, right?"

"Yeah," replied Denny dismissively. "What'll you have?"

"Ale. You got a Highland Springs?" Denny filled a mug with Burton's from a keg and pushed it across the counter. "Close, just down the street," referring to another of the several breweries located along Heath and Terrace Streets on Parker Hill. Moore laid his ten dollar bill on the counter and told Denny, "Keep it."

"So who you looking for?" Denny pocketed the ten spot.

"Customer of yours. Goes by the name Nick."

"Lots of guys called Nick."

"Okay. How's the name Nikitin work for you? Not that many of them around."

"Sit over there. I'll give you a nod when he gets here. Should be here soon—*if* he comes in."

During the next half-hour, two guys, then a solo, then three more came in while Frankie was nursing his brew. When a chubby, balding man entered, Denny addressed him as "Nick" just loud enough for Frankie to hear. The Patrolman had two options. Leave Molly's to find a telephone—there wasn't a police call box nearby—that he knew from his rounds. If Frankie left, Denny might tip off Nick, and Nick would have fled before Frankie returned. Moore watched Nick as he walked from the counter into the back room; the suspect appeared to be in his fifties and more fat than muscle, so Moore decided to chance it. Frankie went through the door on Nick's heels and whispered to him. Both men returned to the front room.

Nick's surprise was momentary when he realized it was a arrest instead of a potential deal in stolen goods. He started to run, but Frankie thrust a leg between Nick's, just as he had seen Brody do it, and the tubby fellow fell forward. Moore propelled Nick upright by his coat collar and out the door. Twisting one of Nick's arms against his back, Frankie added, "You're wanted for a few friendly questions down at Station Four. Cooperate, and the Inspector won't charge you. Try to run, I'll break your arm."

It took several blocks of walking up Washington Street, threatening and shoving his suspect, before Moore was able to hail a hackney. As it was obvious that one of them was not a willing party, the hackney tried to drive past them, but Moore yelled and flashed his badge. The cabman braked, picked them up and drove to Lagrange Street.

CHAPTER 61

Late Thursday Afternoon: Once Again Into the Breach

Tommy had bathed the night before, so it took only a sponge bath in the metal tub to freshen up after working in the yard. Lavinia was pleased that his foot seemed improved—how fast the young heal. "It's coming along nicely. Any pain."

"Naw."

"You're sure?" Lavinia had swabbed the cut with more iodine and was wrapping it with gauze.

"Just a little if I stand too long."

"Such as cleaning up the yard?"

"It's good now."

"In that case, Tommy, do you think you could help me clean up after dinner? Florrie and Mr Boniface have to run a few errands."

"Sure, Miss Lavinia."

"When you finish dressing, come back to the kitchen and watch what we do. When I need you, I'll tell you exactly what to do. After the lodgers eat and we have our dinner, you can help clear the tables in the upstairs dining room—just as you did after lunch—and perhaps give a hand washing up. Is that all right?"

"Sure." Tommy was eager to have something to do. He missed selling his newspapers in downtown Boston and gadding about in his free time. He had yet to read any of the books that Florrie had put on the table by his cot. He had flipped through them, but only *Treasure Island* initially attracted Tommy; its color plates promised adventure with a boy his age as the hero.

By the time Tommy and Lavinia entered the kitchen, Agnes had returned from her few hours off duty and Florrie had popped her casseroles into the oven and had written down the time when Agnes should check the casseroles, adding a note that if they hadn't bubbled and browned by then, to give them another ten minutes. Lavinia resumed taking care of the side dishes, and told Agnes what to put in the salad.

A few minutes earlier, Florrie had stuck her head out the kitchen door. The sky had darkened and there was a nip in the air that threatened a cold, damp night. She went up to her quarters to put on a sweater, scarf, warm knitted hat, one of her cloaks and another of her scarves, a large woven rebozo of red, orange, pink and yellow cotton. As she walked down to hall, she was pleased to see Mr Boniface, sensibly garbed against the night air, waiting for her.

"To be quite candid, Mr Boniface, I'm not at all sure what I expect to discover, but I'm sure there's something amiss at the Tremont. I must confess that even if I knew what we were looking for, I haven't even the slightest idea of how to go about it. Have you any suggestion, Mr Boniface?"

"There is the suspicion that money was being mishandled. And there is the matter of access to keys to all the dressing rooms. Did you intend to ask Mr Weiss about that and the new stage manager?

"Mr Boniface, thank you for turning my vague wonderings into an agenda for action." It took the two billowing-caped shapes—one tall and thin; the other shorter and more substantial—five minutes to reach the corner where Tremont Street intersected Broadway. Florrie broke their silence. "May I request a favor, Mr Boniface?," she asked as she rummaged through her purse, picking out coins. "Would you be so kind as to step into that liquor emporium over there and buy a pint of whiskey—not too cheap and not too dear—for Petey? Once again, I've stepped out unprepared, and one never visits Petey empty-handed. I'll meet you outside that little bakery over there. Perhaps they have a small something we can bring to Mo and Emily."

Thus provisioned, they went first to the Tremont's lobby where Mr Boniface tapped on the closed box office window. Had Laurence Simpson responded, Boniface could always claim to be looking for a few days of box office work. Mo Weiss came to the window and informed Boniface that Mr Simpson had left shortly after the intermission for a meeting at Wood's office. Boniface collected Florrie who was waiting on the sidewalk, anxious to avoid Simpson. Once inside there were several pleasantries to observe before Florrie could come to the point. Hearing the voices, Emily cautiously stepped out from the inner office and smiled.

"Good afternoon, to you, too, Miss Stropell."

"Thank you, Miss Portridge for that lovely toffee yesterday."

This time Florrie had purchased something less problematic for people who probably, unlike herself, had false teeth. She handed Mo a bag containing a half-dozen molasses cookies. "Not homemade, I'm afraid."

"Oh, Miss Portridge, you shouldn't…"

"Please accept them. Perhaps some time when you are both off duty, you'll visit us at Portridge Arms for tea? I can promise home-baked goodies on that occasion."

The invitation occasioned further smiles but somewhat flustered responses that Florrie cut short. "We've come by with a specific purpose, Mr Weiss. As you and Miss Stropell may know, we are helping the police with their investigation of Rosetta Rice's thuggish murder. ..."

Miss Stropell blinked rapidly but said nothing. Mr Weiss tried to utter something, but nervousness garbled the words in his throat.

"We shan't keep you long, but I must warn you that the police will shortly be looking into the Tremont's bookkeeping."

Florrie might as well have hit Emily and Mo.

"Oh, please don't worry, this does not reflect on either of you, but you can be of great assistance to the police—and to us. I know Mr Boniface has worked with you in the box office on several occasions, so perhaps you can explain to him how the money and the tallies are handled from the time you turn them over. Meanwhile, Mr Boniface, I'll hop around back to have a few words with Petey." She forgot the brown paper bag that contained Petey's liquid refreshment until Mr Boniface held it toward her and whispered, "May I suggest, Miss Flora, that after you give Mr Martin his 'treat,' that you begin by asking what happened to Bill Moxley?"

"Capital idea, Mr Boniface. A roundabout foray."

Mr Boniface turned to Mo and Emily. "Please allow me to assure you that Miss Flora's investigations will not implicate you or threaten your positions. We simply need a bit of information, and no one will know from whence it came." If he did not completely assure them, Mo, at least, seemed to find some comfort in Boniface's promise and decided that the quicker he answered Boniface's questions, the sooner he and Emily would be left alone before Simpson returned to the box office.

"Mr Weiss, after you check the money against the number of tickets, what happens next?"

CHAPTER 62

Late Thursday Afternoon: Attack at the Rear

Alleyways leading to the rear of most theatres are dreary approaches. Marquees promise joy within to passersby yet camouflage only the facades of buildings. The other three walls look like windowless warehouses webbed with metal grate stairways leading to fire doors on the upper levels of the auditorium. Were the ordinary citizen to venture into a stage alley, the whole effect might persuade him to the pulpit's accusation that verve and color simply mask the innate sordidness of show business.

The air this October day exceeded crisp and reminded Florrie that autumn was dismissing Indian summer. The waterfront winds seemed to reach her very bones, and today the late afternoon light of the receding sun had already deserted the sides of the tall buildings that closed in on the cobblestone alleyway roughly patched with macadam. At the far end, glowing alone amid the leaden grey gloom, a single electric light perched above the Tremont Theatre's stage door barely hinted at the vibrancy pulsing inside drab russet brick walls.

At this hour, however, the performers and musicians had left the theatre to eat their dinners before the evening show. The alley was absent all life until Petey Martin cracked opened the door after Florrie rapped a second time. He was not happy to see her standing there. As he slipped out, closing the door behind him, Florrie had to descend one step below, but that vantage allowed her to peek through the narrow opening.

"Who's carrying on so?" Florrie could hear someone inside hollering. "Is anything the matter?"

"Naw. Just Gilly yelling at the crew."

"He's the new stage manager?"

Petey nodded and tried to slip back inside, but Florrie's outstretched arm detained him. "Whatever happened to old Bill Moxley?"

"Simpson canned him. Said he was too old to do the job."

"Not too drunk?"

"Maybe that, too. But no worse than Gilly. Look, I gotta get back..."

The door slammed open, nearly toppling Petey over the side railing. Florrie lost her purchase on the handrail, and she slid down six steps to the alley level, where she sat stunned until the pain in her left arm poked through the confusion to persuade her that it was wrenched. The paper bag concealing the pint of whiskey had flown out of her hands, crashed and broke. Petey's eyes sorrowfully traced a rivulet of whiskey as it worked its way between cobblestones to eddy in a pot hole. Neither man offered to help as Florrie struggled to her feet.

Gilly demanded of Petey, "We're not paying you to stand around gabbin'. Who's this old bird?"

"This old bird, as you contemptuously put it, is a member of the 'profession," and I demand..."

"Stow it," snarled Gilly, "I ain't talking to you." He grabbed Petey by his shirtfront, and before he needed to ask again, Petey volunteered that "She's one of the Porridge Sisters that own..."

"One of those nosey old biddies, you mean." Gilly slammed Petey back inside the stage door and bent his burly frame over Florrie. "Sticking her nose into business that ain't none of hers."

If Gilly were about to descend the stairs to further intimidate or harm Florrie, the vision of a tall witness hurrying up the alley persuaded him otherwise. Without a further word, Gilly stepped back into the theatre and shut the door behind him. Mr Boniface reached Florrie just as she sank to a resting space on the bottom step.

"Oh, Lord. That despicable bully!" Her words came in short utterances between long breaths. "You arrived just in time. I'm afraid that awful man was going to..."

"Now, now, Miss Flora, ..."

"You're right, Mr Boniface. Of course. But help me up. I won't stay here. Not another moment. Ooph!" Florrie had forgotten her injured arm as she reached for Mr Boniface's hand. Even for a gentleman of such sensibilities and courtesy as Mr Boniface, there was naught to do but gather her, best as his thin frame could manage—her ample body pressed against his—and pull her to a standing position. Once erect, Florrie's right hand clasped her injured upper arm to stem the pain, and they picked their way as quickly as they could amid the growing darkness and along the irregular surface of the alleyway.

"May I suggest, Miss Flora, that we proceed to the police station? You really should report this assault."

Florrie would have preferred going directly home, but as she recovered her composure, her shock and pain gave way to a more useful mindset.

"Good idea, Mr Boniface. Thank heaven it's just two blocks away."

CHAPTER 63

Late Thursday Afternoon: Lavinia Takes on a New Role

Waiting for Pierce at the front desk of the Touraine were several messages. One was from the Chief Inspector at Pemberton Square; another was from the Governor of Rhode Island. The desk clerk had alerted his boss, so the hotel manager was already acquainted with his guest's importance and readily invited Attorney Dudley Pierce to use his office to return the telephone calls received during his absence. Each of his several return telephone calls was successfully put through and concluded to Pierce's satisfaction.

Barely an hour after Dudley Pierce had departed Portridge Arms, he hired a hackney to transport him back to 146 Castle Street. He alit from the carriage, bounded up the front steps and rang the doorbell. Lavinia Portridge, already cloaked and muffled for the late afternoon autumn weather, stepped out the door, accepted Pierce's proffered arm and the two descended to the waiting hackney.

"Colonial Building on Boylston Street," Pierce instructed the driver. "Opposite the Common." He turned to his passenger: "Miss Lavinia, thank you for making yourself available again today."

"Quite all right, Mr Pierce. Fortunately we prepared dinner early. Still I can't help worrying how well our lodgers will fare at dinner with only Agnes and Tommy to serve them. It's just four o'clock, so perhaps I'll be back in time to supervise."

"I'll do my best to bring you back in an hour or so, Miss Lavinia, but I'm not sure what to expect. I'm rather surprised at what I'm doing. As a lawyer, I prepare myself as thoroughly as possible and take few chances. Yet here I am, attempting what is largely a bluff. Catching them off guard will be key."

"Mr Pierce? Just how do I fit into your sortie upon Ira Woods Enterprises?"

"Both Ira Woods and Chief Inspector Watts have agreed to sequester the books. so Chief Watts detailed a police officer to the Wood's office to ensure that no one tries to remove or tamper with the books until the auditors arrive. Ira Woods, unfortunately, was unable to get a train into Boston today, but I understand that he contacted Nathan Furst who has been able to locate Joshua Woods—no simple task after 2 o'clock when the younger Mr Wood customarily quits his office for the day. Anyway, both

Joshua Wood and Mr Furst should arrive at the office about the same time as we do."

"I still don't understand why you need me."

"Ah, as to that—well, it will be a few days before we can arrange for a team of accountants, and their work will take a week at least. I hoped that, given your management of the Portridge Arms accounts, that you might take a look at Wood's books."

"Good heavens. I wouldn't know what to look for, and, if I did, it would take weeks, not hours. Even were I familiar with whichever bookkeeping system the Woods employ, I doubt I could detect any irregularities. I took over our books out of necessity and I'm self-taught. I imagine that our books are rather elementary compared to the records that Wood Enterprises must maintain."

"Yes, I see, Miss Lavinia, but perhaps you could..." Pierced paused, unsure how to frame a delicate suggestion. "Perhaps you could seem to... Again he faltered.

Lavinia put it into plain words: "You want me to pretend that I know what I'm doing at Woods Enterprises?"

'Not too put too fine a point on it—yes."

"All right. I suppose I can at least sort out which ledgers and papers we need to secure, but don't expect me to make head or tail of them." Lavinia didn't qualify her response further, and Mr Pierce was relieved that she had readily agreed. "We still don't know if anyone at Wood's is involved—or even if there has been any skullduggery at all, but I want to send a signal to all the Wood employees that the company's affairs are under serious investigation."

"I'll play my part, Mr Pierce, although it's more the sort of thing that my sister would relish."

Ten minutes later, a uniformed policeman opened the door of Ira Wood Enterprises only to bar entrance. "Yes, sir?," he inquired.

"My name is Dudley Pierce and this lady..."

"Come in, sir. Expecting you. The other two gentleman are waiting in the next office."

"Thank you, sergeant." Although he did not practice criminal law, Pierce was well able to recognize the insignia denoting various police ranks. "Miss Portridge is here to examine the company records. Miss Markey will assist her. Please extend every courtesy you can, Sergeant...?

"Sergeant Alpert, sir."

"Thank you, Sergeant Albert. Mr Yates and I will join the others in Mr Wood's private office."

"Very good, sir."

Pierce beckoned to Mr Yates. The old man didn't move although he must have heard all that transpired between Dudley Pierce and Sergeant Alpert. "Come along, Mr Yates. We mustn't keep Mr Wood and Mr Furst waiting." Then, turning back to the policeman, Pierce asked, "When did you arrive, Sergeant?"

"Half hour ago, sir; 3:30 on the nose."

"Has anyone removed any materials from this office in that time?"

"Not even the rubbish, sir. My orders were clear, sir."

"Good." Pierce turned back toward Yates, opened the door to Ira's and Joshua's joint office.

A few moments elapsed before Yates heard and complied with Joshua Wood's demand, "Get in here, Owen!"

When the door closed behind the four men, Lavinia walked up to Miss Markey. "Hello, Miss Markey. I'm Lavinia Portridge. My sister Flora and I own Portridge Arms, a boarding house for theatricals. I doubt there is anything you need to be afraid of, Miss Markey," she tried to reassure the white-faced woman nearly petrified with fear, "but you need to help me all you can. We suspect that someone has done your employers a disservice, and you and I are here to sort it out. May I count on you, Miss Markey?"

"I've done nothing wrong, Ma'am..."

"That is precisely why we have asked you to help us, my dear. Shall we get started? To begin with, tell me "Do you receive money in this office?"

Miss Markey was able to summon a whisper. "No."

"Where do the receipts from the theatres go?"

"To the bank. Directly."

"Thank you, Miss Markey. You've helped me already. Now, can you tell me how you know how much each theatre makes?"

"The bank deposit slips. And the box office reconciliation sheets."

"Is there any chance you could make all three of us a pot of tea, Miss Markey?"

Miss Markey, thankful for a temporary reprieve, crossed to a table wedged between two file cabinets and held up an old tea kettle. Then stood there uncertain what to do.

256

"What is it, Miss Markey?"

"Water. I get it from the ladies room."

"Ah. Sergeant Alpert, have you any objection if Miss Markey and I go to the ladies room?"

"None at all, Ma'am."

"Thank you. Miss Markey, shall we go? As they passed by Sergeant Alpert and out the door, Lavinia suggested, "We can't keep addressing each other Miss This and Miss That. I'm Lavinia. May I call you Jane?"

Jane Markey offered a nod and a smile.

CHAPTER 64

Late Thursday Afternoon: Four-Handed Draw

The conversation inside Joshua's office bumped along less cordially. If he was nervous, Owen Yates did not show it. Unruffled, the old man offered maddeningly simple replies to each question, not deigning to amplify or speculate.

All that Pierce was able to wring out of Yates was that he was chief bookkeeper, had been in the employ of Ira Wood for more than a quarter of a century, that the accuracy of his work depended upon the accuracy of the numbers he was fed, and that Ira reviewed the ledgers. It would have been a surprise, had Yates' contempt for Joshua not been quite apparent to all, when the old man added to his response to the last question that "Mr Wood, Senior, only comes in once a week to go over the accounts with me, but I guess it's difficult for him to make the long trip from Nashua more often. Mr Wood, Junior, never checks the books."

Joshua exploded. *"I'm* the one who cuts the deals that gives our customers good acts week after week. All you have to do, Yates—you and that other antique out there—is keep the books straight. It's your damn job, old man!"

Owen Yates drew his thin lips together more tightly, which didn't seem possible, and stared at the young profligate pup who had replaced him as Ira's advisor and had now insulted him.

Furst decided this was the time to risk a new tactic. "Mr Yates, when you phoned my office a week ago, why did you specifically request I book Rosetta Rice?"

"I didn't."

"You didn't request her? The message you left was explicit."

"I didn't contact your office."

"Our receptionist took your name."

"It wasn't me."

"You didn't telephone my office last Friday?"

"No."

"Who did, then?"

"Mr Joshua Wood handles the bookings for all our theatres."

"I never telephoned your office, Mr Furst. I told you, I took the train to Marblehead that afternoon. I was a guest of Miss Pamela Courtney and her parents for the entire weekend!"

"Just a moment, gentlemen" interrupted Furst. "Did either of you gentlemen receive a request from the Tremont for a replacement act?"

"No! I've already told you that when you asked me yesterday or the day before." Joshua was still steaming. Yates simply shook his head dispassionately.

Furst raised his eyebrows and looked at Pierce as if to say 'I'm stumped. Your turn.'

Pierce decided on a different tact. "Do you understand, Mr Yates, that the reason for this investigation is embezzlement?"

Owen's head involuntarily jerked toward Pierce, but his facial expression remained unruffled. "Are you accusing me? If you are, I'm not answering any more questions until I get a lawyer."

Pierce retreated a bit. He had misgauged Yates' equanimity. "No one is accusing you, Mr Yates. We are trying to discover who *is* responsible for the misappropriation of funds and why Miss Rice was murdered and by whom."

An indifferent shrug of the shoulders was as close to an answer as they were going to get from Mr Owen Yates.

"May I use your telephone, Mr Wood?" Joshua pushed the instrument across his desk to Pierce. Patrolman Madden at Station Four informed Pierce that Inspector Brody had left about a half hour ago with three other police officers for the Tremont Theatre.

"Excuse me, gentlemen." Pierce stepped into the outer office for a few minutes to confer with Lavinia. When he returned, he informed them that Miss Portridge had done all she could today and was ready to leave.

Joshua willingly agreed to close the office for the day and not to reopen until Monday, at which time the police presence would be resumed while independent auditors began to conduct a thorough audit of Ira Wood Enterprises. Lavinia and Miss Markey set aside particular ledgers for Sergeant Alpert to secrete in the safe in Joshua's office. Mr Yates and Miss Markey were directed to return to work as usual on Monday to provide whatever assistance was required by the auditors.

All seven left the office at the same time. Only Mr Yates went upstairs—to the office of an attorney with whom he was casually acquainted through their mutual tenancy in the Colonial Office Building. Sergeant Alpert, having affixed police-sanctioned locks to the entrance doors of the two adjoining Wood offices, bid good night to all and walked through the Boston Common to the

Pemberton Square police headquarters. Miss Markey followed the others down the stairs to the lobby level but turned west along Boylston, then north up the length of Charles Street, the primary thoroughfare of Beacon Hill, to her West End rooming house. She hoped that the charming store fronts along Charles Street would divert and calm her.

Pierce, Lavinia, Joshua and Furst, turned east and walked the two blocks to the Tremont Theatre, all the while Joshua sputtering about Owen Yates' impertinence. Nathan tried to change the topic by inquiring of Pierce why Inspector Brody and several policeman had been dispatched to the Tremont.

"Oh, God, not more trouble," whined Joshua. Whatever liquor Joshua had been able to consume before Nate Furst located him had obviously worn off, and the corresponding drop in his spirits had been evident midway in their interrogation of Owen Yates. As they crossed the corner of Boylston and Tremont Streets, Joshua was reminded that behind the Touraine Hotel was the Lagrange Street Tavern, wherein a few comforting glasses of brandy awaited. It took more self-control than Joshua usually demonstrated not to invent a reason to absent himself from his current companions.

Nathan Furst's mind wandered from what to expect at the Tremont to how much business he had lost by being away from his office. A few buildings before they reached the Tremont, Pierce asked his companions to wait while he dashed back across the street to the Touraine. "I'm expecting an important message from my office."

While they stood around chatting on the sidewalk, Lavinia's thoughts turned to Portridge Arms. She hoped that Agnes, whose culinary skills had yet to progress beyond boiling and burning, was not making a hash out of dinner for the lodgers. While at the Wood office, Lavinia had taken the opportunity to use the telephone to contact the girl. Agnes, on the telephone, alternated between huffiness and being sorely put upon with only an "the boy" to help finish dinner. Her attitude assured Lavinia that all was as well as could be expected under the circumstances, else Agnes would have been tearfully abject. Lavinia had explained that both she and Florrie were liable to arrive home later than expected and, without conviction, she assured Agnes that a capable young woman like her could handle everything properly until they returned.

Dudley Pierce caught up with Lavinia, Nathan and Joshua and they set off for the Tremont, only a few buildings ahead. Thoughts about the telegram he had picked up at the Touraine's front desk vied with what had transpired in the Wood office and what possibly awaited them at the Tremont Theatre. A small niggling notion pushed its way to the forefront of his mind. If the afternoon's interview with Owen Yates had failed to implicate the office manager in a misappropriation of finances or the death of Rosetta Rice, it had also failed to rule out either of the two men walking ahead of him.

CHAPTER 65

Late Thursday Afternoon: Bending Fences

Had Mr Nikitin held any hope of bounding from the moving carriage on route to Station Four, it was checked by the policeman's youth and proven strength as well as the stout 12 inch hardwood truncheon that Frankie previously had concealed beneath his coat and now held across his knees.

Once the carriage stopped at the station house, Nicky calmly and agreeably entered with Moore. After all, he assured himself, even if the police tried to charge him with a crime, he could produce witnesses who would vouch for his whereabouts any night of the week. The trick to being a good fence was to remain one step away from the original crime itself. How was he supposed to know goods were stolen? The seller always assured him of lawful possession. Yes, sir, he provided a service, much like a pawnshop's, to those unfortunates in need of ready cash.

Nicky, however, was not prepared to be facing Pop Plunkett the minute he entered the stationhouse. There it was. No preliminaries. Just a plainclothes cop, probably an inspector, asking the quaking old man "Is this the guy you met at Molly's?" Pop was already nodding his head in assent before Brody has finished his question. Pop's ready answer was no less truthful for his desire to return quickly to his cell where a promised three fingers of John Jameson awaited him.

"Well, Mr Nikitin, doubtless our establishment is familiar to you. But which, you must be asking yourself, of my many crimes has brought me back this time." Brody was smiling with confidence that if he didn't charge Nicky with one thing, it would be another—or a host of others copied from a list of hitherto unsolved burglaries that the Boston Police Department would like to see closed.

"I'll talk when you get my lawyer here."

"Sure, Nicky, I can arrange that. Where can I find him?"

"I got his business card."

"Good. You've come prepared. Nothing like experience, eh, Nicky? But maybe I've got a better deal for you than even your lawyer can fix. Whad'd'ya say? Interested?"

"I'm listening."

"Sergeant Riordan, here, has been kind enough to show me Station Four's file on you—I gotta tell you, I'm impressed. You've skunked us: fourteen arrests and only two minor convictions. Now, the Assistant Chief Inspector, Captain Joseph Dugan, doesn't like scores like that; he wants me to win a couple for our side. So here's the deal. We've got more than a dozen open cases we can charge to you. Now, I know, Nicky, that you're well aware of the vast resources that we in the police department have available to us: the courts, newspaper editors demanding to lock up you crooks, informants who'll say anything for a price, and witnesses all too eager to tell us we're right and you're wrong, just to get on our good side."

Brody wasn't telling Nicky anything the fence didn't fully understand.

"Yep, Nicky my boy, we'll take those cases one by one. Your lawyer gets you acquitted on one charge, the next week we arraign you with another until my brother-in-law—excuse me, Magistrate Billy Dyer—His Honor, William F. Dyer to you, Nicky—gets sick and tired of seeing your mug in court every week and sends you to Prison Point just to get rid of you. If you decide to follow that rough path, Nicky, you'll be in court and out of action for at least six months, spend every misbegotten dollar you have on lawyer's fees and probably end up doing a hitch in jail."

"And?" Nick may have been nervous, but outwardly he remained calm. Brody must have wanted something from him pretty badly, otherwise he wouldn't have staged such an elaborate scenario.

"Or," corrected Brody. "You have a choice. We know you've been trading in stuff that Pop and Buddy Plunkett have been stealing out of the rail yards for years. Don't bother to deny it. The old man and his dummy son are going to jail for theft, and, if they thought it would help them, they'd swear that you fenced everything they ever stole. They gave me your name, so I'll go easy on 'em. Now, for me to go easy on you—forget all I know about the stuff you peddled for them, I want a name from you, and you can walk outta here. A deal?"

"What name?"

"The guy that you set up the Plunketts with on Wednesday night.

"I introduce a lot of people to each other."

"Nick, you're too ugly to play cute. I'll ask you once more, and then I'm going to turn you over to Sergeant Riordan and go to dinner while the good Sergeant books you for trafficking in stolen goods, arson and wanton destruction of..."

"Whoa! I didn't say I wouldn't cooperate. What the hell is this about arson?" Brody decided this was the time to relax his manner, so he dragged a swivel arm chair over to the table where Nick was seated and settled himself in it. Brody leaned over the table within a few feet of Nick's face and spoke in mock anguish, as a prosecutor might: "Two old ladies damn near burned outta their home, a young boy almost crippled, lots of fire damage..."

"I never, in my whole life, did that kind of stuff..."

"Always a first time, Nicky. Besides, I'm only gonna charge you as an accomplice. Now that charge I can make stick for sure. Along with a few of the others we were talking about."

Brody's attention was momentarily diverted to a tall, thin man in a charcoal-colored cloak holding open the entrance door while a large woman, also cloaked, bustled into the stationhouse. She marched to the front desk and asked to see either Inspector Brody or Patrolman Moore.

"Gilly," Nick said quietly.

It had taken Brody a few seconds to realize that under their wide-brimmed hats and voluminous capes were two of his luncheon hosts. He smiled and nodded in recognition but raised a cautioning finger to them. Swiveling back to Nick, Brody asked, "Say again?"

"The guy's name is Ed Gilly." Nick had accepted that it was no time to play around.

"Where can I find him?"

"I see him sometimes times at Molly's. Not often."

"Know where he lives? Works?

"Nope. Guys I know don't usually hand out business cards."

"What's he look like? Age? Height? Build? You know."

"Pretty big guy. No mustache or anything. Regular lookin', you know?

"Like a thug?" Nick failed to respond, and the Inspector grasped that he had squeezed all he could from Nick, so he called to Riordan, "Hey, Sergeant? You got anything on file under the name Gilly?"

"Gilly?! That man just assaulted me!" cried Florrie.

CHAPTER 66

Late Thursday Afternoon: Back to the Scene of the Crime

Once Inspector Brody sorted out that it was a man called Gilly and not Nick who had intimidated Florrie (she allowed that Gilly did not actually touch her), the Inspector was inclined to think that while the odds were against lucky happenstance; Gilly was a fairly unusual name around Boston.

"Hey, Nicky, your pal Gilly work at the Tremont Theatre?"

Nicky shrugged. "We don't talk about that stuff." It seemed a reasonable reply.

"Inspector, I am sure it is more than coincidence," cut in Florrie. "I'm sure that such an observant detective as you will recall what was painted on the brick wall at Portridge Arms." Her voice lifted that statement into a question and added a reminder, " 'Nosey biddies get hurt!' Well, Inspector, those are the exact words that Mr Gilly, the Tremont's stage manager, shouted at me just a few minutes ago."

The Inspector weighed the odds and chose to follow the long shot. "Patrolman Moore, see if you can find an ice pack and something around here to make a sling for Miss Flora's arm." Brody took the stairs up to Captain Walsh's office two at a time. When he returned to the main floor, it was with Walsh's permission to borrow three more of his men for an hour.

"Riordan, get another officer to take over your desk duty. Don't worry; Captain Walsh gave his okay. And tell Sergeant Crowder to report down here and bring another uniformed officer with him. We're going to take Mr Nikitin to the theatre."

While he waited for Riordan to return with the other officers, Brody squelched Nicky's protest by promising him that Gilly need not see him, but it was necessary that Nicky see Gilly and identify him if he hoped to get out of custody with only a minor charge. Brody also made clear to Florrie and Boniface, that while they were also needed to identify Gilly, they were to stay well in back of Brody and Moore when they entered from the front of the theatre.

Three officers were hurriedly buttoning the fronts of their frock-coated uniforms as they followed Riordan downstairs. He dispatched one of the patrolmen, Dan Madden, to the front desk and presented the other two to Brody. "Inspector: Sergeant Crowder and Patrolman Kelsey."

"We might get a bit of excitement this afternoon officers," explained Brody. "I expect you heard about the murder Monday night of one of the performers at the Tremont Theatre? Well, men, that's where we're headed now—where we may find another of our suspects. Sergeant Crowder, you and Kelsey cover the stage door. Don't let anyone in or out until Sergeant Riordan gives you the word. Riordan, you and Patrolman Moore bring Mr Nikitin as your special guest. We're going in the front way. Don't let him out of your sight. Or your grip. Let's go!"

Mr Boniface quickly finished brushing off Florrie's clothing with the whisk broom Frankie had provided, and the pair of them followed the police out of the station. Brody was torn between sending Miss Flora home to rest and needing her to point out Gilly. Florrie was not inclined to leave for home and miss the thrill of seeing "that bully of a stage manager apprehended."

On the way to the Tremont, Crowder and Kelsey peeled away from the others and raced down Boylston to the alleyway that led to the stage door. Passing through the lobby, Brody flashed his badge at Mo Weiss and yanked his thumb in the direction of the entrance to the auditorium. Mo quickly complied and ran around to unlock the lobby doors.

As they passed the nervous Mr Weiss on their way through the inner lobby, Florrie pressed a finger to her lips to caution him, and the Inspector jerked his head toward the office as a signal for Weiss to return there without any questions.

Inside, two of the backstage crew were struggling with the rigging, trying to adjust and tie off to the railing the ropes that were used to raise, lower or hold steady each end of the canvas drop that had slipped during the matinee and sagged unevenly on the stage. Gilly, with his back to the audience seats, was yelling at the men to loosen one set of ropes and make taut the other.

The Inspector, Riordan, Moore—still in his civilian attire, Florrie, Boniface and Nick slipped into the auditorium quietly and paused near the back of the house, unlit and shadowed by the overhanging balcony.

"That's him," hissed Nicky. "The big guy hollerin'."

"You sure?" asked Brody, uncertain that most people could identify, sixty feet away on the stage, a casual acquaintance who, for the most part, had his back to them and was illuminated only by a couple of work lights. "Or do you just want to get outta here?"

"Yeah, I'm sure, and, yeah, I wanna get outta here."

"Miss Flora?"

"Absolutely sure, Inspector. That's the man who assaulted me." Mr Boniface nodded in agreement.

"Mr Boniface, I suggest you get Miss Flora home. You can hail a hackney…"

"No, Inspector. I'm really quite all right. It's a short walk, and it will do me good to get all my parts in working order."

"Anyway, Miss Flora, you might want to call a doctor."

"Perhaps."

"At the least, you'll need some rest." Brody hadn't time to waste. "Okay, Riordan. You're the only one in uniform. Take Nick around back and make sure Crowder and Kelsey don't let anyone out—especially our new friend, Gilly." Brody gave them several minutes to get into position, then motioned to Frankie to follow him down the aisle. Florrie, instead of leaving the theatre, started to follow Brody and Moore, and Mr Boniface felt he had no option but to accompany her.

Gilly probably didn't hear their carpeted tread, but the glances from his stage crew alerted Gilly to their approach.

"Hey! What are you doing? Get out. Theatre's closed." Then he spotted Florrie, who, with several scarves flapping about, was hard to miss.

Instead of running or standing his ground and toughing it out, Gilly walked, with seeming calm, into the wings and out of sight. Moore sprinted after him, easily bounding onto the stage. Once backstage, Gilly darted to the stage door exit, but Moore was closing in behind him when the stage manager grabbed the slight figure of Petey Martin and tossed him at Frankie Moore, causing both to tangle and tumble.

Moore extricated himself, jumped to his feet and darted through the back stage area just before one of the startled stagehands let go of his ropes, and his end of the large, heavy canvas drop fell to the floor, barely missing Petey, still struggling to get on his feet.

Florrie and Mr Boniface were little more than halfway down the aisle when they heard the metal stage door slam. As they and Brody hurried down the aisle, they heard it slam a second time. Florrie pointed to a door nearly hidden by a plush curtain leading

267

to the lower level box seats. "That door leads to the back stage, Inspector. If Gilly comes back this way it'll either be through that door or out onto the stage."

The stage door had first banged behind Gilly just as Frankie reached it. Once through the exit, Moore let it slam a second time as he vaulted over the outdoor railing after Gilly. The young patrolman's leap just managed to grab Gilly by his shirt but not bring him down. Crowder and Kelsey, quick off the mark, wrangled the brawny suspect under control.

"You sonafabitch!" Gilly had spotted Nick halfway back in the alley with Riordan. "I'll kill ya, ya snitch!"

"By the time you get a chance," offered Patrolman Moore, "you'll likely be too old and weak." Spending a few days in Brody's service had given the lad a touch of smart mouth.

CHAPTER 67

Early Thursday Evening: Dramatic Conflict

No sooner had the Tremont Theatre's manager, Laurence Simpson, returned to his office from his between-shows dinner, than the commotion inside the theatre brought him running into the auditorium. He spied two of his stage crew standing confounded amid a tangle of ropes, the half-collapsed canvas drop and Petey Martin staggering to his feet. Two successive slams of the metal stage door and some yelling backstage alerted Simpson that there was more to the racket than immediately met his eye onstage.

"What the hell is going on? Where's Gilly?" His eye caught the presence of visitors: "And who are these people?" Three short, loud interrogatories hurled into the air carried Simpson to the foot of the stage. The crew looked blankly at their boss. Knowing not what to answer, they began hastily to tug at the ropes and try to pull the scenic drop upright and tie it back into place. "Don't stand there, Petey! Give them a hand," bellowed Simpson before turning to the two men and the woman who had stopped at the far edge of the stage. "What are you doing in here. Who let you in? Gilly! Where's Gilly?" As if on cue, the stage manager, his hands cuffed behind him, was propelled through the wing space onto the stage by Crowder and Moore with Kelsey behind.

"What the hell is going on here!" bellowed Simpson, looking at Gilly. Obviously his stage manager was in trouble because there were two uniformed officers and another man in plain clothes holding Gilly captive. Simpson's eyes again darted to the three people standing a few yards away from him. He might not know what exactly was amiss or who were these three people near him—although the large, peculiarly attired woman looked vaguely familiar, but Laurence Simpson sensed he had better stop demanding answers if he were to get any answers.

"Inspector Malachi Brody. Boston Police." The Inspector deferred further information, preferring the initiative. "And, you, sir, are…?"

"Laurence Simpson, manager of this theatre. Do you mind…?"

"Not at all, Mr Simpson. We're investigating a serious crime, and your stage manager has been implicated."

"And what is this serious crime, Inspector Brady?…

"Brody."

""What?"

"The name's Brody, Inspector Brody."

"Brody, then." Laurence Simpson had calmed himself considerably but was not about to yield his authority. "In about two hours, Mr Brody, the curtain will be going up—if those two oafs on stage can ever get it set aright—on our evening performance. There will likely be more than a thousand people in our audience. In order for tonight's performance to proceed, I shall require the services of my stage manager, so if you have charges to make, may I suggest that you make them now. I, in turn, shall summon our corporation counsel and have Mr Gilly released from custody so that he can oversee tonight's show."

"Ah, well, Mr Simpson, I see your predicament, but the charges—and there are many—outweigh the old excuse that the show must go on.

"You have yet to apprise me of your charges against Mr Gilly, Inspector."

"Right you are. Mr Simpson. Let's start with the assault and battery of this dear lady here." Brody indicated Florrie.

"I never touched her!," yelled Gilly, still held onstage by the police.

Simpson walked a few paces toward Florrie, looked squarely at her then turned to Brody. "Apart from wearing that arm sling, the lady seems well enough to me, but I'll have the doctor on call to the Tremont examine her..."

"Not necessary, Mr Simpson. I've already had her examined at the police station. Would you like me to continue with the charges?"

Simpson, drew a long deep breath and nodded as if acknowledging the start of a chess game.

"There's resisting arrest, assault on officers of the law, conspiracy in arson resulting in the injury of a child and destruction of private property..."

"Have you any proof of these charges?," interrupted Simpson.

"Proof, Mr Simpson?. That we do, indeed. Proof and witnesses, Mr Simpson. Plenty of witnesses."

"In that case, Inspector, if you'll excuse me for a moment, I had better place a telephone call to our corporation lawyer as Mr Gilly is a Wood's employee." Simpson headed up the aisle toward his office.

270

Brody called after him. "I'd hurry if I were you, Mr Simpson. Try to catch him before he leaves his office for the day—if he hasn't already. You know what short hours lawyers keep. Or would you like to hear the rest of the charges first?"

Simpson stopped midway up down the aisle.

"He's bluffing, Simpson! He ain't got nothing on me."

"Go ahead, Mr Simpson. Make your telephone call. It's a long list, so it can wait until you return. Meanwhile, my poor sergeants, though they are stout lads—each one of them, are nearly overcome with the alcohol fumes issuing from the foul mouth of your Mr Gilly, so while you're placing your telephone call, Mr Simpson, we'll set up some chairs on stage so all of us can sit down and talk this over while we wait for your legal counsel."

Simpson resumed his march up the aisle, and Brody turned to his officers. "Patrolman Moore, find some chairs or whatever you can backstage and bring them onstage. Might as well be comfortable folks. Hey, Kelsey, give Moore a hand." For the next few minutes, there was a good deal of shuffling and banging about as the policeman poked about backstage and brought onto the stage a variety of metal chairs, stools and what obviously was a stage version of a park bench. At Brody's direction the seats were arranged in a wide half circle facing each other as well as the auditorium.

Inspector Brody directed Florrie and Boniface to two of the chairs. Two more chairs were reserved for Simpson and the company lawyer. "Handcuff Mr Gilly to that bench, Kelsey. Nicky, I'm afraid you'll have to make do with a stool, but at least we can take off those cuffs. You won't be ducking out on us, will you, Nicky?" Brody leaned toward Nick and whispered, "Right now you got a sweet deal with me, my lad. If I have to chase you, I'll really stick you."

"We got a deal. Inspector."

"Glad to hear it." Brody resumed standing and moved downstage center where faced those sitting in the circle with some satisfaction. He looked at each person, satisfied that he could watch all of them, just as all of them could see each other.

Laurence Simpson came back into the theatre and walked up to the foot of the stage. Brody beckoned him up and pointed to the pair of metal chairs that remained empty. "We'll hold the other one for your corporation counsel. What's his name?

"John Wheelock."

"Of Harley and Wheelock?"

"Yes." Simpson hid his surprise that an Irish police inspector would be familiar with an old Yankee law firm that, for the most part, shunned criminal cases.

"Good man. Fine reputation." Brody turned from Simpson toward Gilly. "Mr Wheelock's specialty is corporation and tax law and real estate. Wouldn't have thought he'd want to get his hands dirty with arson and murder. Ah, well, maybe he was getting bored. You never know, eh, Gilly?"

CHAPTER 68

Early Thursday Evening: A Gathering of Foes

Before Inspector Brody could resume his questioning, five more people traipsed down the aisle toward the stage. Simpson rose from his chair. "The theatre is closed!" As the group of five walked toward the stage and emerged from under the overhanging balcony into the dim spill of the stage work lights, Simpson was able to see that the visitors included Joshua Wood and Mo Weiss. Simpson also recognized Nathan Furst, but couldn't place the remaining man and the lone woman.

"It's all right, Simpson. These people are with me." Joshua's voice reverberated in the empty theatre. "I asked Mr Weiss to join us."

Brody motioned the group forward, then spun around toward Nicky and Gilly. "Gentlemen, you're in distinguished company, today. Let me introduce you to Mr Joshua Wood, owner of this theatre and several others under the management of Ira Wood Enterprises; the eminent counselor-at-law, Dudley Pierce; and Nathan Furst, one of Boston's most important theatrical bookers. That's Mr Weiss with them. Mr Weiss, if you don't know, is Mr Simpson's number one assistant. Right, Simpson?" The theatre manager didn't bother acknowledging Brody's act, but the Inspector continued undaunted. "The lady with them, and this lady on the stage are the proprietors of Portridge Arms. I'm sure you recognize them. Mr Gilly—you tried to burn down their house..."

"Yer daft!" Gilly bellowed.

"You see the class of criminal I'm dealing with, folks? That's the trouble with muscle; they lash out before their tiny brains can crank up into gear." The Inspector had been vamping, hoping that inspiration would bless him with the right line of questioning as it had other times in the past, but now Brody silently welcomed the intrusion. The more suspects and witnesses Brody had on hand, the more likely his usual ploy—needling people into confrontations and counter accusations—was likely to yield some results. Simpson was fencing with him. Gilly refused to talk. Nicky knew he had Brody's word to go easy on him. Maybe now, with more people in the arena, someone would say something that could upset the current standoff.

"We don't have enough chairs to seat you all on the stage with us, so if our distinguished visitors will take seats in the front row, I'll get on with the show."

"Hey, Nicky, I nearly forgot you were still here, you've been so quiet."

"I got nothing to say, Inspector." Nicky had assumed a poker face. "Like I told you at the station, I perform a public service. Buy people's stuff when they need money."

"Nicely put, Nicky." conceded the Inspector. "But for those of you who weren't present at Station Four to hear Nicky when he was more specific, let me tell you what Nicky means. He's a fence. A dealer in stolen goods..."

"Hey! You got no...."

Brody squelched Nicky's objection: "Hold on, Nicky. I got the stage. Besides, we got a deal—don't we? All I'm doing is explaining to these good folks what you do for a living. Now, this other fellow here, the one scowling at me and going by the name of Ed Gilly, found out that a certain lady was asking questions about the murder here on Monday night. She spoke to you, Mr Weiss, about Rosetta Rice's murder; isn't that so?" Mo Weiss nodded tentatively as he shrank down into his front row seat next to Joshua Wood. "And she spoke to Petey Martin, the stage door... Hey, Kelsey, better check on Martin... Make sure he's tending the stage door."

"He's right here, Inspector," laughed Kelsey, "eavesdropping behind the curtains." Several people chuckled as Petey tried to scamper back to his post. "Patrolman Kelsey, why don't you keep him company at the stage door; the old fella's probably lonesome. If the performers or the musicians start to show up before we're finished here, don't let 'em in until I give you the word."

"Right, Inspector."

"As I was saying, this lady, Miss Flora Portridge, was showing up every day and asking questions. When Mr Gilly got wind of it, he found out where she lived. By the way, Gilly, how'd you do it. Ask Petey? Follow her home? ..."

"I don't know what ya talking about!!"

Flora could hold back no longer. "That's a double negative, Mr Gilly, and you, in effect, have just confessed you did something."

"Butt out, you old biddy!"

"Mr Gilly, that's at least the third time you have used that epithet in regard to me and my sister..."

"What the hell's she talking about?"

Brody cut in quickly. "That lady has just accused you of trying to kill her and her sister..."

"She's crazy!" Gilly jumped to his feet, but the handcuff yanked him back down to the bench.

Florrie rose from her chair, "There are witnesses, Mr Gilly!"

"There ain't!"

"Ask Nicky."

"I tell ya, I didn't try to kill them old ladies." Gilly glared at Nicky.

"Not personally, but remember Pop and Buddy Plunkett?"

"Never heard of 'em."

"Come on, Gilly, even a goon as thick as you couldn't forget meeting somebody just yesterday. Right now, they're sitting in a cell over at Station Four. You'll be visiting them soon enough. You can ask them then. They already told me and these fine police officers here all about it."

Gilly sensed he was trapped and growled, "I want a lawyer."

Brody ignored him. "You hired those two boneheads to do the job. That makes you as guilty as they are. Arson, attempted murder, destruction of property..."

"I want a lawyer!"

"*And...* The Inspector paused dramatically. "...the murder of Rosetta Rice." It was hard to tell who hadn't gasped; almost everyone made some kind of noise, much to Brody's satisfaction. But it was the look of panic on Gilly' face that most gratified the Inspector. Gilly' reflexes worked faster than his mind; he again yanked on the handcuffs, this time in the futile attempt to snap the chain. "I want a lawyer!!!" Finally his brain was sending messages to his mouth. "I didn't do it. This is a frame-up!"

CHAPTER 69

Early Thursday Evening: Offence and Defense

Ill-formed questions and flashes of insight were spinning around in Brody's mind like a fortune wheel, and an old, familiar refrain popped into it "...and where she stops, nobody knows." He covered his uncertainty by walking slowly and purposefully about the stage. Since logic had deserted him, Brody had to take a few stabs in the dark. What was there to lose? At least he had Gilly cold on conspiracy to arson. Looking at Gilly again, he challenged him: "You're the only person beside the actors who has keys to the dressing room, right?"

"No! It ain't true." Gilly was about to say more but Brody caught Gilly glance at someone on stage and hold his tongue. "I told you. I want a lawyer!"

Brody found himself fingering a stout rope tied to a pin rail along the side of the stage.

"Dammit! I want a lawyer!! Hey, Simpson! Get me a lawyer."

"Heck, Gilly, *I'll* send for a lawyer," promised Brody while idly looking overhead at one of the canvas scenic drops suspended above the stage. His eyes followed its ropes down to where the stage crew had tied them off at the pin railing. "Tell me his name? Who'd you want me to get?" The type of rope was identical to those that Brody had worked with 25 years ago as a teenager when he helped repair sails on Commercial Wharf—the kind of rope used on the few remaining large sailing ships that berthed in the Boston harbor. He needed confirmation of something barely remembered. "I used to work on the wharfs as a kid. Before I joined the Police Department. I remember an old timer telling me that long ago the theatres were located close to the wharfs. Have I got that right, Mr Boniface?"

"Yes, sir."

"The scenery was painted on the same sort of canvas as they made the sails?"

"Quite so, Inspector."

"Same rigging ropes? Same tools?"

"Indeed, sir. When young, I was apprenticed to a small theatre in Charleston, South Carolina, located near the docks. East Bay Playhouse. Many of the small theatre companies of the day set up in wharf buildings. Little more than large sheds, really, they were inexpensive to rent and renovate, and they offered artists…" When no more was forthcoming, Brody prompted, "Go on, Mr Boniface. I'm sure I'm not the only one who's interested."

"Oh, by all means, do" enthused Florrie. "Please, Mr Boniface." It wasn't often that Mr Boniface spoke about his past. Florrie suspected that he didn't truly recognize the significance of a career that had spanned half a century and involved backstage and front-of-house work as well as acting. More than his own part in it, it was the history of the stage that fascinated Sidney Austin Boniface. It represented to him a canny reflection of society, industry, ambition and national ethic.

Boniface resumed, "Well, what I was trying to explain was that most of our backstage crew were seamen. A few of their wives worked with us to: making and mending costumes, taking charge of props. I believe this was true in England as well. Seamen's skills were suitable to the stage, whether it was carpentry, rigging, painting or stretching and repairing the old canvas sails that we scavenged and turned into scenic drops. Young apprentices like me worked with the sailors. Learned from them. When they signed on to a new ship and left port, we took over their jobs in the theatre. Even used the same tools." Suddenly, Boniface stopped, embarrassed he had been so uncharacteristically voluble.

"Excellent, Professor," beamed Brody. "Very interesting. I'd enjoy a chin-wag with you about our days on the docks, but for the present, I congratulate you on supplying the key to one of the mysteries facing us."

Brody had grown secure in his own dramatic ability. Quite aware of its effect, the Inspector spun around to the stage manager. "Where's your knife?"

"What knife?!"

"Your rigging knife. You got others?"

"No. Maybe. In my room."

"What room?"

"Where I live. No law against owning a knife."

"No law at all, Mr Gilly. Let's just talk about your rigging knife. Where is it?"

"I don't know."

"You mean you lost it after you slashed her throat?"

"What! No! I didn't do it!" Gilly steeled himself and stopped sputtering. Facing Simpson, he measured out a warning: "Get me a lawyer. Now!"

Laurence Simpson stood and turned to the Inspector. If Brody noticed him, he gave no indication. Simpson, still standing in front of his chair, found his voice. "I think, Inspector, in the interests of justice, I had better telephone our corporate counsel again and have him send a member of his firm here to safeguard Mr Gilly's rights."

"Good idea. It's getting late" Brody casual tone and prompt acquiescence surprised everyone, especially Simpson who, after a moment's pause, turned to the short flight of stairs leading down from the *down right* corner of the stage to a theatre aisle. Brody nodded to Sergeant Crower and Patrolman Moore to follow him. Halfway up the carpeted aisle, hearing no sound behind him, Simpson turned and saw everyone's eyes upon him and two uniformed policemen not 20 feet behind him. Simpson continued onward to his office.

Meanwhile, back on the stage, Inspector Brody marked time until Simpson returned. "Mr Gilly, I advise you not to say anything further until that lawyer arrives—if he ever gets here at all. Of course, you could ask for another lawyer. Right down there in the front row, is Mr Dudley Pierce, one of the biggest and best lawyers in Providence. How' bout him? Ah, but I forgot. He's already representing the interests of Miss Rice, the woman you killed..." Gilly started to protest, but Brody lifted a finger in warning. "...Now, Ed, you don't want to say anything more until that lawyer gets here. It shouldn't be too much longer unless he's already gone home to a swell dinner and few drinks. But, there's probably no need to worry. Your boss, Mr Simpson just went to telephone the company's law firm again, but, you know, Ed, even if he does show up, you got to remember that Attorney Wheelock works for Ira Wood Enterprises. Of course, he may be too busy on a big case. He'll probably send one of his assistants. An apprentice lawyer, like one of those youngsters Mr Boniface was talking about. They get to watch the experienced guys do the work, then they try to do it themselves. Anyway, it doesn't matter much who shows up. His first duty is to Mr Ira Wood, then to Mr Joshua Wood. That's Joshua Wood, sitting right there, between Mr Pierce and Mr Weiss. Then, I suppose, your lawyer's next duty is to Laurence Simpson. You're way down the line, pal, so I don't know if he's the lawyer you want representing you."

CHAPTER 70

Early Thursday Evening: Brody Center Stage

A door from the lobby into the auditorium opened and Simpson passed through it with Crowder and Moore close at his heels. Brody resumed. "But it looks like Simpson's lawyer—I mean the company lawyer—is who you're stuck with." Brody called to Simpson, "Did you contact your lawyer?" The theatre manager nodded as he continued down the aisle. "When can we expect him?" "In about 20 minutes. I told him it was urgent."

"Indeed it is, Mr Simpson. Please take your seat back up here on stage. Your stage manager needs company." Simpson hoped that Brody's remark was devoid of any accusatory implication.

"Now, let's all see if we can make sense of the past week's events. Mr Simpson, you fired The Taylor Twins and moved the Cormier family act out of the fourth spot into the second. Correct?"

"Right. It's not unusual for a theatre manager to rearrange or cancel..."

"No question. I think we all understand how it works after the Monday matinee. But what I do find unusual, Mr Simpson, are two things. First, The Taylor Twins: why would you hire for the most prestigious theatre in Ira Wood's circuit two amateurs whose only stage experience was appearing in a talent night contest in your Lowell Theatre?"

"It's my job to keep an eye out for new talent. Besides, what has that got to do with whatever you're trying to prove here?"

"Just that from what I hear, those girls weren't ready, and you fired them after only one show..."

"That's how it goes sometimes."

"Maybe so. But, if you thought those girls were ready for a professional engagement, why did you arrange the booking of a replacement act before this week's bill even opened on Monday afternoon."

"I did no such thing." Simpson had not expected Brody to turn the interrogation from Gilly to him. What had transpired while he, Simpson, was in his office telephoning Wheelock's office? Either Gilly had continued to stonewall the Inspector or Gilly had turned suspicion on him.

"Are you telling me that you didn't arrange a replacement act for the Taylor Twins?"

"No, I didn't say that. I ordered a replacement."

"When?"

"I suppose I contacted the United Booking Office that afternoon..."

"Which afternoon?

"Monday!" Simpson was beginning to show stress.

"I got my orders on the Friday before." It was the first Nate Furst had spoken from his front row seat next to Lavinia.

"Impossible. I didn't even know I would need a replacement act until..."

Brody stepped in: "If it wasn't you who ordered a new act. Who did? It wasn't Ira Wood. It wasn't Joshua Wood. It wasn't Owen Yates..."

"It could have been Yates," suggested Simpson.

"Nope. We already questioned him. Just an hour ago. While we were sequestering the financial records from the Wood office, this theatre and the ones in Cambridge and Waltham. In short, Mr Simpson, all three theatres that you have been stealing from."

"That's preposterous!," countered Simpson as he rose from the onstage chair, "I refuse to submit to any more of your unsubstantiated speculations. Unless you intend to formally arrest me, I will return to my office until my attorney gets here."

"It's no longer your office, Simpson." Joshua Wood had bounded out of his seat to block Simpson's descent down the stage steps to the aisle. "You are relieved of all your duties until Inspector Brody concludes this investigation." Joshua never liked the man his father had hired to run the Tremont and then elevated to the position of General Manager of all the Wood theatres. Although Joshua was second in command, Simpson treated him with the same highhandedness that he exhibited toward everyone except Ira Wood. It felt good to Joshua to get a bit of his own back from Simpson, and surely Ira couldn't argue with Joshua's decision to suspend Simpson's authority, given the investigation. Brody pointed to Simpson's chair on stage and the suspended theatre manager moved back to it.

Joshua was surprised that the prospect of increased responsibilities and demands on his time actually pleased him. He was sure he could handle Simpson's responsibilities as General Manager for most of the Wood theatres with the help of the managers of those individual theatres. Perhaps Ira could take on Lowell and Nashua, both within close range of his father's home, until Simpson was cleared or, more happily, they chose a capable replacement as General Manager. That still left the day-to-day house manager operations at the Tremont. "Mr Weiss, can you manage things up front for a few days?"

Mo Weiss was dumbfounded. He opened his mouth but no words issued forth.

"Of course you can, Mr Weiss." Florrie had been silent for an unnaturally long time, sitting on the stage alongside Mr Boniface. "Why, just today, Mr Boniface told me that you and Emily were the most conscientious and honest box office people he had ever worked with. Isn't that right, Mr Boniface?"

"Indeed, Miss Flora."

"May I suggest, Mr Wood—by the way, I haven't had the pleasure of meeting you, but my sister Lavinia—sitting there, between Mr Pierce and Mr Furst—anyway, she and I run Portridge Arms, a boarding house for theatricals. Many of the artistes playing the Tremont this week are lodging with us."

"Flora?" Lavinia tried to refocus her sister.

"Oh?, Sorry. But I thought I should explain who we are and why we're here. It was our establishment that Mr Gilly and his cronies tried to burn..."

"Flora?"

"Yes? Oh, all right. Anyway, I thought, Mr Wood, that as Mr Weiss and dear Miss Stropell, his assistant, would now have more work than usual to do this week, that perhaps Mr Weiss might engage Mr Boniface, here, to help. As I believe I've already explained, Mr Boniface has often worked, as needed, on previous occasions here at the Tremont with Mo and Emily. Indeed, he has worked at many other..."

"Thank you, Miss Portridge. A fine suggestion," allowed Joshua Wood. "Of course, that's up to Mr Weiss now. Can you use the help?"

Weiss managed a nod and uttered "Yes, thank you."

"Well, that's settled." Brody grabbed at the reins again, "Now, let's get back to the matter at hand."

"Precisely, Inspector." Florrie hadn't yielded the reins. "Perhaps you should ask Mr Boniface what he has discovered about the Tremont's finances."

Brody had learned that commanding an investigation was an ongoing struggle for the tiller when Flora Portridge was around. 'She's doing it again' was Brody first but unspoken thought. Instead, however, of trying to reverse direction, he chose to cede control, but not to Florrie. "Okay, Mr Boniface. Did you discover anything that could help us with this investigation?"

"I think it may be germane, Inspector, but I'd rather not chance misrepresenting my conversation with Mr Weiss. May I ask him to explain procedures in his own words?"

"Go ahead, Mr Boniface. The floor is yours."

CHAPTER 71

Late Thursday Afternoon: Some Figures Don't Lie

"Mr Weiss. I regret having to put you through this again, but I fear it is necessary. As Miss Flora has explained to everyone, I've worked with you and Miss Stropell selling tickets and counting the receipts and stubs on numerous occasions, but please tell us what then happens to the money and the reconciliation sheets at the end of the day."

Again words gurgled in Mo's throat.

"Mr Weiss, just tell us in your own words," encouraged Florrie.

"Yes, Morris," added Joshua. "just take me through the process, step by step."

"Ah, yes. Well, then Mr Simpson comes in to check our work."

"When is that?, "prompted Mr Boniface.

"About a half hour after the intermission. By then, Miss Stropell and I have tallied the number of tickets sold, according to price..."

"You see, Inspector, there are different prices for box seats, for those in the orchestra and those in the balcony..."

"Thank you, Miss Flora. I think we understand," cut in Brody. "Then what, Mr Weiss?"

"Then Mr Simpson puts the money and the reconciliation sheets into the safe until following noon when he takes the reconciliation sheets over to the office and the money to the bank."

"Whose office?," asked Flora.

"Please, Miss Flora," begged Brody.

"Wood Enterprises', sir."

"Mr Weiss, do you know if that's the way it's handled at the other Wood's theatres?" asked Boniface.

"I'm not sure if it is exactly the same at the other houses;" Mo thought for a second and then added, "but at least the Eliot in North Cambridge and the Park in Waltham must use a similar method because on Tuesdays, Thursdays, Fridays and Saturdays a courier collects the receipts from those houses and brings them here for Mr Simpson to take to Mr Yates."

"What about the other theatres? Up in Lowell and elsewhere?" asked Florrie.

"I think they deposit each day's receipts in their local banks, but I really don't know. Perhaps Mr Simpson…"

"Not to worry, Mr Weiss. You've been a great help." Brody reassured Mr Weiss.

"Sir?" Mo Weiss thought of something else he should add. "I record each show's tally in a second ledger that I keep."

"Let me be sure I understand, Mr Weiss. You, yourself, keep a record of the box office take for every show?"

"That's correct, sir."

"How long have you been doing this?"

"About the last seven or eight years. It was Mr Wood's orders, sir." Remembering that Joshua Wood was present, Mo hastily amended to "Mr Joshua Wood, that is. He used to come by to check my ledger against the figures from time to time against those at the office.

"Do you know why, Mr Weiss?"

"Mr Wood never told me why, sir. It was after old Mr Jimsen retired—he had been manager of the Tremont since it opened nearly 20 years ago, when it was a legitimate playhouse. When a new man was put in charge—oh, not Mr Simpson; he wasn't here yet—Mr Wood instructed me to set up a second ledger and enter the tally after each show."

"Did Mr Simpson know about the ledger you kept for Mr Wood." Brody couldn't mask his smile of satisfaction.

"I couldn't say. I felt it was up to Mr Wood to let Mr Simpson know. Mr Wood had ceased coming by to check it a few years ago, but he never told me to stop keeping it."

"Mr Weiss, you are a marvel!" exclaimed Florrie.

"Mr Simpson? Did you know about this second ledger?

"I think I may have heard of it sometime ago."

"Please, Mr Simpson. I may be a copper to you, but I'm not stupid and neither are you. What theatre manager would not oversee all his financial records?"

Simpson didn't yield on the matter. "I was confident in our figures as reported to the office. No need for a second set of books."

"I'm sure the auditors will find both sets of books interesting, Mr Simpson. In any case, you are the last person to handle the money—or just before the clerks at the bank. Right?" Simpson refused to even acknowledge the question. Before the Inspector could press his questioning further, he was distracted peripherally by a policeman hurrying down the aisle. Brody waited as the officer reached the stage, sped up the steps and handed him an envelope. The Inspector opened it and scanned the two-page report.

Meanwhile, Lavinia leaned toward Mr Pierce to whisper, "I suspect that the auditors will be very interested in Mr Weiss' private ledgers."

Pierce whispered back, "Any discrepancy will point to Mr Simpson. But even if he proves a thief, how do we know that embezzlement was sufficient motive for murder?"

"Okay, Patrolman. That'll be all. Tell Captain Walsh, 'thanks'." The Inspector replaced the sheets of paper into its envelop. "You've been pretty quiet, Mr Simpson," observed Brody. "Anything you'd like to say?"

Simpson steadied his gaze at the Inspector. "If you're charging me with a crime, my attorney will speak for me."

"Have it your way, Simpson." Brody spun on his heel. He was beginning to feel like the conductor of the Boston Pops. "Hey, you! Gilly. When did you come to work at the Tremont?"

"I dunno know."

"You tell me, Simpson, when did you hire this fine specimen? Where did you find him?" Brody rapped the envelop against the palm of his other hand. When Simpson failed to reply, the Inspector added, "According to our records, he's spent more time in jail than outside."

"I know nothing about that."

"Didn't you check his references?" Brody pointed the envelop at Simpson.

"I suppose so. At the time."

"And what time was that?"

"He's worked for Ira Wood Enterprises for a year or so, I guess. Did a good job up in Fitchburg. When I needed to get a new stage manager for the Tremont, he seemed a good choice." Brody stared at the envelop in his hand, then placed it into his inside coat pocket.

"So you wanted your own man on the job here?"

"I didn't say that. All I wanted was competence. A sober hard worker."

"Well, your boyo there acts more like a brawler than a worker, and he's no stranger to hard drink." Brody knew he had to put Simpson and Gilly at odds. "See, Simpson, that's why I have a hard time thinking he murdered Rosetta Rice. He's a dumb oaf. According to his arrest record, he's violent and a crook; but what was in it for him? Whoever killed her didn't take her jewelry or her money. Didn't molest her or beat her. What the hell had you to gain, Ed? Why did you have to kill Rosetta Rice? No answer? Well, let me speculate. 'Speculate.' That means, 'guess,' Gilly. Let's see...You didn't beat her..."

"I tole you, I didn't do it! Where's that goddam lawyer, Simpson."

CHAPTER 72

Late Thursday Afternoon: Deduction

Brody pressed on. "You didn't even know her, right?"

"Like you said, I didn't even know her."

"You didn't kill her?"

"Dammit! I didn't do it!"

"Oh, you did it all right, Gilly, me boyo. And we know you used your rigging knife to slit her throat." A wild shot, admitted Brody to himself, but not without a logical probability. "When we saw her body, we knew a professional didn't do it. You used the serrated edge of the rigging knife, you stupid knucklehead! So don't bother denying it. Like I said, the Chief Inspector wants a conviction, and you haven't got the money or the connections to get yourself a decent lawyer. It's the gallows for you, Gilly, even if you *didn't...*"

"Gilly!," snapped Simpson. "You don't have to answer without a lawyer. He'll be here any minute."

"What an admirable display of solicitude for your employee, Mr Simpson. I know I don't have to explain to an educated man like you what 'solicitude' means, even if you've never displayed it toward anyone else who ever worked for you. What is this bond, Simpson, you seem to share with our Mr Gilly?"

"I've nothing to say until our attorney arrives. And stop badgering me!"

"I'm not badgering you. I'm arresting you."

"Me For what?"

"Embezzlement, Mr Simpson. Of course, that depends on what Mr Wood's auditors find, but I suspect you know they'll find discrepancies. I'm also charging you with conspiracy to murder Rosetta ..."

"I was in Lowell Monday night. You can't possibly imagine I had anything to do with..."

"Yes, I can, Mr Simpson. By the way, Gilly, notice I said *conspiracy* to murder. Simpson told you to do it. I don't know yet what hold he has over you—it's gotta be something more than paying you to do it, but I'll find out. I'll bet you tell me yourself. Right Gilly? Who knows, you cooperate with us..."

"Ed! You don't have to say anything until the lawyer gets here"

"... and maybe you'll escape the noose, Gilly," continued Brody. "Even if you hang, you'll have Laurence Simpson, Esquire, swinging beside you."

"You can't prove a damn thing, Brody." Simpson's composure had evaporated.

"Oh, I think, Mr Simpson, by the time we get to court we can prove a lot. Everybody in your business knew the United States Amusement Company was buying up theatres and leases to set up a rival operation to Keith's. The guys behind United States Amusement Company didn't care who knew they were trying to acquire theatres, in fact, the more word got around, the more it made them seem a real threat to Keith's and Albee's operation and the U.B.O. Naturally, you heard the scuttlebutt that the Wood theatres were in play, and then your pal, Owen Yates let it slip that old Ira had received an offer from Early and..."

Florrie piped up triumphantly, "Abe Erlanger & Lee Shubert!"

Brody acknowledged her help with a nod. "So, Simpson, you had to stop that sale, right? Well, Mr Yates helped you out again; he told you who owned large blocks of shares. Other than Ira and Joshua, there was only one other person was a major shareholder: Rosetta Rice. So if you could buy her stock, you could refuse to sell it to Erlanger and Shubert. But it would be a lot cheaper to simply prevent the sale. In either case, the deal would fall through and there would be no need for an examination of the books. Have I got it right so far, Mr Simpson?"

Sitting stone-faced, he refused to respond.

Brody took Simpson's silence as a signal he wasn't far off track and continued. "You contacted the U.B.O. office after normal work hours last Friday and left the message that the Tremont needed to engage Miss Rice for the coming week and at any price. You wanted to talk to her in person, but you didn't want her to know why until you could see her in person and try to persuade her not to sell. You needed to persuade her, Simpson, because, despite your years of embezzling, you couldn't put together enough cash to match or better her offer from the United States Amusement Company. Mr Pierce, why don't you tell us what your office found out?"

"Certainly, Inspector. When I stopped by my hotel on our way here, there was a telegram awaiting me from my office." Pierce waved the folded telegram. "My office had received an urgent message from the New York law firm that tendered the offer to Miss Rice. They had tried—by both telegraph and telephone—to notify the party who made the offer because he was delinquent in providing proof of good faith, but he never responded. The buyer had missed his deadline to put up a bond or securities as the guarantee that he had the ability and intention to pay the full purchase amount. It was Laurence Simpson who made the offer."

"That is privileged information inadmissible in court," snapped Simpson.

"I'm meeting a lot of jailhouse lawyers today, Mr Pierce. Perhaps you'll help me out."

"Mr Simpson, when you failed to fulfill your part of the deal by putting up a guarantee, the offer was effectively null and void. I doubt that a court will support your contention that an insincere offer to purchase can be considered privileged information."

"Thank you, Mr Pierce. Now, Mr Weiss, can you tell us when Miss Rice arrived here at the theatre on Monday?"

"Five o'clock, Inspector. Perhaps a few minutes after."

"And what did she do?"

"Mr Simpson greeted her in the lobby. He wanted everything to be just right. They went into his private office. Miss Stropell made them tea."

"Thank you, Mr Weiss."

"So, Simpson, care to tell us what you talked about?"

The erstwhile theatre manager broke his silence. "Just a very short courtesy visit, and then I brought her down to meet our music director, Earl Findley, so they could run through her numbers before dinner. That's it."

"But you could have met her later in her dressing room when she returned from dinner. That would have been about an hour before she had to go onstage and sing—am I right Miss Flora?

"Quite right, Inspector."

"You claim you were up in Lowell for the evening performance, Simpson, but you didn't leave this theatre right after you welcomed Miss Rice. In fact, nobody saw you leave at any time. Not Mr Weiss. Not Miss Stropell, Not Petey, the doorman. Anyway, you didn't need to leave here until six-thirty or so and you'd still have time to make the train at North Station for Lowell and arrive there by seven-thirty."

CHAPTER 73

Early Thursday Evening: Redound Aright

"Masterful deduction, Inspector" Florrie never failed to applaud a good performance.

Brody himself thought so, too, and continued in bravura form. "Mr Simpson, before you left the theatre, you met Miss Rice in her dressing room, but she refused to discuss her holdings in Wood Enterprises, didn't she? So you ordered your pet thug, here, to kill her later, after she finished performing!"

"No! I had nothing to do with it!"

Brody ignored Simpson's denial and turned on Gilly. "You ran things backstage, so you were free to slip up to Miss Rice's dressing room during intermission for a few minutes. Mr Edward Gilly, I'm arresting you on the charge of murder and conspiracy in arson."

"Go to hell!"

"Sooner or later, Gilly, you'll tell me how Simpson got you to kill Miss Rice, but there's no doubt in my mind you did it. And, believe me, Gilly, my testimony will make a jury believe it. I've got a good long record as a police inspector. You've got a long bad record as a convicted thug."

"Go to hell!"

"Not yet, Gilly boy. Simpson told you to steal her money and jewelry to make it look like a robbery gone wrong, but you heard someone coming up the stairs or you needed to get back to your post, so you scrammed, thinking you'd come back after everyone had left the theatre and go through her stuff.

"Simpson. I ain't taking the fall here!"

"Now you're starting to show some sense, Mr Gilly. So, once you were back in her dressing room, with all her blood all over her and the make-up dresser, you decided to leave the jewelry. Tell me, Gilly, why you didn't go through with the plan? Were you repulsed by what you'd done. Or did you realize, even with that deficient brain of yours, that if you stole her stuff, that you, a convicted felon, would become the logical suspect, and that, very likely, Simpson had planned it that way purposely?"

"Yeah, I figured that out. He tole me he'd make sure I was sent away for the rest of my life if I didn't do this job for him."

"He's lying!" yelled Simpson.

"How could he force you to murder someone?,"

"I escaped from prison a couple a years back. He knew me."

"Shut up, Gilly!"

"Offered me a job. Then tole me there was another murder I was gonna get blamed for if..."

"You damn fool! You thick-skulled...?" Simpson was yelling. Gilly lunged at him, but the handcuffs still held.

Anything else Brody planned to say was lost in the resultant cacophony. His two suspects shouted threats and denunciations. Gilly, despite several previous attempts to pull loose from the handcuffs, tried again. This time, he succeeded in pulling the heavy bench with him for several feet, just far enough to cause Simpson, unencumbered by restraints. to nearly trip as he bolted. It should have been against Simpson's considered judgment to attempt escape, but panic had trumped reason. He regretted it as soon as Patrolman Kelsey confronted him at the stage door and Patrolman Moore yanked his arms behind his back and snapped cuffs around his wrists.

"All right, men. Let's get these goons to jail," ordered the Inspector.

Simpson, Gilly and Nick in the theatre plus both Plunketts were too many suspects to be held at Station Four, so Brody phoned headquarters for two horse-drawn Black Marias, but not even one was available. Neither were the department's new Stanley Steamer motor wagons. All four of those were in service, as was usual through the evening hours when there was increased vehicular and pedestrian traffic. Brody had no other option except to summon a couple of hackneys, although he knew the grilling he would get over the many cabs he had hired at Department expense these past few days.

"Mr Furst. Would you kindly round up two hackneys for a trip up to headquarters? We'll join you out front." Brody feigned fright, "I daren't dispatch any of my officers, not with such desperadoes to guard as these."

Nathan nodded his assent and started up the aisle.

"Mr Boniface, let's you and I join Mr Wood and Mr Weiss front row center. Gentlemen, I've arrested your theatre manager and stage manager. I imagine all three of you will have your hands full getting things in order for tonight's show." The Inspector lowered his voice to a whisper, "So if any lawyers come looking for Mr Simpson or Mr Gilly, tell them to check with Station Four." The men nodded as Brody left them to tell Riordan to find another cab and get Pop and Buddy Plunkett from Station Four and bring them along.

"Mr Wood, we need someone to manage backstage tonight." Weiss' observation sounded like a question.

"I've had some experience calling a show," volunteered Boniface.

His hangover dispelled and buoyed by his participation in the afternoon's excitement, Joshua fairly exulted, "Splendid! I'm—Mr Weiss and I are indebted for your assistance, Mr Boniface. By the way, as you know the ropes backstage, keep an eye out and let me know if any one of the crew may have what it takes to be a temporary stage manager. Meanwhile, I'll talk it over with my father, and we'll engage a permanent replacement. Now, Mr Weiss, perhaps I can help out front? I used to house manage while I was in college. Shall we get started?" Weiss followed Joshua up the aisle to the box office, and Boniface, with some trepidation, screwed up the courage to face the backstage crew he was to boss.

Instead of heading directly into the box office with Mr Boniface and Mr Weiss, Joshua begged off to offer his thanks to Lavinia, Florrie, Nate Furst and Dudley Pierce, who were clustered on the sidewalk, watching as the police herded Simpson and Gilly into cabs.

"Ah, Mr Wood!," exclaimed Florrie before Joshua could offer his thanks. "I'm sure it has been as exciting and gratifying day for you as it has been for us."

"Indeed, Miss Portridge! I'm very grateful to you all..."

"Tut-tut, Mr Wood. We pulled together. Before you gentlemen leave us, my sister and I would like to invite all of you to Portridge Arms Saturday night for a bit of a celebration." Lavinia shot her sister a look; the invitation was as unexpected to her as it presumably was to the gentlemen.

"Capital! I'd love to come, but I'm afraid I'll be on duty here at the theatre every day until we replenish our staff."

"Many of our boarders, Mr Wood, are on your bill and working as well. I'm sure they would enjoy the chance to meet you. We shan't begin until after 11:00. Just a bit of supper and the chance to let our lodgers know how things turned out and how much we appreciated their help. They're a grand lot."

"In that case, I shall be delighted, Miss Portridge. Thank you all, Now I'd better get to work. I don't want to be late my first night on the job."

"I say, Mr Wood," Florrie called after him, "I hope you and Mr Boniface will bring dear Emily and Morris along. Tell them not to worry how late it will be. We'll send each of them home safely in hackneys. And Mr Pierce, Mr Furst. I hope you'll both come, too." Joshua readily agreed.

"Just a small late night supper," hinted Lavinia, who, unlike Florrie, was thinking of all the extra work as well as the cleaning that would entail as well as the marketing that had to be done tomorrow.

"Would you mind if I brought some wine?," asked Pierce.

"I always go to my favorite Bavarian bakery on Saturdays, may I bring a cake?," asked Nate.

"Thank you both; that will be lovely." Lavinia appreciated people who, unlike Florrie, could take a hint. Before Lavinia could drag her sister off to the pile of work awaiting them at home, Florrie scurried over to Inspector Brody and Patrolman Moore.

"Inspector?" Flora got his attention before he climbed into the cab where Moore and Gilly waited. "My sister and I are having a small supper at Portridge Arms after the theatres let out Saturday night to celebrate the resolution of this case. It's the last show for this week's boarders, and it's been a trying week for all of us at Portridge Arms. Please come. And Patrolman Moore. Will you join us, too? We'd love to have you."

"Sure, Miss Flora, I'd like that."

Brody demurred. "Much as I'd like to, my wife expects me to be home or take her out on a Saturday night; she hasn't seen much of me this past week."

"Of course, Inspector, but perhaps you can persuade her to accompany you? We'd love to meet her," added Florrie. "and I promise you both a jolly time. The performers will be so relieved, and your wife might like to hear how you solved the murder. We'll have food and a bit of music—a celebration of Rosetta's life."

"You make it sound like an Irish wake, Miss Flora. I'll ask my bride. She'd probably enjoy meeting all you people I've been talking about at home. G'bye." Inspector Brody climbed aboard the hackney carrying Gilly and Patrolman Moore and gave orders to both drivers to head to Pemberton Square.

"Goodbye, Don't forget," Florrie called after them, "about eleven or so Saturday night." The two cabs clattered off toward police headquarters. Racing up Tremont Street in a third hackney were Riordan and the Plunketts from Station Four to bring the procession to three.

As they pulled into Pemberton Square Inspector Brody chortled. "Frankie, my young friend, I only hope that some of the top brass is still around to see me parade this lot of villains into headquarters.

CHAPTER 74

Early Thursday Evening: Sisters at Odds

Florrie was waving after the cabs and Pierce and Furst were still chatting in front of the Tremont Theatre when Lavinia yanked on Florrie's sleeve.

"Ow! That hurt. Have you forgotten that thug wrenched my arm?"

"No."

"Why are you so angry with me, Vinnie?"

"Why!? I could throttle you! You've neglected work all week to go gadding off like Nellie Bly. Now you've invited a lot of people to a late-night party Saturday night. And you just called me 'Vinnie'." Lavinia was setting a rapid pace homeward.

"You're exaggerating, Lavinia. Calm down." With Lavinia in the lead, they were crossing Boylston Street.

"It's after six, in case you've forgotten the time, Flora. Our lodgers should be eating a hearty supper. Are they? Who's been at the house to get supper ready? Mr Pierce needed me to examine Wood's accounts. You weren't around. Mr Boniface was with you, and now you've volunteered him to the Tremont box office! Do you realize that getting dinner ready for our guests has been left to Agnes and Tommy. Agnes! For Lord's sakes, that girl can't spread butter without tearing the toast! And can you see Tommy taking Mr Boniface's place, passing food dishes around with dirty fingernails? He didn't know what a fork was until I introduced him to one!"

Florrie stopped short in the middle of the sidewalk. "I'm sorry, Lavinia. I didn't know Mr Pierce asked your help this afternoon, but, if you recall, you were the one that insisted that Mr Boniface accompany me to the Tremont. Also, if I may remind you, I had already done the lion's share of preparing dinner before I left our house. If you've been fretting all the time we were sitting in the theatre, why didn't you tell me. We could have left earlier. You didn't say anything."

"What about the weekly marketing tomorrow, Flora? Because you didn't do a shopping mid-week, we'll have to buy so much more tomorrow. And, then, to top it off, you invent more work for us tomorrow! A late-night supper! A party! Are you going to take care of that? Well, what's done is done. Let's not waste time standing here arguing. The sooner we get home the better." They walked toward home in silence for several blocks.

"Mr Pierce said he'd bring some wine, and Mr Furst is bringing a cake..."

"Yes! Because I very nearly asked them to. What an embarrassing situation you put us in. Us! Why didn't you discuss this with me first?"

"It just popped into my mind..."

"...And out of your mouth—without consulting me."

"Lavinia? I am truly sorry. I should have asked you and I didn't. I got carried away. The whole day was so exciting. Anyway, as you said—what's done is done. Tell me what I can do to help make it right. Please?"

When Lavinia spoke again, she had calmed. "We'll have to be up and out early tomorrow if we expect to find decent produce. You know what it's like at Haymarket on Fridays. You'd better think about what we can get ready for tomorrow's breakfast ahead of time.

"Muffins, maybe? Or, better, how about a coffee cake and a ...?"

The discussion carried them home. By the time they had reached Portridge Arms, Florrie had thought of at least a dozen candidates for tomorrow's breakfast menu. Only one or two could be prepared the night before.

"Florrie, you check on things in the kitchen. I want to see how our lodgers are faring in the dining room."

Lavinia went up the steps to the first floor entrance and then to the second floor. Florrie went though the downstairs' entrance into the kitchen. Agnes was scrubbing pans and Tommy was drying them. Doris Greeley was wrapping up leftovers for the cold storage, and Marla Franklin was emptying the bump-up; her sister Paula had loaded it upstairs and sent down. A chorus of cheery greetings welcomed a startled Florrie. She could feel tears cloud her eyes.

Upstairs, Lavinia walked into the most jovial gathering she had witnessed at their dinner table since the lodgers had heard of Rosetta's murder. Everyone seemed to be laughing as Paula Franklin was playing a bumbling waitress, swaying as she toted a precarious stack of dishes to the dumbwaiter.

After Lavinia bid hello to everyone and thanked them for making the very best of a harried situation, she went downstairs where she found Doris and Marla working in the kitchen. Lavinia realized she hadn't noticed that the two women had not been in the dining room. Embarrassed, Lavinia began to apologize, but Doris laughed it off. "Don't give it another thought, dear. From what Agnes has told us, it seems you had a quite a day.

"Searching out evildoers," injected Marla, a bit tongue-in-cheek.

"We all need a change of pace now and then, Heaven knows." resumed Doris Greeley. "It's fun to have the chance to get away from the same old act once in a while—don't I know," she laughed. "I was happy to help. Why don't both of you sit down and have a cup of tea while I get you some dinner? We've all had ours." Instead of waiting for an answer, Doris opened the oven and pulled out two dishes of warmed-up cheese and rice casserole with a side of beets and carrots.

After Doris Greeley and Marla Franklin had done their bit, they went upstairs to join the other performers. Most had adjourned to the library-sitting room or gone to their rooms. The Franklin Sisters and the Hennigan Brothers went into the music room. The sound of the Victor *Electrola* and tap steps drifted throughout Portridge Arms.

Enjoying their warm dinner, the Portridge Sisters gave thanks that theirs was a lodging house for troupers rather than a mere hotel. Troupers were never more alive than when they were covering for a fellow performer taken ill, a missed cue, a dropped line or a piece of scenery falling.

"Agnes?" Lavinia wanted to gauge her disposition.

"Yes ma'am?" Agnes didn't turn away from the sink.

Lavinia continued quietly. "I want to commend you on how well you handled things tonight. Thank you."

"Oh, yes," added Florrie. "We knew you could do it."

Lavinia gave her sister a look that quieted Florrie.

"What my sister just said is not true, Agnes. I, at least, didn't know you could do it. I'm glad you showed me you could. Again, thank you. I'm afraid, though, things aren't going to get much better until Sunday, if then." Agnes turned around from the sink to face Lavinia. "You, Florrie and I shall have to get up no later than five tomorrow morning if we are to get breakfast on the table and get to Haymarket by eight o'clock. We missed our mid-week shopping, so we'll have a lot to carry tomorrow…"

"I can help!" volunteered Tommy.

"No. You won't be helping us or yourself if that foot doesn't heal properly. Maybe next week, Tommy. And as soon as we finish our dinner, I want to look at your foot. When you finish helping Agnes, go to the water closet and give it a good wash."

"Okay, Miss Lavinia." Although it was a nuisance for an active boy of ten to be encumbered with a bum foot and all that bathing, he liked Lavinia's motherly attention.

"One more thing, Agnes. My sister has planned a party for Saturday night. Late Saturday night. After your usual bedtime, at that, I'm afraid. So we'll need to prepare for that." Agnes, who had neither complained as yet nor shared the sense of adventurous fun exhibited by Doris Greeley or the Franklin Sisters, visibly and verbally soured at the news. She had been hoping to spend some time with her family at their home Saturday night.

"The good news is," cut in Florrie, "that you're invited. We all are. Tommy, too, if he can stay awake that long." None of this cheered Agnes. "Oh, by the way, dear, Patrolman Frankie Moore is coming, too."

Agnes could mask neither her delight nor her blushes, and turned quickly around to finish scrubbing the last crusted casserole dish.

CHAPTER 75

Friday Morning: The Best Laid Plans

Although Florrie had tired by nightfall on Thursday, the excitement of the afternoon's encounter with villains and the promise of a lovely party Saturday kept her busy until bedtime. First, she revised the Saturday menus for breakfast and dinner and added one for the late night celebration. Then she put together a long shopping list for Haymarket.

There was so little left in the larder that breakfast required Florrie to rise to her most inventive. Thanks to Mr Kellogg, there were several boxes of Toasted Corn Flakes from Battle Creek. A bowl of pared fresh fruit would have topped off the dry cereal flakes nicely, but there was no fresh fruit left. Still, she had a supply of raisins and milk. Yet, she remembered, not everyone liked cold cereal. Hot rice pudding! Make it tonight. Slip it into the warming oven when she got up. Just the ticket!—provided there were still prunes around. So what if it were a dessert; show folks welcomed the unusual. And she could boil some potatoes tonight and fry them up in the morning. Oh, and baking powder biscuits. That should fill the bill.

Friday's dinner would be a cinch. The kidney beans had been soaking since mid-afternoon and could remain potted in water overnight. Tonight she could peel and chop the onions, garlic and bell peppers, toss them with herbs and spices. Then, after breakfast, she'd add the mixture to the beans and pop the concoction into the warming oven. That would give her bean dish much of tomorrow to sozzle (another of Florrie's made-up words) while they were out shopping at Haymarket. As for the rest of dinner, collard greens, Irish soda bread and stewed tomatoes, that could wait until tomorrow afternoon when they returned home from marketing.

That settled, Florrie put on her thinking bonnet to devise something special for Saturday's dinner and late-night supper. Pasta! What a splendid inspiration. Tomato sauce didn't need to simmer for hours—not if you used enough herbs, wine, garlic and onions along with the Roma tomatoes that were preserved and shelved in the storeroom. All summer, when there were few guests because many theatres—at least those without air-cooling—were closed for the season, Florrie had plenty of time to jar up fruits and vegetables, but then forgot about them. Well, tomorrow night would be an occasion to set some out. Maybe she would discover a forgotten fruit preserve for Saturday breakfast or jars of applesauce, some chutneys or other preserves in the storeroom.

She was sure she had enough onions and garlic, but to her shopping list Florrie added green peppers, mushrooms and pasta, preferably one of the tube shapes that was easier for her guests than the slurpy long strands that many folks, less accustomed to Italian food, found difficult to fork. Best to pair the pasta with a fresh salad of lettuce, cucumbers and blanched Romano flat beans. Were the beans enough protein? "Aha! I'll prepare some of those meatless meatballs that Miss Tenant made for the Metaphysical Society picnic last summer on the Fenway. Now, what did she use?," Florrie mused. "Some sort of mashed bean—I'm sure I have some leftover baked beans from Friday's dinner. There's onion and garlic already in them, so all I'll need do is add mushrooms, walnuts, currents, mustard and Brewers' yeast all mushed up and held together with Farmers' cheese—or, better yet, why not some of that Chinese bean curd instead? Perfect!"

With Saturday's dinner planned, Florrie's thoughts turned happily vocal to her party. "Mr Furst is bringing dessert from a German bakery, so it's likely to be a very rich confection. Good. Mr Pierce is bringing wine; I hope he knows how much some actors drink. Perhaps Lavinia would let her buy a bottle of brandy as well." But what for the main course? "Potato salad, of course, for those who want plain food. And it will fill up those who are hungry. But I'd better think of something easy to eat as people move about—not as messy as potato salad to spill on rugs and furniture, or Lavinia will get upset. Perhaps a pastry stuffed with mushrooms and cabbage like those Chinese potstickers. I've always wanted to try making those, but for tomorrow perhaps I'd better try to find them ready-made to warm up. I'll bet I can find some in Chinatown Saturday morning. I need something else exotic. Falafel! I can buy some at Sami's at the same time. Stick them with some humus and lettuce in Syrian flat bread and they make handy little sandwiches. Well that's all solved, and now we shan't have to lug everything home from Haymarket."

As Florrie reviewed her menus and list of foodstuffs they needed from Haymarket, she thought to herself. "What a lot of fuss Lavinia made about nothing. Tomorrow's breakfast might leave something to be desired, but they'll get a hearty baked bean dinner, and on Saturday, a much better breakfast—perhaps I'll try Boxty, the Irish potato pancakes and fresh fruit. Dinner will be Italian, and we'll have Chinese and Syrian—an international buffet for our lovely later-night supper party."

It was after eleven o'clock when Florrie finished assembling recipes and doing the advance cooking. Quite exhausted but pleased with herself, she went to bed and dreamt of Saturday night's fun to come.

CHAPTER 76

Friday Morning: A-Marketing We Shall Go

Lavinia had asked Mr Boniface to wake her, Florrie and Agnes as soon as he had cranked up the furnaces. He decided to get up a half-hour earlier than usual to rouse the furnaces, then light the ovens in the kitchen before waking the ladies at the requested time. Neither Florrie nor Agnes realized what Mr Boniface had done. Agnes was too busy grousing and stumbling about the kitchen. Florrie flew about her chores still excited by the week's adventures and the promise of the day. Lavinia thanked Mr Boniface for his kindness. She knew he had to work two shows in the Tremont's box office later that day.

After two cups of coffee, Agnes perked up. Finally, she consoled herself, the sisters were taking her marketing. Florrie had bundled a half dozen woven hemp bags for the groceries they would buy. It was a chilly morning, but the sky was bright—the sort of autumn day that New Englanders bragged was crisp and clear.

Florrie decided to test Agnes while they shopped. Midway, she told the girl to buy five pounds of apples, then stepped back, pulled Lavinia with her and watched.

"Oh, no you don't, Mister. I'll have none of those mushy ones in *my* bag. No! You can just dump them all out and start again. No, I said!! I'm not paying five cents a pound for rotten apples." Agnes was getting louder, so the peddler quickly shushed her, emptied the bag and handed it to her to select her own. Florrie stepped forward. "Good morning, Salvi. I see you've met my assistant. Lovely morning, isn't it. See you next week."

Florrie knew Lavinia hated shopping. Agnes seemed born to it. When they got home, Florrie told herself, she'd ask Lavinia if, in future weeks, Agnes should do the shopping with her, as she was sure Lavinia had enough else to do. It might improve Agnes' disposition to get out of the kitchen at least once a week; let the pushcart peddlers deal with her tetchiness for a change.

With two heavy bags apiece, each chocked-filled, and several tied parcels to balance, the three woman had all they could do to hobble to the subway station without stopping more than twice. The train was crowded, and they had to stand upright as the train rattled to their Dover Street stop.

After clanking down the steep metal stairs to the street, Florrie insisted on stopping for tea and "something sweet" at Walton Lunch, a block away and around the corner on Shawmut Avenue, "before I go another step." When Lavinia reluctantly agreed, Agnes stopped moaning. Sitting with weak tea and a couple of sugar cookies didn't perk them up but at least their bones got a rest.

Lavinia finished her tea quickly and excused herself from the table. She crossed back over Dover Street to Mordecai's. She remembered the place from the receipt Patrolman Moore had given her and was pretty sure of Tommy's sizes. She quickly picked out a pair of long pants, two cotton shirts, underwear, two pairs of socks and some slippers to wear indoors. Agnes groaned when she saw Lavinia re-enter Walton's with another bulky parcel. As Lavinia explained to Florrie and Agnes, the boy badly needed a new change of clothes and his current garb laundered. Agnes muttered "Amen."

Florrie's wrenched arm had benefited from a deep sleep last night, but today's strenuous activity taxed her right wrist, elbow and shoulder. Overloaded and abused as mules, Florrie and Agnes ached, and there was still some seven or eight more blocks before they stumbled into their kitchen. Tommy jumped up as soon as he heard them at the door. Despite protestations, he grabbed two bags. Once all were inside, Agnes, without being asked, headed straight for the kettle and set it to boil.

Lavinia thought to ask "Has Mr Boniface left for the theatre?"

"Yup. A few minutes ago."

"Everything all right upstairs?"

"Yup. He set up the dining room for dinner. Me and him brought all the breakfast stuff down." Agnes looked at the pile of dishes in the sink and groaned. When they finally sat down to a decent pot of tea, Agnes and Tommy tried to get the sisters to talk about the criminals that had been caught and tomorrow night's party, but even Florrie responded laconically.

As soon as they finished tea, Lavinia went to her office to catch up on the week's bills and bookings for lodging, while Agnes and Tommy tackled the mess in the sink, and Florrie put the groceries away.

Fortunately, there was still time for everyone to catch an hour's nap before dinner preparations. Florrie took an ice bag for her arm to bed.

Florrie and Lavinia hadn't realized how much the added chore of detective work had tired them throughout the course of the week. After their naps, they almost sleep-walked as they cooked, served dinner and completed their chores until it was time to go to retire to their rooms for the night.

CHAPTER 77

Saturday Morning: Florrie Tries Stage Managing

Though she had been late to bed and early to rise, Florrie had slept well again. That this Saturday would close with a party made her feel more rested, and her normally high spirits rose even higher.

While sipping her morning tea and munching on fruit and biscuits, Florrie reviewed the day ahead. First thing after making breakfast for the household, she'd stop at Sami's Syrian Bakery. It was less than five minutes walk—a stone's throw across the bridge that spanned the railway tracks and a dozen storefronts down Tremont Street. The shop was new to the neighborhood, so Florrie had done little more than notice it while passing by. The desserts that Lavinia and Boniface bought there a couple of days ago had proved fresh and tasty, so Florrie planned to go into Sami's herself and become acquainted with his stock and prices.

If he had falafel, humus and pita bread in stock, she'd reserve it and pick it up on the way home. If Sami didn't carry such savory items, she was sure she had spotted a couple of Near Eastern grocery shops in Chinatown, although there were fewer Syrians still living in what had become a predominantly Asian neighborhood.

After placing her breakfast dishes in the sink and rinsing them, Florrie hummed as she set about cooking the boarders' breakfast. With Florrie too preoccupied to interfere, Agnes was able make cinnamon buns, coffee and tea without unasked-for advice. Once all was in hand in the kitchen, Agnes went upstairs with Tommy to set the dining room table. When Florrie finished her work in the kitchen she went up to her bed-sit suite to get ready to go out.

It was left to Agnes and Tommy to get the food upstairs while it was still hot, clear the dining room after all the guests had finished eating and then wash dishes. Lavinia stopped into the dining room during breakfast to remind everyone that there would be a late-night party after the evening show: a combination thank you and send off to "a fine bunch of real troupers who helped us put out the fire" and a celebration of Rosetta Rice's life and the swift apprehension of the criminals responsible for her death. Everyone was invited.

As Mr Boniface was needed at the Tremont Theatre all Saturday afternoon and night, Lavinia had insisted that he sleep late in the morning. She got up a bit earlier than customary to stoke the furnaces herself and took the opportunity to show Tommy how to bank the furnaces for the night. The boy was happy to have a man's job to do while he was largely penned in the house all day. Lavinia also had a lot of paperwork piling up in her office, so she was glad that yesterday was the last tlme, at least for a while, that she needed to accompany Florrie to Haymarket. Agnes seemed suited to the haggling, and by next week Tommy should be able to tote a few bags. She dearly loved her sister, but Florrie often vibrated with energy and being in her busy company was often more tiring than the shopping.

Most of the vaudevillians lodging at Portridge Arms were looking forward to the day, especially if their agents had booked them for next week and beyond. Saturday was pay day, and it was bright if cool outside. Perfect for a bit of sight-seeing or shopping before the matinee.

Prospects were not bright for Mrs Renée Cormier. Although the act's week-long engagement at the Tremont had guaranteed her $75, there were no bookings waiting in the wings. The cost of the lodging bill at Portridge Arms, the rail tickets back to their Midwest hovel and food on route for one adult and three children would leave little of that $75 to tide them over until Mrs Cormier could badger some small-time booker into giving Dainty Alice a split week's work in some god-forsaken tank town.

Their week at the Tremont was supposed to have been the act's breakthrough into the better small-time. Instead, it had been a disaster. The cancellation of all the New England bookings for Dainty Alice and Her Chums following their week at the Tremont was the blow that drained her of hope.

True the Porridge Sisters had been kind, as landlords go, and brought Renée, Alice and the two boys their meals in their rooms, but the assumption by many that she had a hand in Rosetta Rice's murder had made her an outcast among the other acts. True, that very first day, in a tantrum, she had tried to sabotage Rosetta Rice's act, and that's what led to Renée being suspected of murder.

But if those other acts knew how hard life had been... How hard she had connived and scrimped to push Dainty Alice into respectable show business... How she had often had to shame herself....

She had slipped to the point of feeling sorry for herself but yanked herself back. Feeling sorry for yourself led you to start kidding yourself. Other acts had it tough, too. They dealt with bad breaks, mean people, poverty, illness and death. "Pull yourself together, woman! Face it all realistically. That temper of yours does you no good. The act is stale. A cute four-year-old tot doesn't need to dance well. A girl of ten does. I shoulda got her dancing lessons. Hired someone to build her a real act. But who had time. Who had money?"

Renée had been sitting on the edge of her bed immobilized by worry and fear when she caught sight of a note being slipped under her door. On it Lavinia had penned, "The police have solved the murder of Miss Rice. My sister and I are hosting a party tonight after the last show for all our friends at Portridge Arms. Flora and I sincerely hope you will join us."

Renée appreciated the note; it had gotten her to her feet, and she felt she could press on with the day. But she would not attend the party. Though no longer suspected of murder, everyone knew she had attempted to ruin Rosetta Rice's act.

Dressed for the outdoors, Florrie checked on Agnes and Tommy before she sailed off to Sami's. If she shopped quickly and didn't lollygag about looking in curio shops, she could be back home in an hour and have both dinner and supper all but cooked and laid out by early afternoon. Then—if Lavinia approved and Agnes and Tommy had cleaned up the dining room and kitchen satisfactorily, Florrie intended to treat the two youngsters—and herself, it must be admitted—to a matinee at the Globe Theatre, one of the newer houses downtown, located on Washington Street at Kneeland, where the theatre district met Chinatown—and where she just might find Chinese dumplings or pot stickers for the party.

CHAPTER 78

Saturday Afternoon: Matinee at the Globe

Before gathering her young companions for the afternoon vaudeville show, Florrie explained to Lavinia, in more detail than necessary, what remained to be done for dinner. Agnes and Tommy had already cleaned and set up the dining room with fresh linens, flatware and dishes. Already Florrie had put the mixture of soaked kidney beans with vegetables and herbs, enough to fill two crocks, into the oven, rolled the meatless meat-ball mixture into dozens of patties, quickly fried them, continually rolling them about in her iron skillets to crisp evenly, and then arrayed them on two large baking trays. "About five o'clock, these should be placed in the warming oven. There's already in the oven a large crockery pot of tomato sauce with green peppers and onions..."

"You've already put onions in the 'meat' balls..."

"You can never have too much onion, Lavinia. Anyway, I've already made the sauce. That's it on top of "the dragon". Leave it there all afternoon, but give it a bit of a stir every hour or so, if you think of it. I forgot to make bread, so while we're out, I'll find some Italian or French bread somewhere. Or maybe bread rolls. When we get back, I'll pull together a salad and boil the pasta."

Lavinia looked about for a few moments. "What is there to drink with the meal, and how about dessert?"

"Oh, bother. I forgot about that."

Lavinia smiled. "You've done enough, and I'll have some free time this afternoon. It'll do me good to get out of the house for an hour, so I'll buy the bread—and how about ice cream for dessert?"

"Oh, Lavinia, you are a dear."

"I was thinking of dropping by Hadge & Lawless and have them deliver a few bottles of brandy for the party..."

"Splendid! And perhaps a couple of bottles of wine for dinner?..."

"Something red?"

"Something Italiano!" Impulsively, Florrie kissed her sister on the cheek.

After Florrie and the youngsters departed for the matinee, Lavinia decided it was best to get her shopping out of the way. She stopped first at Hadge & Lawless to order wine and brandy. By the time she completed her errands and was back at Portridge Arms, she was carrying half dozen long loaves of French bread and several containers of ice cream: vanilla, chocolate, frozen pudding and maple walnut. No sooner had she doffed her cloak and hat than the man with the wine and liquor delivery was rapping on the rear kitchen door.

Agnes and Tommy were as elated as Florrie as they entered the Globe Theatre. Tommy had never sat in orchestra seats before; his theatre-going consisted of a few attempts to sneak into the balcony at the Grand Museum. Once seated, Agnes gawked about, no longer concerned that parishioners from Saint Pat's might see her. Looking up at the ceiling, she was captivated by the glorious mural of Raphaelite maidens and muscular lads with garlands of pink roses and green leaves covering their naughty bits while they swanned about on ivory clouds floating against an azure sky. It was the most gorgeous thing Agnes had ever seen. More gorgeous, in truth, she had to admit, than the stained glass saints suffering martyrdom in St Pat's windows.

Florrie smiled as Agnes, fortified by a single previous experience, explained to Tommy what kind of show to expect. The overture went on too long for Tommy's limited taste in music, but the Vetter Trio nearly brought the boy to his feet. Why not? The jumps, twists, handsprings, rollovers and cartwheels that culminated in a three-high finish by the Vetters was more spectacular than any home run that Tommy had ever seen hit out of the South End Grounds while hiding underneath the pavilion stands.

When the pretty Franklin Sisters, Marla and Paula, came onstage in the second spot, Tommy could barely contain himself and not cheer. It wasn't that he liked singing much, but they exhibited a fresh and saucy good cheer, and, he had actually met them! And met Andras, Karel and Dietmar Vetter, too! Talked to all of them, and they made such a fuss about his bravery the night of the fire.

Agnes also found herself proud that she actually knew those glamorous young people: the Franklin Sisters and the Vetter brothers. She had stared with diminished guilt at the chiseled faces and molded physiques of the Vetter brothers and admired their sinuous movements. Marla's and Paula's dresses were beautiful, and Agnes paid close attention to how they were cut, hoping sometime soon to try to make a similar garment on the sewing machine in her family's flat. She noted the way they did their hair and moved gracefully and flirtatiously as they sang and danced. It was a marked contrast to the blushing, giggly behavior of most of her girlfriends. Just because she was a domestic, Agnes decided, was no reason not to pay more attention to her hair, her posture and the way she conducted herself in front of men.

The rest of the bill, though uniformly enjoyable, paled a bit for Agnes and Tommy. A tuxedoed magician complemented his close-up sleight-of-hand manipulation of coins with some topical patter about last year's bank panic that sailed over Agnes' and Tommy's heads.

A 15-minute melodrama enthralled many in the audience, but Florrie disdained those obvious and overripe depictions of good prevailing over evil, while Tommy seem engaged. The pace picked up with the two turns that closed the first half of the bill.

A quintet of men dressed in army uniforms began to execute a series of drills, marching and twirling their rifles. It had been smartly executed for several minutes when one of the men veered right as they others turned left. No sooner had they straightened out than another man's trousers began to slip. Gag piled on gag and the audience was roaring with belly-laughs.

"Making Yourself at Home" was a mélange of song, dance and rather daffy dialogue between Marion Bent and Pat Rooney II. The audience loved it and called the couple back for an encore and several bows. It took a solid act to be able to follow the wild antics of the Ragged Ragtime Regiment.

A snappily-dressed, fast-talking monologist had the task of opening the second half of the bill, and he acquitted himself nicely. Tommy noted his sharp duds and decided that someday, when he had grown up, that's how he would dress. The stand-up comic first settled, then perked up the audience after intermission, so Tyler & Burton, a roller skating act, merely had to sustain the pace for the audience to send them off with a solid hand.

The energy in the audience cranked up as headliner George Evans pranced onstage singing his new song, "Honey Boy," which that very same season would achieve status as his theme song. A minstrel man to the bone, Evans had recently quit 'blacking-up,' but the songs, a couple with nonsense lyrics, and his deft if not taxing dance of the Virginia Essence were hallmarks of the old-time minstrel. Perhaps the audience loved best the asides and anecdotes with which Evans peppered his turn. It all seemed quite casual, a bit like an entertainer performing for friends and family, and therein lay its charm, but the act was meticulously routined and every iota of material thoroughly honed and tested.

The show closed with a brass trio playing marshal music, and a goodly number of folks in the audience took it as their cue and marched up the aisles. The music had been lively and well-played, but many in an audience felt the show was over after the headliner performed, and it was difficult for the rest of the audience to properly appreciate an act as half the house was getting up, collecting wraps and moving out.

Florrie motioned to Agnes and Tommy to wait although other people in the same row were brushing past as they pushed by into the aisle. Florrie applauded after the trio's first number, then whispered to Agnes and Tommy that they now could leave. There would be no backstage visit that afternoon, Florrie explained. They needed to get home and get dinner on the table, and they would see the Franklins and the Vetters at the party that night to tell them how much they enjoyed their acts.

CHAPTER 79

Saturday Night and Sunday Morning: The Afterpiece, Part I

By the time the clean-up after dinner was finished, it was 8:30. The three women decided they had time for no more than an hour's nap before getting things ready for the party and still leave themselves time to freshen up and dress in their finery before the guests arrived. Florrie took the ice bag with her to her rooms.

As Lavinia passed her office, she remembered the parcel of clothing she had bought yesterday for Tommy. She found the boy sitting at the kitchen table at least a couple of chapters into *Treasure Island.* The book was quickly put aside to open the bundle. Tommy was not thrilled with the staid white shirts or the charcoal trousers, though happy that they were long pants, not the hated knickers. He promised to draw a full bath in the galvanized tub and scrub up before he dressed in the new clothes for the party.

All three had donned work clothes when they reported to the kitchen at 9:30. Asleep at the long table was Tommy, bathed and dressed in his new long pants, shirt, socks and slippers, with his head nestled on the open pages of Jim Hawkins' adventures.

The boy awoke as Florrie, Agnes and Lavinia bustled about. Florrie was dicing potatoes as quickly as Agnes was peeling them.

"I don't know where my head was—-forgetting to boil the potatoes ahead of time so they'd be cold. Ah, well, there's always warm potato salad—German salad with olive oil, herbs and a bit of vinegar. We'll call it The Vetter Potato Salad.

Rather than chance bottles rattling about in the dumbwaiter, Lavinia carried the wine and brandy upstairs two at a time but sent the glassware up in the conveyance. "Tommy? You can help me set out things upstairs. If you promise to be very careful and watch your step, you can carry a few of those bottles—one at a time, mind you. Upstairs Lavinia directed Tommy what to do in each room. In the music room he arranged the wood chairs in two semi-circled rows facing a large open space in the center of the room in case anyone wished to perform. Two nests of small tables were brought out of the corners of the library-sitting room to be unstacked and each one placed near an easy chair for those who preferred quiet conversation. The tables in the dining room were pushed back a bit so there was plenty of room around the sideboards where guests could serve themselves from the buffet spread and mill about.

Downstairs, Agnes selected the prettiest serving plate she could locate for the cake Mr Furst was expected bring. She sniffed the humus as she spooned the smooth beige spread into two medium bowls. Lord, these theatre folk must like their garlic! The falafel balls were placed in a good-sized covered casserole to heat in the oven. When all else had been prepared and set to either warm or cool, Agnes retrieved the colanders of potatoes she had put on the windowsills. Carefully, she turned over the chopped potato contents of each colander so that the pieces in the middle would cool as well as those that had been exposed to the air and placed the colanders back at the open windows. Meanwhile, Florrie was peeling and chopping red onions, green peppers and celery to mix in the potatoes. By 10:30, Florrie deemed the potatoes cool enough to toss with the chopped vegetables, some olive oil, a cup of spiced vinegar, dill, salt pepper and brown sugar.

On the first floor, Lavinia patted down Tommy's hair, told him to tuck in his shirt and dispatched him to wait by the front door for guests. Lodgers were simply to be greeted and presumably they would pop up to their rooms before coming down to the buffet. Tommy was to take the hats and coats of other guests, direct them to the second floor before putting their outer clothes into the drawing room next to the front vestibule.

Nathan Furst picked up Dudley Pierce at the Touraine and both men arrived together in a hackney, bearing gifts as promised. Right behind them was another cab with Inspector Brody and his wife, Carol, and then, on foot, Frankie Moore, who immediately upon arrival, sought out Lavinia to ask if there was anything he could do to help. She suggested he might go down to the kitchen and ask Agnes.

Those acts that appeared during the first half of their bills at the Tremont, the National, Globe and Olympic Theatres arrived next. The Hennigan boys and the Franklin Sisters came together. Right behind them were Doris and Victory Greeley, arriving in a hackney. The Vetter brothers, ever in training, walked from their theatre, as did Mrs Cormier, her daughter and the two boys in the act. By midnight all the lodgers and everyone else who had been invited were eating, drinking and chatting merrily, save Mr Boniface and Mrs Cormier and her children.

Mr Boniface led Emily Stropell and Mo Weiss into the dining room and encouraged them to serve themselves. He stayed with them long enough to introduce them to several knots of people and to let Florrie know they were there. Then he put several slices of cake on a plate, grabbed as many forks and napkins and wearily climbed the two flight to the top floor. He rapped quietly on Mrs Cormier door's, "It's Mr Boniface."

Mrs Cormier opened the door to him and managed a tight smile.

"It's very kind of you, Mr Boniface. The children will appreciate it." Following an awkward moment's silence Mrs Cormier and Mr Boniface nodded goodbye and retreated into their respective rooms.

Downstairs, Brody had pulled aside Lavinia, Florrie, Dudley Pierce, Joshua Wood and Nate Furst to give them the latest news. Magistrate Billy Dyer had found sufficient cause to bound over Simpson, Gilly and Declan Plunkett, Senior and Junior, for trial. What Brody didn't mention was that he had turned Nicky loose as promised, with the understanding that it was a very good idea for Nicky to relocate, at least out of state, unless he wanted to be one of Brody's informants.

The briefing finished, it was time for the celebration to begin. Florrie tapped her glass with a knife a few times. "Thank you, dear friends, both old and new, for coming to our little party. I hope you're all helping yourselves to refreshments. My sister and I want to thank you for putting out the fire and for your forbearance during the past few days. At least a few of you knew Rosetta Rice, as did we. She was rather a private and quiet person, but a good and generous soul." Florrie faltered for a moment. "The circumstances of her death must be known to you all, but some of you may not yet have heard that her murderer—or murderers, I should say—have been apprehended, as well as the men who set the fire here at Portridge Arms." A sincere cheer arose from the guests. Florrie pointed to Brody. "We have Inspector Brody to thank—and Patrolman Moore. Is he about? Ah, well, doubtless he is somewhere among us. Please give Inspector Brody a hand." Performers and actors know how to pick up their cues, and Brody nearly blushed at the applause. Carol Brody beamed.

"Inspector?," called Lavinia as the applause lessened, "I think we'd all like to know the latest news about the case. If you will oblige us?" Her request was seconded by several cheers.

Brody proved less expansive and more reticent when facing a crowd of professional show people than when questioning suspects. After a few 'ahs' and 'ers,' he got started. "First let me tell you all that the Boston Police Department had a lot of help from some of the folks who are here tonight. The Porridge Sisters who..." Guffaws broke out across the room—Brody didn't realize he had slipped and called them by their nicknames, so he stumbled on. "Rosetta Rice's lawyer, Mr Pierce, over there. And next to him is Mr Nathan Furst from the United Booking Of..." a solitary and muted boo greeted the mention of U.B.O., but the voice quickly added, "Just kidding. I need work!," which earned a laugh all around.

Anxious to get out of the spotlight, Brody resumed "and Mr Joshua Wood." Brody didn't mention the stunning redhead at Joshua's side, but no one in the room could have failed to notice her and the bottle green satin dress she had chosen to wear, far fancier than anything worn by the other ladies in the room.

"Hey, Tommy. Where are you?" The boy waved. "Come here, son. This lad is one of our heroes. He caught the fire out back in time and prevented it from spreading. Then positively identified the culprits responsible for setting it."

More applause.

"Where's Mr Boniface?"

Florrie spoke up: "I'm afraid that he's gone to his room, Inspector. The poor man has been working morning and night. But Mr Morris Weiss and Miss Emily Stropell are here," pointed out Florrie.

"Oh? Right." Brody was learning to pick us his cues. "Thanks to the meticulous records that they keep, we expect to have iron-clad proof against Laurence Simpson, the manager...."

"Ex-manager!," Joshua shouted good-naturedly.

"*Ex-manager* of the Tremont Theatre. Anyway, Simpson had been skimming the take from every show at the Tremont, the Eliot and the Park theatres for almost three years. When rumors got about that the Wood theatres might be bought by the United States Amusement..." Boos interrupted Brody for a few seconds. "...Simpson knew that outside auditors would be called in to verify the books before any sale would be completed. He panicked. Taken all together, the estimated total amounts to a charge of grand larceny. There's a good long stretch of prison time facing him.

"Under some pretense or another, he convinced Owen Yates, the office manager at Wood's, to give him unsupervised access to the corporation files, and Simpson discovered that Miss Rice held sufficient shares to block the sale. That Monday night, after the show, he must have tried to persuade her to either not sell her shares or sell them to him. When she refused, he didn't kill her himself. He left that job to Ed Gilly.

"Now, in my experience, most embezzlers don't make the jump to murder, but we suspect that he may have more to hide, and we're delving into his past—the time before he went to work for Ira Wood. A man as respectable as he pretended to be doesn't have friends the likes of Ed Gilly, the goon he hired as stage manager..."

"Ex-stage manager!" Joshua was enjoying himself heartily.

"Well, folks, that's enough from me. If you want more details, ask Mr Pierce or Mr Wood; they can explain the financial shenanigans better than me." Relieved to be quit of performing for a bunch of professionals, Brody returned to his wife's side.

CHAPTER 80

Saturday Night and Sunday Morning: Afterpiece, Part II

Doris and Victor Greeley slipped up to the top floor. Because she seldom questioned or criticized her husband, he paid attention when she did. At lunch today, Doris had convinced Victor that he needed to make amends to Mrs Cormier. "I'll grant you that she is unpleasant, but I imagine that weighs more heavily on her than anyone else. We need to do something to help those children, if not her." Victor who liked to live up to his self-image as a gentleman of grace and no grudges, agreed.

When Renée Cormier opened the door, her face froze. She had not expected to see the Greeleys of all people.

"Mrs Cormier, my husband and I would like to speak with you for a few minutes. May we?"

Mrs Cormier didn't know what to say. She was too depressed to slam the door, and she had nothing against Doris Greeley.

"Madam, please let me tell you how much I regret my intemperate remarks earlier this week. I was upset by the death of a good friend, but that is a poor excuse for my ungallant behàvior."

Mrs Cormier nodded. Perhaps it was an acceptance of Victor's apology.

"Dear, may we sit somewhere and talk for a bit?," asked Doris.

Mrs Cormier opened the door wider as if to give evidence that there was insufficient seating in her room. When Doris peered in, she saw the glum-faced Dainty Alice sitting on the edge of the bed.

Doris suggested, "We can go to our room or the sitting room. Most of the people are in the music room."

Renée was about to demur. She preferred to shut the door and retreat, but Victor Greeley, pleaded softly and gently, "Please. It would mean much to us."

Mrs Cormier looked at them for a moment, nodded, stepped out in to the corridor and shut the door. "I need to tell the children where we're going."

"Why not bring them along. You know Tommy, don't you? The boy who lives here and helps around the house. He's downstairs at the party, but everyone else is a grown-up. I'm sure he would like the company of some children his own age. There's lots of food and desserts."

It was very hard for Renée Cormier to take the next steps forward, but mindful of the resolution she made earlier to stop feeling mad at the world and sorry for herself, and to put the welfare of her daughter and the boys first, she nodded again. "Let me tell them. They'll need to get out of their nightshirts. What room are you in? I don't want to go into the music room alone."

While Doris waited in their bed-sitting room for Renée Cormier, Victor hurried down to the music room and sought out Florrie.

"I think, my dear, that Doris has convinced Mrs Cormier to let the children attend your party.'

"I'm so glad, Victor. They seem so dispirited. A little party will be good for them."

"Do you think you could ask Tommy to take them under his wing tonight? Make sure they get food and talk to them? It'll only be for a half-hour or so."

"I'm sure he will—if I can drag him away from the Vetter brothers and the Hennigan boys. The lad seems to have found a whole set of older brothers, but I'm sure he'll see that the Cormier children enjoy themselves. Tommy's not a shy one; he'll get them to talk."

Victor and Tommy were waiting in the sitting room when Doris and Renée entered with Alice and the two sleepy young boys.

"Hi." Tommy walked over to the children. Want to get some cake?" That was all it took for the boys to follow Tommy, but Alice waited for her mother's signal.

"Go ahead, dear. Enjoy yourself, but we have to pack early tomorrow, so only for a half-hour"

Alice nodded and joined the three boys.

"Mrs Cormier, my wife and I have been in vaudeville for decades—at least I have—and we know how difficult it can be. We haven't changed our act in years, and I don't know how many more years audiences will want us..."

"You've got a good act."

"Thank you for that, Mrs Cormier. But the motion pictures will prove a challenge to us all. Moviemakers are starting to tell stories in film, and every year they are less crude. Someday the camera will tell a story better than live actors can, boxed in on a stage as it were. I've watched the show business change ever since I was a tyke. Oh, yes. I grew up in the family act. A corny old melodrama. I went from playing the babe in the young widow's arms or her little golden-haired daughter to acting the young swain fending off the villain—played by my father—while courting the widow—played by my mother. In between, when I was too old to play the child and too young to play the hero, I became the stage manager for the act. My point, dear lady, is what was an appropriate role for me at two or five was no longer suited to a lad of ten or sixteen."

"My Alice?"

"Precisely, Ma'am. She needs to play her age..."

"She needs to be in school," interrupted Doris Greeley. "In six or seven years what will become of her?"

"What's to become of us, now? The future may look worse, but, right now, it's the present I'm hard up against, Mrs Greeley. No booking, no money and now you tell me 'no act'!"

"I'm sorry, Mrs Cormier, I..."

"No. I'm not stupid. You're right. Even before we left the Midwest, I could see it. She used to be so cute and..." Renée Cormier was determined to face facts. "And, here, in Boston? It was like getting sandbagged. Oh, I blamed everyone else, but I also watched the other acts. All of them. Clever. Fast-paced. I just didn't want to admit it. That the act was finished and I was trapped— back to being a housewife. I suppose I could get work as a housekeeper, but to tell the truth, I wasn't much good at that either."

"You might make a good agent."

"What?"

"You know the business. You push hard for your act. Why not try it? You could get a new act for Alice. I might be able to write something. I wrote our act."

"And the boys? They were my brother's boys. Either they came with me or went to St Ann's Orphanage. My husband didn't want them. He didn't want..." Mrs Cormier halted before she slipped again into self-pity.

"Oh, my dear." Doris reached across and took Mrs Cormier's hand.

"Of course, a new act for all three." Victor was at his best when looking at the bright side of life.

"I can't afford..."

"Not a consideration, dear lady, and I promise no expensive costumes or need for a special scenic drop. Are we agreed? Good. Now, let me think on it, and I may be able to dream up something that will work for a pretty young lady who has to stay home to look after her two rambunctious younger brothers. A little playlet that will allow the children to act a bit as well as dance and tumble. Something that will give you time to consider your options. How's that? Give us your address and I'll mail you something. Meantime, why don't we find Mr Nathan Furst. He's a very important booker here in Boston. With United Booking Office. Perhaps he can give you some advice on becoming an agent or a booker. That is, if you think it would suit you? He may even be able to put in a word with their branch office in Chicago. You never know. No promises, but it might work out. What do you say? Shall we search out Nate Furst?"

It was all a bit much to contemplate, but Renée Cormier never, no matter how bleak were her prospects, let an opportunity pass her by. She looked at both Doris and Victor, offered a rare smile and nodded.

When Cormier and the Greeleys entered the music room, the Hennigan boys were entertaining. Mindful that an important booker and a theatre owner were among the crowd, Ned had dragged his partner Mike over to the piano where Ned played and both warbled "Sweet Rosie O'Grady."

After the first chorus Ned beckoned to Marla to join them. She took over the piano while he rose to do a clog dance. Mike, not his usual shy self with a glass or two of wine inside him, stepped up and precisely mirrored his partner step for step. Then Paula slid onto the piano bench and Marla stepped in between Mike and Ned to make it a three-way clog. Encouraged by the applause, Ned left the others to bow while he went over to the Victrola and put on the top record, "Ma Rag Time Baby," played by the Peerless Orchestra.

"Hey everybody, this is a ragtime ditty that Marla, Paula, Mike and me are going to do in our new act. Wanna see it?"

A renewed round of applause was all Ned needed. By the time the short spoken preamble to the music was over, the newly formed song-and-dance quartet, The Franklin-Hennigan Four, were in place and launched into a percussive dance routine, the wooden heels and soles of their shoes tapping in unison.

Florrie smiled at Lavinia: "I think we know who's the manager of their act."

"They should be quite successful," observed Lavinia. "Not at all bashful, and they came to the party wearing their clog shoes. I hope they don't scuff the floor too much."

The Vetter Brothers were itching to show their act, but the confines of floor space and the normal ceiling height of a residential building denied them the opportunity to show their stuff, but they had the attention of the youngsters present, and Andras, Dietmar and Karel were downstairs in the front hallway teaching Tommy, Alice and her two cousins, Donald and Henry, a few simple tumbling maneuvers.

Although neither Morris Weis nor Emily Stropell could recall an occasion as enjoyable as this had been, they were concerned about getting home. Lavinia, however, had thought ahead and arranged for three hackneys to call at Portridge Arms between 1:00 and 1:30 in the morning. She persuaded Emily and Mo to wait until the first cab arrived and assured them that the expense had been taken care of by Joshua Wood.

As each hackney arrived, its driver was invited in for a drink while his customers got into their wraps and top coats. Tommy had been alerted by Florrie to fill a clean galvanized bucket ahead of time. As each cab pulled up, Tommy was to set the bucket of water for the horse to drink while the driver fetched his fares.

The lodgers had all stored their outerwear in their rooms, so Florrie only had the Brodys, Mo and Emily, Dudley, Nathan, Joshua and his red-headed date to see out.

Although Tommy was on duty on the first floor to make sure all the guests found their outer garments, he was more occupied learning acrobatic tricks from the Vetters. When Lavinia warned him about stressing his foot while it was healed, Tommy countered that he was learning how to somersault and walk on his hands. Florrie appointed herself doorkeeper in Tommy's place but alerted him to water the horses as each cab arrived.

Inspector and Mrs Brody were the next of the "honored guests" to leave the party, mindful that they wished to sleep off the wine and food before attending Mass tomorrow—no!—*this* morning. Carol and Malachi thanked the sisters for a "grand time" and sailed off in the second cab.

Dudley Pierce thanked the Portridge Sisters for their hospitality and expressed the hope that he would have occasion to visit

Boston again in the near future. Should he be "so fortunate, would Miss Lavinia and Miss Flora be his guests at dinner?" Lavinia answered that she and her sister "... indeed look forward to his return, and gladly accept your invitation." In the back of her mind, though, Lavinia wondered if she dared again to leave Agnes to manage another evening meal for their lodgers.

As Nate Furst and Joshua Wood bade good night with thanks to Florrie and Lavinia, Florrie urged them to catch the Vetters' act—"held over for another week at the Globe. Superior in its line, gentlemen."

As they were all heading uptown, Nate, Dudley, Joshua and his stunning red-headed companion had agreed to share the third and last hackney. At the last minute, Nathan asked the others if they would wait a minute for him in the drawing room. Nate hurried back upstairs and told Ned Hennigan to let him know when The Franklin-Hennigan Four were ready to show their new act.

Some of the older folks in the sitting room stopped by the dining room to help themselves to one last bite or a nightcap before finding their way to bed.

Not much later, the entertainment in the music room ended with Marla Franklin at the piano, playing tunes of the day. As the few remaining performers gathered around to the upright to sing, Frankie Moore gave his Irish tenor a workout and persuaded Agnes Rigney to join him and the others.

When at last the young folks decided to call it a night or, more accurately, an early morning, Patrolman Moore insisted on helping Agnes clear the sitting room, dining and music room of dirty glasses, flatware and dishes. Lavinia and Florrie were glad to be relieved of the chore at that hour and decided that it was no business of theirs if there was any courting going on in the kitchen as long as food was being put away and some of dishes were washed.

"I've enjoyed myself tonight, but I expect I'll regret it tomorrow. Come along, Flora; it's well beyond time for us to go to bed. The rest of this mess can wait until morning. Thank heavens Cora and Ida will be here. Tomorrow will be another frantic day; we have eleven guests booked for next week."

"Anyone we know, Lavinia?"

"Only the Howard family, I think."

"Ah, lovely," murmured Florrie as she toddled downstairs behind Lavinia, anticipating the week ahead more joyfully than her sister. They exchanged their usual good night wishes and retired to their separate quarters. As she climbed into bed, Florrie smiled to herself, "New people to meet and new acts to watch. And, perhaps, a new adventure."

AFTERWORD:

As Victor had foretold, the scam threat of deep-pocket competition by Abe Erlanger and Lee Shubert forced B. F. Keith and his second-in-command Edward Albee to negotiate. By mid-November, only a few weeks after Rosetta's murder, the principals, unaware of the role they had inadvertently played in her death, settled. Erlanger, Shubert and their partners pledged to retire from the field of vaudeville for ten years in turn for $200,000 paid them by Keith and Albee, which is really all that old Abe wanted.

Erlanger and Lee Shubert got richer. The Keith and Albee empire was spared a costly battle to defend its hegemony. Tommy the orphaned newsboy found a safe home with Florrie and Lavinia. Joshua Wood buckled down to business. Mrs. Cormier returned to Chicago with a gleam of hope and firm resolve. The Franklin-Hennigan Four developed into a popular act and into two married couples. Agnes Rigby grew less sullen with the start of a romance with Patrolman Frankie Moore. Inspector Brody and Moore added luster to their badges by quickly solving (with the invaluable aid of the Porridge Sisters) the *Murder at the Tremont Theatre*. The only real loser was Rosetta Rice.

Excerpt from

Murder at the Old Howard

The Second Porridge Sisters Mystery

by

Frank Cullen

&

Donald McNeilly

Weather in New England is taken for granted only in the winter. Always cold and windy, it usually rains or snows as well, and Friday, the 12th of January, 1912, proved no exception. The women and girls were more sheltering themselves from the drizzle under their homemade picket signs than holding them aloft as they plod back and forth along Union Street in Lawrence, Massachusetts. Two teenage girls who had been marching together drifted out of the long line, caught up in urgent conversation.

'Why not? I'm pretty enough, I guess.'

'You don't think much of yourself, do you Gracie.'

'Eddie says so.'

'Oh, then it must be true.'

'You're just jealous, Dottie.'

'Jealous of you? When my Bernie likes me as I am?'

'Yeah? Well, anyway, believe me, both of us is better lookin' than the ones they got dancin' now. Scarecrows or cows, the lot of 'em, and ain't none of 'em as young as us.'

'You're serious then?'

'Betcha bonnet. I ain't gonna wait around, livin' at my old Auntie's, for this strike to get settled.'

As the drizzle accelerated into a downpour, Gracie and Dottie skittered over the wet ice to shelter against the stone and brick wall surrounding the Everett Cotton Mills. Dottie held her sign over both their heads for what little protection it offered.

'Bernie says the strike won't last more'n a week..."

'Yeah, well, a week or a day, it's no business of mine any more. Marching around in weather like this is going to get me death of a cold sooner than a raise. What's the point? A few cents an hour won't change my life, and I'm soaking wet, cold, tired and my feet hurt. And, oh, God!, my shoes are ruined! Honest, until today, I was just thinkin' about it, but now, I swear to you, me and the Mills are quitting each other.'

'Jeez, Gracie, you are serious!'

'It ain't just the weather or my shoes, Dottie. Burlesque looks a lot better to me than rottin' away at the Everett Cotton Mills workin' them looms six days a week for nine bucks until someday I croak gasping for breath.'

'But Bernie says...'

'You and me been friends since we were kids, Dottie, but I don't care what your Bernie and his Wobbly buddies say, I'm through with slavin' over those damn looms and I'm through with this burg!' Gracie's voice dropped. 'And I'm damn well through with uncle of mine pawing me.'

'Gracie!'

'Yeah, well, now you know. It ain't as if I can't handle him. Every time he sneaks into my room in the middle of the night I warn him I'll tell Auntie and the parish priest; that sobers him up fast enough so he skedaddles outa my room.'

'Oh, Gracie, that's awful..."

'I don't mind guys lookin' at me. I even like it. But no one puts their paws on me unless I want them to."

'Gracie! Shame...'

'Shame nothin'. You don't let Bernie?'

'No!'

"You don't? Just a little?'

'Well, just a little.'

'See? But it's your choice, right?' Gracie's arms ached, so she lowered her soggy sign. It ripped in half and both of them got drenched. 'That does it! I'm getting' outa here.'

'Gracie?'

'Yeah?'

'You really gonna do it?'

'I'm really gonna do it.'

'What's your Auntie gonna say?'

'Eddie's takin' me inta Boston tonight to see the show. I told Auntie I'm staying overnight with my cousin Agnes. Don't you go tellin' her or no one else no different, Dottie. Promise?'

'Oh, Gracie!'

'Promise me, Dottie?'

'I promise.' The two friends hugged, Dottie reluctant to let go. 'Don't you have to know how to dance to get hired?'

Gracie laughed and pulled away, 'Say, all you need to do is parade round the stage, one foot in front of the other, and not fall over. You give a kick now and then to show them your knickers.'

'How do you know they need any more girls?'

'Eddie fixed it up. He's an advance man for Billie's Belles.'

'Can you trust him? You ain't known him long.'

'Long enough to get the job. Eddie says I'm a cinch to become a featured act. Don't worry, Dottie, you know me. I can take care of myself. I just gotta get outa here, you know?'

'You leaving' town soon?'

'Eddie and the troupe is packing up and leaving Sunday for Springfield, and I'm going with them.'

'That soon? Oh, jeez, Gracie, I'm goin' to miss you. You been my best friend forever. 'Send me a postcard, will you?'

'Say, why don't you come to see the show with us tonight?'

'To the Old Howard?!'

'We wouldn't be the only women there, you know.'

'Really?'

'You could bring Bernie.'

'Oh, no! And he'd never forgive me if I went.'

'Suit yourself. I gotta go. The next time I see you I may be a star and you'll have to call me Grace Kendall—that's gonna be my stage name.'

'Oh, Gracie, I'm gonna miss you. Don't forget to send me a postcard.'

'Me, too.' Gracie called over her shoulder as she scampered and slid away over the icy patches on the street.' Bye!'

Bunny Rosen moved the chair down the row a few feet at a time so he could reach each group of hanging costumes, pulling those that needed mending. He had to make magic out of *bupkis*. Not only had he to spruce up and disguise what remained of years-old costumes every week, he had to devise new dance routines for the chorus girls and rehearse them Thursdays and Saturdays nights after the last show and then again early afternoon on Sundays so they'd know the steps when the new show opened Mondays afternoon.

Bunny kept the dance drills basic, usually a shuffling one step formed into patterns like military parade maneuvers: left, right, reverse and oblique. Despite their limited abilities, the dancers did their best and only occasionally did a girl—perhaps tired, hungry, tipsy or hung-over—trip and tumble.

He felt sorry for his dancers; most of them knew as well as he that they were nobody's idea of Irene Castle, and the twelve bucks a week for seven days of rehearsals and performances offered little incentive to improve.

Only the newer chorus girls had yet to realize that stardom was as far off as the furthest reach of the galaxy, and conditions elsewhere offered little better. Even at its worst, though, all the dancers, women or girls, were thankful they weren't scrubbing floors or working in sweatshops.

The *schmatta* was a different story; there was no excuse for old, spoiled and patched up costumes. But no matter how often he asked management for money to buy some new costumes, they told him the old stuff was good enough, that no one could work wonders with them as he did, that you couldn't tell from the audience anyway, and, besides, what guys in the audience were looking at the costumes, for Pete's sake! Other times, the manager was less polite: "Stop *hucking* me! If you don't like it here, leave!"

Even the *goyem* in show business knew a few Yiddish words, and the manager, Larry McCartey liked to fling them at Bunny.

Although the manager claimed he was Irish, no small blessing in a town with an Irish mayor and largely Irish police force, the spelling of his last name seemed suspect to Bunny.

The one concession he was able to wrest from Mr McCartey was a small stipend—three dollars a week—for a part-time assistant to help mend the costumes. Recommended by a vaudeville double act that had played the Old Howard a few months ago, the wife had some emergency repairs to her gown made handily by Ida Banks who worked Sundays at Portridge Arms, a theatrical boarding house. Bunny had heard Mr McCartey use abusive terms to speak of colored people and would sack Ida if he saw she was a Negress, so Bunny asked Ida to come to the Old Howard after the usual business hours. Ida collected the week's mending at the stage door on Friday evenings and returned the repaired articles Monday nights.

Frank Cullen and Donald McNeilly have partnered in many theatrical ventures over the decades, most notably in the 1982 founding of the American Vaudeville Museum (www.vaudeville.org) and the research, writing, design and publishing of 40 issues of *Vaudeville Times* (1998-2008) and their landmark, two-volume, 1600 page, *Vaudeville, Old & New: An Encyclopedia of Variety Performers in America* published by Routledge Press in 2007 to laudatory reviews.

Made in the USA
Charleston, SC
08 November 2010